IF IT'S THE LAST THING I DO

DAVID FITZ-GERALD

HISTORIUM PRESS

Library of Congress Cataloging-in-Publication Data on file
Library of Congress Control Number: 2023913269

First Edition 2023

Standard Images by Shutterstock & Public Domain
Main cover image copyrighted and protected © Cindy Burkart Maynard
Cover designed by White Rabbit Arts

Visit David Fitz-Gerald's website at
www.thehistoricalfictioncompany.com/david-fitzgerald or

www.itsoag.com

Hardcover ISBN: 979-8-9881815-0-7
Paperback ISBN: 979-8-9881815-1-4
E-Book ISBN: 979-8-9881815-2-1

Historium Press, a subsidiary of
The Historical Fiction Company
2023

This novel is dedicated to
Cindy Turcot
"Queen of ESOPs"
on the occasion of her retirement
from day-to-day work,
in recognition of her decades of tireless service
to the employee ownership community,
and in reverence for her leadership
in the quest to make employee ownership commonplace
and remarkable at the same time.

Advanced Praise

In 1975, Misty Menard, a newly retired woman living in Washington DC, is called home to Lake Placid upon her father's death. Misty is shocked to discover that she has inherited the struggling Adirondack Dowel and Spindle Company, making her owner and CEO. She's torn on whether to personally nurture the struggling business her father loved, or sell it as soon as possible and return to her comfortable life in the city.

Misty soon discovers trouble simmers all around her. A former classmate holds on to a long-standing resentment. Managers at her father's company want her to pack up and leave. Friends and family in Lake Placid have secrets of their own. What Misty decides to do could not only make or break the company, but jeopardize her life.

This book has a unique and creative premise, utilizing a female protagonist who is nearly seventy years old, yet smart and tough enough to tackle any difficulty that comes her way. Conflicts are introduced early on and multiply as the story progresses, which keeps the reader engaged and curious about what will happen next. I learned a lot about the concept of Employee Stock Ownership Plans, and found it most refreshing to read a story that features a conflicted yet capable woman "of a certain age."

Pat Wahler, author of *The Rose of Washington Square*

CONTENTS

IF IT'S THE
LAST THING I DO

1

LAKE PLACID, NEW YORK
APRIL 17, 1975

The smell of cedar makes my skin tingle. I don't know why. Despite the fact that Father had selected the fragrant wooden casket, Mr. McCabe suggested an upgrade to stainless steel and whispered that the price list was in the drawer. He paused for a moment, in case I might encourage him or slide the drawer open, and then asked if I was ready to finalize the arrangements.

"Father took care of all of that himself, Mr. McCabe." The metal box reminded me of a refrigerator and I'm not burying anyone in an icebox.

The mortician cleared his throat, and said, "Yes, indeed he did, Miss Menard. If there is nothing more that you need, I'll leave you alone with the departed."

"Thank you, Mr. McCabe." Whenever men called me 'miss' it reminded me of my advanced years and that I was not married. I supposed there were worse things one could have been called.

He gripped my forearm with his bony fingers and said, "Take all the time you need, dear." Then he disappeared quietly as if wearing velvet-bottomed slippers.

Somber music wafted through the airwaves. I hadn't noticed the dirge earlier, but the muted tones were comforting.

The coffin was closed at one end and open at the other. Instead of looking upon Father's lifeless remains, a nostalgic picture on a delicate table made me long for yesteryear. Looking at the portrait rather than the corpse was a better way to remember the man whose daughter should have visited him more often during his final years. A wave of guilt crashed over me and brought tears to my eyes.

My teeth mashed together. A dainty handkerchief, plucked from my pocketbook, sopped up errant tears. Emotions must be contained, particularly in public. I had scarcely shed a tear since my oldest son's funeral, thirty-one years ago. Whenever I look at the gold watch Junior gave me as he marched off to war, I am reminded of losing him, and want to cry, but a grieving woman should be stoic and keep her feelings inside.

I took a deep breath and stepped toward Father's coffin as a firm hand gripped my shoulder. It could not be Mr. McCabe's skeletal fingers, though I hadn't heard anyone else's footsteps behind me. The man's hand turned me toward him and I looked up into bright green eyes. The middle-aged man smelled of menthol and moss, the instantly recognizable scent of Aqua Velva. Attractive, well-groomed, good-smelling men have always been my downfall, though it was neither the time nor the place for such thoughts.

My expression must have conveyed fear. The man let go of my shoulder and said, "I'm so sorry, Miss Menard. I didn't mean to frighten you. My name is Winslow Gloversmith. I am your father's attorney. Perhaps you remember me."

"Yes, of course, Mr. Gloversmith." Truthfully, I didn't remember ever having met the man. Perhaps he was mistaken about having made my acquaintance. "I was just about to spend a moment beside…." My words trailed away as my gaze drifted back toward the coffin.

"Would you permit a few minutes with me in private? Mr. McCabe has made his study available for our use. There's an urgent matter I need to discuss with you."

My heart began to race. What could be so important? Why would Father's attorney need to speak with me now, before the funeral services? My gaze traveled the length of his rigid arm and I noticed the dark brown briefcase in his hand. His unwrinkled suit matched the color of his attaché.

"Won't you step this way, ma'am?" As if with an invisible arm across my shoulder, Mr. Gloversmith's presence guided me toward a private room beyond a spiral staircase. "Please make yourself comfortable, Miss Menard."

I considered removing my black gloves and descended onto a stiff antique chair.

Mr. Gloversmith removed documents from his leather bag. Then he sat behind the mortician's desk and said, "May I call you Misty, or would you prefer that I address you more formally?"

Something about the man rattled me, perhaps it was the occasion. Maybe it was worry about what he planned to discuss. Having spent decades working at Cracken, Humble, and Dobbs, the famous Washington D.C. law firm, it certainly wasn't the man's profession that caused me to be on edge. My job as the receptionist was to greet clients, make them feel comfortable, and remember the names of the powerful men that came to seek the counsel of our country's leading attorneys.

I turned my body slightly toward the man and reminded myself to maintain my composure. "It would please me if you called me Misty, Mr. Gloversmith."

"I'm glad. And you must call me Winslow."

"Alright, Winslow." His first name sounded even more pretentious to me than his last. Even so, it occurred to me that I liked the sound of his name as it rolled across my tongue. *I wonder if there is a Mrs. Winslow Gloversmith.* It dawned on me that I was blushing and frowning.

"Is everything quite alright, Misty?"

"Oh, yes, of course. I'm just a bit on edge today."

"Most understandable, especially under the circumstances. And I'm sorry to intrude on you as you are grieving, but I have an urgent matter to discuss with you. It's most uncouth to discuss business at such a time, but I assure you that it can't be helped." He lifted a document with a light-blue cover, half as wide as a normal sheet of paper and taller. "It is the matter of your father's last will and testament. Would you like to read it?"

I shook my head from side to side. "No, Winslow. If you don't mind. Could you tell me what I need to know instead?"

He sat forward, his sparkling eyes staring right into my soul, making me feel ridiculous for reacting like a teenaged girl rather than a woman of an advanced age. "Your father has left you his home on Grandview Avenue, and the company. Now, *you* are the sole owner of the Adirondack Dowel and Spindle Company. Papers must be signed immediately so that we can make payroll this week, otherwise, I would have waited until a better occasion to discuss this with you."

My will to maintain my composure caved at that moment and my slouching body crashed from the chair. I felt lightheaded but did not lose consciousness. I thought of all the times I'd seen women faint on the afternoon soaps, and began to laugh.

The man's deep voice turned my head again. He said, "I'm sorry, Misty," and hurried from behind the desk to help me back to the chair.

My laughter went from an uproarious giggle to an all-out, belly-grinding roar. My face felt like it had split apart, and I couldn't control myself. I laughed so hard that tears streamed from my eyes. To my horror, I could feel myself lose control of my bladder, and yet, even after peeing myself a little, I couldn't stop howling. At that moment, I wished that I were a million miles away from that unyielding chair in McCabe's Funeral Home.

Winslow must have prepared himself for a different response than the one he got from me. He said, "Should I leave you alone for a moment?"

My mouth opened and I tried to tell him that it wouldn't be necessary, but another fit of laughter racked my body. I covered my face with the palms of my gloved hands, and then the tears came. Wave after wave and sob after sob, it felt like my chest would cave in. We had just celebrated Father's 90th birthday a couple of months earlier. Of course, we didn't expect that he would live forever. I knew this moment could not be far off. It doesn't matter how old a little girl becomes, or how ancient her father is; no matter what, she is always *Daddy's little girl.*

Winslow Gloversmith, Esquire was to be commended. It takes a brave man to console a woman at such a time. His firm hand on my back and his deep soothing voice in my ear finally brought me back from the edge of a breakdown. I hadn't realized that my hands had balled into fists. Winslow took my hands in his and I watched my fingers relax. My handkerchief fell to the floor, and Winslow quickly retrieved it. When he handed it to me, I quickly snatched it away from him and then realized that I must look frightful. "I'm sorry, Winslow. I need a moment to myself. Do you know where the powder room is?"

As I sped away to the lavatory, I hoped that Winslow hadn't looked at me. Between the tears of laughter, my gut-wrenching sobs, and my hands on my face, what could have become of my makeup? Thank heavens for my hasty retreat. *The mirror never lies.* My foundation was cracked and caked, and mascara had streaked down my cheeks. While reapplying cosmetics, to the highest standard possible under the circumstances, I was glad that I had the good sense to spend a sizable amount of my savings on a facelift and plastic surgery just after retreating into oblivion. If ridding my face of wrinkles meant living on an austerity budget, I had decided, so be it.

When I returned to the undertaker's den, Winslow was standing beside the door, waiting for me. He offered his arm and escorted me back to the chair, and said, "It must have come as a surprise to you, Misty. Weren't you expecting to be your father's heir?"

I shook my head slowly and my voice softened. "I thought he would leave me his house, but I never imagined owning a business and having to be concerned about paying people's wages. Father said he was going to leave the company to the general manager. What happened? Why did he change his mind?"

"Indeed." Winslow rubbed his pointy, clean-shaven chin. "He

never said." Winslow looked distracted and muttered, "Many times over the last ten years, AJ changed his will. For a while, he declared that Doyle Polk would inherit the business, but it never stayed that way for long. Once he changed the will to leave it to his grandson, but then he changed it back to you, Misty."

My breath came faster again, and I said, "What should I do, Winslow? I can't run a business, can I? What if I refuse? I can't be forced to own a business if I don't want to, can I?"

"There, there, Misty. No, you don't have to run the business. We can close it, let everybody go, and sell what remains. Would you like to do that?"

"Oh, no. We mustn't do that, Winslow. How many people work there?"

"Sixty-five, last I knew."

"And it isn't just them, Winslow. We have to think about the people that depend on them. How will they make ends meet?"

"I suppose they'll have to find a way. Maybe they have savings set aside. They could collect unemployment for a while. That's what it's there for, after all, just such emergencies."

"No, that wouldn't do. But, I could sell the business. Someone would buy it, wouldn't they?"

"I expect so, Misty. If it had to be sold quickly, it might not bring in enough to pay the bank loans. If it were properly marketed, it could sell for more as a *stable* company. That could take a year, perhaps two or three even."

"Oh."

"Just because you own the business, doesn't mean you have to run it. You could hire someone to run the business. Or you could let Mr. Polk run it."

"But Father must have had concerns about Mr. Polk."

"Yes, I guess he must have. I wonder why."

A shiver crossed my body and I pulled my arms in close beside me. Why didn't I bring a shawl? With a grimace, I said, "Shall we take care of the paperwork then? I don't know if I'll keep the company, but we must make the payroll this week. What do I need to do?"

"We'll have to make a trip to the bank, and we'll need Bob Peacock's signature on the documents as well."

"Mayor Peacock? For goodness' sake, why? Does the Mayor have that much power?"

Winslow laughed softly, and I felt comforted. "No, it's not that, Misty. You see, Bob and I are on the company's Board of Directors. We'll need to hold a quick meeting and add you to the Board as well. Then, there will be three of us, you see?"

"Oh, I understand. You, Mayor Peacock, and me. *We* are the Board of Directors?"

"Yes, and it is our job, as the Board of Directors, to look after the best interests of the shareholder of the company."

"And that would be me? Good heavens, Winslow. It's a lot to take in." While shaking my head, I imagine Father's ghost hovering over his casket in the other room. *Will Father watch over his company from beyond? Perhaps his essence will haunt the halls of his beloved office at the Adirondack Dowel and Spindle Company. He should have told me that he planned to leave me the business. Better yet, he should have asked me. I should have had the right to know.* "Why didn't he mention it?"

I hadn't realized that I had spoken out loud until Winslow answered me. "I don't know, dear. He must have always thought that he had time, but just never got around to it."

It's funny how familiar people can become when they share an intensely emotional experience. It dawned on me slowly. *Father's lawyer, Winslow Gloversmith, Esquire called me 'dear.' What does that mean? I'm old enough to be the man's… older sister.* I looked back into his arresting eyes and he handed me a letter. My name was on the envelope in my father's handwriting, along with the words, *open in private after the contents of the last will and testament are divulged.*

***

I stayed at Father's house whenever I returned to the Adirondacks. When Father died, I asked the boys to stay with me until after the funeral. The boys included my second son, Harold, my grandson, Presto, and my great-grandson, Four. They lived in small cabins at the edge of the woods.

We sat together in the tidy living room furnished with gorgeous antiques. I told them about the funeral arrangements and relayed the shocking news about inheriting Father's company. "So, I'll be moving back home."

An image of my therapist in Washington flashed in my head. Could good counselors be found locally? Maybe I no longer needed weekly sessions, but after decades of support, it was hard to imagine going without. Then I sighed at the thought of giving up my apartment and moving my possessions.

Harold slouched on the sofa. He had never had very good posture. He folded his hands over his belly and said, "Oh, Mom. You can't stand being away from the city. It's like you told me when I moved to Schenectady. 'That place doesn't suit you, honey. It's not the place for you.' You don't belong here, Mom. You always say there's nothing to do. It's too dark, too quiet, and nothing ever happens around here."

He was right. I had grown up in Lake Placid and considered it a tiny oasis of civilization surrounded by a frighteningly empty wilderness. After graduating from high school, I couldn't wait to move to the city. It didn't much matter what city as long as it was well-lit and the stores were always open. Harold, on the other hand, moved to Schenectady and worked for decades at General Electric. It was always his dream to return to the Adirondacks and live in a cabin in the woods. He never married, didn't have any children, and preferred to spend most of his time alone, but when my oldest son, Junior was killed, Harold raised Junior's son. The two have remained close throughout the years.

Presto said, "You're going to run the company? How are you going to do that? You're just a...." Presto squirmed and paused.

I cut him off. "Woman? I'm just a woman?"

My grandson hung his head and said, "No. Secretary. I was going to say you're just a secretary, but that didn't sound very nice. I'm sorry, GiGi." After Presto's son was born, I suggested my great-grandson could call me that, and Presto followed suit. We call my grandson Presto because he moved so speedily as a teenager, and because it is short for his full name, Preston Palmer the third. My great-grandson, Preston Palmer the fourth is simply called, Four.

"I'm sorry I snapped at you, Presto." My grandson is kind and sensitive. "You are right. What do I know about running a company?"

Eight-year-old Four crowded into my chair and said, "You're smart, GiGi. You'll figure it out."

"Thank you, honey. I'll do my best."

Harold looked at me like I had lost my mind as we talked about my plans to move back to the Adirondacks, and then I retired for the evening. I didn't tell the boys about the letter Father left me, but held it in my hands. It was just a couple of ordinary sheets of paper in a flimsy envelope but somehow it seemed heavy. Thoughts of undertaking the enormous responsibility ricocheted through my head. It was as if the weight of the world were at the tips of my fingers. I knew that making sure everyone got paid was important, but that was before meeting the people that work at Adirondack Dowel.

My fingers plucked the stationery from the envelope and I sniffled at the sight of Father's handwriting. The letter communicated Father's final words to me. As my lips moved, I heard his voice as if he were whispering to me from beyond.

* * * * *

Dearest Misty,

If you're reading this letter, it means that I've passed on.

By now, you know that I've left you the house and the company. I know we discussed leaving the business to management, but something kept changing my mind about that. I can't explain it, darling. I felt compelled to leave it to you. You may not think you were meant to run a company, but I think you are. In fact, I'm convinced of it.

There will be hard times ahead, of that you can be certain. I don't know what it is, but there is something you were meant to do. Nobody else can do it. You'll know what it is when the time is right. It will hit you like a hammer. Don't question it. You may be uncertain, but rest assured, you'll know what to do about the company, even though I did not. Adirondack Dowel and Spindle Company belongs in your able hands. Don't let anybody convince you otherwise.

I love you dearly, Misty. I always have. Mother, Johnny, Junior, and I will watch over you from the other side if we're allowed to do so.

Make sure that Harold, Presto, and Four know that I love them, and take good care of my precious, Calhoun.

Forever your Father, with love,

AJ Menard

*　*　*　*　*

Crying was for other women, not me, yet tears constantly reappeared in my eyes despite frequent dabbing. Blinking away tears made it hard to see while rereading Father's letter over and over again, committing it to memory.

Finally, I set the envelope on a table, sat on Father's favorite chair, and painted my fingernails. My usual choice of polish was a flashy, cherry red, but I remember applying a dusty pink instead, knowing the classic, muted color would be more appropriate for Father's funeral. When the familiar fumes had evaporated into the air, a low, vibrating sound startled me. My eyes grew wide. Was that the sound of a ghost? Father's large Victorian house felt like it could comfortably put up a clatter of spirits. Turning to face the poltergeists, I was amazed to see a fluffy white cat, bright as new snow on old Whiteface Mountain. I always loved cats, but living in apartments in the city meant doing without pets.

I had forgotten what a friendly purr sounded like; cats are great listeners.

2

Calhoun insisted on sleeping between my legs all night long. He was adept at dodging moving limbs whenever I shifted positions and always returned to slumber between my thighs. I hoped that would not become a regular habit and later learned the cat was named after Father's first employee, Sparky. Nobody recalled Sparky's real first name.

When morning came, the smell of brewing coffee and the distant sound of activity in the kitchen roused me. The clanging of lids against pots and muffled conversations were audible even as sleet stung the window panes. The urge to cover my head with a thick pillow and go back to sleep was strong, but with breakfast in progress, there was no choice but to tend to my appearance. Before I finished putting myself together, an impatient fist rapped on the door. Four shouted, "GiGi! Breakfast is ready."

"Alright! I'll be right down."

That boy was a bright light in my life. I thought his numerical nickname was cute and was glad we didn't have to call him Preston, though that name was my fault. When I'd given a son to my ex-husband, Preston Palmer, I figured that he would appreciate naming the boy after himself. If I had known that the skunk would one day run away to California with an ingénue, I would not have named our boy after his stinker of a father. Calling him Junior made it better. It was not my fault that Junior named his son

Preston Palmer. Nor was it my fault that Presto continued the tradition.

So, the youngest Preston Palmer became, simply, Four. There was something about the child that drew me to him, even more so than my boys, Junior and Harold, or my grandson, Presto. The child had a free spirit, and I loved to watch him twirl endlessly without seeming to get dizzy or perform somersaults, cartwheels, and flips, especially into leaf piles or off of diving boards. That great-grandson of mine reigned supreme within my heart. It was entirely mutual; the child followed me wherever I went, inquired about everything I did, and asked the most impossible questions. Sometimes I wondered whether there wasn't something else that he should have been doing. As far as I knew, his only interest was skating: figure skating, speed skating, and hockey. He was more comfortable on blades than walking.

Like I had, Four had lost his mother at a young age. Cancer took my Mother when I was a young girl, and a car crash on a snowy night killed Four's mother when he was a toddler. I thought my unplanned move from Washington, DC back to Lake Placid would benefit both Four and me, and looked forward to spending more time with the boy.

While covering my nightgown with a soft bathrobe and making my way to the stairs, my thoughts returned to Father's funeral. My teeth gritted and I resolved not to have another breakdown like the one Winslow was forced to witness yesterday. My countenance should be stoic and my demeanor reserved. Father was entitled to a hero's sendoff and I was intent that he should have the funeral he deserved.

I didn't expect to see Betty Kramer in Father's kitchen and greeted her with a kiss in the air, beside her cheek. We went to high school together, but she remained in Lake Placid rather than moving away. She became an interior designer and opened a shop on Elm Street, behind the Palace Theater. We had been best friends as girls. In the years since, when I'd come to town to visit family, sometimes Betty and I got together for lunch or coffee.

Betty said, "I thought I would break into your Father's house and fix you all breakfast this morning and it's a good thing I did. Everything in the icebox was rotten, so I hurried home to get fresh provisions."

I scratched my chin and looked at the refrigerator. It seemed beyond neighborly to think of such a thing.

When I invited Harold, Presto, and Four to join me at Father's house, it hadn't occurred to me that they would need to be fed. Grieving didn't do much for my appetite or attention to detail, and all my efforts had been directed at choreographing Father's funeral. Interior designers were magnificent at managing tasks and Betty excelled at it.

I sat in awe at the table watching Betty work, amazed at how efficiently she delivered coffee, cream, sugar, and a spoon in one fluid motion. It was as if she knew exactly where everything was kept. As my spoon swirled in my coffee cup, I watched Betty deliver waffles, with whipped cream, syrup, and sliced strawberries. A minute later, she produced fluffy omelets with a tray of diced condiments. Then she sliced oranges, crossed the kitchen to the pantry, and returned with the citrus squeezer. I wondered how long it would have taken me to find that hand press, but she seemed to know exactly where it was kept. Then it dawned on me: Betty was right at home in Father's kitchen.

Before thinking better of it, I said, "Gosh, Betty. How do you know where everything is around here? I'm always lost in Father's kitchen."

She stopped for a moment and then continued twisting the oranges onto the press. "I know my way around this place pretty well. AJ liked to play cards, and I was his favorite bridge partner, though Winslow kept threatening to steal me away from him."

"Oh, I see." Warily, I thought Betty's familiarity with Father's kitchen went far beyond what an occasional guest might possess. I couldn't help noticing that Betty was on a first-name basis with Father's attorney.

With her back to me, Betty continued. "By the way, Misty, AJ asked me to draw up renovation and decorating plans for the house. It hasn't been updated in decades." She rolled her eyes dramatically like she had been after him for years to let her make such changes. Then she continued, "The basement, attic, garage, and shed are filled with all sorts of junk. It's practically a fire hazard. I know people who can take care of all that clutter if you like. Just say the word." With one hand, she delivered a glass of fresh squeezed orange juice, and with the other, she dropped a dossier on my lap. "No hurry, Misty. You can look at the plans at your leisure and let me know what you think."

Then Betty removed her apron, slipped into her overcoat, and said, "Let me know if there's anything you need. I'll see you at church, Misty. Oh, and if you want to do over AJ's office at the company, let me know. I've got lots of ideas about that too."

A long drawn out, "Oh" escaped my lips. The woman was miles ahead of me.

During breakfast, the sleet changed to snow then converted back to rain as we prepared to go outside. We had hoped for nice weather for Father's funeral, not swirling winds and driving rain.

On the way to church, I wondered whether the departed attended their own funerals. Did spirits rise to heaven immediately upon a person's death, or did they linger for a while before moving on? I hoped that Father's essence would remain with us at least until we finished saying goodbye and praying for his soul. "I'll Fly Away" played as we entered the church.

Walking up the aisle, I thought about the hours spent with Reverend Vigne. He took careful notes as I told him about Father's life, the people who were important to him, and the milestones he celebrated. I thought the preacher's questions were strange, considering Father was a regular attendee and founding member of the Adirondack Community Church and often talked about singing in the choir at its 1927 dedication. Reverend Vigne should know Father, considering he rarely missed a sermon even though he sat in the back and made his donations anonymously. Patiently,

Reverend Vigne encouraged me, "It helps me to hear about the departed in the words of their loved ones." Then we discussed Bible verses and hymn selections. When I asked if there was a way to play Father's favorite, Jim Reeves, Reverend Vigne said, "I think we can arrange that." A portable record player looked out of place among the solemn artifacts on the dais. "Where Do I Go From Here" played on the turntable as mourners settled into the pews behind me. Four, Presto, and Harold sat beside me in the front row.

Reverend Vigne stepped forward to the front of the stage and delivered a short sermon followed by a long eulogy. Instead of thinking about Father and focusing on the celebration of his life, I sat in the front pew wondering whether Father and my best friend from high school had been lovers. I tried to convince myself that it wasn't any of my business. If they had made each other happy, why not? Yet try as I did, I couldn't stop thinking about them.

When my attention finally returned to Reverend Vigne, it dawned on me that the man kept referring to my father as DJ instead of AJ. My head turned and after glancing to see if anyone else noticed, my gaze returned to face the preacher. When Reverend Vigne did it again, my stomach soured. Father should be remembered properly, not forgotten before he was even buried. As the owner of the long-established business, Father was one of the town's leading citizens, and he should not be misremembered at his own funeral. I was horrified by the thought that Father's ghost would be hurt and disappointed in me for allowing it to happen.

I was glad when the eulogy finally ended until Reverend Vigne told us that the organist failed to show up that morning. He said, "It is a good thing that we have the record player." The machine made a harsh screech as Reverend Vigne dropped the needle in the wrong spot before finding the song he was looking for. He gestured with open palms on outstretched hands. We stood and sang along to "May The Good Lord Bless and Keep You." Behind me, a woman's barking cough and her husband's combustible sneezes drowned out most of the song, and they weren't the only ones who were sick on that miserable spring morning. The song's optimistic message drowned under the weight of the choir's delivery. The place sounded more like an infirmary than a church. I had never heard a more disharmonious combination of discordant notes. A loud crack of thunder accompanied the end of the song, and it sounded like lightning would penetrate the shingles on the church's roof.

Before the service ended, Reverend Vigne had a few more words to share. He looked directly at me when he said them, and I wondered whether he meant them just for me or if he wanted everyone to hear his message. He said, "DJ Menard served others, his whole life. When you serve others, you shouldn't require anything more than knowing you helped people. It's not the legacy we leave behind but the act of stewardship that matters most."

It felt as if insects were crawling around beneath my skin. To halt the sensation, I dug my fingernails into the palms of my hands. Again, Reverend Vigne called Father DJ instead of AJ. I took a deep breath and imagined myself as a dragon exhaling a scorching fire bomb. Instead of releasing my breath, I held it and counted to twenty-five, to control my anger. Then, I glanced at the men to my right. Harold was making notes on a piece of paper, and I leaned slightly toward him to see what he was writing down. He had neatly printed the words, *It's not the legacy we leave behind but the act of stewardship that matters most,* and I thought about my younger son's humble, steadfast servitude. He had practically raised my grandson, his brother's boy, Presto.

Reverend Vigne carefully placed the needle back on the record, and Jim Reeves sang, "My Cathedral" as Reverend Vigne walked down the aisle, followed by the cedar casket and its pallbearers. The boys and I followed the funerary box down the egress and into the rain. Despite the inclement weather, it felt good to be outdoors. I appreciated the kind words from Father's friends, yet was glad for the cover of a lacy black veil.

Most of the funeral-goers offered hurried condolences as they scurried away. Mayor Peacock lingered despite the rain. After offering his sympathy, he reached into his suit's inner pocket and pulled out two tickets to The Royal Lipizzan Stallion Show at the Olympic Arena. "The show is on Tuesday. Perhaps you and the young man will enjoy 'The world's greatest equine extravaganza.' That's what it says in the newspaper advertisement, so it must be true."

Four looked up at the man and said, "Golly, thank you, sir." His mouth hung open for a moment and then he continued. "Someday, I'll perform at the Olympic Arena, and I'll make sure you get a ticket."

The kindly mayor patted the top of the boy's wet head and said, "I don't doubt it for a minute, young man." Four beamed up at our town's leading citizen. The gentleman gave the boy a stiff smile and then strolled toward the sidewalk as sleet began to cut through the thick fog.

The family gathered in the North Elba Cemetery. The sleet changed back to rain, then subsided to a drizzle. Raw spring weather dampened the grief of friends and neighbors who otherwise would have joined us at the side of Father's grave. The reverend kept his remarks to a minimum and I was glad that he said Father's full given name correctly before the coffin was lowered into Father's final resting place. When everyone else stepped away, I remained behind. The modest headstone had Father's name carved on the left and Mother's on the right. In between, my brother Johnny's name was chiseled in harsh, angular letters, and Junior's gravestone stood alone to the side. I thought of the letter Father left for me with Attorney Gloversmith, saying that Mother, Father, Junior, and Johnny would be watching over me.

Father once dreamed that Johnny, his golden boy, would take over the company. Johnny was killed in a routine naval exercise and his body was buried at sea. The day we buried Father was very similar to the day we mourned Johnny, in 1927, the same year the new church was built. Father said it was good luck to have a funeral during a cleansing rain, and when the thunder rolled, Father said that meant that Johnny had found his way to Heaven.

Before departing the cemetery, I closed my eyes, tapped the top of the modest gray headstone, and promised Father that one day, I would replace the marker with a more fitting tribute. I turned away from the monument and walked into a woman standing directly behind me. I gasped and stepped back, looking into familiar eyes, yet it took a couple of moments before I realized who she was. I'd recognize her thick pouty lips anywhere, slathered in bright pink lipstick just as I remembered them so long ago. It was shocking to look at someone I hadn't seen since high school and to think of them as that same person despite the passing of nearly five decades. Perhaps she felt the same, looking at me. No amount of plastic surgery can make a woman my age look like she did in her teens.

The immaculately dressed woman stood beneath a fortress of an umbrella. Curtly, she said, "You don't remember me, do you?"

"I haven't seen you in decades. Lois! Is that you?" Betty, Lois, and I had been close friends, but that was a very long time ago.

She turned her head slightly away from me and lifted her upper lip in disdain. "I haven't gone anywhere, Misty. Not since you ruined my life."

Her words and the intensity of her tone startled me. "Pardon?"

"I never got over it when you stole my Preston away from me. I've hated you ever since. Not a day goes by when I don't think of you. I've fantasized about your grisly death in thousands of tortuous tragedies."

"But, Lois. Preston was my boyfriend before he was yours." I didn't remember how many times we broke up, and each time he went back to Lois, but when it came time for marriage, I ended up with the skunk. That's how I began to refer to the stinker after our divorce.

Through pinched lips, Lois growled, "I don't care. I warned you not to marry him, Misty, but you wouldn't listen. And then, you weren't woman enough to hold onto him. I'll never forgive you."

Without another word, Lois Phelps turned away, stepped up the hill, and disappeared into the fog. I stood and watched, shaking my head in disbelief. I hadn't thought about Lois in decades. Meanwhile, *I'd* been on *her* mind every day. She'd spent her whole life jealously hating me, as if Preston Palmer were enviable. If it weren't for my boys, it would be easy for me to say that I wished I'd never met the fink. As I walked toward the waiting car, a foul automotive smell touched my nostrils which reminded me of the odorific radiators of tourists' station wagons descending Whiteface Mountain in the summertime.

Why did Lois approach me at Father's graveside? Of all the days in the almost fifty years since we graduated from high school, why now?

When I opened the door and tucked the black pleats of my skirt beneath my legs, Betty gripped my arm and said, "This weather reminds me of the day that we said goodbye to Johnny." She sniffled and added, "That was forty-eight years ago."

I burst into tears, burying my face in my hands. The poor weather, Reverend Vigne's forgetfulness, the organist's illness, Lois's appearance, and Betty's recollections weren't my fault, but Father's funeral was ruined and my stomach roiled.

3

My 1973 Ford Mustang rolled into Adirondack Dowel and Spindle Company's unpaved parking lot at 6:30 Monday morning. With a yawn so hard it made me wonder if my wrinkles would regenerate, I hefted a bag from the passenger seat, confirmed my punctuality on a delicate golden wristwatch, and stepped toward the building. I wanted to arrive before anyone else and surprised the night watchman, who gruffly challenged me before my feet reached the footpath that led to the front door.

"What are ya doing here, lady? This is private property."

"Yes, I know." I smiled at the man and set the heavy bag on the ground beside me.

"And yet, here ya are. I must ask ya to leave or I'll call the authorities."

"Perhaps I should introduce myself. My name is Misty. AJ Menard is my father. That is…" I cleared my throat and looked back at the unpaved parking lot, and continued, "he *was* my father."

The guard coughed and tried to speak. "I'm sorry, ma'am. I had no idea. It's too bad about your Dad. He was a great man."

I nodded, appreciating his words, and said, "Thank you."

"But what are ya doing here at 6:30 in the mornin'?"

"Oh, I just wanted to meet everybody as they came in." I reached forward to shake his hand.

The bearded sentry looked at my hand and I presume it was my long fingernails that caught his eye. Then he looked back at me. He cleared his throat again, and said, "Stanley Dard." At least, that's what I heard. His rough, thick hand barely gripped mine. Perhaps he worried that my fingers might break if he gave me a proper handshake. When I repeated the man's name, he corrected me. "No ma'am, Stanley *Bedard*. In my line of work, I don't talk too much. So I guess I don't speak very clearly."

"Stanley, please call me Misty. You'll have to excuse me. I've been away from the North Country for a couple of decades and I've gotten out of practice listening to people speaking normally."

The flannel-frocked man grinned. *Perhaps I'm winning him over.*

"Let me show ya in, Misty."

I leaned forward. "Would it make you feel better if I show you my identification, first?"

He shrugged then nodded, and said, "Ya seem very nice, but… kinda. Yeah."

Stanley stared at my license for so long, I wondered whether he could read. Then he looked back at me and said, "Look, ma'am. I don't know who ya think yer foolin', but there's no way you're 69 years old. If y'are, I'll eat my hat."

"That won't be necessary, but you made my day. Why I'm so happy, I could kiss you, Stanley."

The man stood perfectly still, his eyes grew wide, and his cheek started to twitch. He looked a mite distressed, but I kissed him anyhow. "How old are *you*, Stanley?"

The gray-haired watchman said, "Forty-five. And I thought you were my age."

I laughed and said, "How kind! I may have to kiss you again if you keep up all this sweet talking."

He closed his eyes, turned his bristly, weather-beaten cheek toward me, and grumbled, "Well, if ya must, then let's get it over with." After I pecked his cheek, he picked up my bag and led me down the path toward the front door.

Inside, I said, "You'd better check the mirror, Stanley. I think I frosted your whiskers with my lipstick."

He touched his cheek and smiled. Then he led me to Father's office. "It's almost quitting time, Misty. I gotta make a couple a pots a coffee and then I'll get ready to go home. Folks be arrivin' soon. I'll leave ya here."

"Before you go, I've got a little something for you, Stanley. Do you like lemon squares or brownies?"

"Yeah. Reckon so." Both of his eyebrows elevated. "Either one, I suppose."

"How about one of each?" I pulled a pair of treats from my bag and handed them to Stanley.

"Thank you, Misty. Thank ya kindly." Then he turned and left me alone in Father's office.

I glanced around and felt transported through the decades to my childhood. Sometimes, Father would bring me with him to work on Saturday mornings. Usually, it was just us, but sometimes when business was good and demand was heavy, the workers would also toil on Saturdays. The pictures on the walls and the shelved trinkets looked distantly familiar. I stepped toward a tall table near the wall and looked into a small wooden bowl. A pair of antique onyx cufflinks rested in the dusty receptacle. Between my thumb and forefinger, I picked up one and placed it in the palm of my hand, and then plucked the second one from the dish.

Of all the things in Father's office, what drew me to his jewelry? I took a deep breath and began to feel dizzy. The air began to stir, and my body felt like it was spinning amidst a cyclone. It was as if I were surrounded by sparks, such as a Forth of July sparkler throws off. Then I had a vision of Father helping Johnny put on the cufflinks. It was as if it were playing on an old-fashioned television set. My fingers curled over the cufflinks and the image transformed. I was surprised to see Johnny and Betty together in an amorous embrace. A knock on the open door brought my thoughts back to the present, and I felt my body swiftly spin back to Father's office. When I returned the cufflinks to the bowl, Stanley said, "Coffee's ready, Misty."

I turned toward the man, still thinking about the wondrous experience and feeling lightheaded. Something about those cufflinks made me feel as if I were *there*.

Stanley gruffly asked, "Are ya alright, Misty?"

"Oh, yes. I didn't expect to be swept away, but being surrounded by Father's old things brought me back in time, I suppose."

"Understandable. Anyway, I just heard a car, so folks are startin' to arrive."

I said, "Thank you, Stanley." After a pause, I asked him, "Which door do the workers arrive through?"

"This way, Misty." Stanley led me down a hallway into a large, open rectangular factory and led me to a thick door. Beside it stood a rack of cream-colored cards and next to that, a mechanical time clock was mounted on the wall.

Moments later, a young man burst through the door. He was a handsome, brown-haired man with hazel eyes and a neat, reddish beard. A carpenter's pencil peeked from the top of the pocket in his brown and yellow checked flannel shirt. After he punched his card and set it back in the rack, I stepped toward him and extended my hand. "I'm Misty. Misty Menard. What's your name, sir?"

He shook my hand and a flash of recognition lit up his eyes. "Mr. Menard. Is he your Daddy?"

"Yes, he was."

"Nice man. I'm sorry he's gone. I'm Rusty Buckpitt. Nice to meet you...." the young man paused as if uncertain how to address me.

"It would please me if you would call me Misty. May I call you

Rusty?"

He shrugged, cool as a cucumber, and said, "Super! Everybody else does. Well, I better get a move on. Folks'll be piling up here in a minute."

I smiled at the tall, muscular young man and told him to have a nice day. And just as he predicted, his co-workers quickly filed past the time clock. I shook the hand of each one, catching as many of their names as possible. There were five women and too many men to count, but I recalled being told there were sixty-five people who worked at the company. I turned as the time clock clicked and noticed the hands pointed at exactly seven o'clock. A buzzer sounded, and I watched as the workers spread out across the factory. Seconds later, the whirr of motors powering the machinery filled the idle silence with the sounds of commerce.

Nearby, one young man introduced himself to another. I stood and listened but tried to look as if I were intent on something else.

A dimple-cheeked young man in bib overalls placed his hand on his chest and spoke to the second man. "I'm Hogan. Hogan Hoad." He pointed toward Rusty and said, "The foreman asked me to show you what's up."

The taller man hadn't removed his hat upon entering the building and still didn't seem interested in taking it off. Dark hair curled around the edges of his close-fitting toque as if trained to do so. "Bob Holstein. Nice to meet you. Don't see many black guys around here."

Hogan tilted his head forward and spoke in a soft tone as if sharing a secret. "I'm the only one. Not just at Adirondack Dowel." He raised his arms as if suggesting a larger region than just the company's property.

"No offense. I shouldn't a mentioned it."

Hogan shrugged.

I couldn't resist joining their conversation and spoke to the new man. "Today's your first day? We have something in common. It's my first day also."

Bob said, "How about that?"

I gripped Hogan's shoulder and said, "Maybe I should have you show me around too."

His eyes grew wide. "*You* want to run a lathe?"

Before I could answer, Rusty swooped in and marshaled the machinists away. Bob sauntered as he walked alongside his assigned mentor. He moved with a jump in his step as if dancing his way from one place to another. Young people were often full of vigor, but Bob Holstein always had *extra* pep in his step.

A young woman emerged from the office doorway carrying an armload of papers. She tipped her head at me as if she wasn't surprised to see me standing there, and made her way to a small structure that looked like a podium. She set the papers on top of the raised desk and turned back toward the office. Rusty Buckpitt approached her, patted the stack of papers with the palm of his hand, and then the woman returned to the office. From where I stood, it looked like they enjoyed their brief conversation. Rusty watched as the woman bustled off, and when the door closed behind her, he turned toward the papers, rearranged them, and left them on the podium.

For a couple of minutes more, I watched the workers toil. I knew the basic process of converting wood into dowels, spindles, pegs, and buttons, but had never watched Father's workers as intently as I did that day. It had been such a long time. Did any of the workers remember me? I frowned. Certainly, everyone had been hired subsequently.

Finally, I turned toward the office. When I placed my hand on the doorknob and pulled it toward me, a scowling man in a hurry emerged from the other side. He grunted and said, "What are *you* doing here?" He stepped through the open doorway, and held it open widely, gesturing for me to return to the office as if he wished to shove me from the factory. I recognized the dour man as one of the pallbearers at the funeral. He followed me back into the office and said, "We didn't know you were coming today."

I had hoped to make a good impression that morning and tried to overlook the man's greeting. I offered my hand and said, "I don't think we've met."

Doyle Polk seemed about ten years younger than Stanley, perhaps in his mid-thirties, but the perpetually worried look on his face made him look older. He told me that he had been with Father for the past thirteen years. Then he said, "Do you plan to come to the office regular-like?"

"Yes. I do, Mr. Polk."

He nodded understanding, but his sneer wasn't hard to interpret. He said, "Then you'd better stay in the office, Lady Fingers. We got work to do out in the factory, *ma'am*." Though he emphasized the last word, the phrase, lady fingers, tumbled in my head. He turned and blustered toward the factory door and was gone before I had the chance to tell him I would go where I pleased. I fumed at the gall of the man and considered replacing him immediately, but that wasn't the way my first day should go. My eyes closed for a couple of seconds and then I turned back toward the interior of the office.

In the corner, a thin man wearing a shirt and tie was keying numbers on an adding machine and flipping papers as he plunged the keys, looking back and forth from his work to me. Near the front door, the perky young woman's fingers clicked on the keys of an electric typewriter. The equipment in the factory and the rest of the office equipment looked like relics, but the IBM Correcting Selectric II was the latest model.

I made my way toward the woman first and introduced myself. She cheerfully told me that her name was Joanne Sorely and that she was happy to meet me. Helpfully, she said, "If there's anything you need, let me know." She told me that she was the receptionist *and* the secretary, then she returned to her work. I watched her for a minute, and if I made her nervous, it didn't show. Joanne was a fast typist, and I didn't notice her using the correction button even once.

Joanne looked like she stepped out of a picnic basket. Her tidy, modest but slim-fitting, red-checked dress reminded me of a tablecloth. I imagined myself wearing a dress like that to greet the clients at Cracken, Humble, and Dobbs. It certainly wouldn't do for the big city, but Joanne looked right at home at Adirondack Dowel. She impressed me.

I turned toward the man in the corner and walked slowly forward. He looked like a nervous fellow and I didn't want to spook him. He stood when I reached him and looked like he was shaking when he offered me his hand. I wondered if he was a drinker. As an alcoholic myself, I recognized the signs. The balding man looked to be in his late forties and he introduced himself as Art Boykins. I asked, "What's your job here at the company?"

First, he said, "I'm the bookkeeper," and then he corrected himself. "Actually, I'm the business manager," and with a sweep of his arm, he continued. "Doyle runs the factory and I run the office." He looked nervously down at the pile of invoices beside the adding machine like he was eager to get back to his paperwork.

I waved my hand toward the empty office in the corner and asked, "What about that office over there?"

Art said, "That's Stuart's office. Stuart Franklin is our sales manager. He's not an early riser. Unless he has appointments with customers, we're not likely to see him until at least nine."

I could feel Art's beady brown eyes boring into my backside as I made my way back to Father's office. I busied myself examining the papers on Father's desk. Aside from an assortment of sales flyers, newspapers, magazines, and price lists, I didn't find anything that needed attention. Perhaps Father took care of everything that was urgent before he died.

Twenty minutes after nine, Joanne knocked on the doorjamb, looking awkwardly at the open door. It was as if she were used to the door being closed rather than open. A man who looked to be in his early thirties followed her into the room, and Joanne introduced me to Stuart Franklin. He had blond, blow-dried hair, perfectly coiffed, and was dressed in multi-colored plaid slacks and a tight-fitting, white short-sleeved shirt. It was way too early in the season for the country club, but the tiny crocodile's open jaw looked ready to snap up potential customers on the golf course, nevertheless. The young man was polite and made a good impression if not entirely genuine, and after a pleasant conversation, I noticed the small Duck Head tag below his belt on the back of his pants as he returned to his office. He looked like the lawyers I worked with in Washington, DC when they came into the office on Saturday mornings.

When they were gone, I sat behind Father's desk and thought about the people that I had met. My first impression of the workers was positive. Rusty Buckpitt, the man that looked like a young lumberjack stood out in my mind. Joanne Sorely also impressed me. I wasn't so sure about the managers, Doyle Polk, Art Boykins, and Stuart Franklin. The general manager seemed like a tyrant. I wasn't sure what to make of the office manager, and the sales manager struck me as lazy. I told myself to keep an open mind, despite my initial assessments.

That afternoon, I watched the clock in Father's office as 3:00 approached. Then I carried my bag of treats toward the door to the factory. I made my way past the time clock, through the exit, and waited for the buzzer at the end of the day. Father's workers thanked me for the sweets with words and smiles and disappeared into the crisp, sunny spring afternoon. Rusty was the last to leave, and he said, "Aw, you didn't have to do that, Misty." He unwrapped the cellophane from a lemon square and popped it in his mouth. "That's delicious. Sweet and tart, just the way I like 'em." He turned to go, then looked back at me. "Will we see you again tomorrow?"

I shook my head and said, "Yes. I'll be here. See you tomorrow, Rusty."

"Super!"

As Rusty drove away in an old yellow car, I looked at the empty parking lot. I felt a swelling in my chest and was proud of my Father's business. I loved meeting the workers and pictured myself seeing them off every afternoon. Then the door swung violently open and Doyle burst through the exit. He stood in front of me with his thumbs in the waistband of his pants. He barked, "What are you doing?"

I said, "Hello Doyle. I wanted to see the workers off."

"Why? Why in tarnation would you do a thing like that?"

The man's harshness stunned me. I stammered before finding my voice. "What difference does it make? What harm could possibly come from wishing them a good day?"

"Did you raise spoiled children, Miss Lady Fingers? We don't take to coddling around here. I won't have it, do you understand me? Stay away from *my* employees." He turned and walked away as if he didn't care what I thought of his ultimatum.

4

During my first week at Adirondack Dowel and Spindle Company, I learned a lot about Father's employees by greeting them in the morning and seeing them off each day, to the chagrin of the general manager. I was determined not to let The Three Stooges make me lose my cool. But Moe, Larry, and Curly must not be permitted to have their way. Whether they liked it or not, I was the owner and president of the Adirondack Dowel and Spindle Company, and that meant that I had the right to do with the company as I deemed best. The sooner they came to accept it, the better, as far as I was concerned. Despite my determination, I dreaded the confrontation and it rattled me all weekend, knowing that it was coming. Comparing them to famous comedians amused me, but there was nothing funny about my predicament.

After everyone arrived, I asked Joanne to inform Stuart, Art, and Doyle that I wanted to meet with them in my office at 10. Judging by the looks on their faces, they didn't appreciate being sent for. Maybe they didn't like the idea of being called to a meeting, or perhaps they took issue with the short notice. I had set five chairs so that we could face one another.

Doyle crossed his arms over his chest, sat back in his chair, and spread his legs widely. His red cheeks and scowling face made him look angry and there was no mistaking his dark mood.

The business manager's small frame squirmed on his seat, and he cast his gaze about the room as if he were looking for a safe corner in which to hide. His fingers tapped on his leg, one after the other in a repetitive loop. He never made eye contact with me, and I couldn't help wondering why he had brought his briefcase with him. I began to wonder what he carried that was so important to him that he couldn't be apart from it.

Stuart had a smirk on his face and I couldn't tell whether he was amused by the novelty of meeting with his colleagues, entertained by the predicament I had found myself in, or eager to watch the sparks fly. Some people revel in drama at work, to help pass the time or lessen the dullness of their daily routines.

Joanne looked surprised when I called her in and asked her to bring her stenographer's notebook. "Would you take notes for our meeting? I'd like to keep a record of the things we discuss and the decisions we make." Joanne crossed her legs, set the notebook on her lap, and prepared to record the first meeting I had ever conducted at work. At the law firm, I'd attended quite a few, but running meetings was new territory for me.

I took a deep breath and looked at Doyle. "We are the leaders of this company, and I think it is important that we work together to make it better. Every Monday morning, I'd like us to sit down together like we're doing now."

Doyle blew air through his lips like a toddler in his highchair rejecting unwanted baby food. "Why on earth would we want to do that? Meetings are just a waste of time. Every minute someone is talking is a minute they're not working. I've got *real* work to do. There are two lathes out there that need fixing, and dozens of employees that need watching over. Employees slow down to half speed when nobody's watching. You know that, don't you?"

I was prepared for Doyle's arguments. "Communicating is crucial. When we know what's important to one another, we can help each other out. And I'd like to think you could place more faith and confidence in our workers, Doyle."

"Shows what you know. If I don't ride herd on them, they'll take advantage and before you know it, nobody will get anything done. I went to business school, *missy*, and I spent a couple of years in the army. So I know a few things about subordinates, and if I've learned one thing, it is that people need to be told what to do."

I can't help wondering whether Doyle recognizes that the general manager of a company reports to its president. How could he *not* know that? <u>Coolly</u>, I said, "My name is Misty, not Missy. You should be very proud of our workers, but I don't want them to feel like soldiers."

I hoped to move on to another subject, but Doyle wasn't willing to drop the matter yet. He practically spat his words at me. "What's wrong with feeling like a soldier? And since when do we care how they *feel*? They are paid to do a job. I expect them to do it. I'm not going to burp and diaper them or wipe their noses."

Doyle was pushing my patience to the limit, but I reminded myself that I wasn't going to lose my temper. I placed my hands on my knees, leaned forward, and said, "We're not at war, Doyle. People deserve to be treated with respect and decency. Yes, they should do a fair day's work for their pay, but they should also know why they're doing the things they're doing. I believe any task can be performed with dignity as long as one knows why that task is important and how it contributes to the reason we're all here."

The retort came hot and fast. "If I want them to do something, I'll tell them what to do, and they'll do it without a fuss, by God, or they'll find themselves in the unemployment line so fast their heads will spin. As long as I'm the general manager here, I run the factory, and we'll do it *my* way."

That's when I lost it. I could feel my face twist with rage. I was so angry, I didn't know exactly what I was saying, but Joanne wrote it all down. Spittle flew from my lips as I screamed at the man. "This is *my* company. You work for *me*. If I want you to sit in a meeting all day, that's what you're going to do. I'll treat you with respect, but if you can't do the same for me, it will be *your* head spinning in the unemployment line." I could feel the daggers shooting from my eyes into his perpetually worried-looking forehead. My hands balled into fists, and I pounded my knees with each word as I finished, "Is that clear, Mr. Polk?"

He answered firmly with one word, "Yes." But I heard, "Yes, sir." It was clear to me that he understood and was deferring to me because I was his superior officer and for no other reason. That would have to do.

I looked at the clock and was surprised to see how little time had passed. I wished that I could have a few minutes by myself to collect my <u>wits</u> before continuing. In my imagination, a smoke break provided a brief interlude. Instead, I swallowed hard and looked from person to person. "The next thing I want to talk about is our profits. Friday afternoon, I met with our accountant, Vernon Crawford. He has finished the company's taxes for last year. We just barely squeaked out a surplus. The good news is that we will not have to pay a lot of taxes, but Mr. Crawford said that a successful business needs to generate income in order to grow and prosper. If it loses money, it cannot survive, and we came close to losing money last year. I know everyone is working hard but we're not making money. If you have any thoughts about that, I'd like to hear them. If you want to think about it, we'll talk about it again next week. Perhaps we should discuss it every week."

Doyle found his voice again. "Hey, my job is to get the product made and delivered on time. The rest is up to Art and Stuart. Maybe you should get up in their business instead of mine."

Trying to regain my composure, I said, "I don't want to get up in anybody's business. I want to work together so that the company can make a profit."

I looked from Doyle to Art, but Stuart spoke instead. He said, "I thought you cared how the people felt, not about how much money *you* make."

"If we *all* work hard, we should *all* expect to make more money, shouldn't we Stuart?"

The sales manager grinned, shrugged, and nodded.

"That's why I'd like to put in a profit-sharing program. When we make a profit, we should distribute a portion of it as a bonus, and everyone in the company will share it. Most of the profits have to go back into the company, but I think if we're successful, we should be able to give ten percent of it back to the employees."

Art's eyebrows twitched frightfully. "Oh, no, no. That will never do. What if the customers find out? They'll demand we drop our prices. There won't be any money in the checkbook by the time we're through."

"I think it will be alright, Art. As long as we charge a fair price, it is up to our company to decide how to split the profits. Anyway, think about the bonus idea, and also think about how we can make a fair profit. We'll talk again about it next week."

We'd covered a lot of ground, but we still hadn't filled an hour yet. I asked Stuart what he could tell us about his visits with our customers. He sat up and talked about his plans to visit hardware stores downstate, but it was clear that Doyle and Art weren't listening. Warning bells went off in my head, but I stopped Stuart anyway. I said, "I'm sorry, why isn't anybody paying attention to Stuart?"

Doyle said, "That's just sales talk. I don't want to hear about all the time Stuart spends skiing, golfing with customers, and plying customers with martinis during two-hour-long lunches at the country club. I'll pay attention to the orders when they come in. Getting the orders is Stuart's problem. Figuring out how much to charge is Art's job. What's it to me?"

I held my head in my hands, frustrated, and said, "Don't you numbskulls get it? We're all in this together. If we succeed, we succeed together. If we flounder, we all suffer. If the ship goes down, we're all sunk. That's what I'm trying to tell you."

Art said, "It's eleven o'clock. Time's up. I have to get to the post office and pick up the mail, and then the bank." His bony fingers grabbed the briefcase handle as he stood and backed away from the group as if fearful of turning his back to us.

I shook my head and looked up at the ceiling just as a spider dropped from a long strand of web and landed on my face. I jumped to my feet, slapped my face, and knocked over my chair. My management team was gone, but Joanne hurried to my side. Thank heavens for Joanne.

After the lunch break, I closed the door to Father's office for the first time in the week that I'd been there. I thought about dialing the number myself but instead called Joanne and asked her to get Attorney Ted Drake on the line. It felt like forever since I retired from the firm and I missed the camaraderie. I especially missed the enthusiastic young lawyer who specialized in the laws governing retirement plans.

"Misty, is that you?"

"Yes, Ted. It's good to hear your voice."

"Gosh, it's been a long time. I thought you said you were going to stop in and visit every once in a while."

"I know I did. You'd be surprised how busy one can get when they retire."

Ted laughed. "I don't think I'll ever retire, Misty. Maybe if I had a hobby or two. I can't even *imagine* retiring. It will be another century before I'm old enough for that anyway. Oh, listen to me go on. What have *you* been doing?"

"You wouldn't believe it if I told you, Ted." I paused for a moment, took a breath, and said, "My father passed away, and he left me his company, so I moved home to Lake Placid in the Adirondack mountains of New York."

"Lake Placid! Why that's practically in Canada, isn't it? I thought people went south when they retired, not north. I'm terribly sorry to hear about your father, Misty."

"Thank you, Ted. That means a lot. I appreciate it."

"What are you doing about the business?"

"Well, I decided to run it myself, at least for a little while. And I wanted to talk to you about that *thing* you were always bragging about. I can't remember the name of it. All I can think of is esophagus, but that isn't it. Do you know what I'm talking about?"

"Yes. Of course. You're talking about ESOP. That stands for Employee Stock Ownership Plan. Not esophagus. Heavens no." After a brief pause, Ted added, "Why do you want to form an ESOP, Misty?"

It was hard not to get emotional when I answered his question. "Over the past week, I've been amazed to learn about Father's employees. They work hard but never get ahead. They are fiercely loyal, but the longer they work for us, the poorer they become. Our night watchman, Stanley's house doesn't have running water. Poor Hogan's family can't afford electricity. Millie's house only has a dirt floor. It's been decades since the Great Depression, Ted. In this day and age, why are people still living like this?"

"They shouldn't have to. But you are paying a legal wage, aren't you?"

"Yes, but it's not enough. They deserve better. It pains me to hear about their finances. To think of all the money I squandered, by calling Father for emergency loans I never repaid, and what it could have meant to his employees if he paid them more instead of wasting that money on me. And then, to think of how management treats the employees. Why should they have to work for short pay and be harshly treated? They deserve respect, Ted. It breaks my heart." My voice broke and I squeezed the phone tightly in my hand before continuing. "Do you think I could buy an ESOP so that Father's employees could own the business?"

Ted chuckled. "Not exactly, Misty. You don't *buy* an ESOP. You form one. That's the easy part. The rest is a bit harder."

"I was afraid of that. I was hoping it would be easy. Do you think you could explain it to me?"

I hate to admit that my mind wandered as Ted went into the technical details involved in the formation of an ESOP trust and transitioning ownership of a company to it. I pictured the blond-haired lawyer's chubby, cherubic cheeks that reminded me of a cartoon chipmunk, and for a moment I was afraid that I might giggle. When he was done, I said, "Do you think we can manage all that?"

Ted was reassuring and I asked him if he could fly to New York and drive to Lake Placid. He said, "I'd be glad to come, and what's more, if you decide to go ahead, I'll do the legal work for you *pro bono*."

I was speechless, but managed to squeak out, "I'm so grateful, Ted. I can't wait to see you."

Before I let Ted hang up, I asked him whether he had found a wife and settled down. He said, "Not yet, Misty. I guess I work too many hours, but my big news is that I just made *partner*."

"Good for you, Ted. That's fantastic! I'm so proud of you." It was rare for someone to make partner so young, and it was also unusual for an unmarried man to be promoted into the ownership ranks of a prestigious law firm. I thought of Joanne and wondered whether Ted and Joanne would appreciate being fixed up together.

After we hung up, I reminded myself, "Not esophagus. An ESOP for us!"

The evening after my first meeting with the management team, I walked down the sidewalk to the store and purchased a pack of Winstons. The slogan, "Winston tastes good like a cigarette should," ran through my head. I resisted the temptation to light a smoke on the way home. By the time I closed the door behind me, the urge had passed. I tried to think about how many packs I'd bought through the years and later tossed out unopened. If I ever ripped off the cellophane, I was sure I'd be powerless to resist, and if I smoked one I'd be hopelessly hooked, yet again. It was hard to quit drinking, but giving up smoking was even tougher. I slipped the cigarettes into my dressing table drawer and tried to forget they were there.

***

I insisted that Ted stay at Father's house, and it was good to have a visitor. After Father's funeral, Harold returned to his cabin in the woods. Presto and Four went back to their small home, so it got mighty quiet in the breezy old Victorian with just me and Calhoun knocking about the house.

Not only was it my first Board of Directors meeting, but it also happened to be the Annual Shareholder's meeting *and* the Annual Board of Directors meeting. Winslow told me that it was all rather routine, but that we should go through the formality of actually getting together and documenting its occurrence. I suggested we have dinner together at The Woodshed Restaurant afterward. I should have told Winslow that I had invited a special guest. After making such a big deal about communication at the company, it might have been a good idea to consider my own advice. But I was excited about the prospect of the company's employees becoming owners and I couldn't wait to surprise the Mayor and Attorney Gloversmith with the idea.

The meeting itself was held in the dining room of Father's home at four in the afternoon. Mayor Peacock was the first to arrive and Winslow rapped on the front door a couple of minutes later. I introduced Ted as my houseguest, and Ted raised a curious eyebrow at me when I did. I forgot to tell Ted that I didn't explain his reason for being there.

Mayor Peacock shook Ted's hand vigorously and promised the young man that he was in for a treat. "I've made reservations for dinner at our finest new restaurant. The Woodshed Restaurant is in its first season. The owner, Bob Terwilliger, is setting his best table for us, and will personally serve our meal tonight. After we take you out to the Woodshed, Ted, you'll really feel like you've been to the Adirondacks." The restaurant was intimate, classy, and cozy all at the same time. It glowed like a candle, warmed like a woodstove, and smelled like a campfire. I could practically hear the steaks sizzle just thinking about dinner. I was looking forward to a nice evening out as much as Mayor Peacock and hoped that Ted would enjoy himself also.

The Shareholder's meeting lasted ninety seconds. The Shareholders elected the Board of Directors, Winslow Gloversmith, Robert J. Peacock, and me. As the sole shareholder, I voted all of the shares. The Board of Directors meeting wasn't expected to take much longer. We elected the officers of the company. Winslow was named secretary of the corporation, Mayor Peacock the chairman, and I was named president and treasurer. Then, Mayor Peacock said, "I believe that's all the business for the Board to attend to. Are there any other issues the Board would like to discuss today?"

I crossed my legs, cleared my throat, and said, "Actually, I do have a matter I'd like the Board to consider. But first, I should clarify that my guest, Ted Drake is a newly named partner in the law firm, Cracken, Humble, and Dobbs, where I worked as a receptionist before I retired. He specializes in a little-known, brand-new part of the law." I turned to face Ted and said, "What did you call it, Ted? It was something like Melissa, but that isn't right."

Ted's boyish laugh accompanied his mild correction. "Misty means ERISA." Ted went on to explain the new law which governed retirement plans. I watched Winslow's face sag as he turned ghostly white as Ted explained how ESOPs work. Mayor Peacock, on the other hand, looked intrigued and wanted to hear more.

The young lawyer said, "So, we hire a trustee. The trustee has the business appraised. The bank lends money to the trust. The company funds the trust to repay the loan, and participants' accounts grow as the loan is repaid. Employees don't have to pay one dime to become owners and the seller gets to defer the profit on the sale of the stock to the trust. So, everybody wins."

Winslow rubbed his face, releasing a wave of Aqua Velva scent into the room. "So, Misty sells the company for what you call *market value*. She can't use the proceeds from the sale if she wants to defer the taxes on it. The company goes deeper into debt. And all the benefit of it goes to the workers? AJ must be doing somersaults in his grave listening to this. What am I missing?"

Ted grimaced. "The company doesn't have to go deeper into debt. Misty can lend the company the money for the deal, but the bank's loan has to come first. If the bank makes the loan instead of Misty, it is likely they will require Misty to guarantee the loan."

The older attorney groaned and looked toward the heavens.

Mayor Peacock asked, "How is the market value calculated?"

Ted answered, "We'll help the company conduct a feasibility analysis and hire a valuation firm to appraise it. They'll make calculations based on projections, earnings, and comparable companies to determine how much the business is worth."

The mayor said, "Mr. Drake, the accountant's report for 1974 tells us that the business barely made a profit. How much is a business that doesn't make money worth?"

Ted looked at me in horror. "Nothing. If a business doesn't make a profit, it isn't worth anything. You didn't tell me *that*, Misty."

I stammered an apology. "I'm sorry, Ted. I didn't think to mention it. But the company isn't worthless. It provides great value to sixty-five people who support their families with the income that they make."

The mayor came to my defense. "And it provided Misty's father a very comfortable income throughout his long life."

Winslow leaned toward me and whispered at me through his teeth. "Misty, do you realize what's at stake?"

A juicy steak at the Woodshed Restaurant with my favorite attorney and the Board of Directors of the Adirondack Dowel and Spindle Company no longer sounded tantalizing. I just wanted the men to leave so I could have a cigarette. I pictured the pack of smokes in the drawer and yearned to be home. I wanted to go to bed early and pull the covers over my head.

5

Nine months later, I sat in Winslow's narrow, second-story office overlooking Mirror Lake. I tried to convince myself that I wasn't nervous, but my stomach churned. I had managed to resist a smoking relapse, but on New Year's Day, I moved the still unopened pack of cigarettes from the table drawer to the bottom of my pocketbook.

Winslow made himself busy at his large wooden desk, reading some sort of document and flipping its pages. I looked out the window and watched a squall swirl above Mirror Lake and occasionally glanced at my watch. The man we waited for was twenty minutes late and I felt like I had held my breath for a month. Ted had recommended Mr. Benjamin Penchant. The two men had graduated from Columbia University together in 1968, and Ted had worked with the business appraiser in the past. Whatever his strengths, I thought, being on time wasn't one of them. Everything depended on Benjamin's opinion about the value of the company. I prayed that it would be high enough to justify forming an ESOP.

I must have sighed loudly because Winslow looked up from his desk and frowned. "You mustn't worry, Misty."

That was easy for him to say. I had been on edge since my first cup of coffee, well before dawn. My family must have forgotten, and maybe nobody at Adirondack Dowel knew that it was my birthday. It shouldn't have bothered me that nobody recognized my milestone birthday, but it did. I tried to focus on the priority of the day. I imagined myself a convicted felon, awaiting a judge's verdict. How much was the company worth?

When it finally came, I flinched at the loud knocking sound on Winslow's wooden door, and stood up as Winslow called out, "Please come in."

I watched as Winslow greeted Benjamin. The appraiser looked exactly the same as he did when I met him a month earlier. The lake was already frozen and we were digging out from a blizzard. Benjamin's <u>heavy </u>overcoat made him seem twice his actual size.

Benjamin Penchant was shorter than me and as skinny as a teenager, and yet his presence was off-putting. His handshake crushed my fingers, his deep voice rattled my eardrums, and I was still thinking about how loudly he knocked on the door. His dark hair was combed straight back and was so heavily greased that it looked wet and crusty. I swallowed hard and recalled his previous visit when he asked question after question and stared at me through his thick, soda bottle glasses.

Winslow gestured toward the chairs by the window. "Please make yourself comfortable, Mr. Penchant."

The door to Winslow's office flung open and Ted Drake burst into the room without knocking. He panted, "I'm sorry I'm late. I hope you didn't start without me." He raced toward me and momentarily, I was afraid that he wouldn't be able to stop. I imagined him knocking into me, and both of us crashing through the window into the icy lake below. He had an arm behind his back, and as he reached me, a bouquet of flowers appeared before my face, wrapped in paper and open at the top. I glanced at the gladiolas and chrysanthemums, and the balmy fragrance of carnations made me smile.

I said, "Thank you, Ted. You shouldn't have," but I was glad he did.

"That's why I was late. I had almost forgotten what day it was." My favorite attorney remembered my birthday!

I said, "It's so kind of you, Ted." I kissed the young lawyer on his cheek, and then Ted slapped his college buddy on the shoulder.

Winslow took the flowers and set them on his desk as the rest of us claimed our seats. We sat quietly, waiting for Benjamin to speak, and he looked at me like he was waiting for me to answer an interrogation. I felt like I should say something, but Benjamin was the one with the news of the day. Maybe the young analyst enjoyed suspenseful moments, but the awkward silence made me feel like bad news was imminent.

Finally, Winslow broke the silence. "Mr. Penchant, have you completed the appraisal of Adirondack Dowel?"

Benjamin turned toward the older man and acknowledged that he had.

Ted said, "Have you written your report?"

Benjamin nodded. "I have." He sat forward and reached for his briefcase, which looked exactly like the one that Art Boykins carried with him everywhere he went. As Benjamin pressed the buttons on the attaché, the brass clasps violently released with a loud thunk. He removed four neatly bound reports and passed one to each of us. "I'll take you through the report, page by page, but first, I expect you'd like to know what the company is worth."

Winslow made an affirming sound as I nodded and Ted looked at Benjamin, waiting patiently.

"The company has experienced a rough couple of years, recently, but the good news is that last year was a little better. I looked at the results later in the year and they were stronger than at the beginning of the year. The trend supports the forecast of improving results, but the company still isn't producing a lot of cash. As you know, cash is king." Benjamin let his words settle before continuing. "I value the business several different ways and calculate an average of the results." I could feel my heart pounding, waiting for Benjamin to tell us how much the company was worth.

Finally, Winslow impatiently said, "And?"

"And I find the fair market value of the Adirondack Dowel and Spindle Company is $500,000."

Someone may as well have punched me in the stomach. I had hoped that Father's company would be worth more than that. Winslow had supposed that it would be worth a million, but my hunch was that he was just being cautious. My prediction was a value of two million dollars. It was tempting to blame Benjamin. I wouldn't want to admit that the urge to push him down and stomp on his glasses crossed my mind as he began to speak again.

Benjamin said, "In 1974, Adirondack Dowel made less than $10,000 profit. Fortunately, 1975 was much better, generating $90,000 in cash from its operations. If I value the business based on what its assets could be sold for, I calculate $400,000. When I average that with the present value of its projected income stream and compare it to the value of similar small businesses, I'm comfortable that the fair market value of the company is higher than its liquidation value." Benjamin directed our attention to one dizzyingly complicated page after another until we reached the end of his report and my scrambled brain just wanted to ooze from my ears. Finally, Benjamin concluded, "If Misty runs the business for a couple of more years and if the projections become reality, I think she can double the value of the company."

I tried to maintain my composure. I sat stoically in the chair, my hands joined in my lap, and thought that even doubled, the value would only be half what I thought it should be. I tried to console myself with the thought that at least the company was worth something. It *wasn't* worthless.

Winslow sat forward and turned his head to face me. "Would you like to be alone, Misty?"

"No. Let's continue."

"Very well," Winslow said. "Given the company is only worth half a million dollars, I think we should forget selling it to the employees."

I shuddered, squeezed my hands more tightly together, and

said, "Why, Winslow?"

"I should think that you'd want to get every cent you could for the company, under the circumstances, and I guess you'd like to sell it as quickly as possible. What if things go bad, and the value goes down next year instead of up?"

Benjamin nodded and in his deep, growling voice agreed. "If the company's progress halts or its profits decline, it will be hard to sell it at any price." He sniffled, wiggled his nose, and his thick glasses jumped up and down in front of his dark, serious eyes.

Ted reached an arm forward, clasped my knee in his hand, and said, "I'm sorry, Misty."

I knew that Ted was trying to make me feel better, but it didn't work. All day long, my frayed nerves threatened to get the better of me, but at that moment, stubbornness prevailed. "I don't care if the company is worth thirty-seven cents. If the company isn't worth anything, then I will not need to borrow money from the bank to do the deal. I lived on a receptionist's salary, so I suppose I can get by on Social Security. I never expected to inherit the company anyway. I want the employees to own Father's company."

Ted said, "Misty, you don't have to sell the whole company at once. You could sell part of it now and the rest of it later. That way, if the employees can make the company more valuable as owners, you'll benefit when you sell the rest of the company later, at a higher price."

I thought about what Ted was suggesting. "So if I sell twenty-five percent of the company now at a low price, I can sell the rest later at a higher price."

"That's right."

"But then the company will have to go into more debt to buy it from me then."

"That's also correct."

Winslow had heard enough. "But then you'll only own a fraction of the business, not all of it."

Ted said, "That's true, but if Misty still owns a majority of the company, she can make all of the important decisions. As long as she owns more than fifty percent."

Winslow looked at me intently. "I can't let you do this to yourself, Misty. I just can't. I'd be guilty of malpractice. Please reconsider. I'm begging and pleading with you, dear. It's for your own good!"

"I appreciate that Winslow, but I've made up my mind. Draw up the papers."

Ted asked, "By what date do you need them?"

"I want to make it official on Independence Day. The Fourth of July. What better way to celebrate than on the country's bicentennial?"

Winslow shook his head violently from side to side. "That's less than six months away." He turned toward Ted and said, "These ESOPs are complicated. We can't get it done that fast, can we?"

Ted looked at me. The perceptive young man could always tell how I was feeling and he must have taken pity on me. "Yes," he said. "They're not *that* complicated, Winslow. The hard part of deciding to form an ESOP is already done. Besides, most of my deals happen at the end of the year, so I have a little more free time in the spring and summer. If Misty wishes, we can do this."

Winslow tipped his forehead into his fist and grumbled. "Are you certain, Misty? You must be absolutely sure."

I replied. "I've never been more certain of anything, Winslow."

Ted said, "What would you like to name the ESOP?"

"It gets a name?"

"Yes, the trust needs a legal name."

"How about calling it the AJ Menard ESOP? That's fitting, wouldn't you say? The workers adored him."

Winslow looked into my eyes and said, "Alright, Misty. I'll form the trust."

And Ted said, "I'll draft the plan document. Would you like to prepare the purchase and sale agreement, Winslow?" Father's attorney nodded tentatively, and Ted said, "Now we just need to find a trustee."

Winslow said, "Good grief. I forgot to think about that. We can't have the Board of Directors also serve as the trustee."

"No, we can't. The Board is responsible for the company, the trustee has to act in the best interest of the plan participants, and will have to hire their own appraiser for the deal."

Benjamin's booming voice reminded us of his presence. "Ted, the company should hire an independent trustee, don't you agree?"

"Yes, I have a few I could suggest. But they will charge a fee for their services."

Winslow rolled his eyes dramatically though he never failed to miss an opportunity to send the company an invoice. I asked, "Could the employees do the job themselves?"

Ted said, "Yes, they could. Often the seller serves as trustee, but we can't recommend that, Misty."

Winslow stomped his fist on his knee. "I won't hear of it. I will not allow *that*. Misty, if you're going to do this, you must do it by the book."

"Very well," I said as calmly as I could. "We'll hire an independent trustee. Ted, will you recommend one that can get the deal done by the Fourth of July?"

***

After lunch, Ted and Benjamin set out in their rented car for Albany to catch the late flight back to Washington. Winslow and I paid a visit to John Frederick Duncan of Mirror Lake Bank. The man looked like Jackie Gleason, but for his ski jump-shaped nose. I explained my plans to sell a quarter of the company to an ESOP and Winslow interjected the technical details as Mr. Duncan asked questions. The money-grubbing weasel informed me that the bank would allow the change in the company's ownership structure provided I would personally guarantee the bank's loans to the company, even if *I* financed the $125,000 sale of a quarter of the company to the ESOP.

Mr. Duncan said, "You must understand the bank's position, Miss Menard. The company is already in debt, you see, what with the mortgage on the factory and the equipment loans. The bank's *policy* doesn't allow me to make loans to over-extended businesses." I thought I saw a twinkle in Mr. Duncan's eye and his under-developed mustache almost concealed a devious smirk. I imagined that he relished the possibility of repossessing the bank's collateral. I told myself that people can't help how they look and convinced myself that the banker had no interest in owning Adirondack Dowel.

***

That afternoon, I never made it back to the company. Four had been looking forward to the skating competition for eight to ten-year-olds that afternoon. His dedication to the sport was impressive for someone of any age, let alone a 9-year-old boy, and I didn't want to miss any of it. When the school year began, Presto and Four moved in with me so that Four could skate before and after school; that's how serious he had become about his training. Though he enjoyed watching hockey and skating fast, Four had set his sights on figure skating. Presto and I were among the first to arrive at the competition and sat in the front row. Before the sporting event, during their warm-up session, Four skated along the edge of the rink and shouted, "Hi GiGi," as he passed me. Then he looked back and added, "Hi Dad."

The girls went first and it seemed like dozens of them competed. My mind wandered as the graceful young ladies twisted, twirled, and danced on their sharp blades. Whenever one would fall, my attention would return and like the other spectators in the stands, I sat on the edge of my seat until it was clear that the children would be alright. Injuries were painful enough, but in most cases, it was the letdown from having fallen or losing the competition that caused their heartfelt tears.

After the winner of the girl's competition was announced, the boys began taking turns on the ice. There was far less competition for the boy's trophy. When Four skated onto the ice and struck his opening pose, I gasped. A joyful expression radiated from his face as his arms spread wide. It was as if he were embracing the experience of participating in the Olympics instead of a local competition for children. I was transported back in time to when I sat with my father and watched Karl Schäfer of Austria win Olympic gold in men's figure skating at the 1932 Olympics in Lake Placid.

To me, Four looked like he was in fine form in his black polyester slacks, and matching black shirt with bright blue sleeves that made his arms seem twice as long whenever he would spin. He was good at jumps, flips, and footwork, but his dizzying spins were his favorite move, and he was smart to work several of them into his routine. I swooned just watching him twist relentlessly. For a moment, I feared he would drill a hole into the ice with his blades.

When the competition was over, Four hugged a trophy that was almost as tall as he was. I'll never forget that moment when my great-grandson seemed on top of the world.

***

The following Monday, I stood by the window just before 10:00 am and gazed at the brilliant, snow-covered mountains and the cloudless sky. Joanne rearranged the floral bouquet that Ted gave me for my birthday, stirring a spicy scent into the air. Spring was a long way off, but the blinding sun reflected on ice made me long for warmer weather.

Stuart, Art, and Doyle promptly took their regular seats and I greeted the team as Joanne stepped into the room. We had been meeting dutifully every Monday for a year, but the gathering still felt as uncomfortable as the first one did. The men didn't argue about whether they should attend the meetings and they didn't discuss whether any value came from our meetings. Instead, they endured them. Whether they had discussed it, or it just turned out that way, one thing they seemed to agree upon was a strategy of running out the clock. It was always up to me to have discussion topics ready, or we would sit in silence waiting for the time to expire.

I thought about all the questions that Benjamin asked me during his valuation interview over a month ago, and that helped me think of new topics to discuss with the group. After each man gave his update and answered my questions, I took a deep breath. I looked at each man for a moment, finally resting my gaze on Doyle. All weekend, I rehearsed the words I would use when we met today.

My eyes closed for a second and I thought of Father. I wish that he were here to witness the gift I was about to bestow upon his workers, in his name. "I've decided to sell the company to the workers. The sale will happen over the course of several years, and the first transaction will happen on Independence Day. I plan to hold a big luncheon on Friday to tell everyone the big news, so I want you to keep it to yourselves until then. Maybe you've never heard of ESOPs, but under a new law, employees can become owners through an Employee Stock Ownership Plan."

Doyle was the first to speak. "What kind of an idiot are you?" Truthfully, the man added an expletive before the word *idiot*.

Thanks to Art, I didn't have to categorize for Doyle just what sort of an idiot I was. The business manager said, "Why would you go and do a thing like that?"

Stuart's perpetual grin became a guffaw and he slapped his thighs. "Doesn't that beat all? What will you think of next, Misty?"

Doyle added. "That'd be like putting the students in charge of the high school. How can you expect the principal to do his job?"

Art added, "Or putting the prisoners in charge of the jail. What's the warden to do?"

Stuart laughed and held his sides like it hurt to have to laugh so hard. "Oh, or like opening all the cages at the zoo and expecting the animals not to eat each other." I looked at the sales manager and imagined a lion chewing on his carcass.

Doyle said, "Next thing you know it, Misty'll want everyone to sit around in a meeting, holding hands, and singing songs."

Stuart began singing, "I'd like to Teach the World to Sing (In Perfect Harmony)." I smiled at the thought and the five-year-old song played in my head.

The door between the factory and the office swung open and Millie shouted, "Come quickly. There's been a terrible accident. Call an ambulance."

6

That night when I got home, I went straight to my bedroom. Calhoun looked up from the center of the bed where he had been napping as the door clicked behind me. I removed the unopened pack of *Winstons* from my pocketbook and packed the smokes with a few raps of the box on my wrist and then peeled the cellophane from the box. I plugged the end of my brass cigarette holder with a smoke and flipped the top from my matching butane lighter. The ornate smoking relics were a wedding gift from my brother, Johnny. I guess that's why I kept them when I quit smoking. Perhaps, also, I knew I would need them again someday.

As I drew my first puff of smoke, I felt like I had been reunited with an old friend—one that I had missed terribly and longed to see. A friend that made me feel giddy when we got together, but a friend that I knew was no good for me. Even as the tingling feelings rushed to my head, I knew that I would suffer to have to quit again, but at that moment, I didn't care. After the traumatic day, I was powerless to resist the addictive urge to surround myself in a cloud of smoke.

I'll never forget the horrible moment when we raced into the factory. The workers darted around, panicked, trying to turn off all the machinery. Several people screamed at the sight of all the blood, and I thought I would faint. People had gathered around Rusty Buckpitt who looked lost, like he couldn't make sense of what was happening to him.

Joanne screamed, "I found Rusty's finger!" The young woman was more level-headed than me. I was still trying to make sense of what was happening, but she was already helping.

Fortunately, the ambulance came fast. The medics took Rusty's finger with them. I blindly followed Joanne and climbed into the passenger seat when she hurried into her ugly green, Ford Granada, and raced the ambulance to the hospital. Somewhere along the way, I pulled myself together, just as Joanne started to crumble.

In the waiting room, Joanne looked at the blood stains on her blue and white floral dress and began to wail. Between sobs, she moaned, "Poor Rusty. What will he do? What will become of him if he isn't able to work anymore?"

I couldn't answer Joanne's questions but held my arms open and Joanne sagged into my embrace. I said, "There, there, honey." I had heard of fingers being reattached, but I didn't know how common it was. Could the doctors in Lake Placid perform such medical miracles? They were acutely aware of how to mend broken bones. The steep, icy mountain nearby sent many shattered arms and legs to the Lake Placid Memorial Hospital. Perhaps they would also know what to do about Rusty's finger.

We heard a commotion and it sounded like an alien spacecraft was landing on the hospital's roof. A passing nurse stopped in her tracks and told us not to worry. "That's just a helicopter. They're taking a patient to Boston for emergency surgery."

Joanne said, "Do you think they're taking Rusty to Boston?" Before I could answer she said, "Should I go with them? Would they let me?"

As it turned out, Rusty *was* airlifted to Boston, but they wouldn't allow any other passengers. Joanne and I returned to Adirondack Dowel and looked into Rusty's file in the cabinet to see if we had emergency contact information. I remember hearing that Rusty Buckpitt was from nearby Tupper Lake, but the single man didn't list any next of kin. Joanne looked distraught and said, "I shouldn't have let him leave that part blank. I always make sure employees complete their paperwork. What should we do, Misty?"

"I don't know, honey." I thought about suggesting that we drive to Boston. "Maybe we can phone the hospital later." Joanne looked at me expectantly as if I had made a good but incomplete suggestion. I added, "Perhaps we could drive to Boston tomorrow to see how Rusty is doing."

That seemed to delight Joanne. She said, "That'd be super!" Then she drew her arms to her side and rocked back and forth, demurely. "Now I sound like Rusty. He's always saying that word, *super.*"

When Joanne mentioned it, I realized that she was right. Nobody said super more than Rusty did. I glanced around to make sure that Stuart, Art, and Doyle were nowhere nearby, and said, "You're sweet on Rusty, aren't you, honey?"

"I guess, maybe. Do you think he's noticed?"

I laughed in a way that I hoped Joanne found reassuring. "I don't know if he knows he's noticed, but I've seen him watching you. Why don't you tell him that he should ask you out?"

Joanne smiled at me but didn't say anything more.

One cigarette wasn't enough. After years of deprivation, I immediately needed another. I flipped the lighter's lid and inhaled a satisfying puff as the doorbell chimed. I looked at the cigarette and thought about ignoring the evening caller. I felt like I had been caught stealing. Confound it, if I wanted to smoke, I would. It's not like it was illegal. Whose business was it anyway? I snubbed the coffin nail, spritzed the perfume atomizer, popped a mint, and trotted down the stairs. I opened the front door without checking to see who was there. "Oh, good heavens, Betty. It's you." Usually, Betty just let herself in the back door rather than making a formal call at the front door.

"Of course, Misty. Remember, we had an appointment." She carried several large picture books beneath her arm. This wasn't a personal call.

"I had forgotten, but please come in." I suggested she make herself comfortable in the living room, but she wanted to use the kitchen table instead.

As if to make up for having forgotten our appointment, I told Betty about Rusty's severed finger.

I had put Betty off for months but rather than forget about making over Father's home and office, she persisted. Didn't she have enough clients? She flipped pages to pre-marked exhibits, pointed, and looked into my face to see if any of the images elicited a flicker of enthusiasm within me. I was glad when the tea kettle whistled but Betty frowned at the interruption.

She followed me to the kitchen counter. As I dangled a tea bag into a cup of hot water, Betty said, "I've been after you for months and you keep putting me off. I'm beginning to think you don't want *me* to make over your home. Why won't you let me redecorate for you? I thought you liked my work."

Absentmindedly, I spooned five teaspoons of sugar into my teacup. Betty interrupted me and pointed out what I had done. I pushed the sweet water away and turned toward her. "I love your work, Betty. But Father didn't leave us cash, just the house and business. And I squandered most of my retirement funds on a sports car and a younger face. Besides, I like everything just the way it is."

"Oh Misty, I should have made myself clear from the start. I never intended to charge you. I wanted to redecorate as a gift for you and for… oh, dear. What do you mean, you like it the way it is?"

"As a gift for me and who else, Betty?"

With an exasperated flush of breath, Betty said, "For your father, Misty. He said you were a city girl and the only way you'd stick around is if the place looked more cosmopolitan. AJ made me promise to replace all of these worn-out old antiques with the latest, most fashionable furnishings. I agreed to waive the fee and he paid in advance for the appurtenances."

There was something Betty wasn't telling me. I decided the time had come to smoke it out and the idea of changing the subject appealed to me. I poured another cup of water, dropped a tea bag, and sprinkled one level teaspoon of sugar over the surface. Then I looked Betty in the eyes and said, "Tell me about you and Johnny."

The question caught Betty off guard. She glanced at her left hand, looked back at me, and sat down. "What would you like to know?"

She wasn't going to make it easy. "I don't know how I missed it at the time, Betty, but there was something going on between you. Why should it be a secret?"

Betty's eyes filled with tears. "Johnny was my first love." She turned her head and shielded her face with her forearm. "I knew that Lois wanted him, and yet I fell in love with Johnny anyway. I couldn't help myself. He asked me to marry him after he finished serving in the Navy. One night when he was on leave, we went dancing. Passion overtook us and we couldn't wait for marriage." Betty looked up the stairway as if she were planning a trip to Johnny's room. "AJ worked at the company late nights and I hid away in Johnny's room until his furlough ended. On the last night, AJ came home early and, er... caught us. I was so embarrassed, I thought I would die. I expected AJ to go off the rails, but he was very sweet. Nine months later, Johnny's baby was born dead. Your father was the only one who knew. I never got to tell Johnny about the baby."

"So, you were pregnant at Johnny's memorial service?" Betty sniffled and nodded. I said, "I'm glad you and Johnny had each other. You should have told me."

"I suppose. The thing about a secret is the longer you keep it, the harder it becomes to tell it."

"If I had been more perceptive, perhaps I would have known. You're going to think this is funny, Betty, but last year, at Father's funeral, I had a feeling that something strange was going on. It crossed my mind that instead of Johnny, you and Father were lovers."

Betty's eyes grew wide and her face reddened. Her shoulders sagged and too much time passed since I had spoken. "That's why I never told you, Misty. AJ was very understanding. I was inconsolable after Johnny died and then when our baby was born dead, AJ was the only person who could comfort me. AJ was so much older than me, and it didn't seem right to love him after having loved Johnny. We suffered for years to prevent it, but we became best friends. Eventually, we became lovers also."

It was a lot to take in. I gulped hard and told myself that Betty's revelation didn't matter. As I stood and swept Betty into a friendly embrace, I wondered if I was being honest with myself. It was shocking news. Did Betty's revelation change anything between us? How could such a thing not matter? Yet, who was I to judge? How could our friendship remain unchanged with my new knowledge of their relationship?

Betty whispered, "I've never been with another man. Just Johnny and your Father."

What if it did matter what I thought? I was glad to know that Father was loved, but what would people think of *him* if they knew Betty's story?

As I walked Betty to the door, I said, "I want to keep Father's office and the house just the way it is. If we don't change anything, it's like he's still here with us."

***

The next morning, I arrived early, as usual. I enjoyed visiting with Stanley before everyone else arrived, and I'd come to realize that the man was much more perceptive than anyone else knew. As the months went by, I began confiding in him more and more, and his counsel was as valuable to me as the company's professional advisors. For a loner who avoided people, his helpful human relationship advice impressed me as ironic.

On Thursday morning, Stanley asked me if he could borrow a couple of hundred dollars until next week. He said he had made some miscalculations. His checkbook didn't add up straight and he didn't have any savings. I asked him if two hundred dollars would get him through, and he assured me that it would.

Doyle Polk was coming up the sidewalk as I pulled my wallet from my purse and handed cash to the night watchman. I glanced at the general manager and saw his frown, and in that instant, I knew he didn't approve and I was going to hear about it. I didn't have long to wait. Stanley's Plymouth had barely left the parking lot when Doyle confronted me. "What are you doing, giving that man money?"

I felt my face tighten defensively. "He said he needed money, so I agreed to help him until next week."

"And what will you do next week when he needs money for something else, Lady Fingers?"

"I don't know, Doyle. I guess I'll worry about that next week."

"And what will you do when Stanley's coworkers find out you lent Stanley some money? Won't be long and you'll be making dozens of loans."

"Good heavens, Doyle. I never met anyone with such a dismal outlook."

"You don't know these guys like I do, Misty. Give 'em an inch, they'll take a mile. Give 'em a dime, they'll steal a dollar, and ask you for change for a twenty."

"How did you get to be so jaded?"

"Did I mention I've been here for a long time? When I started out, I lent a guy a hundred dollars. Just like I said, before I knew it, everybody was asking me for money. I felt like a flippin' bank. Learned my lesson and stopped that right away. These guys lead a hardscrabble life, Misty. They go from one emergency to the next as fast as you turn the pages in the Lake Placid News. You gotta harden yourself to it. You've heard the story about the swimmer drowning the lifeguard, ain't you? If you get too close to 'em, they'll drag you underwater. Gotta stay aloof. That's what I always say. Unless you gonna give everybody two hundred dollars, don't give anybody money."

I thanked Doyle for his advice and I was glad that it was almost seven. The rest of the employees would be along shortly, and I wanted to tell them about Rusty. Of course, Doyle still didn't approve of me greeting everyone in the morning or seeing them off in the afternoon, but he stopped complaining about it months ago.

As folks arrived, I told them about Rusty's helicopter trip to Boston. I shared the news that the hospital called me after his reattachment surgery and they sounded encouraged. Then I told them that Joanne and I were driving to Boston to check on him. Just after nine, we left Joanne's car in the parking lot. I stomped on the gas pedal. The Mustang's wheels sent gravel flying and then left a long skid mark on the paved road.

***

Monday morning, before everyone else arrived, Doyle asked me, "Don't know why you went off to Boston. If the doctors there can't help him, don't know what *you're* gonna do for him, but, whatever. That don't surprise me though. What I don't understand is, why'd you take the girl with you? I don't pay much attention to the paperwork, but it looks like they fell behind while she was gone."

"Joanne is very compassionate, Doyle. But let me ask you something. Does Joanne ever take a day off?"

"Not that I know of. Neither does Art, come to think of it. Stuart on the other hand takes enough time off for all of us." With a harrumph, Doyle was gone. I scratched my chin as he departed. People should take vacations. Nobody should have to work every single day. I resolved to follow up on that later. That day, I wanted to tell the employees about becoming owners. I had meant to do it the previous Friday, but Joanne and I didn't make it back from Boston in time.

***

I told Doyle to shut everything down a half hour early that afternoon. At 2:30, with everyone gathered, I stood on a box in my favorite white dress and spoke to Father's employees. "I've got big news to share with everybody, but first I want to tell you the latest news about Rusty."

The rumble from the crowd made me feel good. Despite Doyle's pessimism, everyone cared to know how their coworker was doing. I continued, "A helicopter took Rusty to Boston. The brilliant surgeons reattached his finger. It's too soon to know for sure, but now they are more confident. They're pretty sure Rusty will keep his finger. It's going to hurt for months, and be sensitive for years, maybe, but it looks good. They're sending Rusty home tomorrow."

My smile widened as everyone cheered. I stood and waited until they became quiet again. "The other thing I wanted to tell you is this." I paused until everyone was staring at me. It's funny how silence can make people listen. "The Adirondack Dowel and Spindle Company is going to be employee owned." The silence was deafening. They looked at one another like they didn't understand what they had just heard. Then they looked back at me, dumbfounded. "We'll start off slowly at first, and then we'll go faster as time goes along."

Millie shouted out, "What do you mean, employee owned?"

I thanked Millie for asking and said, "I'm going to sell the company to a Trust, called an ESOP. ESOP stands for Employee Stock Ownership Plan. So, during your working years, you will earn shares and when you're old like me and retire, you'll cash the shares out."

Bob Holstein, the young man who joined the company on my first day shouted, "What if I go work somewhere else after a few years? What then?"

"The ESOP is a long-term benefit and we'd like you to stick around, Bob. It takes a few years to vest in the plan, but let's say you start when you're twenty and go somewhere else when you're thirty years old. You have a right to the value of your shares, but it is supposed to be for your retirement. You'll get paid out in installments, but the value of the shares will be *yours*."

Leo asked, "How much is this gonna cost me? Do we pay for it out of our checks each week?"

"No, that's the best part. You don't pay for it at all. Nothing comes out of your pocket. You pay for it with your work through the years."

The always skeptical Francis said, "What's the downside?"

"I have to be honest with you Francis. I'm not the expert. There aren't a lot of ESOPs yet, and I've never done anything like this before. We'll all have to work at this together. I guess the downside is that we'll have to be patient. I'm told that employees can make a lot of money in their ESOPs but it is not a get-rich-quick scheme. If the company does well, you do well, but slowly. Not fast."

Leo piped in again and said, "When do we get started? I'm not getting any younger!"

"This year, Leo. I plan to sell 25% of the company to the ESOP this year, on the Fourth of July. How's that sound?"

Hogan hooted and the rest of Father's employees echoed his enthusiasm.

When the crowd quieted, Francis pouted and shouted at me. "You're not going anywhere are you, Misty?"

I laughed and repeated what Leo said. "I'm not getting any younger either. In fact, I just turned seventy. But I will be here for at least a couple more years. So be patient with me. We've got a lot yet to learn about this, but we'll keep you posted. In the meanwhile, if you have any concerns, let me know."

As I shouted out, "Hip, hip, hooray for ESOP," I thought about my high school cheerleading days.

Father's employees shouted back, "Hooray."

We repeated the cheer twice more before I wished everyone goodnight and told them that Doyle would punch them all out at three. I had let them go ten minutes early. The general manager scowled at me, but I didn't care. We were going to be employee owned, and I remember thinking of that moment as a happy ending. What could possibly go wrong now? I had absolute confidence in Father's employees, like Millie, Hogan, Bob, Leo, and Francis. I was so certain about Ted's *ESOP for us.*

As I followed the employees to the parking lot, I watched Bob with amusement. The young man in the ski cap danced his way from one place to another and if anybody else had tried to do it, it would have seemed awkward. It's just the way Bob was. The beat he lived his life to was fast. Faster than everybody else's. One day I asked him if he had ants in his pants and he laughed at me.

Bob admired my Mustang with a lecherous whistle. "I'd sure love to have me one of those."

"Maybe someday you will, Bob."

He rubbed his chin and said, "Not on what I make, I won't."

"How about when you retire? Maybe you can use some of your ESOP to buy a sports car, Bob."

He cast his gaze downward. "Pshaw. That'll be the day." Then he looked at me with a naughty grin and said, "Could I take yours for a spin?"

The few remaining employees loitered and looked astonished as I handed Bob my keys. "Would you like me to take the top down?"

"In January? I'll freeze to death!" He knocked his forehead with his knuckles and said, "And, I might lose my hat."

It didn't take long for Bob to race the Mustang up to the Olympic Ski Jumps, turn around, and zip past the factory before turning around again and driving back to the parking lot. His eyes sparkled and his grin seemed eternal.

When everyone was gone, Doyle said to me, "You let that goofy kid drive your car? What did you do that for?"

"Why not? What's the harm? It probably made his day and nothing bad happened."

"I heard he's trouble. Drinks too much, stays out late, and doesn't take work serious. I've had several complaints."

"But he works hard."

Doyle grumbled and offered no reply.

"Maybe if we show him kindness, he'll turn his life around."

In a mocking voice, Doyle said, "Wouldn't that be *nice*? Everything around here is so *nice* now."

He puffed his cheeks widely and blew air through clenched lips. "I hate this thing. *You* make me miserable enough as it is. Now with everyone thinking they own the place, *they're* going to make me miserable too. Of all the places I could have worked, I had to join this freak show. I might just as well have run away and joined the circus. How can I talk you out of this, Misty? There's gotta be a way."

He didn't wait for an answer to his question. As Doyle walked away, all I could think of was, *Why don't you just keep walking?*

7

A week later, as I sat at my dressing table in front of my mirror, smoking the day's first cigarette, I watched my reflection as the gray fumes billowed from my nostrils. I was disgusted with myself. How could I have allowed myself to get hooked again? When Father passed away, I was tempted. I even bought a pack of cigarettes, but it wasn't until the horrible day that Rusty's index finger got buzzed off that temptation overtook me. But if it hadn't been that, it would have been something else. As the months went by, I could feel my willpower vanishing until I couldn't stop myself any longer.

As I inhaled the soothing smoke into my lungs, I reminded myself of all the reasons I hated smoking. It caused cancer, bad breath, and wrinkles, if nothing else. I decided to set a new quit date. I had already chosen July Fourth to sell a quarter of the company to Father's ESOP. What better day to quit smoking than that?

Later that morning, at our management meeting, after we updated each other according to our new custom, Art blinked rapidly, cleared his throat, and shifted nervously in his seat. In a high-pitched voice, the business manager said, "We have something for you, Misty." He stood, crossed our circle, and handed me a document on legal paper, folded into fourths. "It's an offer to buy the company. Doyle, Stuart, and I are offering three times the earnings for the Adirondack Dowel and Spindle

Company. Mr. Duncan at Mirror Lake Bank says that he'll release you from your personal guarantee and that he will lend each of us $100,000 to pay you for our thirds."

I was stunned. I stared at the twitchy man not knowing what to feel. How could I sell the company to management after promising the employees that they would become owners? What would Father say if I sold his company for only three hundred thousand dollars? Yet Father had employed this management team. He must have seen something in Stuart, Art, and Doyle that I didn't see, and yet, at the last minute, he decided to bequeath it to me instead of Doyle Polk.

Most days I felt like I could run the company. Despite the fact I spent my working years as a receptionist, which was hardly the sort of job one takes if they'd like to become an executive, the company seemed to be doing better in the year after I inherited it than it did in the year prior. I loved Father's employees, and yet I often reminded myself that I was seventy years old. I knew I should be retired, enjoying my golden years, and spending all my free time baking cookies for Four, feeding birds, and collecting antiques. Why was I running a manufacturing company? My dream was to open an antique store, not a woodworking factory.

Ted told me that Adirondack Dowel should be making more money, perhaps something like half a million dollars a year. Benjamin said that if the company made that kind of money it would be worth upwards of two million dollars. I wished that we could find a way to help the company become what it should be.

As insulting as management's offer was, I knew that I could afford to open a cute little antique shop if I accepted it. The Lake Placid tourists would love the kinds of artifacts I could place on the shelves, and I could spend the day listening to records and rattling around the shop with artifacts.

I felt like the proverbial deer in the headlights on a foggy mountain morning. Stuart began laughing. I looked at the man in the neat white sweater holding his arms at his sides. He said, "So what do you think, Misty? Do we have a deal, or do you want to think about it?"

Doyle said, "It's a fair offer, Misty, especially considering your father practically promised to leave the business to me. Er, I mean, us."

Art said, "That's right, Misty. Don't know what came over the old man at the last minute, but Adirondack Dowel should *already* belong to us."

I muttered. "I had no idea Father told you that." That's when I understood why I had so much difficulty with Father's management team. Father told me that he intended to leave the company to Doyle, but I didn't know he had told *them* anything. Evidently, it wasn't just Doyle, but Art and Stuart also believed that Father intended to include them in his will instead of me. They felt entitled to the company. It was as if by honoring Father's wish that I own the company, I had cheated them out of what was rightfully theirs. I looked back and forth between them and said, "I had my heart set on the employees becoming the owners."

Art said, "We won't make them owners, but we'll take care of them."

Doyle said, "I'm not going to coddle them like you do, Misty. I'm not going to kiss them good morning and tuck them in at night, but we'll pay them good and employ them as long as they keep their work standards up."

Stuart suddenly became serious, leaned forward, and suggested that I sign on the dotted line. His buttery voice assured me that it was in my best interest to do so. I almost felt hypnotized for a moment, before I blinked free of Stuart's attempt to close the deal and seal the company's fate. I ended the meeting by saying, "I never imagined this. I'll have to think about it."

I glanced at Joanne who had stopped scribbling notes. She seemed like she wanted to cry. I looked back at Stuart and said, "Ask me again next week."

***

The next morning, I couldn't find Stanley anywhere. His old truck was parked in the usual spot at the edge of the parking lot, but he wasn't in any of the places I normally found him. I searched the office, then the plant, and finally walked the exterior perimeter of the building. I found him behind the factory, on his back in the snow, clutching his chest and moaning.

I tried to communicate with Stanley, but he didn't seem to realize I was there. I said his name over and over again and slapped his face lightly to try and get his attention. Finally, he began to say my name when he moaned.

"I'm going to call for an ambulance, Stanley. I'll be right back." I kicked off my shoes and ran barefoot through the snow as fast as my legs would carry me until I reached the front door.

I dialed 911 and begged them to send an ambulance quickly, then I hung up and raced back to Stanley. I unbuttoned layers of flannel knowing that the medics would need to be able to reach his chest. Stanley was still breathing and moaning. His body was mostly still, but he kept trying to reach for his chest. If I needed to administer CPR, it would be helpful to have fewer layers of thick cloth in the way.

The wild screams of the ambulance sirens reached the parking lot as I unbuttoned Stanley's fourth shirt. I ran my hand across his forehead and told him the professionals had arrived. "You're in good hands now, Stanley." I kissed his forehead and stood up as one of the medics checked his pulse and the other placed a flimsy stretcher next to his body.

When they were gone, I sobbed into my hands. *Stanley's too young to die. The man is only forty-six. He just has to be okay.* Then I thought about management's offer to buy Father's company from me. *Owning a company the size of Adirondack Dowel isn't an easy job. Maybe it's not* fair *to ask the employees to become owners. Maybe I should sell out.*

Though I couldn't feel my toes, I stood behind the factory until my tears subsided and then I looked at the beautiful, icy river a short distance away. I thought, *By now, Stanley is at the hospital.* I said a quick prayer for Father's night watchman, my beloved crusty friend, and asked myself, "What would Stanley do?" Maybe the better question was, "What is best for Stanley?"

***

The following day, I was leaning toward continuing my plan to sell the company to the ESOP. After a strong cup of coffee and tending a short stack of paperwork, Joanne accompanied me on a wintery stroll through her dormant garden. It was hard to imagine the tulips that would bloom in a couple of months.

Joanne said, "What if the company is like a garden?"

"What do you mean, honey?"

"Well, I take care of it. I give it everything it needs. When it's dry, I water the rose bushes. In the spring, I prune the shrubs and clean out the beds. A couple of times each year, I fertilize and feed the roses, and every year I freshen the mulch. Mostly, the tulips and roses put on a good show by themselves, but sometimes, I need to help them along a little bit. It's kind of like when you greet the employees in the morning and say goodbye to them at night. So it's like gardening, wouldn't you say?"

"What a lovely comparison, Joanne." I thought of what the preacher said at Father's funeral. *It's the act of stewardship that matters most.*

We talked for a while about the ESOP plan. Not many people would have asked a young lady in her mid-twenties for her opinion on business matters or about the sale of their business, but Joanne was a quiet observer, an intent listener, and spoke in a way that made people want to be with her rather than against her. I asked, "Do you think it is fair to ask employees to assume the responsibilities of owning a company? It can be a mighty burden sometimes."

"I know what you mean, Misty. Sometimes I see the same look on your face that I used to see on Mr. Menard's. It seems like you carry the weight of the world on your shoulders, and most of the people who work here have no idea."

"So you don't think it is *fair* to ask them?"

Joanne's head tilted forward, and her lip curled into a slight smile as she glanced at me. "Have you ever tried to move a big sofa by yourself?"

I laughed. "Yes." I held an arm forward and tried to pose a muscle. "I couldn't push it very far, and certainly not up the stairs."

"So what did you do?"

"I got a couple of friends to help me."

Joanne nodded crisply and her eyes twinkled. "So, the sofa was too much for one person, but not a problem for a couple of people working together. Wouldn't it be something if your ESOP was like that?"

I shook my head in wonderment, "Not my ESOP. I would like to think of it as Father's ESOP." I touched her elbow briefly and said, "You are a remarkable young woman, Joanne. I don't know if you realize how special you are." My resolve had wobbled, but I felt the strength returning to my conviction.

Joanne blushed, then turned her head slightly away. "Oh, go on, Misty!" We completed a lap around the garden, and then she spoke again. In a voice barely louder than a whisper, she said, "Actually, Misty, *you* are my hero. I've never met a woman like you before. Imagine, being a boss and owning a company. Who ever heard of a woman doing such things?"

I felt a wave of goosebumps wash across my back and another rush of them on my shins. Her words meant more than anything anyone had said to me in years. I said, "You'd be surprised, honey. Maybe you have heard of Golda Meir, the prime minister of Israel, or Indira Gandhi, the prime minister of India, and then, of course, there's Queen Elizabeth in England. Despite what some might have you believe, women do amazing things. I don't think history gives us enough credit for our accomplishments, but things have been changing over the last couple of decades. In the future, you'll be surprised to see what women can achieve." I turned to Joanne and said, "Do you know I was a receptionist at a law firm in Washington DC until I retired?"

"Gosh, no. I knew you worked in Washington, but I didn't know you worked in a law firm."

"The thing is, Joanne. My job was to greet the clients, make them feel comfortable, and help the attorneys make their rich and powerful customers feel special. Some of the young lawyers weren't very good at making conversations with people. My role was important, but what you do for Adirondack Dowel is way more difficult than the work I did. When I think of all the things you do, I'm just amazed. I couldn't have done half of what you do."

The normally cheerful young woman looked down at her boots and said, "Thank you for saying such sweet things. I'm going to miss you when you sell the company."

"Joanne, do you think I should sell the company to Stuart, Art, and Doyle?"

She looked up into my eyes briefly, shook her head, and looked away. "No, but I'll understand if you do it."

I told her I didn't want to sell to them but that I had to think carefully and be sure. Then I asked, "What about Rusty?"

Joanne said, "He told me I look like an angel and thanked me for coming to visit him in Boston."

"Did you tell him he should ask you out?"

"Not yet. But I might."

I told her, "If you don't, I will. Don't you think we'd make a cute couple, Joanne?"

The girl smiled at me and I wondered if she imagined me on a date with her dreamy young lumberjack.

***

That evening, I visited Rusty at home and was surprised to find Joanne there, fixing him dinner. Bob Seger's album, *Beautiful Loser,* was playing on the turntable.

Rusty was sitting up on the couch. He held his bandaged hand in his good hand, and his eyes followed Joanne as she bustled around his small apartment. His hair was messy. His normally neat beard looked scraggly, yet his bright, attentive eyes and welcoming expression were reassuring.

I sat on a threadbare chair across from Rusty. He tried to focus on me, but he kept looking away, distracted by Joanne's movement. Did he enjoy the fact that she was there, or did her presence in his apartment make him nervous? I said, "I can't stay very long, Rusty, but I wanted to see how you are holding up. Are you doing alright?"

Rusty held up his bandaged club of a hand and said, "I'm fine, except for this. I can't wait to get back to work, Misty." He bit his lip and the worry was plain to see on his sagging eyebrows. "Will you hold my job for me?"

I sat forward and patted his knee. "Count on it, Rusty. Actually, I was thinking that you could fill in for Stanley at night until he returns. It might be a challenge with one hand."

The light returned to Rusty's eyes. "Yes, I could do that. I know I could. How is Stanley?"

"I wish I knew more. He's taking a lot of medications, but I'm not sure what else they can do for him. The doctors say we'll have to wait and see how he does as the days and weeks go on, but that he should stay out of work for at least a couple of more weeks."

Rusty asked me to tell Stanley that he wished him well.

"There's something else I wanted to talk to you about, Rusty. Do you remember what I mentioned about forming an ESOP? What do you think about becoming an owner of Adirondack Dowel?"

Rusty sat up even taller and his chest seemed to swell as he spoke. "Aw, I don't know about that, Misty." He looked over at his hi-fi and said, "I never owned much of anything before." The needle lifted from the record, swung back to its cradle, and then returned to play the first song on that side of the record, "Travelin' Man." He made a face at me and it was an expression I'd never seen before. "Sounds like a whole lot of responsibility." Then he looked at Joanne who approached with a big plate of food.

Joanne draped a large cloth napkin on his lap and set the dish on his thin legs. I looked at the meal she had prepared. The pork chops looked juicy and my mouth watered. I couldn't help but notice that she had thought to slice the meat so that Rusty could skewer chunks one-handed. A small patch of vibrant spinach accompanied a steaming heap of bright, mashed sweet potatoes. As I stood, Joanne said, "Will you join us, Misty?"

I rose to my feet. "It looks delicious, but no, I have to be going. I want to check on Stanley before it gets too late. Thank you, honey." I looked at Rusty who was staring at the mountain of yams. I wonder if he was trying to imagine how he could eat that much. I said, "I'll check on you again in a couple of days, Rusty."

As I made my hasty retreat, I hoped that Rusty and Joanne would benefit from being alone together. I wanted to know what Stanley thought I should do about management's offer, but decided not to burden the man with my conundrum.

***

On Friday, I had lunch with John Frederick Duncan. The banker always took his mid-day repast at the Lake Placid Club and had a regular table in the White Birch room. Mr. Duncan ordered for me without asking me what I might like but proudly bragged that the steaks were shipped directly from Omaha, Nebraska. He chose an expensive wine to accompany his meal, and said, "You're a teetotaler, aren't you? Would you like something else to drink?"

I thanked him and requested an iced tea. Despite the company, I enjoyed the hearty meal. The ornate, decorated dining room was a celebration of opulence and rustic beauty at the same time. I liked to call the Adirondack style of decorating, where crystal and silver coexisted with bark and twigs, *pine cone chic*. The attentive service and delicious dishes reminded me of the finest restaurants in the nation's capital, though I rarely had the opportunity to dine in those. The quantity of food brought to Mr. Duncan's table would have been enough to satisfy a crowded orphanage full of growing teenagers.

When the waitstaff suggested dessert, Mr. Duncan patted his bloated midsection and said, "I'd better not. I'm trying to watch my weight. Just a cup of coffee," and with a twirl of his hand, the remaining dishes were removed from the table. Then Mr. Duncan turned to business. He raised his chin, looked down his nose, and said, "Miss Menard, I must encourage you to accept management's offer. If you don't sell, I'm afraid the consequences will be dire.

The company is deeply in debt and hardly <u>ekes</u> out a profit." He raised an eyebrow and feigned a frown. Then he scratched the tip of his nose with his index finger, rubbed his chin, and continued. "I must answer to the bank's Board of Directors, and I'm afraid we cannot endlessly extend credit to the company." I couldn't help but think that Mr. Duncan's advice sounded more like a threat than a prediction. His voice dripped with chauvinism and he tapped my wrist with his chubby fingers as he said, "You did the best you could, darling, but it's time to let the men take over."

I took a deep breath and said, "Mr. Duncan, I have decided that I would like to sell the company to the employees. I appreciate management's offer, but I've made up my mind. So instead of lending Stuart, Art, and Doyle $300,000, I need to ask the bank to lend money to the trust to buy a quarter of the company."

The expression on Mr. Duncan's face soured. "Sorry, Misty. Can't do it. The only way I can make that loan is if you pledge the proceeds of the sale to the bank, and hold it in an account at the bank until it is fully repaid by the company."

Mr. Duncan gave me a lengthy lesson in banking practices. He talked endlessly about balance sheets and income statements and the necessary balance between debt and earnings as well as the optimum ratios between the bank's investments in a company when compared to the owners' investments in an enterprise. Usually, when a man talks to me like this, I imagine him as a bawling infant, complete with flailing arms, kicking legs, and a stinky nappy. Perhaps I should have listened to his warnings instead of picturing him peeing in the midst of a diaper change.

When he finally stopped talking, I conceded. "Very well, Mr. Duncan. I will pledge the proceeds of the sale to the bank."

He shook his head from side to side and said, "I hoped that you would listen to reason, Misty. You mustn't blame me if the bank is forced to foreclose." I couldn't help but think he didn't look sincere when he said, "I would hate to see that day come, Misty. Your father worked so hard, his whole life, building the company, only to see it all get washed down the drain."

I held my hand on my stomach as we departed. I was glad

lunch was over. At that moment, I was determined to prove Mr. Duncan wrong, no matter what it cost me. I hoped that I wouldn't change my mind again.

8

The following week, I had dinner with Mayor Peacock and his wife, Leola, at the stately Mirror Lake Inn. Bob and his wife ordered the prime rib special, au jus, and I feasted on rich crabmeat Newburg. After dinner, we lounged in plush leather chairs near a large stone fireplace. Mounted denizens of the forest witnessed our conversation from wood-paneled walls, another take on pine cone chic. I declined the offer of brandy and pulled a cigarette from my purse. I asked Bob and Leola, "Do you mind if I smoke?"

Bob said, "Be my guest." Then he inquired, "Have you reached a decision, Misty?"

I shook my head as I blew a puff of smoke from the corner of my mouth, hoping to send the vapor away from my friends. "I can't seem to stick with a decision. If it weren't for Father's employees, I'd be glad to let the business go, even if the offer is insulting."

Bob leaned forward and said quietly, "Are you sure you haven't made a decision, dear? It sounds to me like you know what you want to do. What's keeping you from moving forward?"

I looked at my left hand, dappled with a constellation of age spots, and looked back at the mayor. I said, "I'm not getting any younger, Bob. I already retired once. Working at Adirondack Dowel is sometimes rewarding but often stressful. I guess you know Stuart, Art, and Doyle would rather I vanished. I just can't help feeling like the company needs me. I think there's something Father wants me to do. It was his dream, his greatest love, and it is up to me to oversee his legacy." I could feel my eyes growing wider as I looked directly into the mayor's eyes. "Father must never be forgotten."

Leola leaned against her husband's shoulder and said, "It does sound like Misty has made her decision."

I looked at the woman and nodded. "You know what, you're right. I have. I guess I knew it all along. If those bozos don't like it, they can quit, but I'm going to see this through."

Bob said, "I think you've done a good job so far, Misty. Keep at it. I think you'll succeed."

I felt my lips tighten firmly in resolve and nodded slowly. "You're right, Bob. I can do it. With the help of Father's employees, we can make it better than it ever was before. Long after we're gone, the ESOP that will bear his name will take care of generations of employee owners. How about that for a grandiose vision." My laughter sounded confident even to my own ears.

Bob and Leola lifted their glasses and cheered my pledge as if it were a toast.

***

Every couple of days, a new version of the documents arrived in the mail. Winslow would call me to let me know, and I'd rush downtown to review the changes with him. We frequently dialed Ted on the speaker phone for consultations. I had become impatient with all the details that needed to be tended to, and just wanted to get the deal done.

When the Fourth of July was only three months away, Winslow received a letter from Alice Blankenfritter of Albany. We chose her from Ted's list of independent fiduciaries. Her job was to represent the ESOP Trust when the ESOP purchased my shares of stock in the company. We interviewed her over the phone and were impressed with her qualifications. The woman had spent twenty years working for the Internal Revenue Service, and another ten years at the New York State Department of Taxation and Finance. Ted said that she was very thorough, and described her work as ironclad. He added, "She's a stickler for details."

Mrs. Blankenfritter's letter said that she had reviewed the copies of the check register we sent her and the bank statements since the beginning of the year, and warned that she had some concerns. She insisted on coming to Lake Placid for a tour of the company. Then she suggested a meeting with the bookkeeper in such a way that made the request seem more like a demand.

On the phone, Ted said that Mrs. Blankenfritter's requests should be honored. Whatever she asked for, we must provide. If we couldn't satisfy her, the deal would never happen.

The dour woman arrived during an early spring storm. Heavy rain slid off her thick raincoat, and a shower of raindrops drenched the carpet as she shed her outer layer just inside the front door. Joanne offered Mrs. Blankenfritter a cup of coffee or tea, but the expressionless woman just answered, "No. I'm here to see Misty Menard."

I stood a few feet away, and said, "Here I am."

The woman said, "You're Misty?" Evidently, I was not what she expected. She looked me up and down then said, "Who is going to give me a tour of the factory?"

"Doyle Polk, the general manager, is in charge of manufacturing." I turned to Joanne and asked her if she would get him. When I turned back to address Mrs. Blankenfritter, she was standing on her tiptoes in a corner of the office looking at a stained ceiling tile. The woman wore an ankle-length, dark gray skirt, a man's suitcoat, and a plain black blouse with no frills. Her straight gray hair was pulled back into a bun at her neckline. Most women wore some sort of adornment, but Mrs. Blankenfritter was devoid of accessories. Nary a necklace, pin, broach, shawl, or scarf decorated her utilitarian outfit.

I followed the trustee as she badgered Doyle at every step of the tour, with questions like, "When did you buy that? When was that last inspected? Has that been properly maintained?" She was built like a battleship, yet crawled into every nook and cranny of the factory, squatted in every corner looking for flood damage, and several times she climbed a ladder to look at the top of a wall or ceiling. The woman was just as thorough when she examined the exterior of the building, and I wondered whether she would climb onto the roof.

When we finally returned to the office, Mrs. Blankenfritter tortured Art with dozens of questions about vendors. She demanded to see the cards that showed how much customers owed us and the corresponding deck that detailed our debts to suppliers. Several times, she passed a card back to Art, telling him that he had made an error. When she finished her interview with the business manager, she said to him, "You must be more careful in your calculations, Mr. Boykins. Your handwriting isn't very neat and you make too many mistakes."

Stuart didn't chuckle or smile when the trustee grilled him. She asked him as many questions as she did Art, questions like, "Who's the owner of this business? When was the last time you visited them? How long have they been a customer?" She also asked dozens of questions about the customers' other choices and it sounded like she was very concerned about our competition, Crabapple Dowel in Albany.

Doyle stood beside me and whispered through clenched teeth. "Get that old battle axe out of here. How humiliating. How dare she ask such insulting questions?"

I was exhausted and relieved when Mrs. Blankenfritter finally left the building. The sun came out when she was gone, but I worried about her impression of our company. What if she didn't approve of the deal?

A month later, a letter from Alice Blankenfritter arrived in Winslow's office. She demanded that the price for a quarter of the company be lowered from $125,000 to $100,000.

Two weeks before the closing, the trustee sent another letter, insisting that the list of seller's warranties be expanded. Most importantly, Mrs. Blankenfritter demanded I certify that my title to ownership in the company was clean and undisputed. In the event that someone challenged Father's last will and testament, and succeeded, I would have to hold the ESOP Trust harmless and provide restitution. All the legal implications were dizzyingly detailed and threatening.

We called Ted to discuss the letter. Mrs. Blankenfritter had carbon-copied him on her correspondence. With Ted listening on the speaker, Winslow asked me, "Are you still intent on going through with this, Misty?"

I'm sure my expression showed my dismay. "I'm not happy about lowering the price, but I've gone too far to turn back now, Winslow."

Ted's voice crackled in the phone's speaker. "The changes Mrs. Blankenfritter is asking for in the contracts may sound excessive, but they *are* reasonable."

***

I was glad that Ted offered to spend the week before the Fourth of July at Father's house. Each day, when I went to the factory, Ted went to Winslow's office, and on Friday, they got a letter from the trustee saying that she would appear at the company's offices at noon on Sunday. Her letter declared that her rate for attending the closing on the holiday would be double her regular, daily fee. She enclosed a long list of changes that she demanded to be added to the documents. Changing the paperwork required Ted and Winslow to work most of the weekend. I was amazed to see how much work it took to make Father's employees into my co-owners.

I tried to focus on the outcome rather than get mired in the details. I trusted Ted and Winslow, and stodgy Alice Blankenfritter's nettlesome attention to detail inspired my confidence too. Technically, she was working for the other side of my transaction with the ESOP, but in my heart, I was more committed to the other side's interest than my own. I imagined cheering the newly declared employee owners and anticipated a jubilant celebration of Father's legacy at the same time as everyone recognized the 200th anniversary of America's independence. It was to be the most memorable event in the history of the Adirondack Dowel and Spindle Company.

Though it was a holiday, I was proud that all of the employees showed up to celebrate. Stanley's pallor still looked gray, but he insisted on attending and barbecuing chickens over charcoal in what looked like metal barrels cut in half lengthwise. My family grilled hamburgers and frankfurters, for those who preferred not to eat chicken.

Rusty stood nearby. The young man's bright red eyes showed what a difficult time he had adjusting his sleep schedule to the nocturnal habits of a night watchman. His unbandaged hand looked terrible. He held it up like a pirate holds a hook. The attachment seemed successful, but his wound kept opening and getting reinfected.

I was surprised when Joanne pulled into the parking lot driving a brand new, rose-colored AMC Pacer. She later told me that it cost her four thousand dollars. Mr. Duncan insisted that her father cosign her car loan. Bank policy required male cosigners when single women borrowed money. It didn't matter that she had been continuously employed by Adirondack Dowel for five years. I wanted to laugh at her funny-looking car with rounded back windows that resembled a fishbowl. When she opened the back hatch, the shape of the car from behind reminded me of the Swiss chalets that were popular in the Adirondacks. It was astonishing how many side dishes Joanne had packed into the back of her new car, especially when the casseroles, baked beans, coleslaw, and salads were laid across the several serving tables we had set up.

Bob Holstein pulled in after Joanne in his clunker. Each door was a different color, like a patchwork quilt. The replacement doors were in better shape than the rust-pocked body, and it sounded like the muffler had a hole in it. Doyle had warned me not to interfere, but I would have liked to give the young man a raise so that he could afford a safer automobile.

I asked if his parents had given him the car, and he scoffed. "You kidding me?"

He hiccupped and I realized that he had been drinking.

"They didn't give me nothing, and if they did, I wouldn't have taken it." Though it was mid-summer, the young man still wore the ski cap that seemed like it was a part of him. I only saw him without the hat once, and his straight dark hair with the wide curl at the end looked out of place.

"Did you have it bad growing up?"

"I don't know about that, Misty. They fed and clothed me, but that's it. Maybe they care about my sisters, but nobody in that house ever spoke to me. The day I turned 18, I was out of there, and I ain't never going back."

Bob's words reminded me that I spent far too much time away from home as Father grew older.

After lunch, I watched as employees and their families participated in a rowdy sack race. I would have much preferred to race around before a meal rather than afterward. One little girl stood off to the side, bent over with her hands on her knees as if she were prepared to lose her lunch.

Next, contestants lined up to compete in a pie-eating contest. It was hard to imagine anyone had an appetite for custard pastry, but ten brave souls stepped forward. The spectators complained about the heat as they baked in the sunshine, and mosquitoes didn't wait for dusk to drill into the crowd. It took a long time for the fastest pie eater to beat the competition.

Activity on the other side of the river made the gathering seem larger than just sixty-five Adirondack Dowel families. The annual Lake Placid Horse Show was well underway. The elite jumping competition crowded our village each summer, yet I always enjoyed it when our equine visitors came to town. The show grounds bustled with movement, sounds, and smells. The downside was an onslaught of horseflies and deer flies, and people complained about the insects' voracious appetites. The sound of a commotion interrupted my thoughts about the horse show and blood-sucking bugs.

One man shouted insults. Bob taunted him by singing Miller Beer's theme song, with the famous line, "If you've got the time, we've got the beer." They danced like boxers, hands balled into fists, and a crowd formed around them. I was grateful for Doyle's presence when the general manager separated the young men and shouted into their faces, but I was saddened by the bloodied lips and noses. I later learned that Bob refused to pay up on a bet.

It was almost two o'clock by the time the pie-eating contest and the resulting scuffle concluded. It was time to sign the documents. Some families looked like they were ready to depart. Gathering clouds tempered the heat, but made the ravenous skeeters even more annoying.

I stood at a custom-made table built out of dowels just for the occasion and waited as the employees gathered around to watch. Nearby, a transistor radio played. I listened as a popular song called, "Today's the Day" ended, and "Making Our Dreams Come True" from the new television show, *Laverne & Shirley,* came on. I imagined the young women from Milwaukee becoming owners of the brewery where they worked.

Joanne turned the radio off just as carillons began ringing. A man in the village had an enormous bell which he struck like a gong, filling the valley with a deep resonant tone. Anyone who had an instrument capable of producing a chime joined in and participated in the nationwide event, and I'm not sure whether there were more tings coming from the Horse Show grounds across the river or from our celebration.

Accompanied by tintinnabulation, I picked up a pen and signed the purchase and sale agreement, and then passed the ballpoint to the beaming trustee. It was surprising to see that even Alice

Blankenfritter enjoyed the symbolism of signing our official documents at the exact moment the Declaration of Independence was ratified, precisely two hundred years earlier. When Mrs. Blankenfritter was finished, Ted whispered in my ear that a witness was needed to sign the documents as well, and I waved Joanne over. "Would you do the honor of officially witnessing the signing, honey?"

When the bells stopped ringing and the signing was finished, Joanne turned the radio back on, and the song "Misty Blue" by Dorothy Moore caught my ear. Joanne immediately realized what song was playing, and turned the volume up as loud as she could. I stepped forward to say a few words, prepared to project over the music, but was interrupted by the crowd who had joined in, singing along with the radio. It was like they were singing the song as a tribute to me.

I was stunned. It was such an unexpected honor, but I was horrified. I had a long speech prepared. The purpose of our celebration was to recognize Father's legacy, founding the company and nurturing it through the decades. The wind picked up as they sang the short song, and the hot sunny day suddenly threatened rain.

When they finished, I barely had time to thank them and congratulate them before the sky opened up and a deluge cut me off. I had to complete my tribute to Father in three short sentences as my audience scrambled away to their automobiles, gathering their families and belongings, and leaving just a few of us to clean up.

I wished the celebration could go on forever, but the moment I had waited for so long was over. Despite the fistfight, sunburns, insects, and the unexpected cloudburst, the deal had been consummated. The Adirondack Dowel and Spindle Company was finally employee owned, at least twenty-five percent, anyhow.

I didn't dare look for a mirror. Bouffant hairdos, like mine, didn't take kindly to heavy rain. I covered my head with a big silky handkerchief from my pocketbook, and when everyone had departed, I stood in front of the factory and smoked what I told myself was my last cigarette. Addictions had a way of making liars out of would-be quitters.

On my way home, I drove the Mustang down Main Street. The midsummer holiday visitors slowed traffic to a crawl, but I couldn't help driving among the throngs and feeling like a part of the ongoing celebration. I noticed a long line in front of the Palace Theater, which was celebrating its 50th anniversary by airing the award-winning film, *One Flew Over the Cuckoo's Nest*. I did a double-take when I realized that Lois Phelps stood in line. She scowled at me from behind sunglasses that reminded me of Jackie Kennedy, and as my Mustang made its way slowly up the street, Lois turned and glowered at me. Despite the summer heat, I shivered as I remembered what she said at Father's burial: I ruined her life, she hated me, and she was never going to forgive me. Her shielded stare made me wonder, was there something more to my former high school friend than her disdain for me? I couldn't help feeling that I should worry about my safety and wished that I were home instead of stuck in traffic.

The next day had been declared a national holiday. The Fourth of July had landed on a Sunday depriving the nation of a day off from work, so the government corrected the calendar and our celebration continued into a third day.

The men who built the special desk of dowels for the signing of ESOP documents also built a raft of dowels to be placed on top of two weathered canoes with a pedal boat in between them. The final event planned for Lake Placid's Fourth of July celebration was the Bicentennial Moonlight Regatta. Our entry was the last to depart from the public beach at the south end of Mirror Lake, and I was impressed by the festive boats that preceded ours.

I beamed with pride while watching our volunteers hastily assemble our entry as the flotilla waited for us to join the parade on water. Everything had been planned and tested so that it would be ready for showtime. With the desk placed over the pedal boat, and the long dowel raft completely covering the canoes beneath, it didn't even look like a boat. Our props and decorations conveyed the signing of the Declaration of Independence. I dressed up as George Washington, Joanne portrayed Thomas Jefferson, and Millie looked surprisingly like Benjamin Franklin. My kindred spirit, Bob Holstein enthusiastically volunteered to serve as the engine and shimmied into the narrow opening that allowed just enough space to access the pedal boat.

A big sign with letters large enough to read from the shore towered over our floating desk. It featured the company's name and the words, "employee owned." After that, it said, "The AJ Menard ESOP." I was delighted with the festive, red and blue letters on a field of white.

Everything went well at first. The parade of boats began to make its way up the long, west side of the lake. After a couple of hundred yards, the raft began to tilt. Millie slid over the edge, and Joanne slipped in quickly after her. I watched as the dowel desk pitched over the edge and splashed into the lake. I managed to keep my footing on the raft of dowels until it slid from its perch on the canoes. Then I fell down and rolled over the edge into the chilly lake.

An army of canoeists and kayakers descended upon us and fished us from the water. We were paddled to the edge of the lake and wrapped in blankets. I sobbed as I watched men in boats search for Bob. The empty canoes and the vacant pedal boat were retrieved and towed to shore, but Bob was nowhere to be found. Someone handed me Bob's waterlogged ski hat. How could his hat be found but not the man?

The last thing I remembered was collapsing to my knees.

9

Bob Holstein's body was never found. As the days went by, we hoped for a miracle that didn't arrive. The passing of almost four years failed to lessen the catastrophe.

We checked Bob's personnel file, but his next of kin read: Idonna Wannatell Yanuthin and the phone number listed was all nines. Rusty said that Bob left home at a young age, but the kid didn't talk much about his past. I had hoped to get to know the young man better. He was an entertaining guy who danced as he walked. It was as if everything he did was a cause for celebration, except when he was drinking. Then he was unpredictable. Not knowing what else to do, I placed a marker for Bob in the family plot, near Father, Mother, Johnny, and Junior. Then I hired a private investigator, who didn't offer me much hope of finding Bob's kin with nothing more to go on than a name, Social Security number, and a faded knit hat. On the other hand, Bob's unique middle name and the first several digits of his Social Security number could narrow the search.

A couple of times a year, I received a letter from the detective updating me on his lack of progress and billing me for his services rendered. As the years passed, I'd given up on ever finding Bob's family. His tragic disappearance and assumed drowning were sad enough, but to think that nobody else in the world cared about him made me melancholy. Every day since I have thought of him. I had spent thousands of dollars on the investigator through the years, and yet I still felt guilty about poor Bob's drowning. The detective suggested that the search be suspended, but I had stubbornly held out hope. Whenever I thought about it, I would get a sick feeling in the pit of my stomach, especially when I thought about the money I wasted trying to find Bob's family. I knew I needed to be reasonable and quit frittering away money on a pointless pursuit, but I couldn't quit on Bob, at least not yet.

When the 1980 Winter Olympic Games came to town, I was determined to take off as much time as I could. It was my first vacation since Father's death and I needed a long, well-deserved break from the company. Lake Placid had the unique distinction of hosting the world twice.

The last time was in 1932 and I remember attending the Opening and Closing Ceremonies with Father and Junior. Harold was too young to go and stayed behind with Nanny Peggy. Father attended every hockey game he could, and I didn't miss any of the figure skating events. Junior liked bobsledding and was infatuated with ski jumping.

I looked forward to attending the 1980 Games with Four. The boy was constantly beside me, except for when he was at school or skating. It was a treat for local children to have an extended break from school due to the Olympics.

The 13-year-old relentlessly trained and hoped to be an Olympic figure skating champion in Sarajevo. Four never complained about the endless hours of practice, but he did grumble about not being able to skate until the Games were over. Usually, kids whine when they have to work too hard, but Four became irritable when he couldn't be on the ice. It had become his only passion and sole purpose on earth. I worried that the boy's obsession had become unhealthy but I enjoyed watching him from the stands. I wasn't an objective judge but thought he was a gifted skater. He was good at the dance steps and his jumps were explosive but spinning was his specialty. The coaches were impressed with Four's world-class ability to endlessly whirl while maintaining perfect form. Just watching Four twist made me queasy and I wondered how he managed to keep from getting seasick.

At breakfast, I gave Four a gift, wrapped in flashy red paper, like a Christmas present. He ripped the paper off the box, pulled the cardboard flaps away from the brim, and tugged out a stuffed animal. Four looked at me with a grimace. "Gosh, GiGi, it's a toy." He was silent for a moment as if considering whether to hurt my feelings or be honest with me. Finally, he said, "I'm not a kid anymore."

I said, "I know, honey. But it's not a toy so much as it is a mascot. Think of it as a keepsake — a souvenir to remind you of the Lake Placid Olympics. His name is Roni. It means raccoon in the Iroquois language. He can sit on your dresser or bookshelf. I know you're not a kid, but look: he's a skater. And who knows, someday, Roni might become a collector's item."

"Thanks, GiGi." Roni disappeared behind Four's back as if he hoped to hide the sight of the athletic raccoon, though there was nobody in the kitchen except for me and Four. I wished that kids wouldn't be in such a hurry to grow up. There would be time for adult burdens and responsibilities later, though Four had known more than his share of hardships and troubles already.

When Four disappeared briefly, I brewed coffee and while it percolated, I retrieved my scrapbooking project. Father collected local newspapers his whole life, and I'd spent a year going through box after box of them, clipping articles that mentioned Father or the company. I was glad that the local paper only came out once a week rather than daily. Four returned to the kitchen as I was pasting a brief article into the book and asked me what I was doing.

"I'm preserving the history of Adirondack Dowel so that the employee owners of the company will know the story of how Father built the company from nothing into whatever they'll turn the company into in the future."

"Oh. Is Adirondack Dowel famous? Like...." The boy repeated the last word as if searching for the thought of a company he considered notorious enough to mention. "Like Ford or McDonalds?"

"No, I guess not, honey. It's more of a local thing. It's a part of Lake Placid and supports local people who depend on their wages and salaries to feed and house their families. The money they spend at other businesses makes Adirondack Dowel even more significant, and then think about the products the company makes and sends to customers hundreds or thousands of miles away."

We sat at the table, and Four helped me paste newsworthy articles into the book. When I stopped to stretch an ache from my shoulder, I noticed a strange object hanging from his neck. Curiosity sparked my question. "What's that necklace you're wearing?"

The boy twisted his body away from me as if protecting the object, or trying to hide its appearance. Then he frowned and relaxed. "It's just a piece of junk I found in the attic, but I like wearing it. The cold metal reminds me I should be skating."

"Can I see it?"

My great-grandson held the pendant in his hands and paused for a long moment. His eyes rolled behind his lids and he blinked oddly. The boy's fingertips seemed to glow. Was I imagining that? Was he having some sort of vision?

I thought about what had happened when I held the cufflinks in Father's office, almost five years ago. When Four lifted the medallion over his head and passed it to me, I considered asking him what happened when he touched the adornment. Instead, I focused on the unique object.

The back was white enamel, bright as children's teeth. On the front, a continuous line linked three spiral circles together, like an endless shamrock. I had been interested in antiques for decades but had never seen anything like it.

As I ran my finger along the ridge, I felt the sizzle of a mild electrical current and a brief flashing vision of a wild, woodland boy flickered on and off, alternating with Four's image, like a neon sign on the fritz. The sensation was mild and dark compared to the vivid images of Johnny and Betty when I touched the cufflinks. I blinked rapidly and handed the necklace back to Four. "That's extraordinary. What do you make of it, Four?"

He shrugged as if the answer were obvious. "It connects us to our ancestors."

"You think it was passed down through the generations?"

Four nodded and said, "It shouldn't be hidden away in the attic."

Did the object compel Four to climb the attic steps and retrieve it from storage? I chided myself for the fanciful notion and for attributing human motives to an inanimate object. "I wish we had time to hunt for other treasures up there."

The boy chewed his cheek as he lifted the necklace over his head. Then he closed his eyes for a moment as if seeing something in his mind's eye again. It had happened to me twice in the last five years. Was it possible the same thing or something like it was happening to him? From his expressions, I was certain that his visions were stronger than my own. It made me proud, yet just a tad envious as well.

When the telephone rang, Four disappeared again. It was the reclusive sculptor, Webster Givens of Saratoga Springs, who had been avoiding me for over a year. I hired Web to sculpt Father's bust just after we formed the ESOP. I hoped that I would be able to dedicate the statue and present it to the employee owners on the first anniversary of the day the employees became owners of the company, but Web told me right away he had at least two years' worth of backlogged commissions to deliver before he could even start on Father's likeness. I hired the famous sculptor anyway. When I hung up the phone, I was elated. Web offered to personally present the sculpture at Founders Day on the Fourth of July.

After I hung up the phone, I hummed happily as I put away the scrapbooking supplies. Four materialized again and I told him it was time to take a shower and get ready to go. I warned him,

"Dress warmly, we're going to be outdoors all afternoon."

Four twisted his face in protest. "Why do I have to take a shower just to sit around outside?"

I said, "How about just to make me happy?" Then I threatened to pinch his cheeks and kiss him if he didn't do as I asked.

***

As we waited for the opening ceremony to begin, I felt like a schoolgirl waiting for lunch or recess. We could have watched the afternoon festivities from the roof of the factory, just across the river, but I was glad we had reserved seats with a great view. The sparkling snow and ice contrasted with the brightly-colored waving flags of the participating countries, and the majestic, snow-covered high peaks rose dramatically behind the open-air parade grounds. Dramatic red carpets led up steps to an elevated platform and beyond, another crimson rug introduced the waiting Olympic cauldron.

Beside me, Four snapped pictures on the Instamatic camera and I wished he would stop. I cautioned, "Slow down, honey. You'll run out of film." He looked forlorn. I seldom admonished him. "Don't you want to save some for later?"

Four pouted and nodded. It was as if he wished it were possible to have an unlimited supply of film. He said, "I guess," and snapped another couple of pictures as golden costumed skydivers dropped from the clouds. I wondered how many parachutists he managed to capture. It was hard to photograph a moving target especially from far away.

I frowned when Four took a picture of Vice President, Walter Mondale standing on the platform. I had only given the boy two rolls of film. The gala was just getting started and he was well into the second roll. There was a reason sensible adults didn't let children take pictures.

Mercifully, the politicians spoke briefly. President Carter left the job of welcoming the world to his vice president, probably because of his promise to boycott the summer Olympics in Moscow in response to Russia's invasion of Afghanistan. The triumphant music and fluttering flags added to the pageantry. The Olympic Orchestra, a university chorus, and a fife and drum corps warmed the winter air with song.

As the Parade of Nations began, Four tugged at my elbow. "The camera's broken, GiGi."

I removed my white mitten and cranked the lever advancing the film from the last picture to the end of the roll. "It's not broken, honey. You took the last picture."

The disappointed boy exhaled with a multi-syllabic version of the word, "Oh."

I tilted my head and looked down at him. I touched the tip of his nose with my index finger and said, "I have one more roll of film. Then that's it. There isn't any more after that." I pulled a small yellow box from my pocket, tore the metallic wrapper that protected the film cartridge, and popped it into the rectangular camera. "Pace yourself, kiddo."

Despite my warning, I could hear the quick succession of snapping clicks as the US athletes paraded by. The sight of them filled my chest with pride and the young men and women looked gorgeous in white cowboy hats, cream-colored sheepskin jackets, tan gloves, and Levi's blue jeans. Their bright red sweaters reminded me of the welcoming runway carpets, and the blue and white stripes near the jacket collar symbolized the US flag, Old Glory.

Four exclaimed, "Look, GiGi. The skaters. There's David Santee! Charles Tickner! And look who is carrying the flag. Scott Hamilton. Wow! Why does *he* get to carry the flag?"

"I don't know. What an honor."

"They should have let David Santee carry the flag."

"Why, honey?"

"He's been in the Olympics before. Remember Innsbruck,

GiGi?" We had watched the 1976 Games together on television.

Behind us, a middle-aged woman coughed and sneezed. I felt bad for the lady who should have stayed home to nurse a cold rather than risk her health outside on a frigid winter day.

I hadn't realized that Mayor Peacock was to participate in the ceremony. I watched with pride as the Chairman of the Board of Directors of the Adirondack Dowel and Spindle Company received the Olympic flag from the Mayor of Innsbruck, Austria, and the orchestra played a medley of music reminiscent of the 1976 Games. The Olympic flag skated up the towering pole and a flock of two thousand pigeons took flight.

The Hymn of the Olympic Flame blazed. In a golden suit, the torch bearer sprinted into the stadium and circled the parade grounds while racing birds returned to their keepers. The runner stepped to the cauldron and lit the sacred fire, which magically floated from the runner's feet to the top of the tower. After the Olympic Oath, a brief figure-skating show starring Dorothy Hamill, called "Ode to Joy" dazzled the crowd. With a loud whoosh, dozens of hot air balloons lifted into the air and drifted over the crowd. Thousands of colorful, helium-filled orbs danced in the breeze and millions of feathery rose petals fell like snowflakes from the sky. A skywriter traced five rings in the sky and spelled out the words, Lake Placid and the impressed crowd sighed.

Four laughed as he looked above my head. "GiGi, your hair is full of flowers." I tried to freeze his expression of wonderment in my mind. Such moments were fleeting, yet they made life worth living. Light reflected from Four's antique medallion.

I shook my head and looked at my gold watch. An hour had passed since the ceremony began. I couldn't believe how much happened in such a short amount of time. Normally, such events could be stodgy. Music played as the athletes marched from the stadium. The crowd began to dissipate, and I said goodbye to the woman behind us. I said, "I hope you're feeling better, honey."

***

On Monday, we sat in the arena and waited for the compulsory figures. I pressed my fingertips to my temples and worried that my head would split apart. What would it feel like to have an aneurysm? Migraines happened frequently enough that my jackhammering head wasn't a mystery, though this was more intense than usual. If only crawling into a corner and curling up into a ball were possible. Fond memories of attending the 1932 Games with Father remained with me through the decades. This was Four's chance to make a memory that would last and we were staying no matter how my head hurt.

One after another, the skaters entered the rink and performed their technically required moves. Four chattered in a whisper near my shoulder, and I barely heard him.

To my right sat a man who smelled so bad I wanted to vomit. Sometimes nausea accompanied my headaches, and the combination of body odor and stale beer made my stomach roil.

Four tugged at my sleeve like a toddler rather than a young teenager and asked, "Why do they call him Dick Buttons?" He snickered and said, "He's such a nice guy. Why would they name him that?"

Somehow I managed to hear his question, and I expect other spectators near us did also. I tried to pretend I wasn't ill, turned toward Four, and said, "Dick is short for Richard, honey. I'm sure his full name is Richard Buttons."

"But why wouldn't they call him Rich, Rick, or Rickie instead of *Dick*?"

"I don't know. I guess that would be better."

Mercifully, the next skater, Brian Pockar from Canada appeared on the ice and prepared for his routine. The compulsories only counted for twenty percent of the score. I would have liked to enjoy watching them, but my open eyes failed to see beyond the throbbing red thunder in my head. I wished for the strength to survive until it was over and looked forward to climbing beneath my blankets when I got home.

When the Canadian's performance was over, the lights filled the arena and the crowd roared. The light and noise collided in my head and felt like lightning and thunder behind my temples. I feared I might collapse. Lake Placid wasn't far from the border, and many exuberant Canadians attended the 1980 Games. I wished our noisy northern neighbors would settle down and hoped that they hadn't qualified any more of their citizens in men's figure skating.

A couple of rows ahead of us, a loudmouthed man began heckling the skaters. Evidently, his favorite had already competed. The man used foul language and appeared to have consumed a lot of alcohol. Four glanced at me a couple of times, and I patted him on the leg, reassuringly. Someone should speak to that man about his behavior or remove him from the crowd. Finally, someone fetched the authorities and the man was escorted from the building.

When at last, the compulsories were over, the crowd chattered noisily as they filed toward the exit. I just wanted to retreat to the silence of my bedroom and the soft vibrations of Calhoun's purring. On the way out, we overheard grumbling about the German skater, Jan Hoffmann, who stood in the first place position after the day's performance. The home crowd would have much preferred one of the Americans, or even the Canadian or British skaters. For all I cared, Godzilla could be in first, followed by King Kong, and Batman. I held onto the backs of chairs as we made our way slowly through the arena. Four chattered, "GiGi, do you think Santee can do it? Do you think he can catch up and take gold? He's better than Hoffmann and Tickner, don't you think?"

"I suppose so, honey."

"We shouldn't have to worry about Scott Hamilton, should we? It would be pretty hard to come from 8th place and take first, wouldn't you say so?"

I was confused by his twisted-up questions, and couldn't figure out whether yes or no meant that I agreed with him. I said, "It would seem like he is too far back to take gold, honey." I know it is hard for fans of any age to separate themselves from the letdown when their heroes fall short of victory, yet only one skater can win. I stopped for a minute and leaned against a metallic column and took a deep breath. My head throbbed, and I tried to focus on what to say. "I know you want David Santee to win gold, but just making it to the Olympics is a huge accomplishment. It would be nice if your favorite skater won a medal, but even if he doesn't, he should be very proud of himself."

Four said, "I know, GiGi. But if I were Santee, I would not be thinking how great it is that I'm one of the 16 best skaters in the world. I would want to win gold, not bronze."

I said, "I hope the young man takes the time to enjoy himself. For most athletes, having a chance to compete is a dream come true." I swooned and gripped the post tightly.

Four said, "Gosh. Are you okay, GiGi? You don't look so good."

"I'll be alright, honey. I just have a headache. I'll be fine once I take some aspirin and have a nap."

"I'll help you get home." Four put his arm around my waist and gripped my arm with his other hand and escorted me home. I didn't want to alarm him, but I was afraid that I would pass out and crumple to the ground.

***

Fortunately, my migraine went away, but the next morning I woke up stuffy. I had a sore throat and congestion. I thought of the woman from the opening ceremony and wondered if she had given me her cold. I shuffled off to the drugstore and invested in what I hoped were the most powerful remedies available. I called Presto and Harold, and between them, they took my tickets for the next couple of days' events. I hoped to feel better by Thursday evening.

I should have known I couldn't get over a cold in a couple of days. It seemed like colds were more severe and lasted longer the

106

older one got, and the foggy haze of medications made me feel every one of my seventy-five years, whereas normally, I felt years younger than my actual age. Nevertheless, I was determined that I was going to take Four to the men's finals. My cold had progressed to the point where my nose no longer ran constantly, but it was hard to suppress my cough and breathing was a challenge. I sucked on one Sucret after another, emptying tin after tin of the lozenges.

At the finals, Four raved about Scott Hamilton's footwork. Four clapped enthusiastically for the young skater when he was done and again as the young man stood in front of a wall of yellow flowers as the marks came in. Watching Four as David Santee skated in his red suit with sparkling gems at his waist, collar, and wrists made the whole night seem worthwhile. The famous skater had once spoken to Four's skating club and spent a couple of minutes answering questions. Ever since then, the young man has been my great-grandson's hero.

As the last couple of skaters performed, Four began singing, albeit quietly, the song, "Crazy Little Thing Called Love" by his favorite band, Queen. I thought about what we'd endured from other spectators during the Olympics and would have let Four continue but a man behind us tapped me on the shoulder. He looked at me with a deeply furrowed brow and a harsh stare. "Can you make that boy stop, Lady?"

I leaned toward Four and whispered, "The man behind me would like you to stop singing."

Four nodded. His stomach growled, and he whined, "I'm hungry."

It's no wonder, I thought. The boy barely eats enough to keep a pigeon alive. I dug in my pocketbook and handed him a box of animal crackers that looked like a circus wagon train car. I sat staring ahead and worried that Four would be insulted that I had offered him a child's snack. Then, when he bit into a crispy cookie, I worried that the man behind me would complain about the crunching, but he did not.

When the skating was finished, my heart ached for Four when

it became clear that the gold medal would go to the graceful Robin Cousins from Great Britain, and the silver to the veteran, formidable skater from East Germany, Jan Hoffmann. I felt bad for Four and for the skater from Illinois when the other US skater, Charles Tickner took third instead of David Santee. I didn't know how the judges made their decisions, making subjective choices with precise scoring when a sliver of difference separates one magnificent performance from another. When a tear sailed down Four's cheek I looked away and forced myself not to wrap my arms around him. I thought of Roni, the stuffed raccoon, and knew that Four would not appreciate me making him feel like a child. I sat still and watched, waiting for the end of the show, and we filed out of the arena quietly.

We didn't talk about it until we got home. When the door closed behind us, I said, "I'm sorry it didn't work out the way you hoped."

Four shrugged as if he didn't care, but I knew that he did. He said, "That's alright. I guess only one man can win and only three get medals. Somebody has to be in fourth place."

I agreed. "That's true and it doesn't diminish the extraordinary young man's talent. He should be very pleased with himself."

"But it's not fair. Santee spins like a top, and Tickner had a bad jump."

"I know." I didn't know what else to say, so I said, "That's the way the cookie crumbles." I spread my arms wide, and Four allowed my embrace.

He said, "Thanks for taking me to the Olympics, GiGi. I'll never forget it."

I felt groggy and ready for a dose of sleep-inducing cold medication.

When we returned to the Olympic Arena for the closing ceremonies my cold was practically gone. I sat listening to Chuck Mangione play "Fun and Games" on the flugelhorn as blue and white balloons dropped from above and the medal-winning athletes basked in the glow of the television cameras. I wished the Lake Placid Olympic Games could go on forever.

10

Sometimes I liked to sit in the lobby as if I were visiting Adirondack Dowel while enjoying a coffee break. It provided a different perspective than sitting invisibly behind a desk. I decided to relax for a few minutes and then make a list to see what else needed to be done.

Founders day was coming again, and I wanted it to be a memorable occasion. There was much to do to finalize preparations for the celebration and I felt frazzled. I couldn't seem to focus on organizing everything that needed to get done or wrap my arms around the plans for the big day. I hoped that my short break would settle my nerves.

I took a sip of coffee and watched Joanne roll a piece of stationary into her electric typewriter. As her fingers danced across the keyboard, I marveled at her posture. I remembered mentioning it once, and she said that her typing teacher told her she'd get a hump if she didn't sit perfectly straight. Her style hadn't changed since Father died. She still made her own old-fashioned dresses that resembled tablecloths, and the pretty girl looked remarkably comfortable despite being seven months pregnant with her second child. In August 1977, Joanne married Rusty Buckpitt. Their woodland wedding ceremony was like a scene from the animated classic Disney movie, *Bambi*, and baby Olivia was born on Thanksgiving in 1978.

My gaze shifted. I watched Art insert a check into the Paymaster check-writing machine. He was still sore at me for asking him to write a $500 check to Father's alma mater, Rutgers College in New Jersey. The donation was for a chair in the college's library and would feature a brass engraved plaque with the company's and Father's names on it. Art wasn't pleased to have an unexpected task added to his morning routine. His rushed fingers quickly lifted levers to the required digits, and then he deftly crunched the handle down until he was sure that the amount was deeply embossed onto the draft. He inspected the check, returned to his desk, inserted it into an envelope, licked the flap, and added it to a pile of mail. The business manager frowned at me when he noticed me watching him. Then he spun the combination on his briefcase, placed the mail inside it, and departed for the post office.

It was a great comfort knowing that Art took care of all of the company's deposits and disbursements, and kept the books, but the passing of time hadn't improved our relationship. It wasn't just Art Boykins. Neither the general manager, business manager, nor sales manager had changed one whit. No matter how hard I tried, the triumvirate blocked changes, avoided me, and tried to pretend the employees hadn't become owners after all. Sometimes I fantasized about firing one or all of them but always talked myself out of it. I imagined I saw glimmers of potential and hoped for a breakthrough that never materialized. Four years after founding the AJ Menard ESOP, the stubborn trio hadn't changed one iota. For all of their faults, each man took care of the matters they were supposed to and the daily business was conducted in an orderly fashion.

The air felt fresh and bright whenever Joanne and I were alone in the office. When the men were present, I felt the weight of a dark, heavy, oppressive curtain hanging over us. I longed for a day when things would be different. When Art made his frequent trips to the bank or post office, Joanne and I would chat, conduct business, or talk about what we could do for the employee owners.

As my mind wandered, my coffee had gone cold, and I returned to my office to make a final list of things to do before tomorrow's celebration. Instead of buzzing for Joanne to step into Father's office, I took my list to Joanne's desk and sat in a rigid chair beside her typewriter.

I said, "Can we go over the plans for tomorrow?"

Joanne turned to face me, with her hands folded together in her lap. "Sure can." She quickly reassured me that everything had been properly planned and all the details arranged. Stanley Bedard, who had returned to work as night watchman after his heart attack took care of the menu, and Joanne took care of the rest of the details. I was left with three tasks: making sure the sculptor arrived with Father's bust, completing the scrapbook, and delivering my speech.

"Are you sure about Millie, honey?"

Joanne held up the envelope that contained Millie's check. The woman had retired in December, and we had to wait until the books were closed for the year to make her distribution. "She promised to come, Misty."

"Did she say if she was bringing her family?"

The pitch of Joanne's voice raised slightly, and she lifted her hands from her lap. I recognized her gesture of uncertainty. "No, I asked, but she wasn't sure."

Millie's husband had passed away a couple of years earlier, and her children lived downstate. I sat forward and said, "I hope they can make it. It will be nice to have them join us."

Joanne asked, "Have you seen the statue?"

I could feel my lip curl and answered. "No, the artist insists on dramatically unveiling it at the ceremony. Creative types can be so mysterious. I can't wait to see it."

"He sure has kept you waiting."

"I was beginning to think he would never finish."

The bright-eyed young woman smiled and said, "It pays to be patient."

The door to the factory burst open and Rusty stepped into the office. His hand had healed and yet he always held it skyward, like the Statue of Liberty bearing her torch. I wondered if he would ever break the habit. I supposed it didn't hurt anything, but it always reminded me of the horrible day his finger was sliced off and made me feel guilty. Rusty said, "We're finishing up the Buffalo order. What's next?"

Joanne stood and handed him a small stack of papers. "I was on my way out with the paperwork."

"Super!" Rusty winked at his wife, nodded at me, and sauntered off to deliver the rest of the day's work to the factory.

I glanced at Joanne from the corners of my eyes and saw what looked to me like adoration as she watched her husband depart.

The phone rang and Joanne gracefully glided toward it. She answered, "Adirondack Dowel and Spindle Company, employee owned since 1976, this is Joanne. How can I help you today?" The pleasant woman didn't sound rushed, and though she said those words dozens of times a day, they sounded as fresh as dew-kissed morning glories. She listened to the voice on the other end of the phone and then she said, "Yes, Mrs. Blankenfritter. Misty's right here. Let me connect you."

Joanne stood and handed me the phone and I sat down at her desk.

The voice on the other end of the line said, "Good morning, Misty. This is Alice Blankenfritter. I'm sorry, I'm not feeling well. I will not be able to make it tomorrow."

I told her not to worry, that we'd be alright and that we hoped she would be feeling better soon.

When I hung up the phone, I said to Joanne, "What are we going to do?" We had come to rely on the trustee to explain the company's value to the employee-owners and to answer their questions. Could I do it without her? It was hard to imagine how.

***

Stanley, Rusty, and Joanne had everything ready at noon, and a few families began to arrive. I chatted with Stanley for a few minutes. He asked me if I thought he should wait, or whether he should begin cooking. As we chatted, I thought about the man who had a heart attack a few years earlier, and how lucky he was to survive it. The guy who had dined mostly on donuts, chips, and canned meat had lost weight and crunched on carrot sticks that magically appeared from the pockets of his multiple flannel shirts. Finally, I said, "Why don't you go ahead and get started?"

As Stanley began grilling frankfurters and hamburgers, I counted the families that had arrived. As he cooked, a few more cars pulled into the company parking lot. Twenty-five families was a long way from the total number of employees that worked at Adirondack Dowel. Did a Fourth of July parade prevent more families from arriving on time?

A sinking feeling dropped to the pit of my stomach. Last year's Founder's Day celebration wasn't well attended either, but there were lots more families in attendance then, compared to this year. Maybe they don't care? They probably had better things to do. Holidays were for families, not for work parties. It had seemed like a good idea to establish the ESOP on Independence Day during the bicentennial. I loved the symbolism of it but was it fair to ask employees to celebrate with their fellow owners during their personal time?

I felt abandoned, but what really rankled was the thought that the employees had forgotten Father. Most of them had decided not to attend the Founders Day celebration and the disappointment stung. Should we stop celebrating the occasion, or recognize it differently, perhaps on another day?

I looked over at the table where I had set the scrapbooks which contained the company's history. I finally finished the third and final volume after midnight last night, pasting the news of the company's becoming employee owned on the last page. I had spent years working on the project and I guess I didn't really want to finish it. For weeks, I was conflicted about whether to include clippings about Bob Holstein's disappearance during the Bicentennial Moonlight Regatta. I was tempted to brush that painful memory aside but finally decided to include the tragic moment in the company's official history. It was a lonely moment of deliberation, and I blinked away tears as I pasted the newsprint onto the pages. I felt empty when I tagged the final article in the scrapbook. The task was done. Working on that project was like spending time with Father, and I had enjoyed myself, but it was time to do other things instead. I watched as children chased each other on the lawn and their parents chatted in little clusters as the smell of picnic foods made my stomach gurgle. Nobody was interested in flipping scrapbook pages or reminiscing about the past, and it made me sad to think that the world had moved on.

Joanne pumped balloons with helium from a round tank and tied them to long strings while Joanne's mother bounced Olivia on her hip. Rusty encouraged children to throw bean bags to flip squares on the tic-tac-toe, Toss Across game. Older folks played cards on picnic tables, set up on the shady side of the building.

The oppressively hot sun poured down on me and I squinted, constantly glancing toward the parking lot. It was after one o'clock and Millie still hadn't arrived. Where could she be? What was keeping her? What if she didn't come? I had also been watching for the arrival of the sculptor who said he might be a couple of minutes late, but it was way more than that.

We had planned to gather everyone together in Joanne's picturesque rose garden in front of the building, but it was too hot and there was no shade out front. Rusty asked, "Do you mind if we celebrate Founder's Day here instead of out front?"

I nodded. "That's a good idea." Rusty was right, but I was disappointed. In my mind, Father's bust stood proudly on its fancy pedestal with a backdrop of shiny foliage and crimson rosebuds.

A vehicle backfired and I looked toward the parking lot. A rickety old truck sputtered as its engine shut off. Web Givens, the sculptor had arrived just in time. I'd never met the man, having only spoken to him on the phone, but it had to be him. He wore tight-fitting blue jeans, flared at the ankles, and an olive-green smock made of a coarse-looking fabric that might have been hemp. A spray of long, dark chest hairs sprouted from his v-necked shirt, and a camel-colored slouchy beret melted over the side of his head. The middle-aged man looked like he was dressed for a picnic ten or fifteen years earlier.

Rusty and several other men hurried toward the parking lot to help the artist, and I followed quickly behind them, shouting as we got closer. "Mr. Givens! You made it. I'm Misty Menard, and I'm so glad you're here."

He said, "Call me Web." He reached for my hand and bowed like a minstrel at a Renaissance fair.

"Can I see the sculpture?"

"No, no. That won't do." He shook his finger, dramatically emphasizing his disapproval. "You must wait for it to be unveiled at the ceremony."

I glanced into the bed of his antique truck. The statue was shrouded beneath stained sheets and bundled with frayed twine. Web offered me his arm and gestured toward Rusty and the men as if directing them to bring the statue. Web didn't look back to see if they followed.

Millie arrived as the men lugged the heavy bust across the lawn. I hollered. "Look. It's Millie! She made it." She moved slowly and carried a cane. "Let's help her." A couple of young men hurried to her side and escorted their former coworker to the picnic tables.

When I caught up to them and saw Millie's face, I said, "Oh dear, Millie. What happened?"

The good-natured woman laughed. "I took a tumble down a steep hill. Sometimes I forget I'm an old woman." She touched her scarred and scabby cheek gently with the tips of her fingers. "I roughed up my face and hurt my knee but it'll take more than that to do me in." She laughed as if daring the fates to do their worst.

I helped Millie sit at a table in the shade and Joanne brought her a plate of picnic food. "Can I get you anything else, Millie?"

She said, "Thank you, Joanne. Do you have any of those potato chips with the deep ridges in them?"

Stanley joined Millie while she feasted and the men cut the twine from the statue and placed it safely on its pedestal. I carried the scrapbooks from the distant table and set them near Millie in the shade and waited for her to finish eating. A couple of families apologized and said they had to hurry off to another holiday event before departing. I couldn't wait much longer. The already small gathering of employee owners was shrinking fast.

I cleared my throat. In my loudest voice, I shouted. "Happy Founder's Day and Happy Independence Day everybody. I know it is a holiday, and I'm so glad you could come." I felt a wistful pang blow through me, longing to have Father there, and wishing that all of the employee owners could have been present.

My voice cracked. "Usually, Mrs. Blankenfritter discloses the stock value, explains our ESOP, and answers questions, but poor Alice is under the weather. She sends her regards and a letter." I opened the letter and read it out loud. Though the company had lost money the previous year, it managed to generate enough cash to preserve most of the company's value. The stock value decreased by ten cents a share, but because of new shares allocated, most people's accounts had gone up a little bit rather than down. Joanne passed out envelopes that contained employee owners' annual statements as I finished Mrs. Blankenfritter's letter which wished the employees a better year in 1980. I read a paragraph that talked about the effects of inflation and high interest rates. The language sounded worrisome.

Millie had finished her picnic lunch and I was ready to present her distribution check. Joanne handed me a fancy pink and red envelope that looked more like a valentine than a bank draft or employee benefit statement. I wished that I had found more eloquent words to announce that Millie was the very *first* retiree to receive a distribution check from the AJ Menard ESOP. I watched the woman open the envelope and desperately wished that the check could have been larger.

The woman looked at her check, rolled her tongue in her mouth like she wanted to say something, and put the check back in the envelope. She held it over her heart, and for a brief moment, I felt that special feeling I had longed for all day. Finally, Millie said, "Thank you, Misty. It was a pleasure working with you all. I'm sure going to miss you."

Everyone clapped and I said, "We're going to miss you too, honey. Could we take a picture for the scrapbook?"

"Oh, no. I couldn't. I look just dreadful." Joanne had appeared with a camera. Millie covered her face with her hands and begged, "Please, put that thing away."

I said, "I understand," and waved Joanne off. I probably would have felt the same as Millie did, but I wished that we could preserve the historic moment so future employee owners could see what happened on the day that the first employee owner cashed in her chips.

Then, with much fanfare, I delivered a shortened version of the speech I had prepared. I could see that people were in a hurry to depart, so I told a brief story about how I found the renowned artist and commissioned him to preserve Father's image in stone. "Avery Johnson Menard loved this company. He built it from nothing and saw it through good times and bad. The company survived two world wars and a great depression. I know he would be proud of the job everyone is doing as employee owners. Together, you'll see this company through good times and bad, yet to come. Whenever you look upon Father's bust, I hope that you'll see it as a symbol of this company's ability to survive *anything*. I know you'll do Father's memory proud."

I turned toward the artist and asked, "Are you ready, Mr. Givens?"

He called back, "Without further ado, I am ready, Misty."

When Web proudly pulled the sheet from Father's bust and I saw it for the first time, I burst into tears as Joanne clicked a picture. I covered my face in shame. I knew I was behaving like a spoiled child but I couldn't help myself. Father looked like a hideous troll rather than a distinguished businessman. The sculpture looked nothing like the handsome gentleman who had founded the company. It wasn't even close enough to laugh it off as a caricature. The last thing I wanted to do was display that hideous monstrosity in the factory, lobby, or even at home. It was as if Father had just died rather than five years later. I didn't want to remove my hands from my eyes and face the artist. I couldn't think of a thing to say to him and the employees were watching.

I was horrified and wanted to bolt.

11

How did that horrible sculpture find its way to Father's office? The morning after the Founder's Day celebration, coffee spilled on my favorite dress when I walked into Father's office; the bust frightened me so. I asked the men to put it in the corner, on the other side of the doorway. The next morning, I draped a beautiful tablecloth over it. I wanted to destroy the ugly hunk of stone, lest someday anyone think that's what Father really looked like, but after spending thousands of dollars on the one-of-a-kind tribute, I couldn't bear to think that I had squandered so much money for nothing. Instead, I let the bust show off the gorgeous linen that was too pretty to risk staining with food.

The following day I telephoned a woman named Philomena Grant. Betty had recommended the portrait artist after placing many of her paintings on the walls of her clients. Betty said that Philomena had a gift for elevating her subjects and capturing the light in their souls. The way Betty described the artist's gift sounded a little spooky, yet that was just what I had hoped for: a work of art that preserved Father as he should have been remembered.

Like the sculptor, Philomena had a list of orders to fulfill before she could begin painting Father. After Betty and I made an overnight trip to Wappingers Falls, south of Poughkeepsie, I left a thousand-dollar deposit with the artist and waited endlessly for

Mrs. Grant to begin Father's rendering. The steep price tag smarted and I knew that Father's accountant would think I was frittering away a fortune, yet again, but after seeing Philomena's gallery, I was powerless to resist.

I had almost forgotten about the painting when the phone rang a year and a half later. It was January of 1982, and Philomena triumphantly declared that she had finished Father's portrait. Adrenaline shot through my gut, and I was tempted to get in my car and drive straight away to Wappingers Falls. The artist told me that Betty had arranged to pick it up along with a truckload of custom-made furniture that was on its way from New York City to one of the elegant chalets that Betty had been hired to decorate. I promised to mail Philomena the other half of her fee, without delay, thanked her for painting my father, and prayed that I would love it. Just thinking of the hideous troll that lived in a dark corner under a shroud in Father's office made me shiver.

***

The painting became an obsession and waiting for its delivery was excruciating. Days went by, and each evening I phoned Betty to ask whether the van had come. Finally, on the last day of January 1982, Betty said that it had arrived and that she would bring it over tomorrow.

Joanne took the day off to stay at home with her toddler, Oscar, who had a cold, so I took over her work for the day. The employees were on break when I delivered the orders to the expediter's podium.

John Smithers, a lathe operator, bit into a bologna sandwich and waved at me. The cheerful, hard-working machinist never missed an opportunity to greet me. I smiled and waved back at John.

A developing situation beyond John caught my attention. I had heard that our newest employee, Buster Snodgrass was disagreeable and had a temper but hadn't witnessed it myself. The hot-headed young man was shouting at his co-worker, Hogan Hoad. As I got closer, Buster uttered a series of obscenities and he capped off his diatribe with racial epithets. Finally, he said, "I've had enough of that whining twang. What are *you* doing listening to that junk?" It was as if he couldn't understand why a black person would listen to country music.

Buster reached for a thick dowel and I screeched, afraid that Buster was going to whack Hogan with the thick cylinder. If Buster heard me scream, it didn't show. Hogan stood, stoic in his bib overalls, but the anger was apparent on his dimpled cheeks. Buster raised his arm and smashed the rod onto Hogan's transistor radio with a loud, crunching thunk. Little bits and parts flew everywhere yet I was glad that Buster hadn't assaulted Hogan. The melodic object that had been playing Kenny Rogers' song, "Coward of the County," was in shambles and Hogan's hands balled into fists at his side.

"Stop that right now, children. Enough is enough." I don't know why I called them children. It just came out that way.

Buster turned toward me. He was surprised to see me standing there. His cheeks were bright red with rage.

I leaned forward and pointed to the lockers where the worker's kept their personal belongings. "Get your things, punch out, and go. You don't work here anymore, Buster Snodgrass."

"You can't fire me." Spittle flew from his mouth as he unleashed a string of profanities. My body shook. What if the man struck me? Did I quiver with fear or rage? Perhaps both. Buster finally concluded by making it clear what he thought of me. "Who wants to work for this lousy company anyway? I quit! Take that, you old hag."

My lips puckered in anger and my fists clenched in rage. I despised that word and the fact that it had been pinned on me made it even worse.

John Smithers stepped forward to defend me, but Buster

sneered at him and said, "Step back." He held his hand out like a school crosswalk guard. "I'm going. You ain't gotta worry about me no more."

I thanked John and turned back to check on Hogan. I would hate to admit having had favorites, but I always enjoyed talking with Hogan Hoad. We shared a love of country music and I remember the first time we talked about it. I had asked him if Charlie Pride was his favorite. He shook his head and said, "I get that a lot. No, Conway Twitty is the best there ever was or will be."

Since then, we've had a running debate as to whether his favorite or my beloved, Tammy Wynette, was the greatest singer the world has ever known. Her sobbing lilt squeezed emotion from the lyrics of every song she recorded and compelled me to purchase every record she made. I'd had the chance to see her in concert many times, though not since Father died.

Hogan's head hung low as if he were looking at the sawdust on the floor. I took his chin in my hand and lifted his head. His eyes looked wild for a second. "I will replace your radio, Hogan. That should never have happened, and I am sorry it did."

Hogan's shoulders sagged. He said, "I hate to see a guy get fired. It's hard enough to get a job these days. What will he do now?"

My head shook in wonder that the aggrieved man would be concerned for the other guy's well-being. I patted his shoulder and said, "Don't worry about that, Hogan. Hopefully, Buster has learned his lesson and will be a better co-worker in the future."

The harsh jolt of a buzzer blast echoed throughout the factory. It signaled the end of the employees' break, but not the end of trouble for the day. As I turned back toward Father's office, Doyle Polk stomped toward me. "What happened? I just saw Buster peel out of the parking lot."

"I had to let him go, Doyle. He broke Hogan's radio and threatened us with violence."

"No, missy. You do not fire *my* employees. Only I can do that.

We had a deal and if you can't keep your part of the bargain, I'll quit. Then you can see just how fast this place goes bankrupt. If you *ever* do that again, so help me God, I'll walk out that door. Do I make myself clear?" The towering tyrant turned away and left without waiting for my reply.

Anger rose from my gut to my cheeks. Doyle made me feel like a scolded child. It rankled knowing that Hogan, John, and the others had witnessed Doyle's outburst. Yet, if I had to do it again, I would have fired Buster Snodgrass, no matter the consequence.

***

Later that afternoon, I sat in the stands as I often did, and tried to watch Four work with his coach and a couple of other skaters as they practiced jumping. The experts agreed that his step work was excellent, and his spins were other-worldly, but his jumps needed work if he was ever to become an Olympian, so Four practiced them endlessly.

Instead of focusing on the skaters, my thoughts kept returning to the trouble between Buster and Hogan. The memory was bad enough, but Doyle's threatening nature concerned me even more. My hands wrung in my lap and I fumed at the thought of Doyle's claim that the company would go under if he were not in command of the factory. Surely someone else could run the shop. The employee owners might even thrive and work better for a more humane boss. Everyone could be replaced. Why keep Doyle Polk? How many years had Father been gone now? Why tolerate this man who despised me? I still owned a good percentage of the company. At last, it was time to escort the dictator to the door.

My eyes returned to the ice. I watched as Four leaped high into the air. I was no expert, but something looked wrong. I jumped to my feet and my pocketbook fell to the floor with a thud, spilling its contents. When Four's skates hit the ice, one skate struck the other and his legs became unnaturally twisted. His shoulder brutally struck the ground and he skidded across the ice into the surrounding plywood walls.

As I hurried down from the bleachers, the coach hollered, "Call the Doctor. Now!" Four's body didn't move and I feared the worst as I scrambled toward the scene. I imagined that I could hear a faint, disoriented moan.

***

Presto and I spent the night at the hospital beside Four. I thought about how happy Presto and Cookie were when Four was born and I couldn't believe that fifteen years had passed since then. Presto was a good father, but it hadn't been easy for him after that tragic night when Cookie was killed in a car crash during a snowstorm. Presto was quiet, gentle, and a supportive single parent, but looking at his bandaged son in the stark hospital bed made him angry. He kept looking at me with a pitiful, guilty scowl and uttering, "How could I let him do this to himself?"

"Oh, Presto, how could you stop him? As long as I can remember, skating is the only thing Four wanted to do." We both knew that the only reason Four worked hard in school was so that he would be allowed to skate. I hated the idea that all of his happiness was wound up in just one thing and I often tried to convince him to find a second passion, something else that he enjoyed doing in addition to skating. Four had his heart set on Olympic gold and all he could talk about was competing in Yugoslavia.

I dabbed the corner of my eyes with a Kleenex. It was hard to look at the young man, bandaged like a skeleton. The doctors said he had a broken leg, shoulder, three fractured ribs, and a concussion. I didn't have the heart to ask how long it would take before the boy could skate again. The Sarajevo Games were only two years away. To be competitive in 1984, Four would need to be able to compete against the best in the world for a year or two prior. I couldn't imagine how he could make it after having suffered such injuries.

When Four woke up, he seemed disoriented. He asked, "What happened?" and tried to get out of bed.

Presto explained Four's injuries and I held his hand while tears streamed down his face. I wanted to collapse at the sight. Four didn't speak again that night. Eventually, he cried himself back to sleep. I felt like I had just witnessed the death of the young man's dream and my head hung with despair.

***

I hardly left Four's side during the next week. The doctor ordered him to stay off skates for six months. Poor Four alternated between fits of anger and waves of tears and at times was inconsolable.

When we met with Four's coaches, they told us his chances of making the 1984 Olympic Team were meek. They advised Four to set his sights on the 1988 Games in Calgary, instead. Even that would be a long shot and would require constant training once his injuries healed. The determined young man said, "I won't give up on 1984 but if it's got to be Calgary, so be it. I can wait if I have to."

Though I was away from Adirondack Dowel most of the week, my thoughts kept returning to my difficulties with the management team. For years, I had tolerated a bad situation and instead of getting better with time, it had become worse. I had finally convinced myself that I needed to fire Doyle Polk, but it wasn't just the general manager. The rest of the team wasn't any better. Art avoided me entirely and evaded answering my questions directly. Stuart's long absences and unaccounted-for time made me increasingly uncomfortable. Whenever I inquired about his customer visits, he smirked and asked me what I'd like to know. I knew I shouldn't have to ask the man twenty questions about his trips or the company's clientele.

When I consulted with Winslow about making management changes, he frowned. Father's attorney sat forward and softly said, "I know it must be difficult, Misty. Believe me. I understand how you feel." Winslow's frown became a grimace. "You should probably speak with John Frederick Duncan before making any drastic changes. Given the company's indebtedness to Mirror Lake Bank, you should be very careful about doing anything that would rock the boat too much, especially if you intend to sell the rest of the company to the ESOP. I'm afraid that you will need to keep on Mr. Duncan's good side, especially given the sad state of the economy. So that means you shouldn't do anything significant without first talking to John Frederick."

My nose crinkled at the thought. "That man gives me hives, Winslow. There's just something about him. I can't put my finger on what it is."

"I feel the same way, Misty, but Mr. Duncan is a powerful man. If the company were in better financial condition, I would suggest looking for a different bank, but under the circumstances, you need Mirror Lake Bank much more than they need you."

After visiting with Father's lawyer, I called the bank and Mr. Duncan's secretary scheduled an appointment for me on Friday the 12th at 1:30 pm. I arrived promptly and was invited to wait in Mr. Duncan's office. His secretary took my winter coat and said, "Mr. Duncan should be along shortly. Can I get you a hot beverage or something?"

"No, thank you just the same."

As the door closed behind me, I looked around Mr. Duncan's spacious office. On the main street of Lake Placid, square footage was scarce, yet the bank president's office was palatial. Black and white photographs from the 1932 Winter Olympic Games hung on his walls, precisely positioned. The frames were neatly aligned and the distance between photographs was identical. Except for a telephone and a brass light with a green shade, there wasn't anything on John Frederick's massive oak desk. On a matching bookshelf there was a picture of his family on the top shelf, and nothing else. The other ledges were also lightly-adorned and devoid of dust. The room smelled like furniture polish and window cleaner. Did his secretary clean his office while he was at lunch? It wouldn't have surprised me.

I turned and looked at the wall behind me and saw a framed certificate rather than pictures of athletes. I stepped forward and stared at a document that thanked John Frederick Duncan for his generous donation to St. Kateri Orphanage in Wanakena, New York. The silver frame looked like it was worth even more than the banker's contribution.

My fingers touched the frame and sparks flew from my fingertips. My field of vision narrowed and I experienced a vision of a woman who looked like a nun hunched over the banker's desk, delicately scrawling calligraphy on the fancy framed document. Something seemed familiar about the woman, yet I could not see her face. My fingers felt hot. I felt my pulse quicken and I snatched my hands from the edge of the frame. Why did an innocent thank-you note carry such an aura of danger?

My digits still tingled as I turned away from the back wall of Mr. Duncan's office and I stared at my hands trying to make sense of what had just happened. It didn't happen often and the first time was a curious enough matter. This was the third time I had such an experience and it still amazed me. The door swung open and I flinched when John Frederick suddenly entered the room.

"Good afternoon, Miss Menard. It's lovely to see you. You should have come earlier in the day. We could have had lunch together again."

I thought of the last time we went to lunch and said, "Perhaps next time. Thank you for seeing me, Mr. Duncan."

"Of course, Miss Menard. At your service, any time." The banker jostled himself into the big chair behind his desk and invited me to make myself at home. Politely, he inquired, "How's the dowel business? Doing any better?"

I paused. There was no way to make it sound better than it was.

"We're holding on as best we can, Mr. Duncan. Inflation makes everything more expensive, and because of the recession, our customers don't order as much or as often. I know unemployment is a problem across the country, but if business doesn't pick up, we may have to let a couple of people go."

Mr. Duncan folded his hands together on his desk and sat forward slightly. He looked amused, but his words conveyed sympathy. "Sounds dreadful. What can I do for you, Miss Menard?"

I looked at the vast expanse of the desk between us, took a deep breath, and said, "I have two things I'd like to discuss with you today. First, I want to proceed with the ESOP. Second, I want to make changes to the management team."

The man's sympathetic expression soured. "Why would you make a sale when the company is doing poorly? Surely, the stock value will go down this year. You'll get even less for your stock than you did last time."

"Yes, I suppose so." I shrugged like I didn't care, but I was starting to worry that there wouldn't be enough money for my family and me by the time I was done selling Father's company. "The employee owners will get the stock at a bargain, so it will be good for them."

Mr. Duncan grunted judgmentally. "That's foolish, Misty. What would your father think?" The man's cheeks danced like he was swooshing mouthwash. "I suppose you want me to lend the ESOP money to do it."

I nodded. "Yes, if you please, Mr. Duncan." Why did Mr. Duncan make it sound like he would lend the money personally? Perhaps he thought of the bank's money as if it were his own.

"Very well. The deal will be the same as last time, Miss Menard. The bank will hold the proceeds of the sale as collateral until the loan is repaid. Is that acceptable to you?"

"I suppose so."

"And what is this business about the management team?"

Mr. Duncan's demands and inquisition began to wear thin. With a sharp tongue, I told the banker about firing Buster Snodgrass. The look on his face made me realize that the tone of my voice sounded harsh, like there was a chip on my shoulder. After a brief pause to adjust my timbre, I admitted to arguing with Doyle Polk. "Ever since I inherited Father's company, the management has been cold, distant, and even hostile at times. Often, they barely speak to me. It's almost as if they don't think I own the place."

Mr. Duncan lifted his hands from the desk as if appealing to the heavens. "Perhaps it's because of this ESOP nonsense."

"But Mr. Duncan, ESOP or not, I am the president and majority shareholder of the company."

He tilted his head slightly as if understanding management's position. "Misty, men aren't accustomed to having women bosses. You must understand *that*, don't you?"

I was sure Mr. Duncan was correct. "Perhaps that's part of the problem. But I don't know, it seems there's something more to it. And it isn't just Doyle. Art and Stuart aren't any more welcoming. I'd like to fire Doyle and see whether things improve with Art and Stuart. If they don't, I may need to replace them as well."

Mr. Duncan spread his arms wide and gripped the sides of his desk. In a booming voice, he growled, "Absolutely not, Misty. Doyle Polk is a seasoned manager. He knows the business and from where I sit, I think he is single-handedly keeping the company afloat." He released his hold on the desk and slammed his fists violently in front of him. The lamp shook and the phone jostled in its cradle. "As long as Adirondack Dowel owes Mirror Lake Bank, Doyle Polk and the others must stay. If you fire them, I'll be forced to call the loan." He bared his teeth at me and said, "Do I make myself clear?"

As I left Mr. Duncan's office, I felt like a dog with her tail between her legs. I glanced at the line of people waiting to conduct transactions at the tellers' windows. A woman in a dark, hooded cloak caught my eyes and I recognized Lois Phelps. I tried to remember the last time I had seen her hate-filled expression glaring back at me through oversized sunglasses. She stared at me as I made my way to the front door of the bank. A creepy sensation crawled along the back of my neck and I quickened my pace.

12

When Betty brought Philomena's painting to the house, we unpackaged it together. It had been carefully crated to ensure that it could not be damaged. Finally, the only thing covering it was a light cloth which Betty carefully unwound. She told me to sit down as she finished and then dramatically turned the big portrait toward me.

Philomena's painting took my breath away and I was glad that Betty suggested I sit down. I gasped and felt my chest tighten. The subject of the portrait appeared to glow from within his core. The radiant subject looked like a Biblical figure or a renaissance angel, and yet I felt more connected to Philomena's painting than the artwork at church. The artist had matched Father's clothing to the picture I had sent her and he was posed the same. She had captured the shape of Father's features and the expression on his face, but something wasn't right.

Betty propped the painting against a chair and sat down beside me. I turned toward her. Her eyes grew wide and her fingers touched her lips. She said, "It's stunning, Misty. An absolute masterpiece and it looks just like AJ, only...."

"I know, I know...." It was too much. I had wanted to preserve Father's legacy, not deify him.

This was a portrait of Father, not Zeus. Salty tears formed behind my eyes. I looked at Betty and said, "What should I do?"

She turned toward me, but her peripheral vision remained focused on the portrait. Finally, she said, "Why don't you look at it again tomorrow and see what you think of it then?" Then she looked at me and her lip quivered. She stood up, turned away from me, and said, "I still miss him, Misty." She picked up the painting and propped it against the living room wall. Did seeing the painting make it harder for her?

We never talked about Betty and Father's relationship. I'm not sure whether it was on her account or mine. I didn't want to know the details of their romance, but mumbled, "Me too." As she backed away from the painting, I suggested, "Let's have tea."

On the way to the kitchen, Betty said, "I never got over him, Misty."

As the water boiled, Betty's mind seemed to wander and she said, "He always dreamed Johnny would take over the business." She picked up a pen on the counter and fidgeted with it, clicking the top in and out. "It was like he kept waiting for Johnny to come back so he could teach Johnny everything he knew. It took decades before he realized that he should leave the business to you instead."

"What made him think that I could run Adirondack Dowel?"

Betty looked at me as if she were surprised by the question. "He said that watching my decorating business made him understand. Women can be successful entrepreneurs."

"Maybe he should have left Adirondack Dowel to you instead of me."

She frowned. "The idea never came up. I always had plenty to do in my business anyway."

The teapot whistled, briefly interrupting our conversation. When we returned to the subject, Betty said, "You should have come home sooner, Misty. AJ needed you. He didn't have the heart to ask you to come."

I looked down at the table as she spoke. What she said was true. The thought hadn't formed in my head, but now that she had said it, I knew she was right. If I hadn't been so selfish, I would have realized it then. If I had returned to Lake Placid ten or fifteen years sooner, things could have been different. I might have learned the business properly and helped Father when he needed me most. I frowned at the thought that Stuart, Art, and Doyle were my fault, to begin with.

Then Betty vigorously pressed excess water from a tea bag. She squeezed it so violently, I thought it would rupture. Then she set the spoon on the saucer, looked at me, and said, "Why don't you invite me to your family events anymore? You always used to. I don't understand. Did I do something wrong?"

I heard myself stammer. In my mind, I ticked off the various small dinners, birthdays, and holidays and realized that she was right. I mangled a weak apology.

"I don't have any right to attend Founder's Day celebrations at the company, but I would like to go just the same."

"You're right, Betty. You should be there." She neither married Johnny nor Father, but she was part of the family nevertheless. "I'll make sure you're invited whenever we celebrate milestones."

"I'm sorry, Misty. I'm acting like a spoiled brat lately." She spun the lid on top of the sugar bowl. "I've been thinking about the hereafter a lot lately. What if I have to choose between Johnny and AJ on the other side, and...." she sputtered. "What if they don't want me around?"

What could I say to console her? Perhaps I should have spent more time thinking about death and beyond, given my advanced years, but I had my hands full with the present. I doubt she found solace in my lame assurance. "I'm sure everything will work out fine, honey."

"I don't know about that, but what can I do anyhow? Listen to me, blathering on."

Our conversation lulled, we finished our chamomile, and Betty excused herself to meet a client.

I wandered back to the living room and imagined hanging

Father's portrait at the company. It didn't belong there, but Betty was right. The next morning, I looked at it again and decided to display it proudly like the work of art it was. It would be the focal point of Father's living room. The rest of the fixtures and furnishings would disappear into the shadows as the illuminated portrait gormandized the spotlight.

Still, there wasn't a fitting tribute to Father that I could leave at the company he built. My latest new therapist and sponsor was bound to hear it all as soon as I could book my next appointment on her couch. The poor woman always had to cut our appointments short, between listening to me complain about my age, being a woman in a man's world, and trying to keep my addictions at bay, I filled her ears with my problems faster than she could make notes.

***

Despite my therapist's attempts to constructively channel my anger, my temper simmered for weeks after meeting with Mr. Duncan. How dare he try to run Father's business? I was furious with the domineering lender. It wasn't right for *him* to tell me how to run the company, but Adirondack Dowel owed Mirror Lake Bank a fortune and even the ESOP was in debt to it. My stomach boiled in turmoil and I began to wonder whether I had an ulcer.

Four's convalescence was trying. It was hard to keep teen-aged boys cooped up and being stuck inside made him irritable. It wasn't like he could have done the one thing he wanted anyway. I tried to tempt him with potential new hobbies, but he refused my suggestions. Sometimes he seemed like he was in a trance, with his open palm covering the medallion that rested on his chest. The only thing he seemed willing to do was to help me piece together puzzles, so we spent each evening snapping tiny chunks of cardboard together. In hopes of improving Four's mood, I let him control the radio dial. At first, I thought his favorite songs were strange. It was as if the performers went out of their way to be as shocking as possible. As the weeks went by, I found myself enjoying the unusual music. I even purchased a couple of record albums by *Blondie* and *The Human League*, which we enjoyed listening to together, but I wasn't sure I cared for *The Cure*, *Depeche Mode*, or *New Order*.

When Four's cast came off at the end of March, he began physical therapy. The exercises caused him pain, but he refused to complain. I said, "It hurts, doesn't it, honey?"

Four shrugged. "If I want to skate again, I have to suck it up, GiGi."

I was worried. "Don't push yourself too hard, at least not at first."

He shook his head vigorously and his layered hair tumbled about his head. "I gotta. Every week that goes by is another week wasted. I have to get back to training."

Even at Adirondack Dowel, I was often distracted, thinking about Four and his rehabilitation. I scarcely heard the rapping sound on Father's office door when the business manager knocked. When I realized he was there, I stood up and invited him in. Art rarely came to see me. Usually, he saved things he needed to tell me and would blurt them all out when I passed by his desk.

Art pleasantly asked, "How's your great-grandson doing, Misty?"

The business manager rarely inquired about anybody's well-being, let alone their loved ones. I told him about Four's efforts to regain his strength.

He said, "I hope the boy is able to get back to what he loves doing. It's hard to see children in pain."

I thanked Art for his concern and wondered if, after all, maybe there was hope that we could be friends.

He stepped closer and gripped the back of the guest chair in Father's office. It struck me that he was using the big chair as a shield, and yet I didn't recall him ever seeming so accessible. He said, "I wanted to ask you about the orphanage. It is time for the annual Easter appeal. Would you be willing to support the children again this year?"

I remembered the frame on Mr. Duncan's wall and realized that Art was asking for a donation to the very same charity. I must not have realized how confused I looked.

"Maybe you don't remember, Misty. Last year you donated $250, and the year before you gave $200."

"Of course, how silly of me, Art. Let me get my checkbook. Remind me how to make it out."

"You can pay to the order of St. Kateri Orphanage. I've been raising funds for them for over twenty years. Everybody at the company makes a contribution each spring." Art looked down and away and it seemed that he was overcome with emotion. He finished his thought "…and I appreciate it."

I considered asking about his connection to the charity but decided against it. I asked, "Does the company make a donation also?"

Art's face twitched when I asked him that, and he answered. "Yes, Misty. The company gives $1,000 every year. The sisters say that they couldn't feed, clothe, and keep the Indian children warm all winter without our support. It's not just us. All the businesses in town make a contribution."

"I see." I blew the ink dry and ripped the bank draft along the perforation. Mr. Duncan's framed thank-you note crossed my mind as I handed the check to Art. I cleared my throat and said, "At the bank, there's a letter of appreciation from the orphanage. Do they send letters to all their donors?"

The man's cheeks reddened. He spoke fast and said, "Yes, they send a letter to each company. I don't keep them. Would you like to see it when it comes in the mail this year?"

I stood from behind Father's desk and shook my head. "Oh, I don't need to see it, but maybe it would be nice to frame it and put it on the wall as Mr. Duncan does at the bank."

The spindly bookkeeper backed away toward the door and said, "Why not?" He pivoted quickly, added "Thank you, Misty," and whipped around the corner into the hallway.

Everybody had a soft spot. I would never have figured that Art Boykins' weakness was needy children. To think that it took me seven years to realize the man had some humanity to him.

The following week, our CPA sent the final numbers for 1981. They were even worse than I thought they would be. Customers' orders came less frequently and they were smaller than they previously had been. Meanwhile, the cost of everything skyrocketed, especially the heating bills.

On Monday, April 26th, the trustee's valuation adviser arrived to do the work for his annual appraisal of the company. Each year the process took longer, the questions seemed harder to answer, and the man seemed more distant every time he came to town.

A couple of days later, I was looking out the window toward the parking lot when Alice Blankenfritter pulled her brown, Chrysler K-Car into the parking lot. She maneuvered the boxy vehicle in and out of her parking space until she was certain that it was perfectly centered and then marched up the walkway in her drab gray dress.

The valuation advisor hemmed and hawed as he presented his report to Mrs. Blankenfritter. He said, "It's a sign of the times, I'm afraid. It's the same thing everywhere I go. I'm sure it will rebound, Mrs. Blankenfritter." He didn't sound reassuring at all, and it was hard to digest that the stock value was nearly half of what it was when the ESOP did its first transaction.

Mrs. Blankenfritter turned to me and asked, "Are you sure you want to sell the rest of the company *this year*, Miss Menard? Nobody is selling companies right now. It is not wise."

I shrugged and whispered to the woman. "I must, Mrs. Blankenfritter. I am not getting any younger."

She suggested, "Why don't you do a small amount this year, and then you can finish in a year or two when things get better? Going to fifty percent employee owned would be enough of a milestone for now, would it not?"

"I suppose so." I had hoped to go directly to one hundred percent, but Mrs. Blankenfritter assured me that it wouldn't be prudent. As trustee, the ESOP would have gotten the company for a song, and Mrs. Blankenfritter's obligation was to them. Could the no-nonsense woman have taken pity upon me or was she shrewdly looking out for the benefit of the employees?

Instead of leaving town when her work was done, Mrs. Blankenfritter stayed an extra day. I sat beside her as she grilled one man after another. After a dozen questions, I was afraid that Doyle was going to jump across the desk and strangle her. My mind wandered as I imagined them wrestling, and it wasn't hard to picture her getting the best of the burly general manager.

Art writhed in his seat and twisted like a pretzel trying to answer her questions. None of his replies ever seemed to satisfy her, and the man often concluded his explanations with, "I don't know what else to tell you about that."

When Stuart tried his usual tact with the trustee, she sneered at him and said, "Wipe that wiseacre grin off your miserable face, young man, and answer my questions or I'll get the lawyers in here to question you. Sometimes, I swear, there's something fishy going on around here."

I was amazed to see how quickly Stuart came around and answered all of Mrs. Blankenfritter's questions. He didn't hold back as he usually did, and answered beyond her questions. I hadn't heard such a robust account of our customers' troubles as I did that day. It wasn't just us, our customers were experiencing great hardship in the troubled economy as well.

When Mrs. Blankenfritter finished her interviews, she stepped into Father's office without knocking. She said, "Miss Menard, please come with me." She led me to the waiting room and pointed at the newly framed letter on the wall. She pointed at the document, tipped her head forward, and sternly asked, "Please explain *this*, Miss Menard."

I stammered and felt like I did when John Frederick Duncan told me that I could not fire the general manager. It seemed like everybody wanted to tell me how to run the business. My voice sounded unnaturally squeaky even to me as I lamely defended the donation. "The company has a tradition of supporting the orphanage. All the businesses in town do."

With the backs of her hands on her hips, Mrs. Blankenfritter leaned forward and shook her head slowly from side to side. "Miss Menard, companies should not make charitable donations. If the company were wildly profitable, that might be another story. As trustee, I do not want to see the company giving cash away, especially when the company is losing money and short of funds." She paused for a moment and my gaze got lost in the deep trenches of the wrinkles on her forehead. "Do I make myself clear?"

I realized that my mouth was hanging open, so I closed it, and nodded, dejected.

Mrs. Blankenfritter relaxed her stance. "Very well, Miss Menard." As we passed by Art's desk, she said, "Tell me more about the orphanage. I might like to make a *personal* donation."

I stopped her and suggested she ask Art about it. I stood by as the nervous bookkeeper told the trustee about the Indian boys and girls who depended on the citizens of Lake Placid for their survival. Art printed the address for Mrs. Blankenfritter and thanked her for her interest in the cause.

Before Mrs. Blankenfritter left, she sat with me and told me to look closely at every expense. "If you don't need it, cut it. You can't be too cheap, Miss Menard. Tell the employees to bundle up in the winter and turn down the thermostats. In the summer, cut the grass every other week instead of weekly. You must cut Stuart's expenses as well. Instead of sending him on the road all of the time, perhaps he can phone the customers. The travel and entertainment expenses are way too high for a company your size, and you must get a handle on his perks. Do your customers really need to be entertained so lavishly to purchase hardware for their stores? I should think not!"

When Ted Drake came to Lake Placid a few weeks later, he echoed Alice Blankenfritter's advice. "I hate to see you go broke,

Misty."

"Do you think that could happen, Ted?"

"Yes. I hate to alarm you, Misty. I am very worried."

At that moment I felt a sharp pain, leaned my head forward, and clutched my chest. Was it a heart attack? I remembered finding Stanley in the grass and panicked. I couldn't die. Not yet, anyway. My mind went blank as my body sagged.

13

When I regained consciousness, sirens screamed in my ears. When my eyes opened, seeing the interior of the ambulance alarmed me and made my heart race. Is this what dying felt like? I knew I was getting old, and many of my high school classmates had already passed away, but Father had lived to ninety. I figured I still had many good years left, but who knew how much time remained on one's life clock?

A handsome young man in a bright blue jumpsuit spoke to me in a deep voice. A patch on his chest said his name was Zack. "Please try to remain calm, Miss Menard. We'll take good care of you." I looked into the man's deep blue eyes and batted my lashes. For a moment, I had forgotten that I was an old woman making an emergency trip to the hospital. I thanked him for rescuing me and he said, "My pleasure, ma'am. Please just relax and breathe steadily. We'll be at the hospital in a minute." I looked at his mouth as if trying to read his lips. He said, "They'll take good care of you there."

Betty and Ted followed the ambulance. Ted was asked to remain in the waiting room, and Betty was invited to sit by my side as the doctor completed his examination of me. Finally, the doctor cleared his throat and said, "You're a lucky lady, Misty. Rather than a heart attack, I'd say that you have heartburn. Gastroesophageal Reflux Disease. Your stomach acid has boiled over. It's possible that you have an ulcer, too." The doctor gave me a list of foods and beverages to avoid, recommended I pick up some Pepcid AC, and referred me to a specialist. "We don't know why you fainted."

"I panicked and became light-headed. That's all I remember."

The doctor made me promise to make an appointment with a gastroenterologist and released me from his care.

On the way to Betty's car, I said, "I thought I was a goner, Betty."

My friend laughed and said, "It will take more than spicy food to do *you* in. It's a good thing Ted Drake was there to catch you or you could have busted your head open when you fell."

Ted caught up to us and said, "I'm glad you're going to be alright, Misty." The young lawyer chuckled and asked, "Have you made a will, Misty? In all seriousness, it doesn't matter how old you are. You should have your final wishes made clear. Promise me you'll talk to Winslow about it."

***

Four spoiled me all weekend. The kid kept telling me I needed to rest and then woke me up whenever I nodded off to ask me if I was thirsty. The antacid worked fabulously and I felt better by Monday, but the doctor demanded I take a week off before returning to work. He told me, "It isn't just spicy foods and late-night snacks, Misty. Some experts think that stress contributes to the situation. You'd better take it easy for a little while." I didn't appreciate it when the juvenile doctor uttered the cliché phrase about spring chickens and told me I wasn't one of *them*.

Wednesday night, I had a nightmare. When I woke up in the middle of it, I had the sense that the frightening dream was all too familiar.

The sound of breaking glass made me jump from the bed. Calhoun shrieked as he crashed to the floor. Loud music and a beeping horn reached my ears and I hurried to the window and saw the tail lights of a speeding vehicle racing away. It looked like a car full of teenagers or young adults with their heads and arms outside the windows, but I couldn't make out more details than that.

I raced down the stairs and saw the shattered glass in the dining room. Four appeared beside me, rubbing his eyes. "What happened, GiGi?"

All I could think to say was, "We've been vandalized. Would you call Betty for me? And put on some shoes. You don't want to cut your feet on broken glass. I'll get the broom and dustpan." Without getting near the shards, I turned on all the lights I could reach.

A policeman arrived as I tied my shoes and told me to wait until he was gone before sweeping the floor. Betty rushed through the doorway moments later and wrapped her arms around me. "Oh, Misty, how awful. Are you alright?" Before I could answer, she dragged Four by the hand to the kitchen and said, "We'll make coffee."

Things like this rarely happened in Lake Placid. Officer Wilder Wideawake introduced himself and asked about a hundred questions. He scribbled notes on a small pad. "I'm going to have to put all of this in my report." The policeman pushed the drapes aside with his baton, squatted briefly, and stood up again. He turned back toward me and held a brick forward in his hands. The man sounded like he had stepped out of a television western. "I reckon this is what broke your window, ma'am. Do you mind if I set it on the table?"

A massive flashlight appeared in Officer Wideawake's hand and a beam of light flooded a common brick. I peeked around the policeman's shoulders. There was a note attached to the masonry, tied to it with fabric ribbon like the edging of an apron. The handwriting was as neat as the bow but the words made me shudder. I read the threat out loud. "Shove off, lady. Get out of town while you still can." Then I muttered the words a second time and began to sit down.

"Miss Menard, you'd better not sit here. There could be broken glass on the sofa. Let's mosey on into the kitchen." I clung to

Officer Wideawake's muscular arm as we stepped away from the crime scene. He inquired, "Any idea who would do such a thing? Anybody you can think of who would want you *gone*?"

"I'm afraid I can think of a number of people who would like to see me leave town, but I can't imagine any of them doing a thing like this." My hand released the policeman's arm and I rubbed my temples. "I feel a headache coming on." I sat at the kitchen table and Betty placed a tall glass of orange juice and a bottle of Tylenol in front of me. "The truth is, I was having a nightmare when it happened." I glanced at Betty, afraid to speak the name of the villain in my dream. "A woman in a dark cloak with an ancient dagger was about to stab me. She screamed about revenge, but the car that sped away looked like it was filled with young men."

The policeman rubbed his chin. "I don't believe in coincidences, Miss Menard, but I can't put your dream in my report. Just the facts, ma'am. If it weren't for the note, I'd say it was just delinquent teenagers. In the coming weeks, I'll drive past your house a couple of times a night and see if anything looks out of sorts." He tipped his cap like it was a cowboy hat and said, "Call me if anything else comes to mind."

By the time Officer Wideawake had completed his investigation, the sun had begun to rise. Betty helped me clean up the mess and tacked cardboard boxes into the window frame to keep the elements out until new panes could be installed. She spun a quick breakfast together and then she drove Four to school. "I can walk," he said, but Betty insisted on taking him in her car.

I took a nap before noon and tried to forget about the bar of mud and clay that someone hurled through the window. My stomach gurgled when I woke up a couple of hours later. I was tired of following the doctor's orders and ready to get out of the house. I told Presto that I was meeting Joanne for dinner in Saranac Lake and would be home late. "Be vigilant and keep away from the windows, just in case, honey."

***

Joanne was sitting straight and tall, with perfect posture, as always, when I arrived at Casa del Sol.

"This is my favorite restaurant." I sat down across from her, pushed the menu aside, and glanced at the drawing of a sun, rising or setting behind steps that looked like the profile of the adobe cantina. The structure looked like it belonged in the desert rather than an alpine town which was known for its low temperatures. Saranac Lake often boasted the coldest temperature in the country on the morning news. I smiled at the words on the cover of the menu which promised, "A Taste of México." I don't know what foods tasted like south of the border, but the Adirondack chimichangas were a delicacy.

My dinner companion had a concerned frown on her face. After the waiter filled our water glasses, Joanne said, "Aren't you supposed to avoid spicy foods, Misty?"

My medication worked miracles and I assured Joanne that I would avoid using the hot sauce. Tasty as the red and green salsas were, it was not an insignificant compromise. Eager to change the subject, I asked about her test. After seven years of attending North Country Community College part-time, she was completing the last class she needed to get her associate's degree in business administration.

Joanne raised an eyebrow and said, "I think I answered everything correctly."

Try as I might, I couldn't recall which class she was taking. "Remind me, honey. Which subject are you taking this term?"

She rolled her eyes. "Computers. The professor says that someday, there will be a computer on everybody's desk. Not just at work, but at home and in schools also, and not only that, there will be a computer in every room and strapped to everything, like cars and refrigerators. Can you imagine that, Misty?"

"Every room?" I tried to imagine a computer in the bathroom but pictured a robot instead. "I'm not so sure I want to be surrounded by that much technology."

After the waiter took our order, I asked Joanne if she enjoyed the class and whether she liked her instructor.

She tilted her head as if fondly remembering something. She said, "Mr. Compeau is my favorite professor." A rare smirk crossed Joanne's face. "He's smart and witty with a dry sense of humor. He reminds me of David Letterman, often talks about Led Zeppelin, and chides the students in such a way that most don't realize he's teasing them. When nobody else can answer his impossible questions, he turns to me. And before class, we sometimes talk about babies and children as the 'traditional' students slump into their seats. But despite his futuristic predictions, I don't care if it's the last one left on earth. I will not part with my Selectric." As the waiter delivered sizzling plates of scorching chimichangas, Joanne leaned forward and said, "Can you believe *I* wrote a computer program, Misty?"

Neither of us could finish the deep-fried, torpedo-shaped tortillas stuffed with savory ingredients. Finally, I set my napkin on the table and answered yes when the waiter asked if I would like to take the rest to go and whether coffee sounded good. As I stirred Sweet'n Low into my cup, I said, "I don't know what to do next, Joanne."

"What do you mean?"

"In Father's memory." I closed my eyes, pictured the statue hidden beneath a tablecloth in Father's office, and felt a frown cross my face. "I can't seem to find a fitting tribute, and I'm not getting any younger. The statue is hideous, his beautiful portrait would be out of place, and it's all we can do to keep his business going."

"Why do you do that?"

"Do what?"

Joanne reached across the table and took my hands in hers. "Mr. Menard has been gone a long time now, Misty. I know you still miss him, but maybe it's time to let him rest in peace. Does he really need monuments? Why do you refer to everything as if he owned them? Even after all these years, you say, 'Father's home, Father's business, Father's employees, Father's door,' even. I loved Mr. Menard and I'll always be grateful that he hired me, but most of the employees barely knew him." She glanced away from me and continued. "The last couple of years, he barely left his office, and I had to read his mail to him." She squeezed my hands and looked me dead in the eyes. "I don't mean any disrespect to Mr. Menard, but *you* are my hero, not him. And it's not 'Father's company' anymore. You own half, *we* own the rest, and we should fight for that instead of living in the past, commemorating things nobody remembers."

I felt a tear skitter across my cheek.

"I'm sorry, Misty. I shouldn't have said all of that. I don't know what I would do if something happened to my father and I'm sure I just don't understand."

Tears threatened to overwhelm me. I patted Joanne's hands, closed my eyes, and shook my head. "I'm glad you said those things. I want you to tell me what you're thinking and how you feel. Mr. Compeau, your college professors, and I know how smart you are. It's time that others did as well. You should share your wisdom more." Her words about my being her hero crossed my mind and engulfed me. I blinked the waterworks from my eyes and looked away. "Forgive me, honey, for blathering on. I don't usually get so emotional."

After excusing myself, I retreated to the ladies' room and entered the farthest stall. I had almost regained my composure when I heard the bathroom door open. Whoever had entered took a couple of steps into the room and stopped. Then the lights went out. At first, I wondered if there was a power outage. Then a deep voice spoke. It was disguised as if a woman were trying to sound like a man, yet the tone was distantly familiar. The words were the same as the ones attached to the brick. "Get out of town. While you still can. You may not get another warning."

The door opened and the threatening presence left the room. I was left in darkness. My heart pounded and I froze in fear. Finally, I blindly made my way from the lavatory and scraped my arm on a waste bin before finding the door.

Joanne proudly said, "I paid the bill." She looked at me. I'm not sure what she saw. She said, "What's wrong, Misty? Are you alright?"

***

On Monday morning, everyone was so kind, asking me whether I was all right after my week away. As the morning buzzer sounded, I was shocked to see Buster Snodgrass sauntering through the doorway. He looked down at me with glee, nodded his head, and flashed his brilliant white teeth at me in a gloating, closed-mouth smile. I raised my hands in front of me, asking with a gesture, "What are you doing here?"

He said, "I've been hired back." He tilted backward and laughed. "It seems Adirondack Dowel can't get on without me." Then he turned and made his way into the factory as I stormed toward the office.

Doyle sat, tilted back in his office chair with his boots on his desk and his phone wedged between his cheek and shoulder.

I felt the taste of bile in the back of my mouth. My feet clomped toward the ogre, and it felt like I was wearing bulky ski boots. When I reached his desk, I extended my hand toward his telephone and depressed the switch hook, disconnecting him from his call. I closed my eyes and tried to collect my composure. "I need to see you in Father's..." I stopped mid-sentence and corrected myself, "*my* office at once, Mr. Polk." My finger retreated from the desk phone and pointed the way as if the general manager required directions. I could hear the growl in my own voice, "Now."

Doyle followed me and slouched into the guest chair. I stood behind the desk, placed my palms on its surface, and leaned toward the man. "What is Buster doing here?"

"Oh, that," Doyle said as if he didn't know why I was so angry and made a comment about my bunched undergarments. He said, "We got a big order, a couple of people called in sick, and I remembered what a hard worker Buster was, so, I called him back. He promised he would be on his best behavior and that he would stay away from Hogan Hoad."

I turned away from Doyle and looked out the window searching for words to say to the man. I took several deep breaths, returned to my desk, and sat behind it. "Mr. Polk, I do not interfere with your authority. I go out of my way to defer to your manufacturing expertise. I leave the factory and the workers to you to manage. I believe the Buster Snodgrass incident is the only exception. We can not tolerate discrimination or violent behavior. I don't care how busy we are or how hard Buster works. Do you understand me, Doyle?"

The general manager grunted, scowled, and rolled his eyes.

"Mr. Polk, during your military service, did your superior officer not command respect from his subordinates?"

Doyle gripped the sides of the chair and clenched his jaw. I wondered if I had stepped too far into sacred territory. A place where women weren't allowed. "As the president and majority owner of this company, am I not entitled to the same degree of professionalism? When you disrespect me in front of our employee owners it damages the company. In the future, I will require your support in public. You may say what you want to me in private. Do we have a bargain?"

"Very well, Misty." Doyle cleared his throat and took an envelope from the wide inner pocket of his denim jacket. "I was going to wait until this afternoon, but now seems as good a time as any." Doyle leaned forward, set the envelope on the desk, and slid the parcel across its surface. "This is another offer for your interest in the company. It's not worth as much as it was when you owned the whole thing and times are tough. Fifty thousand dollars each is all we can offer. If you say no, the way we're going, you'll have to beg us to take the company off your hands. Isn't it time to let it go, Misty? Haven't you had enough? Is this *really* how you want to spend your *golden* years?"

My toes clenched in the tips of my shoes. I could feel the muscles bunch in the small of my back. I didn't know whether I wanted to kick the man or pounce on him, of course neither would have been an appropriate response to his question. How I wished to spend my golden years was none of his concern. It took all the fortitude I could muster to keep my rage contained.

I opened the envelope, looked at the numbers on the document, and returned the papers to the envelope. "Thank you for your concern, Doyle." My polite words were contrary to my feelings. I wanted to slap the man's face like women did in the movies. I extended my arm but Doyle rejected my attempt to return the envelope.

The man frowned, shook his head, and stood to leave. "I reckon you'll be sorry, Misty." His words sounded genuine rather than angry. "Take a few days and ponder the offer. Maybe you'll come to your senses." Doyle shut the door loudly behind him when he left, though everyone knew that I never closed the office door. I felt like a caged animal and wanted to scream. After seven years, Doyle and I were no closer than when we began. I had tried everything I could think of to win him over. I couldn't get rid of him, because if I did, the bank would call the loans. The only way to be rid of him was to accept his offer and sell the company. I didn't want to consider the paltry sum they suggested my stock was worth, and I had promised the employees that I would sell my stock to the ESOP.

But Doyle had a point. Was it time to let go? Perhaps I had been through enough. How much should any one person have to endure? Maybe I should have closed the factory, sold everything, and let the employees find other jobs. They would have had a far easier time getting replacement jobs back then than they would now.

I sat behind the closed door feeling sorry for myself, thinking about the threatening encounter at the restaurant and wondering why everything had to be so hard. It seemed like everything was conspiring against me. I still yearned to open a small antique shop. When I returned to Lake Placid, I thought it would take me a year or two, and then I'd be in business. But still, there I was, no closer than before. Was I too old to start a business anyhow? If only I could pay off the bank and be rid of John Frederick's demands, requirements, and meddling…

While sitting and stewing, I remembered my nightmare, the vandalism that interrupted it, and recalled the voice telling me to leave town.

I picked up the phone and slammed it back in the cradle. Twice more I picked up the hand piece and thrashed it back down. The fit of anger provided the satisfaction of hanging up on somebody who deserved it without creating unnecessary drama that would just cause more problems later.

14

When the workers left for the day, I headed downtown for a late afternoon appointment with the lawyers. I let myself into Winslow's office without knocking. Winslow and Ted stood briefly and quickly returned to work on documents on the table before them. I crossed through the room and stopped by a mirror on the wall. People always told me I looked decades younger, but my critical eye knew better. The older I got, the less I liked to look at my reflection. Sometimes I wished I hadn't wasted money on a facelift, and other times I wished I could afford *more* plastic surgery. The truth was, I wasn't just past *normal* retirement age. I was a decade beyond that. Doyle hadn't used these words, but his voice in my head said, "What business does an *old dame* like you have trying to run a man's company?" I frowned at my reflection and recalled Buster Snodgrass calling me a hag.

Winslow looked at me and said, "Can I get you a cup of tea, Misty?"

I declined with a dismissive wave and made myself comfortable in an easy chair. My thoughts drifted across the surface of tranquil Mirror Lake as I gazed out the window. Winslow returned his attention to Ted and I barely heard the men as they talked about the closing checklist for the coming transaction. I set the envelope containing management's offer on the coffee table and looked back into the room. It occurred to me that I should stop Ted and Winslow. Instead of working on documents to sell another fraction of the company to the ESOP. Should I tell them that I had decided to sell it all and move back to Washington? I had been happy in the busy city before. Perhaps I should never have left it.

Finally, I cleared my throat and suggested that the men join me.

Ted rubbed his eyes and said, "We could use a break, Misty. We've been stacking papers and rearranging files all afternoon."

I smiled at the chubby-cheeked young lawyer, then I gazed into the eyes of the mature attorney who represented Father before me. If only he were older and I were younger, I would set my sights on the man. I took a deep breath and told myself that I was too old to begin a new romance and that lawyers were forbidden from having such relationships with their clients anyhow.

Finally, I said, "Winslow, did Ted tell you about my trip in the ambulance?"

When I glanced at the young counselor, I saw his cheeks redden.

Winslow smiled warmly and said, "Yes. I am glad your heart is strong, Misty. You must have had quite a shock."

"Thank you. I know I'm lucky. I presume the mettlesome child lawyer told you to get to work on my will?" I smiled at Ted who was accustomed to my jokes about his age. I added, "I shan't live forever, you know, counselor."

Winslow gripped his knees and leaned forward toward me, sympathetically. "It would be prudent, Misty. Even healthy as you are, you just never know. It's better that you decide than to leave it to the court."

I looked down at the stark, legal-sized envelope on the table and said, "Before we talk about my will, we should talk about *that*." I pointed at the offensive document and noticed the knobby knuckles on my aging index finger. Maybe the shiny red polish on long, fake nails was more noticeable than the age spots on the back of my hands. I found my vanity a welcome distraction given the weighty topics on my mind.

Winslow picked up the envelope, removed its contents, and I watched his green eyes zip back and forth as he began to read. I turned to Ted and said, "My management team has offered to purchase seventy-five percent of the company for fifty thousand dollars, each." I turned back to the window and watched a canoe glide across the surface of the lake. I realized that I had said, "My management team," rather than Father's.

When I looked back at Winslow, I said, "There's something else you should know." I told him about the threatening note delivered on a brick through the window and the frightening encounter at Casa del Sol. My head tipped forward slightly and I said, "Maybe I should just give up, Winslow. Everything seems to be conspiring against me and I'm not getting any younger. I try to deny it. I never planned to age gracefully anyway. Instead, I fight it as hard as I can. But it is a losing battle." I looked back up into Winslow's face and added, "If Father couldn't save the business he built, how can I?"

Ted interjected. "I don't think it's you, Misty, and the employee owners are hard-working."

I nodded. "Yes, they are very dedicated and we're lucky to have them." I thought about Buster Snodgrass and frowned. I thought, perhaps the young man deserved a second chance, and had to admit that I was glad Doyle had given him one.

Ted continued. "Then what's the problem, Misty? According to the valuation report, similar businesses are weathering the troublesome economy. Why isn't Adirondack Dowel doing as well?"

I touched my lip and muttered, "I wish I knew. Much as I despise the general manager, I have to admit that he gets the job done. The employees do as he demands and they never let our customers down."

"How about the business manager and the sales manager?"

"Indeed." I thought of Mrs. Blankenfritter and told Winslow and Ted about how the trustee always seemed to have doubts about Stuart, Art, and Doyle. "The last time she was here, she suggested that we cut as many unnecessary expenses as possible."

Ted laughed. "Mrs. Blankenfritter is a professional skeptic. She doesn't trust anybody or anything, but you could do worse than follow her advice, particularly in troublesome times."

Winslow said, "Sometimes businesses hire an expert to do the hard job of cutting expenses during downturns."

Ted added, "I've heard about these *turn-around* specialists. Sometimes they can save a company. They know where to look and how to question things. Like a fresh set of eyes, or looking at something from another angle."

I asked, "Do you know anybody in that line of work?"

Ted said, "I'll have to think about that. Maybe I could ask somebody. Often, bankers have a list of such contacts. You might ask Mr. Duncan."

I thought of John Frederick. The idea of asking for his recommendation turned my stomach. Sometimes the remedy is worse than the malady, but if it could help our employee owners, I would ask for his referral list.

Ted said, "Whether you hire a consultant or not, Misty, it would seem as simple as this: charge more or spend less."

"Aren't consultants expensive?"

"Yes. It seems counterintuitive, doesn't it? But sometimes you can pay them a percentage of whatever amount they save, so if they don't bring solutions, you don't have to pay."

Winslow said, "But if you're going to accept management's offer, then it isn't up to you to engage a consultant. And then, there's the matter of your will. If something were to happen to you before you sell the rest of the company to the ESOP, who would you want as your heir?"

Though I should have, I hadn't given the matter enough thought. "Harold is a kind and decent man. He spent decades working at GE in Schenectady, so he understands manufacturing, but he's never shown any interest in Adirondack Dowel. Presto works with Harold at the campground in the summer and on Whiteface in the winter. He never asks about the company. And Four is only fifteen, besides, all he cares about is skating. I want to take care of them, but I can't imagine asking any of them to run the company or own the business." I thought about what Joanne said to me at dinner last week and said, "Even though they don't appreciate Father, I'd like to leave the company to the ESOP if anything happens to me. I just wish I didn't have to saddle them with Stuart, Art, and Doyle."

Winslow looked at me with a grin and a twinkle in his eyes that surprised me and said, "Very well, then we'll have to take very good care of you and make sure that nothing happens to you."

Ted added, "Good plan. That and fix the business. The sooner the better, Misty."

Winslow stood and walked to the window. He was silent for a moment, and then turned and leaned against the windowsill. Finally, he said, "So, Misty. If you want to sell to management and wash your hands of it all, nobody can blame you. You've worked hard your whole life and don't owe anyone anything. I know it is an insulting offer, but it does give you freedom. You could spend your days as you wish. Go where you want. Wouldn't you like to relax? It must be stressful having to worry so much all the time."

"Thank you for understanding, Winslow. I think back to the offer they made a few years ago. What would life be like if I had accepted it?" My mind wandered away for a moment. A picture of the antique shop I always dreamed of appeared in my mind, and then an image of waltzing with a handsome older gentleman replaced it. Getting old didn't seem to stop my dreams but perhaps they had become more like fanciful notions, unlikely ever to come true. When I returned from my visions I said, "And what about the threats? Do you think my family and I are in danger? When do I have to decide?"

***

I tried to remember the last time I visited the cemetery. When Father died, I made the trip whenever the seasons changed but as the years went by I visited less often. Perhaps a year had passed since the last time I stood before Father, Mother, Junior, and Johnny. Sometimes, it would cross my mind to go and I would feel a pang of guilt, then something would come up and I'd forget to go. Tuesday afternoon, with a head full of impossible questions, I decided to catch up with the deceased.

As I stepped into the cemetery, a small headstone caught my eye, and I suddenly remembered my promise to replace Father's marker with a more prominent monument. My heart sank for a moment. What if something happened to me? I should have done it straight away, but just never got around to making arrangements.

Joanne's words crossed my mind. "Why do you do that? Does he really need monuments?"

A swift breeze swirled the air around me and I walked slowly through the cemetery. I felt alone, abandoned even. After nine decades on earth, and seven years in the hereafter, Father's memory had faded into oblivion. I doubted whether anyone ever thought much about him anymore, other than me, and I hated to admit that some days Father didn't cross my mind either. I lived in his house, worked in his business, sat behind his desk, and tried to take care of his employees and yet Joanne was right. They didn't belong to Father anymore.

I stopped for a moment, opened my hand, and gazed at the green marble I had brought with me. The shape of its inner swirl reminded me of a cat's eye and I thought of Calhoun. Father's cat had probably forgotten him weeks after he died. I rolled the marble with my index finger and looked at it from different angles. Every time I visited Father, I left another glass orb at the base of his headstone, and the caretakers carefully landscaped around them. I returned the sphere to my pocket and flipped a penny between my fingers. I always left a penny at the center of the headstone, above Johnny's name. My gift to Junior protruded from my pocketbook. My heart always ached for my lost son. Placing a red carnation on his grave reminded me of how much I loved to picture him on the night of his high school prom, wearing his black tuxedo with the fragrant flower pinned to his lapel.

Something didn't feel right. My stomach tumbled and I tried to remember whether I had taken my medications that morning. I began the day with a bland breakfast to keep my stomach acid from boiling over, yet my innards churned. I felt like I might crumple to the ground and yet I increased my pace.

When I reached Father's grave, I was horrified at the sight. The headstone had split in half like someone had taken a sledgehammer to it. Father's half had fallen to one side, Mother's had crashed to the other side, and Johnny's name was split in the middle. In drippy red paint, the words, "GET OUT" made it clear that whoever had desecrated Father's grave was also responsible for vandalizing Father's house.

I looked around quickly, afraid to be alone, but more afraid to find whoever demanded that I leave. My legs gave way and I fell to my knees. I hurriedly swept marbles together and placed them back at the base of the broken headstone, added the green marble from my pocket, hastily placed a penny nearby, and quickly left Junior's carnation by his untouched stone, scrambling back the way I had come. When I got to the car, I rifled through my pocketbook, looking for the card that Officer Wideawake gave me, but couldn't find it. Instead, I sped away in the Mustang toward the police station across from the Olympic Speed Skating Oval.

***

When I got home, I called Harold and asked him to come to Lake Placid at once. When he arrived fifty minutes later, I sat down with Harold and Presto and talked about my dilemma. I wanted to know whether they thought I should keep or sell Adirondack Dowel, but they refused to tell me what they thought.

In the hours since visiting the graveyard, fear had given way to anger. If it were just me, I would not submit to the will of a bully, but what if something were to happen to my family? Whoever was terrorizing us had struck at home, my favorite restaurant, and at the family plot in the cemetery. This wasn't work-related. It was personal.

I didn't want to tell Four, but we agreed that he needed to know. When he joined us at the dining room table, the teenager was the first to say that we should be brave. I clenched my teeth and forced myself to be silent as my emotions burned hot inside me. I gripped the edge of the table so tightly, my fingers hurt while Harold and

158

Presto agreed we should avoid being alone. I felt my lips clamp together, infuriated at the thought that we should have to take such measures for the sake of safety.

The boys wouldn't tell me what to do about the company, but I tried to trick them into revealing their thoughts. Instead, they kept turning my questions back to me. I was good at reading faces and noticing body language, but if Harold, Presto, or Four had an opinion, I couldn't tell what it was. One thing they agreed on, however, was that I was not to be driven out of town.

Our conversation ended when the phone rang. It was Officer Wilder Wideawake on the line. He told me that he had visited the cemetery and promised me that he would conduct a thorough investigation. Before he hung up, he said, "Did you know that most homeowners' policies cover headstones and cemetery plots?" That was news to me and I made a note to contact Phil Stanwick at the insurance agency.

When I hung up the phone, Harold told me that he was moving into Father's house, at least temporarily. "We need to stick together, Mom."

I rubbed my eyes and felt my body sag. Then I looked at Harold and said, "I hate to have you do that." He loved the anonymity of his cabin in the woods. Harold had worked in Schenectady for decades but never was happy living in a city, town, or even a village. Some people belonged alone in the woods, and that's how Harold was.

He said, "Don't worry, Mom. My place will be there when all of this blows over. I'll pick up my things after work tomorrow. Tonight, I'll sleep on the couch." I kissed him goodnight and made my way up the stairs.

I sat before the mirror and looked at my reflection. Danger had brought my family closer. I wanted to be glad that my boys were all together under one roof, but felt isolated. As I removed my makeup, I seemed less and less myself and more forsaken. It was the most lonesome time of the day. As I wiped away the layers from my face, I aged decades in minutes, and then I slipped into bed alone. The truth was hard to ignore. I was an old woman, long abandoned, and the urge to take a drink was never stronger than in those moments. If it weren't for Calhoun and his warm purr, I'm sure I would have given in to another temptation. Father had left me his beloved business, his fancy home, and all of his possessions, but it was the fluffy Turkish Angora that I cherished.

Calhoun pushed his face into my elbow and I caressed his back. I muttered, "What should I do, Calhoun? Why can't anybody answer my question? If only *you* could tell me."

***

In the morning, Stanley said, "You don't seem yourself today, Misty."

"I've got a lot on my mind, I suppose." When he asked if I wanted to talk about it, I felt my face twist.

Stanley told me that my nostrils flare when I'm angry. He was an expert at reading people. I handed him the envelope that contained management's offer to buy my shares in the company, stomped my foot belligerently, and looked up at the security guard. "But Stanley, I have even worse news." I told him about the threats and vandalism. "Please be careful at night. Should I hire another watchman? Maybe it isn't safe having just one."

Stanley placed his hands on my shoulders, reassuring me. In a passionate voice, he said, "Thank ya for letting me know, Misty. I'm not afraid, but I'll be on the lookout. You're not going to sell, are ya?"

"I don't want to do it. Maybe I should, but I just can't." I petulantly huffed. "I don't care if I live to regret it. I'll be hanged if I let those rats run me out of here. I promised all of you that you would own it and own it you will. I don't care if I have to retire on cat food and die penniless. I'm selling my stock to the ESOP if it's the last thing I do."

Stanley wrapped his arms around me and I relaxed. Doubt and anger melted away and I knew that I had made the right decision. As our embrace ended, I noticed the smell of vegetables. The night watchman pulled a slice of celery from a pocket and placed it between his lips like a cigar. He said, "You're one of a kind, Misty. If ya need anything, let me know. Any time, day or night, don't hesitate ta ask." Then he turned away, to make coffee, I presumed. I felt at peace knowing that I had reaffirmed my commitment.

I was ready when Doyle came up the walk, envelope in hand. Curtly, I said, "No deal, Doyle. I'm rejecting your offer and I want to see you and Buster Snodgrass in my office, ten minutes after seven. Is that clear?"

Doyle shook his head, blew air from his lips, and looked down at me with disgust. He snarled, "We made a reasonable offer. Every year Adirondack Dowel loses money and its value drops. You ain't got no business being here." His upper lip curled and he added, "It's a disgrace. You're going to bankrupt the company. You should know better. What the dickens is wrong with you, lady?"

15

Harold bought me a pistol. He said, "You can keep the handgun in your purse. I'm sure you'll never need it, but just in case you do, you'll have it."

The small-bore, .32 caliber Beretta Cheetah had a short, 3.8-inch barrel and took a single stack cartridge of 9 rounds. Harold tried to teach me how to use it, but I struggled to hit a target.

Stanley took me to his game club on Saturday mornings, and I practiced relentlessly until I could fire the pistol without cringing or jumping at the sound. I was glad that the gun had almost no recoil. Whenever my purse opened, I stared at the Cheetah and shivered at the thought of what might happen if I had to rely on it to protect myself. I never got good enough at firing it that I could hit a bullseye, but sometimes I came close. Stanley joked that I could fill in for him when he took a night off, which he almost never did.

Instead of celebrating Founder's Day on the Fourth of July, Joanne suggested we have a breakfast party in the factory on Friday the second. I was determined not to make the day about Father's legacy. Of course, it was, but it was time for the company to move on from its founding. In order to assure Adirondack Dowel's future, we needed to focus on the present. Our employees needed to understand that they owned half of the company. It was one thing to know it, but another to feel it.

Thursday afternoon, when the workers left for the day, Joanne helped me set up. We decorated the walls with colorful streamers and hung signs that proclaimed, "50% Employee Owned," and "We're Halfway There!" We unfolded metal chairs and crowded them together facing a row of stools near the time clock.

We tied brightly-colored helium balloons to the back of each chair and I placed a quarter-pound box of fudge on the seat of each. Every box contained two flavors. I wasn't sure whether the milk chocolate or the maple walnut signified the ESOP's share or which symbolically represented my interest in the company, but the local chocolatier told me they were the two most popular flavors.

A boombox thumped as employees clocked in. The song, "Don't You Want Me," by The Human League ended as the buzzer sounded.

I asked everyone to write their name on a small piece of paper and to complete a sentence that began, "We go together like…." To prompt them, I suggested peanut butter and jelly as an example. Then I told everybody to fold the paper in half and passed through the crowd carrying a large glass bowl. I chirped, "It's easy to play and you could win a cash prize."

When everyone who wanted to submit an entry had completed their sentence fragment, I reached into the vessel and stirred the slips of paper. To add to the drama of the moment, I stirred the slips longer than necessary and then pinched a piece of paper from the bottom. "The winning answer is, Willie and Waylon, and the grand prize goes to Hogan Hoad." I noticed a scowl on Alice Blankenfritter's face as I motioned for the young man to step forward and collect his money. The trustee never approved of frivolous spending. I opened my pocketbook and tried not to think of the handgun which rested on top of the hundred-dollar bill.

A couple of people clapped as Hogan returned to his seat. I looked away briefly and didn't see who did it, but somebody tripped Hogan and he crashed into Joanne and Rusty Buckpitt. I glanced through the crowd of employees and saw Buster Snodgrass, laughing on the opposite side of the room. If he didn't trip Hogan, then who did? I had planned to read all of the contest entries, but my mood had spoiled. Joanne and Rusty helped Hogan regain his feet and the young man returned to his chair. My eyes followed the path Hogan had taken but I couldn't discern who had toppled him.

Hours later, I read the rest of the entries. Some I understood, others I did not. but here's what the bowl held: E.T. and Elliott, cake and ice cream, music + television = MTV, leather and lace, Charles and Diana, Hall and Oates, Reagan and Bush, surf and turf, vodka and orange juice, salt and pepper, Sandy and Danny, Bo and Luke, bacon and eggs, Johnny Carson and Ed McMahon, J.R. and Sue Ellen, mac and cheese, french fries and milkshakes, zombies and flesh-eating bacteria, and death and taxes. Nobody cared to write their name on the last two slips of paper. I remember thinking, there's good and evil contained in every group of people, and also, no limit to the creative possibilities. I could have sat and thought all day long and not come up with half of those answers.

There were so many things I planned to say to everyone, but anger chased them from my mind. Instead, I introduced Alice Blankenfritter and perched on a stool behind her.

The trustee stood in front of the employees and spoke to them in a commanding voice. The no-nonsense woman's voice boomed, "There's something wrong with this place." She stared at the crowd accusingly. I could hear the seconds ticking away on the time clock behind me. She turned her head from the right, to the center, and then to the left of the crowd and I imagined her eyes locked with one employee after another.

She turned and marched a few steps to the side and faced the audience again. Her meaty hands joined together behind her back. "The first time I visited Adirondack Dowel, it crossed my mind. There's something fishy going on here." She leaned forward, waited several seconds, and barked, "Can you feel it too?" Her bark transitioned to a growl. "I'll bet you can."

She pivoted and stepped purposefully past the point where she began speaking and turned back toward the crowd. "And yet, I can't explain it, there's also a lot of heart in this company. Of all the companies I've been to, Adirondack Dowel is my favorite."

Alice Blankenfritter masterfully employed the use of pregnant pauses. Then she whispered so loudly I could hear her from behind her battleship gray skirt, "It's such a shame." Alice looked up at the ceiling as if appealing to God. "Heaven help you. At the rate you're going, this place is doomed."

The trustee spun, faced me and the management of the company, and raised her arms as if she were performing an exorcism. "Raise prices and cut costs now." Her right arm twisted in its socket and she pointed back toward the employee owners behind her. "If you don't do this now, they'll own half of nothing and be unemployed as well." She looked each of us in the eye, and when Art failed to meet her gaze, she said, "Look at me when I'm talking to you, Mr. Boykins."

The business manager squirmed and wilted under her gaze.

Mrs. Blankenfritter stepped toward the bean counter until she stood inches away from him. He looked like he wanted to do a backward flip off his stool. She said, "Do I make myself clear?" Then she jabbed her index finger at Stuart. "Get those prices up, hear me?"

Stuart quickly nodded. His expression was devoid of its characteristic smirks. She stared at him for a few seconds, and he didn't bother telling her that he thought it wasn't his job to determine the prices of our products.

Then she turned her attention to Doyle Polk. She jabbed her hands onto her hips and said, "What do you have to say for yourself?"

Doyle sat still and tried to wait her out. Finally, he shrugged.

Alice scoffed and said, "That's what I thought."

Finally, the trustee turned back toward the employee owners. I could see their mouths hanging open and their bewildered expressions showed that they had never expected to witness anything like Alice Blankenfritter's presentation. The sound of her voice changed and she sounded like a grandmother rather than a drill sergeant. Warmly, she said, "When I come to Lake Placid, and I watch you work, I'm so impressed. I wish that I could show the world what I see when I look at you. I've never seen such dedication, diligence, and teamwork. That's why it's such a heartbreak to see this company struggling. I want better for you and so does Misty. You deserve better."

Mrs. Blankenfritter turned her back on her audience, stepped forward, picked up her stool, and carried it forward until she was practically sitting in the front row. She sat on the tall chair and said, "Let me begin again. My name is Alice Blankenfritter. I am an independent trustee. I work for the ESOP Trust, you are participants in the AJ Menard ESOP, and so I work for you. It is my job to determine the stock value. In order to do that, I hire an appraiser to tell me what he thinks the company is worth. We call that Fair Market Value. I read his report and ask a lot of questions." She raised her arms slightly and made a self-effacing joke. "I bet it doesn't surprise you that I ask *a lot* of questions." The trustee was rewarded with a collective chuckle. "Based on the appraiser's work, I determine the value of the company. Then I divide that value by the number of shares. There are 20,000 shares of stock in the company. You already own five thousand shares. Misty owns fifteen thousand shares. When we sign the documents on that table over there, you and Misty will each own ten thousand shares of stock. You can think about the shares as little bits of ownership. Each bit makes up the total. Do you understand?"

The audience sat spellbound.

Mrs. Blankenfritter barked, "I said, do you understand?"

Everyone nodded and replied.

"Good. So, as of December 31, 1981, the company was worth $320,000. Divide that by 20,000 shares, and the value per share is sixteen dollars. Your ESOP Trust will buy five thousand shares for $80,000. That's sixteen times five thousand. Do you know why the company is worth $320,000? The company didn't make money last year and it ended the year with less cash in the checkbook than it had at the beginning of the year. You owe the bank a small fortune, and yet your building, machinery, and inventories have some value. Your customers owe you money for sales you haven't yet collected. But, in the future, if your company can make the kind of money it *should* be making, then your company will be worth a lot more money than it's worth now. If you could make half a million dollars a year, then your company could be worth two and a half million dollars instead of $320,000. How does that grab you?"

A murmur spread across the crowd and it grew into a cheer.

Sarah Jones raised her hand and asked, "How much a share will the stock be worth then?"

Alice raised her arms forward and asked the crowd. "Can anybody answer this young lady's question?"

Kevin Doolittle raised his hand and shouted out, "One hundred and twenty-five dollars. That's $2,500,000 divided by 20,000."

The trustee turned her head and scanned the audience. "How do you feel about turning $16 per share into $125?"

The employee owners cheered, goosebumps shivered down my legs, and I nodded my approval. Alice Blankenfritter had them in the palm of her hand.

"So what's the problem?"

Sarah shouted out. "You said we spend too much money."

"And we don't charge the customers enough," Sam Nelson added.

Kevin pointed at management. "Maybe we need to fire those bozos."

Alice spread her arms wide as if embracing the crowd. She said, "Yes, yes, and maybe so. You also need to pay your bank debt. You owe Mirror Lake Bank way too much money. There are lots of things *you* can do. At the very least, *you* can show up every day and work hard. *You* can ask questions and look for ways to work smart. *You* can make sure that your products meet the customers' specifications. Happy customers stay put. *You* can look out for one another, help a friend when they need a hand, and teach people what *you* know. When new people join the company, make sure they feel a part of things because if they don't stick around to take over when you're gone, then the company won't be worth a cent. Any questions?"

Rusty raised his hand and Mrs. Blankenfritter called on him by name. He asked, "What about the economy?"

Alice's head lolled slightly to the side. She said, "Alas, that's the one thing we don't seem to have any control over. Interest rates, inflation, the stock market, supply, and demand are altogether known as *the economy*. If you live long enough you'll see that it rises and falls. The best *you* can hope to do is build *your* company so it can weather any storm. Build it to last and it shouldn't let you down. Do you remember, from your childhood, the story of the three little pigs?"

Rusty answered from the crowd. "Are you kidding me? I have to tell that one every night before our kids will go to bed. I don't know why, but Olivia and Oscar love that story."

"There you go! Build your company with bricks, not twigs or straw. Any more questions?"

Kevin asked, "What if there's not enough work to keep us busy? It seems like business gets slower every week. If I'm an employee owner, can I be fired or laid off?"

Alice answered sympathetically. "Sometimes we say employee owner like it's one thing, but it's two different hats that you wear. As an employee, you *can* be let go. As an owner, if your shares are vested, you have the right to be paid the value of your shares at some point in the future. The details about that are in the distribution policy." The trustee turned toward me and said, "Misty, do you want to talk about the company's policy with respect to economic layoffs?"

I slipped down from the stool and stepped to Mrs. Blankenfritter's side. "I hope we can keep everybody we have. It's a tough call though. If there's not enough work to keep everybody employed, is it better to provide 65 part-time jobs or 40 full-time jobs, for example? If it were up to me, I'd keep everybody and divide the time evenly, but if I were a long-term employee with a mortgage, car payments, and kids in college, it would be tough to get by on part-time pay. I wish it were an easy question to answer."

Kevin said, "So you can't guarantee jobs for employee owners."

Sarah said, "And you can't guarantee that the company will be worth anything when it's time to pay off our stock."

Alice Blankenfritter said, "That's why I think you need to ask a lot of questions and run a tight ship, to keep it afloat. Everything comes with balance. You have to take some level of risk to achieve a reward. If you want rights you have to accept certain responsibilities. If you want to be trusted, you have to deliver. If you want to be a part of a team, you have to be vulnerable. But I think asking important questions means holding each other accountable. I've always believed that if something looks wrong, it probably is. That's what worries me. When I tell you something seems fishy, my instinct tells me somebody isn't asking a question that sorely needs an answer. You need to find out what stinks around here."

Buster Snodgrass lifted his arms and pointed his nose toward his armpits and made a show of sniffing one and then the other. "It ain't me," he proclaimed. Several guys near Buster chuckled.

Ignoring Buster, I thanked Alice and waved Ted forward. I said, "For those of you who don't know him, Ted Drake is the ESOP's attorney. Ted, Alice, and the company's attorney, Winslow Gloversmith worked on the documents that need to be signed today. Do you have everything ready to go, Ted?"

"Yes, Misty. We just need a witness."

I said, "How about Joanne? She's probably got the neatest handwriting." I remembered that Joanne had witnessed the first transaction as well.

Ted waved Joanne forward. The employees watched while I signed the purchase and sale documents as the seller, Alice Blankenfritter signed as the buyer on behalf of the ESOP, and

Joanne Buckpitt signed as the official witness to the transaction, although everyone present had seen it happen.

After the documents were signed, I turned around to face the audience of employee owners. In a loud voice, I trumpeted, "Congratulations. Now, you own half the company." As if on cue, the lights cut off. A jolt of panic pinched my chest. The power had gone out. Somebody screamed and I tried to remember where I put my pocketbook. What if I needed my handgun?

Doyle was seated near the exterior door, and when he opened it, there was enough light for everyone to make their way from the building.

On the way out, Alice asked, "Shouldn't you have emergency lighting in the building, Misty? They should come on automatically when the power goes out."

After an hour of waiting around for power to be restored, we let folks head out into the holiday weekend. The weather didn't provide an excuse or explanation. Doyle dragged a couple of chairs to the sidewalk and we waited for several hours until a lineman arrived. It took a while until he repaired the wire. He said, "I don't understand it. Someone flipped the power main and the line was severed, clean. It was no accident. It's like somebody wanted the rest of the day off."

I couldn't imagine who would do such a thing. It couldn't have been anyone listening to Alice Blankenfritter. It had to be somebody else.

***

The next morning when I arrived at Adirondack Dowel, the front door was wide open. I fished the Cheetah from my pocketbook and stepped inside. A ribbon of red spray paint ran across the factory walls and continued into the office where the words, "GET OUT" threatened me in the hallway. The office furniture was smashed and I wondered whether the sledgehammer that broke the family headstone had also destroyed the desks, chairs, and file cabinets. Papers were strewn all about.

Stanley was nowhere to be found.

16

I took several steps backward, tripped over a wastebasket, and crashed into a wall. As I slid to the floor, the Cheetah exploded in my hand and blew a hole through the framed letter of appreciation from St. Kateri Orphanage. Glass shattered and rained onto the floor. I covered my face with my left hand and wept. My right hand maintained a firm grip on the pistol.

A thumping sound interrupted my sobs. I was immobilized by fear and my half-shed tears froze in a flash. A garbled voice sounded like someone trying to shout with a mouthful of food. The sound came from the small closet where we hung the coats of our guests. I climbed to my feet and took a few wobbly steps forward, lifted my gun into position, and turned the doorknob.

When I saw him, I screamed. "Stanley!"

A coarse, burlap bag covered the night watchman's head. His arms and legs were tied and a short length of rope connected the bonds from his wrists to ankles. I was surprised that the burly man fit in the small closet. Even though he had steadily lost weight over the last couple of years, I still thought of the man as burly.

"Oh, Stanley. What has happened to you?" I set the gun on the floor and hurried to untie him, trying to reassure him that he would be alright. When I had freed his arms and legs, he wriggled from the closet and I pulled the sack from his head.

Stanley gasped for air and then panted like a runner who had just finished a marathon. Between breaths, he said, "I'm glad to see you, Misty! I thought for sure, I was going to suffocate."

A loud voice behind me made me jump and I dove to the floor, desperate to get my hands on the Cheetah. The man said, "What the dickens happened, Misty?"

I turned from the floor and was relieved to see Doyle Polk towering above me. My body sagged with relief. "We've been burgled, Doyle. I feel…" At a loss for the right phrase, I finished with the word *violated*.

Stanley added, "Someone got the drop on me, dagnabbit."

Doyle Polk crouched and helped me back to my feet. "Has anyone called the police?"

I shook my head and wondered why I hadn't thought to do that myself.

The general manager found a phone on the floor. I watched as he placed the handset in its cradle, counted to ten, then picked the handset back up. The sound of the dial turning and then retreating to its home position filled the quiet room as the dial on the rotary phone spun.

Stanley stumbled to the small kitchen and brought the Bunn-O-Matic to life. The plundering barbarians had spared us the luxury of coffee.

Doyle frowned and gruffly said, "Pull yourself together. The police are on the way and my employees will begin arriving soon." His eyes met mine and he didn't look away. His tone softened and he reached toward me, patted my shoulder, and said, "I'm sorry this has happened, Lady Fingers." His head swung slowly back and forth and he added, "What's wrong with people?" Papers stirred at his feet as he made his way back to the factory.

The damage was heaviest in the offices whereas, in the factory, the vandalism was mostly superficial. I was glad to see Officer Wilder Wideawake when he rapped on the door. Within a couple of sentences, we were back on a first-name basis.

A short while later, Phil Stanwick, our insurance advisor

arrived to assess the damages. The middle-aged man spent a little time with me each year when he presented our policies and requested payment for our policies. I never realized how many different types of insurance there were until I met Phil. He was quick to process the claim for the window at the house, but as he toured Adirondack Dowel it looked like he had blinking dollar signs in place of eyeballs. The man who I had never known to be slowed down by a detail suddenly moved at a snail's pace.

Wilder and Phil spent most of the day with Art, Joanne, and me, assessing the damage. Phil scribbled endless notes about each object that had been destroyed and tried to estimate replacement values. Wilder made his own notes, but mostly just stood shaking his head in disbelief. Such crimes were uncommon in Lake Placid.

Several times, the policeman offered his opinion on the value of things, and whenever he did, Phil cringed and crossed out what he had previously written. Wilder thought everything was worth almost twice what Phil estimated.

Art was grateful that his Paymaster machine had been spared, and Joanne was delighted to find her Selectric still worked. I was glad that the coffee machine and refrigerator had survived the attack. Other than that, it was hard to find anything that wasn't destroyed. The worst damage was found in my office. I still hadn't boxed up Father's possessions, and now it was too late. Everything was ruined, including Father's bust which had been smashed to smithereens. I was happy to tell Phil Stanwick how much the sculpture had cost. His eyes spun into his head in shock. I was glad to know I had a chance to get back some of the money I had wasted on the hideous tribute.

In my office, Wilder rubbed his chin and said, "Misty. Is anything *missing*?"

"What do you mean? Practically everything is destroyed."

"That's right. It's a mess and a downright shame, but burglars usually steal valuable things. So far, I haven't heard you say anything is missing. I think whoever did this wants to scare you. Did you see the words on the wall? They match the graffiti on your family's headstone and the note on the brick that shattered your window."

"I think scare is too mild of a word, Wilder. I associate scare with a mild prank. This is much more terrible and threatening."

Wilder suggested that I step outside with him for a private discussion. Near the parking lot, the officer said, "You must have some idea of who could be doing this to you. If I were you, I'd be making a list of suspects. The more time I spend with you, Misty, the harder it is to imagine anybody wanting to harm you."

It took about an hour to tell the short version of my romance with Preston Palmer, Senior, and his on-and-off relationship with Lois Phelps so many decades earlier. Wilder was particularly curious about Preston's horrible habit of sending mean postcards and Lois' threatening words at Father's funeral. Other than appearing in my nightmares, the woman had kept her distance for the last seven years. I also told the policeman about my troubles with the banker, the management of the company, and the young man I fired. "If I've made any other enemies through the years, I can't think of who they might be."

"Could I see the postcards?"

I shrugged. "I hardly even pay them any attention anymore. I know he blames me because our son Harold will not speak to him and he also thinks it is my fault that our son, Junior joined the military and died overseas." I looked up at the handsome young officer and said with tongue in cheek, "After years of counseling, I casually decided that if Preston wanted to go on blaming me, I should let that be his problem. As far as I know, he never leaves California anymore, so I doubt he's got anything to do with all of this."

"Do you mind if I speak with this *Lois* woman?"

I don't know why I grimaced at the suggestion. I muttered, "Better you than me, I suppose. I still don't understand why she blames me for stealing her man. He was my boyfriend first. It's not like he turned out to be worthy of such envy."

"Where might I find Lois Phelps?"

I turned away from Wilder while I struggled to recall where she lived. I realized that if I ever knew her address as a child, I couldn't remember having been there. Nor had I bothered to inquire about where she lived when I returned to Lake Placid. It might have helped to avoid the woman if I knew where she resided.

"Do you know anybody else who knows her?"

My head shook slowly and I said, "Maybe Betty knows. As schoolgirls, Betty Kramer, Lois Phelps, and I were friends. Betty's an interior decorator. She knows a lot about real estate. She didn't move away from Lake Placid as I did, and she's been in almost everybody's home."

"And she hasn't…" Officer Wideawake scratched his head pensively and continued, "retired yet either?"

"No. She works less than she used to, but loves what she does too much to stop entirely." I told the policeman where he could find Betty and gave him her phone number. When Wilder was gone I wondered whether Betty would be able to help him find Lois or whether he would need to do some investigating. I hadn't seen her that many times since Father died and I returned to Lake Placid, just often enough to remember her bizarre threats that rainy spring day in the cemetery.

At the end of the employees' shift, Doyle gathered them together near the time clock. I told them what I could: the insurance man had spent most of the day with us; a policeman was conducting an investigation; and we were doing everything we could to figure out who had rampaged within the company's walls overnight.

Before I let everyone go, an idea crossed my mind. Impetuously, I said, "Let's take advantage of this opportunity to make a fresh start. We can reinvent ourselves. Remember everything Alice Blankenfritter said? We should make a plan, a strategic plan. We know what we've been. We see what's happening now. Let's figure out how to become what we'll be in the future.

Just imagine what we can do. Let's write it all down, make a giant to-do list, and pick the company up by its bootstraps. I bet we can make Adirondack Dowel and Spindle Company better than it's ever been before.

When the employees were gone I sat down, exhausted. It was a lot easier to be a cheerleader in high school than a motivational force in my seventies. I should have gotten out while I could. I thought, *There's no escaping it now. I'm in too deep.* I thought about the ESOP and revitalizing the company. I recalled saying I would do it if it's the last thing I do, and that's what I intended on doing.

*****

It took us a week to clean out the office, salvage what we could glean from the blizzard of paperwork on the floor, and set up cheap, utilitarian furniture to conduct the company's business.

A week after the barbarian invasion, which is how we had come to refer to the incident, I asked Stuart to step into my office. I sat up straight, cleared my throat, and spoke directly. "We need to make some changes, Stuart. It's time for a new sales strategy."

Stuart sat forward eagerly and said, "I agree. The first thing I want to talk to you about is the company car. It hasn't been replaced in years. It's embarrassing to show up at the customers' businesses driving a ten-year-old jalopy. I've got some ideas about a new set of wheels." Stuart handed me a brochure for a flashy BMW and said, "If this doesn't impress our customers, I don't know what will."

I said, "Stuart! Haven't you been listening? Don't you remember, Mrs. Blankenfritter said we need to cut costs? She did not suggest we spend a lot of money on a luxury automobile."

"Nonsense. That old battle axe is a blowhard. Think of the car as an investment, Misty, an investment in our future sales. We can't go wrong with a machine like that."

"No, Stuart. We're selling the company car. We will not purchase a replacement. When you need to make a business trip, the company will reimburse you for the use of your personal automobile and we'll pay you the IRS-approved rate. From now on, you'll make your sales calls using the telephone rather than in-person visits."

"But our customers expect to be pampered. If we don't wine and dine them, they'll buy from the competition."

"No, Stuart. From now on, our promise to the customer is that we will deliver quality products to them as quickly as possible for a fair price. I'm going to cancel the country club memberships. If you would like to pay for personal memberships, you are entitled to do so. And no more tickets to ball games in the city or seasons' ski passes at Whiteface Mountain."

"Why, you can't do that. I had an agreement with… with… I had a deal with your Father."

"That contract has *expired*. From now on, you will submit your expenses to me for approval. Do not give them directly to Art. Furthermore, *you* are now responsible for customers' prices. Have Art explain to you how he makes the calculations. Then, make sure we are charging each customer an appropriate amount for their goods."

"What if I don't want to do all that?"

"These are the conditions of your employment at Adirondack Dowel, Stuart. If you don't like *this* job, you can seek another one. In the meantime, we've got work to do here. I hope you'll want to stay and be a part of the future success of our company, but that is up to you."

Stuart scratched his nose, rubbed his ear, and slid his hand down his chest. Then he crossed his arms and said, "I… I… I don't know what to do."

I said, "That's alright. Art will tell you how. If he does not, then you and I will figure it out together."

Stuart stood and I followed him from my office. Then I asked

Art to step in. He grabbed his briefcase and followed me. The business manager looked at the sales manager as if hoping for clues as to what I said to his colleague. I don't know what Art surmised as a result of the look they shared with one another and I didn't much care.

I said to Art, "Please be seated." Then I made my way around the desk. I tipped my head forward and asked, "Do you remember when I said it was time to reinvent ourselves? It was just last week, after the offices were destroyed."

"Yes, Misty. I remember."

"Do you remember when Mrs. Blankenfritter said we needed to raise prices and cut costs?"

"Yes."

"Do you have any ideas, Art?"

The business manager's eyelashes fluttered. He tried to speak but his tongue quickly became tangled. Finally, he said, "No, but I can make a list of things. Let me go back to my desk and think about it first."

I said, "Very well, Art. I would appreciate that. In the meantime, I want to make you aware of my meeting with Stuart a few minutes ago." His eyes grew wider as I told him what I had communicated to the sales manager. Then I said, "Another change I am making is that, from now on, I will sign the checks. That way, I can better understand how we're spending the company's money."

Art blinked rapidly, his teeth chattered, and he said, "Yes, ma'am. Will that be all?" He pulled his briefcase into his lap and shivered. He always was a jumpy fellow.

When Art was gone, Doyle stepped into my office. He said, "I guess I'm next. What's going on around here?"

I shrugged and said, "Nothing that impacts you directly, Doyle, but it might help if you knew." I told him about the changes I was making to Stuart and Art's jobs. Then I said, "I tell you what, Doyle. I was proud when Mrs. Blankenfritter praised our workforce. You built that team and guided them down a successful path. If it weren't for you, I don't think the company would have survived to this point." I paused and hoped that my words sunk through the man's thick hide. I didn't compliment him very often. I would have liked to suggest he utilize a kinder, more respectful approach in the future, but I'd done enough for one day. I added, "If you have any other cost-cutting ideas, I'd like to hear them. We need to look under every rock, stone, and pebble."

Doyle muttered half-heartedly, "Isn't that *your* job, not mine?"

After complimenting the man, I didn't want to conclude our meeting on a sour note. I focused on speaking in an upbeat tone, and said, "We all owe a duty to this company, Doyle. I *don't* think it starts and ends with ironclad boundaries. A job isn't property. It doesn't belong to somebody. I think it generally defines what we are primarily responsible for taking care of, but it isn't just the workers that need to look out for one another. The management needs to do that too. *You* are *also* an employee owner. Think what would happen to *your* ESOP account balance if the stock value went from $16 to $125 per share."

Doyle grumbled and dismissed himself, sounding more like a wounded bear than a seasoned manager. He'd never turn into Mary Poppins, but perhaps he had a soft side to him after all.

***

The next morning, John Frederick Duncan stopped in. It was rare to see the banker visit the company. Usually, I was summoned to meet the man for lunch. When we were alone in my office, he said, "I hate to kick you when you're down, Miss Menard. I'm sorry about the hooligans who ruffed up your place, but I've got some bad news." He cleared his throat and continued, "Mirror Lake Bank's Board of Directors has reviewed your loans, and in order to continue lending money to Adirondack Dowel, you will need to increase your equity investment in the company. You have ninety days to inject $100,000 into the business or we will be forced to call the loans and liquidate the company. I'm so sorry, Miss Menard." With his right hand on his chest, he dramatically concluded, "It pains my heart to have to be the one to tell you, dear."

17

February 14, 1983

It was a scramble to raise the funds. Phil Stanwick begrudgingly delivered a check for $65,000 representing the proceeds from our insurance claim. We had hoped for more, but Winslow suggested we settle our claim rather than negotiate for a larger sum. I closed my savings account, sold some jewelry, and withdrew most of what was left from my pension fund in Washington. I was still a couple of thousand dollars short. I considered selling the Mustang or mortgaging the house, but instead, I took a cash advance on my credit card. I joked about converting all the money to pennies and delivering rolled coins to John Frederick Duncan's office at the bank, but Winslow frowned and advised against it.

The stubborn economy failed to rebound. We slashed expenses, customers cut their orders, and everyone wondered how long the financial drought would last. Every month we struggled to increase our checkbook balance. Meanwhile, I rallied the employee owners to make big plans for the future. We formed a committee, made a logo for the business, had stationery professionally printed, and adopted a drawing of a moose as our official mascot. The new branding proudly proclaimed that our employees owned the business. The improvements we made felt good, but nothing we did seemed enough.

In July, we received a letter from the IRS that said they wanted to audit the company's tax returns for the past three years. When Art read the correspondence he sank into his chair and endlessly stared at the paper as if the words might change if he only scrutinized them more intently. He whined, "It will take months to gather everything the government needs." His lips quivered every time he reread the letter and I thought a flood of tears was imminent.

In October, Mr. Duncan said that the bank was concerned about the company's monthly financial statements and demanded that we hire a turnaround specialist to diagnose what ails the enterprise. We had already planned to do so but hadn't gotten around to it yet. Mr. Duncan said, "I would personally recommend a brilliant man named, Toby Waters. You should ring him at once. I told him you might be in touch. Here's his number. If he can't save Adirondack Dowel, I don't know what more *I* can do for you, dear."

The banker looked up and I thought of Jackie Gleason's catchphrase, "Bang. Zoom. You're going to the moon." Poor Alice Kramden. Luckily, she was a fictional character rather than a real woman.

Instead, Mr. Duncan tilted his head and chirped, "The bank should have done you the favor of demanding such a consultation years ago. You obviously don't know how to run a profitable business. Toby does."

In November, Stuart received a phone call from Joseph Jeffrey King at the Catskill Hardware Emporium based in Krumville, New York. The salesman was delighted when he hung up and raced about the office proclaiming that our troubles were over. "The Emporium is stocking up their warehouses and filling their shelves. They're getting ready for a robust economic recovery in the spring and are planning a huge promotion." Stuart showed me the order he had made out and my eyes bulged. Our Krumville customer's purchases would exceed our sales to all the rest of our customers put together for the next two months. Even Doyle, who never cracked a smile, grinned when he heard the news. Our employee owners were thrilled to have the extra overtime pay before

Christmas, and everybody seemed to catch the holiday spirit.

When Toby Waters walked through the front door, I was surprised. Based on Mr. Duncan's description of him, I expected him to be younger, but he looked to me like he had to be fifty years old. I had expected Art to be skittish when he arrived. Perhaps after spending months being audited by the IRS, he had become accustomed to oversight. From a distance, it looked like Art and Toby were working together on a school project rather than middle-aged men running a fine-tooth comb through the company's books.

As Thanksgiving approached, Stuart said, "Look at them. They're just like two peas in a pod."

I said, "So it would seem."

Doyle overheard the sales manager and shook his head. "They barely seem to notice anyone else when they get together. Sometimes I think they're going to bump heads. The way they peer at them papers makes them look like they're trying to find a leak in a tire."

I chuckled at Doyle's observation. "I hope they can find it and plug it fast."

Doyle added, "And look. Art's briefcase is open, wide as can be. You don't see that very often." I tried to recall whether I had ever seen the mysterious valise's interior.

By mid-February, I began to wonder whether Toby was ever going to conclude his work. Each month he sent me an invoice for five thousand dollars. I brought the first one to the bank and asked Mr. Duncan to take a look at it. He said, "I know it seems like a big expenditure, Misty, but when he's done I'm sure it will pay off. He has a brilliant mind for business and I expect you'll see a remarkable payback when you implement his suggestions."

"How long is this going to take, Mr. Duncan?"

The banker raised one eyebrow, let it fall, and then raised the other. When John Frederick began to speak, he sounded like he was talking to a child, and I struggled to listen. I never could concentrate when men spoke to me that way. He said, "When a troubled business has been mismanaged as long as Adirondack Dowel has been, it takes time to make note of everything that is wrong with it. Unless you have a wealthy benefactor, I don't see what choice you have but to see this through. It's the only way. I'm sure it won't take long for the doctor's diagnosis now, Misty."

Disaster struck on Monday, Valentine's Day, 1983.

After a deep freeze in December and a cold January, the weather was uncharacteristically mild. It had rained all weekend and everyone was concerned about the loss of snow on the mountain. Warm winters had a devastating impact on tourism. Lake Placid's Main Street businesses struggled when skiers canceled their winter vacation plans, but Adirondack Dowel was working overtime trying to catch up with its regular customers after months of stocking up the Catskill Hardware Emporium's warehouses. A new work week hadn't put a stop to the soggy skies. As we arrived at work, a penetrating rain drenched us. The morning went on and the wind howled. A driving rain jackhammered the roof.

Even over the din, a frightening jumble of ghostly sounds reverberated through the valley. I had heard similar echoes in the past when ice jams blocked the AuSable River. We were surrounded by creaking and cracking noises. Otherworldly moans and groans twanged like gigantic rubber bands. We didn't hear the sirens when three police cars sped into the parking lot. Officer Wideawake and two of his buddies ran through the building screaming, "Evacuate immediately. The river is gonna blow."

Employees screamed and ran from their workstations without shutting off the machinery. Officer Wideawake pointed toward the door and commanded, "Get in your cars and drive away from the river. Get to high ground. Now!"

When everyone was gone, Doyle flipped the power main switch. The machines shuddered to a stop and Adirondack Dowel went dark. Doyle struggled to lock the door and escorted me to my car.

It was raining so hard that my vision was limited. It was impossible to see through the blinding rain and the swirling winds made it seem like a tempest. River Road wasn't known for traffic jams, but our employees' cars inched slowly toward the turn onto Cascade Road.

I turned from our parking lot onto River Road, and Doyle was right behind me in his pickup truck. I leaned forward and peered through the window, trying to see the road as pelting rain bounced off the windshield and the wipers furiously flapped from side to side. I strained to see the taillights in front of me and feared that I would bump into the car ahead of me.

A roar drowned the sound of beeping horns. As I neared the end of the bridge, I was jolted by a vehicle from behind, yet I couldn't stop. I couldn't fault Doyle for barreling into my Mustang. I'm sure he had as much difficulty seeing as I did. I glanced out the side window and was unable to see the massive Olympic Ski Jump Tower which was normally impossible to miss.

I heard a roar and then a deafening crunch. It sounded like whatever made the noise was going to come through the back windshield and I wished the cars ahead of me would go faster. If they did, there was a chance that the motorists would go off the road, but it was hard to be patient. Any moment that fire-breathing dragon might come through the back windshield. I tried to convince myself that I had left the raging ice flow as I nudged the Mustang from Cascade Road onto the Old Military Road and crossed John Brown Road. The cars ahead of me moved a little faster, but I remained anxious about crashes. I couldn't make out the cemetery to the right, but the entrance to the hospital was unmistakable. I turned into the parking lot, stopped the car, and collapsed in my seat. It was a relief to know that I had reached high ground. Maybe I could have made it home but I was glad to sit in the car instead of risking a serious accident. I calmed slightly but a nagging worry troubled my mind. I hoped that everyone made it home safely.

Hours later, the rain finally let up and it looked like just another cloudy day. Instead of turning up the road toward home, I drove back toward the factory. I was shocked to see the bridge over the river had been washed away. The flow had left a wake of icy boulders, toppled trees, and debris all along the banks of the river. Across the chasm, I could see what was left of our building. It was impossible to know how damaged it was, but I could see that the nearest corner didn't look good.

After reversing my direction with a three-point turn, I stopped and worried that a motorist would accidentally drive off the road and into the river, not realizing that the bridge was gone. It was plain to see, now that the rain had stopped, but I worried about what would happen if it began to snow or rain again. I sat frozen in my car, blocking traffic, though none materialized. Finally, the State police arrived on the scene and magically produced a trio of red traffic cones to safely block the road. I asked them about the bridge at the other end of River Road and they assured me that it had survived.

I desperately wanted to go home and lie down. I yearned for the warmth of my soft, silky comforter and Calhoun's contented purr lulling me into worry-free slumber. Instead of napping before supper, I had to get back to the factory. How could I relax without knowing what had happened there?

The alternate route to the workshop took me through the village, slowing my pace, and heightening my anxiety. I made my way along Main Street and on the other side of the village, the crowded tourist road became a windy rural route. Finally, I came to the bridge which had survived nature's fury. I crossed the expanse, turned onto the north end of River Road, and pulled over to the side of the street. I got out of the car and my feet sunk into the wet sandy soil as I gaped at the full display of nature's power. A wide swath of devastation framed the riverbanks. The icy flow, like frozen lava, wiped out everything in its path, toppling tall trees and relocating massive boulders.

My stomach grumbled as I climbed back into the car and I realized I hadn't eaten all day. When I left the house, I planned to have a light breakfast at the office but never did. The gnawing emptiness in my mid-section was compounded with worry. My gloomy mood grew to a state of doom. Even though I convinced myself to expect the worst, I couldn't help crumbling onto the steering wheel when I saw how the roof had collapsed along the crumpled steel wall at the southeastern side of our building. My arm accidentally blew the horn and I jumped, surprised by the honking. I covered my face with my hands and cried, glad that I had the chance to get my first look at the damage alone. I would need to be stronger when others saw what had happened.

I hadn't realized that the car radio was on Four's favorite station, I was so focused on the wreckage. The song, "Do You Really Want To Hurt Me," by Culture Club was playing and I turned the key, shut off the car, and silenced the hopeless love song. I picked up my pocketbook, stepped from the car, and marched forward wondering what fate had in store for us next.

It was plain to see that a river of icebergs had ripped and torn the steel wall like it was made of paper. A large hemlock tree impaled the office. I crouched through an opening and tiptoed into the rubble. The office was destroyed. I couldn't find the front door to the factory, and the time clock that monitored everyone's comings and goings was crushed beneath a jagged ice slab. The river of detritus had spared the rest of the building, including the machinery we depended on to turn out dowels, spindles, pegs, and buttons. The documents that substantiated our transactions fluttered in the breeze and blew across the low-lying field between the factory and the river. I stood and contemplated chasing the paperwork across the landscape, but it was hopeless. I might retrieve a handful of documents, but that would only be a fraction of the thousands that we would never find.

A horn trumpeted behind me and I turned toward the parking lot. Rusty, Joanne, and the children spilled from the doors of Joanne's Pacer. I wrapped my arms around them, comforted by their presence even as they groaned, looking beyond me toward the ruins. Rusty said, "Have you been inside?"

I nodded and frowned sadly.

He said, "Pretty bad, hunh?"

Joanne rocked baby Oscar on her hip. "Oh, Misty. I'm so sorry."

"Me too. I should have sold the company. I'm sorry I burdened our employees with this. Who wants to own half of a wasteland?"

Joanne said, "Remember, Misty: A burden shared is a burden halved. Look how far we've come. We shall just have to overcome this as well. Perhaps it will look better in the morning. Do you think we can take a look inside?"

I shrugged, reached for Oscar, took Olivia's hand, and watched Joanne and Rusty step toward the remnants of our business.

When they returned a few minutes later, Rusty glowered sullenly and shook his head. Tears ran down Joanne's face and she sniffled. As she took the baby back in her arms she rolled her eyes and blinked. "You'd think I lost my best friend to look at me. Imagine shedding tears over something as silly as a typewriter when *everything* is gone. Everything in the office anyway."

Rusty's somber expression faded and he said, "I know it is hard to look on the bright side, but at least we can still make dowels. Maybe we can just go from there."

Joanne shook her head but said, "You're right, but it won't be easy. Wait until Art sees the office." Her wet eyes stared into mine and she said. "The Paymaster is smashed and the Bun-O-Matic too." She hung her head and said, "Good thing you didn't let Stuart buy a fax machine."

It wasn't funny. There was nothing amusing about our situation, but laughter burst from within me. Joanne began to giggle and Rusty guffawed. Between outbursts, I said, "Saved us $20,000. Good heavens, who needs a fax machine?"

The fact was, nothing looked better in the morning. An emergency call to the electrician at least kept the factory going. Stuart did his best to remember our upcoming orders and we worked on approximations. Art spent the morning calling vendors and asking them to mail copies of invoices.

I was glad to have Winslow by my side when Phil Stanwick arrived at ten. Winslow extended his hand to the insurance man and said, "Fortunately, I have copies of the insurance policies in my office. It's a good thing AJ insisted on being overinsured."

Phil glanced around and gasped. "It's going to take weeks to process this claim. I hardly know where to begin."

Winslow challenged him. "Can't the insurance company send experts to help?"

Phil frowned and said, "Wouldn't hurt to ask."

Winslow warned. "Don't try to cut any corners, Phil. We didn't negotiate the last settlement, but this time, the company will need every cent it has coming to it. And don't forget the business interruption policy."

Phil argued. "But I see that the machinery is operational. Business is not interrupted."

Winslow said, "The office is interrupted and the paperwork is part of the business. I must insist that you not allow my client to be defrauded by overlooking any aspect of their coverage. Do I make myself clear?"

Phil puffed his cheeks full of air and released his breath slowly through his lips as he glared at the river.

Winslow said, "They also have flood insurance, Phil."

The insurance man said, "I know. I know they do."

While Phil had his back turned to me I mouthed the words, "Thank you" to Winslow. I smiled when he winked at me and thought about Father's good sense to set us up so well. It's hard to write the checks when the policies are presented each year, but on the worst of days, it's the difference between failure and survival.

***

Just as Art Boykins and Toby Waters finished preparing the final financial statements for 1982 we got devastating news. The

Catskill Hardware Emporium had filed for bankruptcy protection. Unsecured creditors, like the Adirondack Dowel and Spindle Company, must wait for a chance to receive a fraction of the money owed to them.

Our year-end windfall was a sham. We spent a fortune stocking Joseph Jeffrey King's shelves and now we had to book a total loss on our statements. Toby suggested we file for bankruptcy protection also. Our suppliers would have to understand; it wasn't our fault. We could just pass the blame along. If only there were insurance policies that would cover bad debts.

18

As it turned out, there *was* such a thing as credit insurance. It was rare, but Father had always purchased the coverage. If I had paid more attention to the policies and Phil's explanations of them, I would have known better.

Somehow, after the dust had settled, the proceeds funded the reconstruction of the factory offices and damaged office equipment. Because the factory and our equipment had been fully depreciated, we booked a substantial gain on the flood loss. When I delivered the 1983 financial statements to Mr. Duncan he frowned as if he would prefer to see us lose money but he said, "That's wonderful, Misty. You have not tripped any bank covenants." He looked at me and I could imagine a twinkle in his eye as he said, "This year." If I didn't know better, I'd think that man hoped we *would* default on our loans.

The year that followed was marginally better than the preceding years. Even without the benefit of an insurance gain, we managed to make ever so small a profit and increased the balance in our bank account by twenty-five thousand dollars. Mr. Duncan praised the brilliant Toby Waters for our progress, but I couldn't identify one thing he did to increase sales or reduce costs. Instead, he left a long list of schedules, checklists, and analysis work to be added to Art's duties, most of which he gave to Joanne to take care of. Though she efficiently performed the tasks without complaint, I wondered what was the point. Perhaps someone should do something with all of those reports.

Four's rehabilitation improved his skating and by the beginning of 1984, he was back to jumping but still had a long way to go before reaching the elite level required for Olympic competitions. He frowned at the news when he didn't qualify to compete in Sarajevo but didn't complain. Instead, he worked harder than ever to improve, and I spent more time attending practices, meets, and competitions than ever before. Four dominated the local competitions, always won at the sectional level, and often was a contender at the national competitions. He rarely qualified internationally, and when he did, he failed to medal, but sometimes he got close. His coaches had almost forgotten the injury that he had overcome and outlined a path for Calgary. Four would be 21 years old in 1988, the perfect age for men's Olympic figure skating gold medalists. When I looked at the heavily-laden shelves in Four's room, I couldn't believe how many trophies, medals, ribbons, and keepsakes he had won through the years. If pride were a function of hardware, it's hard to imagine anyone's ego required more than the accolades he had already earned. But, Four said, "It doesn't matter if every inch of the house is filled with trophies. If I don't have a gold medal, I'm a flop. In order to win gold, I need to win national and world championships. I've still got a long way to go, GiGi." I told him I was proud of him already. I didn't care if he never won anything else. He was already my hero. He looked at me like I was naive, underinformed, and perhaps bordering on senility.

Soon I would be eighty and I felt fortunate to possess good health, except for the occasional flair-up of reflux. Sometimes I forgot where I put things or where I was going when I did housework, but I usually did well at the office, particularly in the morning. It seemed like the business was doing well enough that I could complete the transition to employee ownership. It should have been done ten years sooner, but finally, we were planning to finish the long overdue conversion. As they did in 1976 and again in 1982, Ted and Winslow began work on the documents, and we waited for the appraisal of the company and the trustee's determination of the stock price. Alice Blankenfritter had just turned 65 but had not mentioned retirement, and I was glad that she would continue as our trustee for at least one more year. Other than selling the rest of the company to the ESOP, all I had to do was name a successor.

The challenge was ever-present in my mind and I had spent most of the last two years thinking about who should be the next leader of Adirondack Dowel. Some might think it was an easy choice to make, but who could really guide the company forward into the future? The general manager wanted to own the business and managed the factory well enough, but showed no interest in other tasks. They were always somebody else's job as far as he was concerned. The office manager wasn't good at working as part of a team or communicating beyond the minimum requirements. The sales manager wasn't selfless enough for the job and required close supervision to be good at what he did. Nobody would expect me to promote anybody else, but Stanley had good judgment and could read people. Rusty had an upbeat personality and people naturally followed his lead. Joanne was organized, respected, and had a Midas touch, but who made nurturing a top criterion for selecting a chief executive? Imagine what people would think if I promoted a night watchman, manufacturing supervisor, or receptionist directly to the president of the company. I should have given all three of them bigger titles as the years went by because all of them did so much more than their labels imply.

Whenever I began to think that the thug or deviants who had it out for me had given up or moved on, something else happened. It was as if they wanted to remind me that they were there and could strike at any time. The police had grown tired of following up on sparse clues that didn't lead to suspects. The threatening words had grown more worrisome, and after a barrage of frightening phone calls, I purchased an answering machine. Unfortunately, the ominous disguised voice sounded even scarier and more threatening on the cassette than it did live.

I still wrote monthly checks to the private investigator who spent a few hours each month trying to locate Bob Holstein's family. Every time I made out a draft, I pictured the young man who danced when he walked and always wore a ski hat, even in the summer. I thought, by now, perhaps he would have become a husband and father. Maybe he would have changed. I could have helped him overcome his alcoholism. Maybe I could have been his sponsor. What if he had the potential to become a candidate to succeed me as president? Often people stay the same, year after year, but some people make radical transformations over the course of a decade. Whatever potential Robert Jonquil Holstein may have had, it was sad to think about the day we tragically lost him in a freak accident. I don't know what I could have done to prevent it, but I still thought of it as my fault.

After a ten-year break, I yearned to return to my retirement. After all, they were my hard-earned, well-deserved, golden years. I had done the best I could for Adirondack Dowel as Father hoped I would, and I was ready for its next transition.

The valuation was completed and the documents were ready. Instead of completing the deal on Independence Day as before, we planned to ink the deal on April 15th, until Stuart blew it up. A month before closing, Stuart knocked on the door to my office, walked in, and sat down. His customary smirk fluttered on his lips. He proudly announced, "I'm giving my notice, Misty. I'm going to Crabapple Dowel in Albany. I'm going to be vice president of sales and I'm taking my customers with me."

"What do you mean, *your* customers?"

"That's right. Three customers have already said that they'll follow me to Crabapple Dowel, and I'm sure it's just a matter of time before others switch over as well. I'll miss having Wednesdays off and skiing all the time, but I'll have to make up for it by taking European vacations. With commissions, I'll make almost twice as much as I do now and get a new company car every three years. Beat that?!"

It was hard to tell whether he seriously hoped that I would

match or beat his offer. I was sure we could find or appoint a better sales manager, but it was frightening to think of what the loss of sales could do to the company's income. As I stood and wished Stuart much happiness, I tried to calculate in my head what the loss of sales would do to our bottom line. When he turned to go, I called him back. "Would you get the team together, Stuart? If you don't mind, I'd like you to let everybody know at once. A two weeks notice goes by mighty quickly."

After a brief staff meeting, I asked Joanne to step into my office and close the door. I looked at her for a moment before I began speaking and imagined I were a customer. The cheerful, nurturing woman with perfect posture still made her own dresses. I hadn't looked at them closely in many years, but it looked like the design hadn't changed. Perhaps the prints were different, depending on what was available, but her modest attire still reminded me of a picnic tablecloth. She might not look like a typical salesperson, but I thought the customers would enjoy working with her. If I had to bet on Joanne versus Stuart, I'd bet on her any day of the year. I thought, perhaps we should set our sights on Crabapple Dowel's other customers, and not just try to retain our own.

"I'd love to be our sales manager, Misty. I should have said something sooner, but I've always thought I could do that job."

I stood and hugged Joanne. "I know you can do it, honey. Do you suppose Rusty and your mother can wrangle the kids if you have to be on the road sometimes?"

"I'm sure they can. Mom's always trying to get us to go away on vacation so that she can have the kids all to herself, and Rusty does pretty well. He's really good with them. I'm very lucky."

"That's good. I think Oscar and Olivia are lucky too. Anyway, it would be a good idea if you could try to visit all of our customers in person, right away. Over the last couple of years, we've kept Stuart in the office as much as possible, in order to manage expenses, but I think our customers would benefit from the personal touch right now. It wouldn't hurt to visit the competitors' big customers as long as you're at it."

"Do you think I could practice? Maybe I could pretend you are a customer and see what you think of my pitch, though I've been rehearsing it in my head for years."

With that settled, I asked Joanne about her job in the office. She volunteered to find and train her replacement and I was delighted to take her up on it.

A couple of weeks later when Stuart separated from Adirondack Dowel, we sent him off with pale blue cupcakes and an earnest greeting card. I'm sure he would have preferred a fancy luncheon with cocktails at the country club and perhaps a round of golf. Three sizable accounts followed Stuart as he said they would, and Mrs. Blankenfritter demanded the valuation report be updated to incorporate new projections. "I'm sorry, Misty. I know this will put a damper on your sales price, but I have to keep the best interest of the participants in mind. I can't allow them to pay too much for the company."

I still thought the company was worth much more, but I didn't argue with the trustee or complain about her request for an update to the valuation. Her appraiser recalculated the projected earnings after losing Stuart's accounts and presented a worrisome appraisal. After ten years, the company was worth the same amount as when we did the first transaction. We hadn't kept pace with inflation, but at least we had survived hardships and persevered.

The new valuation was shocking. After losing a problem employee, three customers, and a phenomenal secretary, the value of the business was deemed to be worth only $300,000. I thought back to the first ESOP transaction. That's the same figure that Stuart, Art, and Doyle offered me for the company in 1975.

At my age, I couldn't afford to wait much longer. I called Mrs. Blankenfritter and said, "What if we wait a couple of months? Maybe we can get the lost customers back. Perhaps we can win new business elsewhere. What if the remaining customers order more? Could we revise the projections again and increase the value?"

The skeptic on the other end of the line said, "Hm... Do you think you can do it?"

"I'll bet with a little bit of time, we'll have the best sales manager in the business and I'm willing to bet on her." I told Mrs. Blankenfritter about promoting Joanne and the trustee approved of the decision.

Mrs. Blankenfritter said, "Very well, call me in a couple of months, Misty. We'll take another look at it then."

The phone rang the instant I hung up from talking with Mrs. Blankenfritter. Instead of letting Joanne answer, I picked up the phone. It was Andy Branchport from Ithaca Accoutrements, our largest customer. He said, "We've got an incredible opportunity, Misty. Now that the economy is rollicking, we've taken on more business than we know what to do with. We're expanding into Pennsylvania *and* Ohio. We need you to fill a rush order. If you can handle our order in 60 days, the business is yours. If not, we'll pull our business and award it to one of your competitors. I wish I didn't need to put it to you that way. You and your father always treated us well, but we must rise to the occasion. So must you. What do you say?"

Before I knew what I was saying, the words tumbled from my mouth and spun through the curly cord that connected the handset to its base. "Count on it. Send the order right over and we'll get the job done for you."

"Thanks, Misty. I'll fax it to you."

"Oh, I'm sorry, Andy. We don't have a fax. Can you give me the order over the phone?"

The voice on the other end of the line clucked judgmentally. "Tsk, tsk, Misty. You'd better get with the times. We don't have time to read orders over the phone or send them in the mail. Why don't you mountain people modernize a little bit?"

I promised to invest in a fax machine by the time Ithaca Accoutrements placed their next order, and in the meantime, Andy handed the phone to his assistant who read the order to me, line by line. After forty-five minutes of transcribing pages of order quantities, I had to admit that if a fax machine could beam a sheet of paper through the phone lines, it must be a useful invention. I only hoped we wouldn't have to spend $20,000 to get one. It had been a couple of years since we priced them. When Joanne found a place that would ship us one for less than $4,000, I considered it a bargain.

Minutes after receiving the impossible order, the phone rang again and Mr. Duncan's Honeymooner voice bellowed, "I told you not to change the management team, Misty."

"I didn't change the management team. Stuart Franklin resigned. I can't force people to remain at Adirondack Dowel against their wishes, Mr. Duncan. You know that."

"You could have retained Mr. Franklin with an appropriate counter-offer, Misty. I don't suppose you thought of *that*!"

"Would you have me promote him, double his salary, and buy him a BMW, Mr. Duncan? I think we're better off letting the competition have him."

There was a moment of silence before he continued. "Perhaps you're right, Misty," Mr. Duncan replied, crisply. "I have another reason for calling you today. The Mirror Lake Bank's Board of Directors has met and decided that your business isn't sufficiently solvent. The bank will need $150,000 of enhanced collateral and if you want to sell the remainder of your stock to the ESOP, you will have to finance it yourself. The bank will not object if you subordinate seller financing over a long period of time." It struck me that Adirondack Dowel must be the subject of every Board meeting the bank held and I wondered who served on the bank's board. I thought, *I shall have to ask Winslow next time I see him.*

To Mr. Duncan, I said, "How long would that be? How long must I wait for the company to pay me?"

"Ten years."

It seemed like such a long time. I couldn't help but wonder whether I'd live to see the day when the loan was fully paid. I'm sure an exasperated sigh traveled through the phone line, and I said, "Very well, Mr. Duncan. Ten years, but no collateral enhancement."

"No, Misty, I'm sorry. The collateral enhancement and the seller financing are non-negotiable. If you can find another lender who will give you a better offer, we'll not stand in the way. Gotta go."

Mr. Duncan roughly dropped the phone onto the plungers, ending our call. I stretched my hand forward, looked at the handset, and placed it gingerly in its cradle. I wondered why *he* seemed angry. If anyone had a right to be mad, it was me. My stomach roiled and I reached for the Pepcid AC. We had sixty days to deliver an order that was bigger than our whole year's sales. I had ninety days to come up with $150,000, which meant mortgaging the house. I counted off the days on the calendar. We had until July 5th to satisfy our customer and a month longer to placate the banker.

Though they struck me as the famous last words of a fool, I wondered, *What else could possibly go wrong?*

19

The next morning, I asked Doyle to round up the employee owners. There wasn't time for setting up chairs or decorating as we did at other times we gathered. I stood on a box and said, "We have an impossible opportunity. Ithaca Accoutrements has placed a huge order and we only have sixty days to deliver. Somehow, we'll have to come up with enough wood on credit, find a way to get the work completed, and get it to their warehouse in Ithaca, New York. If we fail, they'll pull their business and give it to one of our competitors."

My words hung in the air and our employee owners looked at me and blinked. They didn't say anything. They just stared. Did they hear me? Was I unclear, or was the idea of such a thing so unfathomable that they had been rendered speechless? Finally, I said, "What do you think?"

They turned to look at each other and then back at me.

Rusty raised his hand, his errant index finger pointing skyward. "Maybe we could all work overtime. I'll pull double shifts during the week."

"Thank you, Rusty. We'll need all the help we can get."

A bunch of hands shot up and most employee owners followed Rusty's lead, either volunteering to start early or stay later. Many offered to work weekends. Joanne scribbled notes, making a long list of everyone's extra time commitments.

Stanley had stuck around rather than leaving promptly after everyone arrived in the morning. The night watchman stepped forward and said, "I've got five brothers. If you want some help, temporarily, maybe they could sign on for a few weeks. Also, instead of policing the property at night, I could work on filling orders too."

I beamed, proudly. "That's a great idea. I didn't think of that, Stanley. Does anybody else have friends or family that could join us for a couple of months?"

The employee owners' response was encouraging but I was worried at the same time. Even if we tripled our regular volume, there wasn't any chance of filling Ithaca Accoutrements' order. It would take more like *nine* times our regular volume and every week we fell short would put us deeper into the hole. My face burned hot when I thought about what I had done to the company, accepting an order that we didn't have a chance of completing. When we failed, we'd lose our biggest customer and our reputation would be damaged. I imagined Stuart Franklin sweeping in, romancing Andy Branchport, and securing our most important account. There had to be something we could do, but what?

When our meeting ended, we brought Joanne's lists back to the office and began making schedules. We planned extra shifts and staffed them as fully as possible. It was a good thing so many of our employees had large families. I hoped that when they went home they'd return in the morning with the names of other relatives who were willing to work for *us* a couple of extra hours each week, on top of their regular jobs.

Even with all the extra help, it still didn't seem like it would be possible to make three million dollars worth of dowels, spindles, pegs, and buttons in time. Sometimes you had to begin a big project, even if you couldn't imagine how you might finish it. Some things must be taken on faith. I had to place my trust in our employee owners to make the impossible possible. We just couldn't let Andy Branchport down.

Joanne had constructed a larger than life poster and hung it on the wall near the new time clock. We needed the visualization to help everyone understand our progress. It looked like the carnival game where horses galloped along a racetrack as players squirted water from plastic pistols into a clown's mouth. The only problem with the display was that it was clear to everyone we were already falling hopelessly behind.

Two weeks into our sixty days, we should have completed a quarter of Ithaca Accoutrements' order but we had only managed half as much as that. We operated the business at full tilt, and yet, we were falling way short. It felt like a Herculean task, one that we weren't capable of achieving.

I stood in the office kitchen with my arms crossed, lost in thought while waiting for a pot of coffee to brew. I jumped when somebody tapped my shoulder and turned to see who was there.

Doyle leaned his shoulder against the frame of the doorway and casually crossed one work boot over the other. Despite his informal body language, the expression on his face conveyed worry. He began to speak and his words sounded sympathetic rather than insulting. He said, "It's all too much, Misty. You did your best, but what chance did you have? You don't know what you're doing. Never did." Doyle tipped his head forward and frowned. "You're too old for this, but you gave it an honest try. It's time to admit defeat. Forget about Art and Stuart, I'll take the company off your hands. You can walk away owing nothing. I'll even let the ESOP keep half of the company. Don't worry. I'll take care of everything. It's for the best, wouldn't you say so, Misty?"

His words shouldn't have come as a surprise after working with him for a decade, but I was stunned nevertheless. I thought of the employees' lost expressions when I told them about the impossible order, and I suppose I had the same look on my face after Doyle's latest proposition. I stuttered when I began to speak and the coffee maker sputtered as it finished its brew cycle. "Good heavens, Doyle. I don't know what to think or say. The only thing on my mind is how to get the rod out."

Doyle said, "Here's what we'll do. We make as much as we

possibly can, and then I will call Andy in a couple of weeks. I'll tell him that you've had a medical emergency that required you to sell the company and retire at once. I'm sure that he'll be sympathetic and extend the deadline. How about that for a plan? Should work like a charm."

I tilted my head forward, tapped my chin, and hated to admit to myself that Doyle's plan could work. But why should I have to give away half of the company? Maybe I could be talked into giving my shares to the ESOP, but not to Doyle. If the man had offered to pay me a fair price while promising to let the ESOP own the other half, I might be more inclined to accept it. Yet Doyle's offer would allow me to walk away. I wanted to reject his overture outright, but instead, I said, "I don't know, Doyle. I'll have to think about it. Meanwhile, we must find a way to produce more dowels. Do you have any ideas? There must be something we haven't thought of."

***

At dinner, Four complained about his calf. It wasn't like him to mention aches and it wasn't common for him to acknowledge being sore, even on long training days. If anything, Four seemed to welcome pain as evidence that his workouts were succeeding. After picking, poking, and prodding his food with a fork, and eating far too little of it, Four limped away from the table and I shot out of my seat. That never happened. I said, "Can I take a look at your leg?"

Four blinked rapidly. "There's not much to see, GiGi. I checked it after practice a couple of hours ago. It hurts on the inside, not the outside." He sat on a bench, kicked off his sneakers, lifted the hem of his sweatpants from his ankle up to his knee, and then pulled his white athletic sock off using his thumbs. It looked like he was trying to avoid letting the fabric rub his skin.

I was concerned and dragged a chair from the dining room

table to sit on while looking at Four's injury. "Set your foot on my knee, honey."

It surprised me to see gold metallic polish on his toenails. Earlier in the year, Four began painting his fingernails. When he asked me to help him, I felt strange and honored at the same time. I never had the chance to brush a daughter's hair or teach a granddaughter how to apply makeup. It never occurred to me that I might one day give my great-grandson a manicure. It was rare for men, but I had noticed an increasing number of boys in their late teens who wore dark-colored varnish. Most of *those* kids dressed exclusively in black, shared Four's musical preferences, and dyed their hair unnatural colors.

Four wanted to get the Olympic rings tattooed on his chest and he asked his coach for permission. He was advised that the conservative judges frowned upon unwholesome mutilations. Four suggested that the judges would never know. He was warned that the arbiters would find out, and his coach said, "It's better to maintain a fresh-faced innocence than to follow the latest perverse fashion fads." If he weren't a figure skating prodigy, Four would probably have a new wave hairstyle like A Flock of Seagulls. I considered a person's choices their own business, but frowned at the thought of my beloved, Four, pestering his father to sign permission slips allowing him to pierce his lip, ears, eyebrow, and who knows what else.

I looked closely at the young man's hairy shin. "Can you point to where it hurts?"

Four pointed to the meat of his calf and I turned my head to examine it. "Would it be alright if I touched it?"

I patted and then rubbed his leg while watching his face. Then I lightly jabbed his skin with a finger. He didn't blink or wince, but I saw him clench his jaw. I said, "That hurt, didn't it, honey?"

He frowned and nodded. I said, "It looks a little red and puffy. Can you show me your other leg?" When he removed his other shoe and sock, he sat back on the bench and rested both his feet on my knees. I looked from one leg to the other. "I think it's a little swollen too. Not just the rosy part, but your ankle also. Do you think we should have a doctor look at it?"

Four scoffed. "I'm sure it's nothing, GiGi. I shouldn't have mentioned it. I expect I'll forget all about it by tomorrow."

I tipped my head forward and sternly said, "I shall not forget it, Four. I want to look at it again in the morning before you go to school."

"Okay, alright. If you insist." Four chuckled at my worries as his feet returned to the floor. He gathered his socks and shoes, but his laughter stopped when he took a step. Clearly, he was in pain. I worried as he walked away. In another month, he would be graduating from high school. If only there were time to plan a graduation party for him instead of being preoccupied with the massive order for Ithaca Accoutrements.

A good night's sleep did not improve the situation. Four stood while I kneeled on the shag carpet in his room. He pinched his eyes closed. His full-faced grimace reflected the pain he experienced and Four didn't protest when I said, "We're going to the emergency room, honey." Presto drove his son to the hospital and I followed in my car.

Four's eyes grew wide with surprise when the emergency room doctor took a razor to his leg. The physician said, "I need to get a better look at this, son." The doctor hemmed and hawed as he examined Four's leg and then asked about the pain.

"Every step is painful. It's alright when I don't move, but it hurts when I walk." Four looked away and continued. "Sometimes, it feels like someone is trying to pull my bones from my body through a tiny hole. Other times it feels like my leg is going to explode. This morning I was afraid my bone had shattered." He looked back at the healer and said, "I can't have a bum leg, Doc, I gotta skate. I got a competition coming next week."

The physician's sour expression worried me. While Four described how his leg felt, the doctor pursed his lips. When the boy talked about skating, the man in white shook his head. "We'll see about that, son." Presto and I watched as the doctor drew on Four's skin with a blue ballpoint pen, tracing the round red rash. "Go home. Stay in bed. Don't wash. Come back tomorrow."

I was surprised at the doctor's simple instructions and asked the nurse if we could give him something for the pain. She shrugged and said, "I'm sure it would be alright to take aspirin or Tylenol."

It was shocking to look at Four's leg the next morning. Instead of a round rash, there was a long red line extending from the blue circle left by the doctor's pen. The mark stretched almost to the back of Four's knee, well beyond the area the doctor had shaved. I couldn't wait to get back to the hospital. Something was wrong and we needed to find out what it was. Harold joined Presto and Four. I followed, though I wasn't optimistic about making it to work that day.

When the doctor looked at Four's leg, his eyes met the nurse's and I was afraid to know what the look conveyed. A shiver ran up my spine as the doctor grumbled, "I was afraid of that." He retrieved his razor and removed a wide swath of leg hair, up to Four's knee and well beyond it. The doctor said to the nurse, "I want to get a picture of that leg, on the outside and the inside." Then he spoke to Four and said, "After your X-ray, I'll examine you again."

It turned out to be more than an X-ray. The doctor had also ordered an ultrasound. I had never heard of the process being used except with pregnant women and I wondered about the difference between the images an X-ray and an ultrasound provided. We sat in the waiting room for hours. Harold paced, Presto drummed his fingers on his leg, and I fidgeted while Four slept. The pain in Four's leg must have prevented him from getting a good night's sleep last night.

Shortly after noon, we were called into an examination room. The Doctor looked at all of us and then started to speak. "Please be seated. This is going to be hard news to hear." I'm sure I flinched and must have frowned, dreading what the doctor would say next. I thought about getting a second opinion but hadn't yet heard the first. The laconic physician looked directly into my eyes and said, "The boy has a blood clot." The doctor nodded to confirm his diagnosis as if adding, "Yes, it's true."

Presto gasped and Harold repeated the diagnosis as a question. "A blood clot?"

Four said, "What's a blood clot?"

Presto stood up and said, "I thought only old people got blood clots. Like President Nixon. Didn't he have a blood clot in his leg?"

The doctor said, "Yes, now that you mention it, I believe he did. I'm sorry to say, it isn't just old people, sir. Blood clots *can* happen to anyone." The doctor looked at Harold and said, "Perhaps you have heard of deep vein thrombosis, otherwise known as DVT."

Four's voice raised octaves higher than normal. "Get rid of it, Doc. I want it removed. When can you operate?" His eyes filled with tears. "I gotta get this over with."

"It's not that simple, son. I wish it were. They used to operate on DVT, but too often the results were fatal. Instead, we prescribe a week of bed rest, anticoagulant treatments, and compression stockings."

Four blinked rapidly, clearing the moisture from his eyes and his cheeks turned red. "Stockings? Like, tights? Like gymnasts and figure skaters wear?"

The doctor nodded. "That's right. For circulation. These stockings only go halfway up your legs."

An indignant huff escaped Four's lips. "Can I still skate?"

The doctor rubbed the back of his neck. He replied, "I don't know." He thought for a moment and added, "I suppose so, but not for a week."

Four said, "Good. Stockings it is." He rolled his eyes and then shivered.

I was afraid that the doctor didn't fully understand. It was important that he knew what the boy was asking him. I interjected,

"Four spends hours a day on skates. He's training for the 1988 Winter Olympics in Calgary."

A long, knowing, yet doubtful, "Oh" came from deep in the doctor's chest. "I see. I'm sorry, I don't know about that. I thought you were asking about casual skating. It will require an expert to answer that question. Now is not the time to worry about 1988. Blood clots are a very serious condition. He will need to be admitted to the hospital immediately. We'll administer the anticoagulant treatments and carefully monitor the clot and the level of thinners in his blood. The clot is the size of a marble and it needs to shrink quickly. The boy will probably always require blood thinners to prevent future blood clots. If one ever made it to his brain, heart, or lungs, it would probably be fatal."

I blinked rapidly. It was hard to hear the doctor say that Four's condition could be life threatening. My mind drifted back to the day I learned that Junior had died. After all these years, I still think of him every day. Losing a child isn't something one gets over, but mostly I steer my thoughts to happy moments, like Junior on his way to prom. Just the thought of losing Four scared me senseless and I wished I could trade places with him.

Four sputtered. "But, but… but. Admitted? Can't I just take a couple of pills or something'?"

The doctor turned toward Four. "Maybe. Not at first. For the first couple of weeks, you'll receive Heparin injections in your stomach. Every day, we'll test your blood to make sure we've got the proper dosage for you. There's not much *to* you. How much do you weigh?" The doctor reached for the chart, choosing to rely on the nurse's note rather than the boy's answer. "Yes, it could be a little tricky. We're used to patients who weigh twice as much as you do, young man. Then, maybe you can learn to administer injections at home or we can try Warfarin which you can take orally if your system tolerates it."

Four sneered. "Shots in the belly?" He glared at his father and then looked at me. "Can I give them to myself?"

The doctor seemed to remember he had other patients in the

hospital and stood abruptly. "We'll see. Too soon to know." He turned to the nurse and said, "Get him into a gown."

***

Harold, Presto, and I took turns sitting with Four throughout the afternoon. Four didn't complain about the intravenous solution, side effects from the medication, or when they drew blood, but I bristled when they mentioned the varnish on his nails. Four always turned bright red and explained that the golden polish reminded him of his purpose and commitment. He would always say, "It's a constant reminder of everything I need to do to win a gold medal in the Calgary Olympics."

Late in the afternoon, I took a couple of hours and visited Winslow's office. When I knocked, he greeted me at the doorway, kissed me politely on the cheek, and took my coat. I stepped into his narrow office and made myself comfortable on the sofa overlooking Mirror Lake. Then I looked into Winslow's emerald eyes and burst into tears. He poked a handkerchief into my hand and I covered my face. Winslow sat beside me on the sofa, extended a comforting arm across my back, and pulled me slightly against him. He said, "There, there, Misty," and made other comforting sounds as well. After a couple of minutes, I sat up and explained Four's medical situation to him.

When we had finished talking about the blood clot, we talked a little bit about the impossible order. Winslow said, "An attorney who went to law school with me has a friend who owns a woodworking company. Would you permit me to contact them and inquire whether they have any excess capacity?"

"Oh, could you? That's a fabulous idea. Thank you, Winslow. If something like that could work, it would save the day." I stood and told Winslow that I should get back to the hospital, but he suggested I sit back down.

Winslow bit his cheek and looked at his hands. "I have some

news and I hate to share it, but it is information you need to know."

I slumped against him. It sounded like bad news. I didn't know if I could handle any more misfortune.

Winslow clicked his tongue and said, "I have a list of Mirror Lake Bank's Board of Directors. I copied it onto that piece of paper for you." He pointed to a piece of stationery adorned with pinecones, pine needles, and a blue bird in a nest.

I picked up the paper and read down the list. When I reached the bottom, I looked up from the roster and gulped hard. "Lois Phelps!" I practically spat her name from my lips. "*Lois* is on the bank's Board of Directors?"

Winslow nodded. "It's worse than that, even, Misty. Lois chairs the Board."

20

I couldn't believe my ears. Lois Phelps was Chairman of the Mirror Lake Bank's Board of Directors. A tumble of questions crashed through my brain. How could it be? Of all the people on Earth, why Lois? They didn't just pick everyday people to serve on a bank's Board as they do for jury duty, did they? What power did Lois wield? Was Lois the reason that Mr. Duncan seemed bent on the annihilation of Adirondack Dowel? That wasn't legal, was it?

My heart thumped and blood raced through my veins. I leaned forward and whispered to Winslow. "What do we do, now that we know?"

Winslow's eyes narrowed, and he said, "I know it will be hard, Misty, but we need to play it cool. Tell nobody. Understand? Absolutely nobody. Not Betty, your family, or anyone at work. Do not tell a soul. I want to find out more about Lois Phelps *and* the rest of the members of the Board while I'm at it. The only person I will tell is Ted Drake. He may know how to help. Until we've done our homework, nothing changes."

"But the bank can't harass Adirondack Dowel just because Lois hates me, can it?"

"There are laws, rules, and bank policies. Financial institutions are regulated. It's not my area of expertise, Misty, but I expect you are right. Lois has a personal vendetta and it doesn't seem to be a coincidence that the bank keeps tightening the noose around your neck."

"At this rate, we'll be hung before we know it!"

"That's why we need to pretend we don't know about this. It isn't enough for us to *be* right. We need proof of malfeasance *and* criminal intent." Winslow's eyes sparkled. "In all my years as a lawyer, I've never dealt with anything like this. I usually stick to the basics. It makes my blood boil. Are you going to be alright, Misty?"

"I don't know." I turned away from my attorney and thought for a minute about what to say. "It's a lot to take in. Between Four's blood clot, the order for Ithaca, and the bank lowering the hammer on us, it's…" I tripped over my emotions again and looked back toward the man beside me. The words caught in my throat. "It's overwhelming, Winslow."

He stood, turned toward me, and offered his hand to help me stand. Then he wrapped his strong arms around me, enveloping me in a comforting embrace. The vibrations of his deep voice from within our hug comforted me. "Leave Lois and the bank to me, Misty." We stepped away from each other. Winslow continued, "Let Harold and Presto help with Four. You need to focus on Ithaca Accoutrements. By the way, my friend says his business can help if you need them as a contract manufacturer. They can take on a quarter of the business at your prices, or a third of it for a premium. Here's his name and number. Give him a call, Misty."

"Oh, thank heavens, Winslow. If they can make a third of the order, we'll only have to make two million dollars worth of dowels." My lips quivered as I finished. "I don't know how we can get one million dollars of production through the doors, let alone two million dollars." I closed my eyes tightly and wished my problems would vaporize.

Winslow said, "You'll think of something, I know you will." He took a step toward me, placed his index finger beneath my chin, and tipped my head upward. His penetrating eyes drilled into my soul. "Keep your chin up, sweetie. If you need anything, call me. It doesn't have to be a legal matter. Even if you just need a shoulder to cry on. These are trying times." Winslow turned his head and placed a comforting kiss on my cheek.

***

I spent most of the week at the hospital.

Four was despondent, Presto was depressed, and Harold was lost trying to figure out what he could do to help. Instead of just tending to Four, I had to console all three of them.

In the quiet hours, as Four slept, while he was reading, and when the doctors were examining him, my troubles invaded my mind. When not at Four's side, I often sat in the visitor's lounge. I wanted to remain by his bedside, holding his hands, and comforting him, but the company needed me too. My thoughts kept spinning back to business. What were we going to do about Lois, Mr. Duncan, and the bank?

The ticking clock in the waiting room clicked off the seconds, minutes, and hours. Sitting quietly on the sofa should have relaxed me but made me squirm instead. I wanted to jump from the couch and scream. "It's too much! I can't take it anymore." Had I convinced myself to let Doyle have my stock? I began to think so.

I thought of the general manager's hateful words but realized that he needed to be sharp, direct, and to the point. I wouldn't have heard them otherwise. There wasn't a kind way to blunt the obvious assessment. I *was* kidding myself. I should have known better than to think *I* could run a company. I gripped my knees tightly and rocked back and forward. My brain continued to self-evaluate. My job performance was dismal and my heart ached. I never was much more than a hostess. When it came down to it, I was a cheerleader who grew up to be a receptionist. I should work at the Holiday Inn pouring coffee and delivering clam rolls instead of presiding over a company. People depended on me. I let them down. I should just walk away. How could I deny my age? The calendar was not my friend and time was not on my side. There came a point when it was time to accept the facts and at 79 years of age, I had no business leading Adirondack Dowel. I didn't want to die in Father's office chair, like he did, at 90 years of age. Yes, it was time to face the inevitable.

The pay phone in the waiting room rang and startled me. I lumbered to my feet and answered it. Joanne's soothing voice asked, "How are you holding up, Misty?" I told her we were doing as well as could be expected. She said, "Don't worry. We're taking care of everything over here." Her words sounded reassuring, but the calm, efficient woman's tone sounded scared. I thanked her for calling and told her I planned to hop over after Four had lunch.

Another woman in the waiting room frowned at me when I hung up the phone. A little bit of noise traveled far in quiet spaces. I was glad the call was brief and that I hadn't said anything confidential. I desperately wanted to confide in Joanne but knew that Winslow would disapprove. I trusted Joanne completely, but Winslow demanded we keep the secret about the bank's Board. I also trusted Winslow.

To the chagrin of other patients' loved ones, the coin-gobbling monster in the waiting room became my temporary office. The beast consumed several pounds of change rendering my pocketbook weightless as I dropped an endless stream of coins into the hungry phone's slots. If I decided to dump the company onto Doyle's shoulders, I still had many obligations to face before throwing in the towel. I phoned Winslow's friend and accepted his offer to manufacture a third of the impossible order, surrendering all of the profits on that portion of the business, plus a little extra. Then I called Joanne back, and she seemed ecstatic to hear the news. I still yearned to tell her about the bombshell Winslow dropped. Then I called Winslow to thank him for introducing his friend.

When I returned to the Four's side, he closed a book and frowned. "I finished it, GiGi. Could you get me another?" Then he placed his hand over the medallion on his chest, closed his eyes, and appeared to float away. It was as if he were lost within the celestial scene on the cover of the book he was reading.

Four read gothic and horror fiction, nonstop, and whenever he'd finish one book, he'd send me off to buy another. On one trip to Bookstore Plus on Main Street, I stopped at Mirror Lake Bank's competitor and applied for a mortgage on the house. It felt good to do business with a different lender, and yet I felt disloyal at the same time. For sixty years, the family had always patronized Mirror Lake Bank. On another trip to the bookstore, I visited the realtor's office and listed the house for sale. It was time to let it go, perhaps well past time. Even so, it felt like I was abandoning a beloved friend. I should have discussed the matter with my family, but I made the decision on my own. I swallowed my guilt. Calhoun and the boys would have to adjust to the change. I choked on tears every time I thought about somebody else living in our family's home, but was determined to move on. Even if Harold, Presto, and Four moved to a new home with me, we could get by on half the square footage.

The boys were mad when they saw the sign on the lawn and I apologized for not telling them. When Harold and Presto confronted me, Four pressed the button on the hospital bed, sat forward, and a tear rolled down his cheek. "It's because of me, isn't it? It's my fault we have to sell the house."

I protested. "No Four, it's not because of you. It's the company and the bank. I need to sell the house so I can put more money into the business."

Presto said, "Again? Why does this keep happening?"

I tried to assure them that everything would be alright and wished that I could convince myself. I attempted to make it sound like a good thing. "I've got my eye on a cute little Victorian a couple of blocks away. We don't need to live in a mansion anymore, do we, boys?"

Harold said, "I'd be happier in my cabin." Presto agreed. Four just blinked. Then they got quiet and I stepped away for a couple of hours.

***

I headed straight for the office. I had lost control of things there and had no idea how we were progressing with the impossible order.

When the Mustang pulled into the parking lot my jaw dropped in shock. A dozen tents stood near the edge of the river. Sheets of plywood rested on wooden pallets. Burly men that I didn't recognize operated shop equipment on top of the makeshift manufacturing space. Clouds of sawdust swirled in the breeze and curled wood shavings spun to the ground as the bearded, flannel-clad men operated machines that looked like they had been brought from their sheds and garages.

I smiled and nodded at them while hurrying past the outdoor factory. Hogan Hoad passed the time clock as I entered the building and he stopped for a minute to talk with me. It bolstered my mood to speak of inconsequential matters with a friendly soul, and it slowed my pace.

The door between the factory and the offices was wedged open. I stepped in quietly and was surprised to see Joanne behind Art's desk. I froze and watched as she turned the dials on either side and popped the tabs on the mysterious box. At the sound of the snap, her head jerked toward the bathrooms, and then she glanced at the clock on the wall. It was precisely the time of Art's predictable afternoon constitutional. It was as if the man's bowel movements were scheduled in his daily planner. Joanne swiftly lifted the top of the briefcase open and removed a small stack of papers. She knew exactly what she was looking for. After a minute, she stepped to the copier and Xeroxed a bunch of papers, and then bustled back to the attaché case. I heard the faint sound of a flushing toilet through the bathroom walls. Then I heard the snap of the latches on the briefcase tabs closing. Joanne took time to slowly spin the dials and I realized that she was returning them to a specific position. She must have observed where the dials rested when the briefcase was locked and closed. Joanne was smart. It would have been just like Art to notice if his precious valise had been tampered with, otherwise.

Joanne and I had always giggled about what Art kept in that blamed lockbox. I took a couple of small steps backward, returning to the factory, stood for a minute, and thought. My trust in the young woman was unshakeable. It was unlike her to violate someone's confidence. What was she doing in the business manager's private property, knowing full well that space was his own? What if she wasn't as trustworthy as I had thought? My head began to ache. It made me sad to see my beloved secretary snooping in an unauthorized space but I had to admit my curiosity equaled hers. I tipped my head forward and walked quickly back into the office. I had to catch up quickly and get back to the hospital.

Other than Joanne's violation of Art's briefcase, everything seemed in order. Doyle and Rusty followed me into the office and within a couple of minutes, they explained everything that had happened during my absence. The tent city between the factory and the river was populated by Rusty's uncles and cousins from Tupper Lake. They hadn't minded setting up equipment outside, in fact, the lumberjacks would have been unhappy working indoors. Doyle lifted his head proudly and said, "This week we are on pace to make $200,000 worth of dowels, spindles, buttons, and plugs. That's a record, Misty."

My arm shot forward and I shook his hand. "How wonderful, Doyle."

He frowned. "It will not even be enough to stay on pace, Misty. What chance do we have of catching up? We must do more. We have to go faster. There are only six and a half weeks remaining, and we'd need to make $425,000 more product to get this forsaken order filled."

Joanne said, "What if we go to Sears and buy more equipment? Just like Rusty's relatives brought with them."

Doyle said it wasn't as good as having industrial machinery but admitted the flannel mob was helpful.

We were interrupted by a ringing phone. Joanne answered it, asked the caller how he was feeling, and then passed the phone to me.

Four said, "Would you pick up *The Armageddon Rag* by George R. R. Martin at the bookstore for me, GiGi?"

After a quick promise, I hung up the telephone and told my colleagues it was time to get back to the hospital.

Joanne said, "Give Four our love."

Doyle said, "I'll walk you out to your car, Misty."

I thanked him, knowing what he wanted and why he offered to escort me. As predicted, when we reached the parking lot, Doyle said, "Have you made a decision, Misty? Will you accept my offer to rid you of all your troubles here?"

I shook my head and said, "Almost, Doyle. You'll have my answer tomorrow or the next day at the latest."

***

When I returned to the hospital, Four buried his head in his new book. I sat quietly beside him for an hour and then gripped his arm. "You're turning pages quickly. It must be a good book."

"Yes, I like it." He placed a bookmark between the pages. "I'm sorry, GiGi. Do you want to talk?"

"I was thinking of going home, honey. Do you mind?"

He glanced at the cover of the book and said, "It's okay. I'll be lost in there." He pointed at the book's cover. "Thanks for picking it up for me." He looked at me pleadingly before I could respond and said, "How much longer do I have to stay here? I want to go home and I need to get back to my training. My leg doesn't hurt anymore."

We'd already been at the hospital longer than the specialist had told us initially. "I don't know, honey. Soon, I hope."

Four was way too old for a great-grandmother's kiss on his cheek, but he allowed it nevertheless. My head turned back from the doorway as I departed and he had already returned to reading. I tipped my head to the side and reflected on my love for the precious child. He was practically grown and I longed for days gone by.

The phone rang as I walked through the door, mail tucked beneath my arm. I wanted to drop the receiver at the sound of the voice on the other end of the line. It was Eloise, my ex-husband's wife from California. We never spoke to one another. The call was mercifully brief. The news was preceded by a sniffle. "Preston is dead. I don't expect you to come but I figured you should know. Click."

Eloise didn't wait for a response or provide details about the cause of his death. Preston Palmer, Sr, the father of my sons was gone. The man who flitted back and forth between Lois and me in high school, like a butterfly in a garden, and then ran away with a starlet after our second son was born, was dead. I stood, bewildered, waiting to feel something. What was the proper way to mourn somebody you once loved but no longer did? Somehow, the death of this 81-year-old man stunned me.

The receiver returned to its cradle and I absentmindedly looked at the mail on the floor. A postcard caught my eye. The hateful things had been coming weekly since Preston divorced me. This one said, "Better off without you. The sun always shines in California. Glad you're not here." He never signed his name, but he didn't need to. There was no mistaking who the greeting came from. I flipped the card and looked at a row of suntanned, bikini-clad babes on beach chairs and tossed it into a box with the others. Perhaps that would be the last spiteful postcard I would receive. He left me for someone else, yet it was he that held a grudge against me. I never could figure out why he maintained the habit of sending mean postcards decades after our divorce.

I snatched my pocketbook from the counter and walked to the drugstore. I knew where I was going and had no intention of talking myself out of it. I purchased three packs of Winstons and returned home. I still didn't know if I was celebrating or grieving but the familiar cigarette holder on my lips brought me back to my first years alone. Looking back, I'm grateful that the nanny who raised me was there for my boys during my drinking years. The irresistible urge returned. It wasn't enough to feel the tingle of nicotine in my brain. I needed the bite and burn of alcohol as well.

It wasn't deliberate. I didn't have a plan. It was as if I were a zombie in a trance and had lost control of my destiny. I knew that I should dial my sponsor and let her talk me out of it, but didn't want to. *What is her name? Where did I put her phone number? Who cares?*

As if duty-bound, I teased my hair, unloaded a quarter can of Aqua Net, sculpted a swirling stack of silver tresses above my head, and painted my face without looking at the wrinkles I plastered over. I put on my favorite, blinding white evening gown. The antique dress was fresh as new snow. I covered my shoulders with a soft, luxurious shawl. At the edge of my closet, an old pair of shoes I hadn't worn in decades caught my eye. Twenty-five years earlier, my friends in Washington Christened my heels, 'The Homewreckers.' They were my lucky shoes and I felt alluring when I wore them. I pulled them from the shelf, put them on, and stepped into the past. My reflection looked at me from the mirror on the back of the closet door. I needed to escape. Before reason got the better of me, I closed the door and made my way to the Old Red Canoe on Mirror Lake Drive.

***

As I walked up the sidewalk in the early evening, heads turned and people stared at me. It wasn't unusual for people to wear fancy clothing in the upscale tourist town, but perhaps my old-fashioned dress made me look like a time traveler. My antique dress unwound dozens of years as long as I didn't look too long into a mirror.

Luxury vehicles lined up along the street in front of the elegant Mirror Lake Inn. I considered changing my plans and walking up the steps to the exclusive lodge and glanced up at the resort. A woman stood at the top of the steps, looking down at me. She wore a dark, elegant cape and stood with her arms crossed. She was just close enough to see her glowering stare. Despite cloaking her face behind long, stringy hair and covering her head with a fashionable hood, there was no mistaking the contempt in Lois Phelps' eye. She couldn't have known I would walk down the sidewalk that evening, and yet there she was at the top of the steps. Was she there for a meeting of the bank's Board of Directors? Did she know about Preston's death? She wouldn't hear the news from me. I forced myself to look away and my pace quickened as I stepped toward the pub.

Seeing Lois always ruined my day. I tried to forget about Lois, Preston, and a world full of problems as the Old Red Canoe beckoned me inside. It was the sort of place that looked rustic on purpose. When the furniture was new, it was intentionally weathered to create the illusion of a comfortable cottage. The boat that it was named for was split in half, and both halves were mounted on the wall. Shelving was added just beneath the lip, and a row of bottles was an arm's length from the bartender's reach.

Despite the casual interior, the homey establishment was frequented by wealthy, well-dressed patrons. A good-looking young man placed his hands on the bar in front of me, leaned forward, and said, "What will you be having, ma'am." He wore a boat-shaped name tag and I glanced at it. He smiled and said, "My name is Don, what's yours?"

I felt naughty telling the bartender my name and asking for a Hanky Panky. Doubt niggled at me. I distracted my hesitation by worrying about what the kid thought of an old woman saying such a thing. "It's a cocktail. Maybe nobody orders them anymore." I blushed at my thoughts as if the man who was decades younger than me might mistake my drink order for a flirtation.

Don assured me that he had made a few and that his training had included the historic beverage. I watched as he splashed gin, vermouth, Fernet Branca, and orange juice into a cocktail shaker. I fired up a Winston as Don passed my Hanky Panky through the

Julep strainer. At that moment, I would have sold my soul for an apéritif. When Don placed the amber composition before me I reached for my pocketbook, and he said, "Would you like me to run you a tab?"

I turned away from my purse and said, "Why not? Thank you."

Don turned away to wash a glass in a tiny sink behind the bar. I closed my eyes and lifted the drink toward my lips. I paused before taking a sip and inhaled the woodsy aroma. Excitement tugged at my belly and the smallest possible sip passed between my lips. I might have come to my senses and left it at just a taste so small that it could be denied. Before the glass reached the bar, I lifted it again for a bitter mouthful. I held the forbidden elixir in my mouth, thought about my decades of sobriety, and it dawned that I could spit the beverage back into the glass. I didn't care about the consequences any longer. Preston was dead and I was glad. Doyle could have Adirondack Dowel. What chance did I ever have anyway? I should have let him have it to begin with. I tried to convince myself not to fall under the spell of addiction again, but surrendering meant liberation.

With a hard swallow, the nostalgic burn flooded my esophagus. After decades of abstinence, one antique cocktail followed another, as I drank my way through the decades. Who knew how many drinks I had? I recall feeling like the belle of the ball but can't remember how many distinguished gentlemen told me their stories. I would never remember when the dashing Don told me that he thought I'd had enough and asked me if there was somebody he could call to come and get me. Maybe, if I racked my brain, I would remember appreciating the comfort of a friend's arm escorting me into the crisp evening air and making sure I made it safely home. If only I could remember what happened next.

21

Dust swam in the beams of light that filtered through my bedroom window as I blinked my eyes open. My temples throbbed and the back of my head ached. I sat slowly forward and began to recall the day before. I remembered the sound of my ex-husband's wife's voice on the telephone and the sight of Lois glowering down at me from the top of the steps at the Mirror Lake Inn.

I flushed with guilt as the realization dawned that yesterday, my thirty year run of sobriety came to an end. After tossing caution to the wind, letting my hair down, so to speak, and feeling free of worry, trouble, and doubt for a couple of hours, remembering what happened after falling from the wagon was beyond my reach. What happened after I gave in to temptation?

My stomach lurched. The water was running in the master bathroom. I leaned forward and gulped as the deep sound of a man humming caught my ears. My hands reached for my aching head as panic overtook me. My pretty bouffant had collapsed since I last looked in the mirror. What a horrible sight. Confound it, who was in the bathroom? I didn't know whether to race for the phone and dial 911 or hurry to my dressing table and try to make myself presentable. What was I thinking, getting drunk and bringing a man home at my age? I was certainly old enough to know better. I tried to remember the various wealthy gentlemen who joked, flirted, and told me stories last night. Did one of them bring me home? If only I could remember. I reached for a headscarf and covered my head just in time. My feet swung from beneath the covers and I prepared to take flight as the bathroom doorknob turned.

A gasp of relief escaped my lips as Winslow stepped into the bedroom. I looked from his head to his feet and back to his head again. My mouth and eyes were parched. A lump appeared in my throat when I swallowed hard and my eyes blinked as Winslow stopped in his tracks. My lawyer stood in my bedroom wearing sky-blue boxer shorts, a white, v-necked cotton tee shirt, and nothing else. All I could say was his name. When I did, he stepped toward me quickly, cupped my cheeks in his hands, and kissed my lips so gently they barely touched.

"Can I get you some coffee or orange juice, Misty? Both, maybe?"

My head bobbed.

"Are you alright? You're probably more than a little bit hungover."

"What happened?"

"You don't remember, do you, dear?"

I crinkled my nose. "Did we… Good heavens, Winslow. Isn't it illegal to…"

"Sleep with your attorney?"

My head dropped and my eyes closed. "Yes. What have I done, Winslow?"

"It's alright, Misty. We won't be in any trouble. You fired me last night, so I no longer represent you."

"What? How could you let me fire you?"

Winslow laughed. "There was no stopping you. You were angry at me for interrupting the good time you were having and you threatened to rip the bartender's face off for refusing to serve you anymore."

I wanted to sag in a heap. "But he was such a nice young man.

What have I done, Winslow? And," I swirled my hand around in front of me, hoping to emphasize the fact that he was practically naked with just a gesture.

"You really don't remember, do you?" He pursed his lips and shifted them from side to side. He continued, "I was expecting that." He looked away so quickly I was afraid he'd suffer from whiplash. "You said you love me and I told you I felt the same way." Winslow turned his head back toward me, ever so slowly, watching my response from the corners of his eyes.

I wondered what my expression revealed, but to me, my words sounded surprised but not alarmed. "We did?" The two short words sounded much longer than single syllables. "What else happened?"

"Nothing, Misty. The next thing that happened was your eyes teared up. You told me about your husband's death and that the boys don't yet know. Then you said you were tired and didn't want to sleep alone. You asked me to hold you. I began to climb into bed with you, fully clothed, but you told me I couldn't wear my trousers to bed."

"That's all that happened?"

"You sound relieved."

"It's true, Winslow. I am. If we're going to be together, I want to remember it. When did I fire you?"

"Just after you said your prayers."

"Good heavens, Winslow. I *never* say my prayers. What did I pray for?"

"I'll never tell. I won't soon forget it, Misty. It was the sweetest, most beautiful prayer I ever heard, but I don't think it should be repeated."

As Winslow climbed into his trousers, I said, "What shall I do without a lawyer?" I giggled, though it made my headache worse. "Are you my boyfriend now? Are we going steady?"

"I'm not your lawyer, but I can still advise you if you want my counsel." After he buttoned his shirt, he kissed me again, not as gently as before, and then hurried off to make coffee while I dragged my haggard body toward the shower.

***

I had barely finished in the bathroom when the boys pulled into the driveway. During their unexpected arrival, a pot of oatmeal boiled over on the stove and Winslow became agitated, mumbling about how he hated to cook. Harold and Presto glared at the man from different directions. I could tell they wondered why my attorney was cooking breakfast. The fact that my hair wasn't fixed, my face wasn't made up, and I was wearing a bathrobe must have also roused their suspicions. If Four had any such thoughts, he didn't voice them. There were more important matters to confront, anyhow.

While Winslow attempted to salvage breakfast, I asked the boys to sit at the table. My head throbbed and I wished that I had a Bloody Mary. Was that the only cocktail I didn't drink last night? I turned away from my son, grandson, and great-grandson, and began to speak. "I have something to tell you."

I turned around, crossed my arms, and looked at the boys. Harold was irritated. Preston seemed disappointed. I guessed that Four's arching eyebrows meant that he didn't know what to expect or how to feel; he was probably just glad to be released from the hospital. I dropped the facts in as few words as possible.

Harold's eyes grew wide. "My father is dead? I thought you were going to tell us you and that lawyer got hitched last night."

I laughed nervously at the thought, before catching myself. Then, I forced myself to look sympathetic, considering my son had just lost his father. Harold bit his lip and looked at his hands on the table.

Presto stood and gave me a hug. He was always very sensitive. "Are you okay, GiGi?" The way he pronounced it sounded like jeedge, close to the word judge.

Harold stood up and said, "I guess he'll stop sending those durn postcards. Might have been hope for him someday if it weren't for that." He shook his head and scoffed. The passing of the man that fathered my son garnered no more thought than that.

Presto inquired, "We going to California?"

I said, "I'm not."

Harold added, "Me neither."

Presto tilted his head forward and sighed. "I barely knew the man. It's sad when families aren't close."

I clasped Presto's shoulder and squeezed gently. "I know."

Four stood up and grumbled. "I don't want to go to California anyway. I just want to graduate from high school and go to Calgary." He frowned deeply, scratched his elbow, and said, "I need to get back to training."

Harold dropped a ball cap on his head and said he was going in to work for a couple of hours. A few minutes later, Presto grabbed his wallet. "The cupboards are bare. I'm going shopping." He jingled the keys in his pocket and said to his son, "Want anything at the store?"

When Harold and Presto were gone, Four shuffled about the house. He said, "It feels good to stretch my legs, GiGi. If I had to spend one more day in that hospital bed, I think I would have gone crazy." He made several journeys through the house, up one staircase and down the other, in a continuous loop. After many laps, Four passed through the kitchen and stopped. He said, "Where's Calhoun?"

My body tensed.

"It's okay, GiGi. I'm sure he's just asleep in a laundry basket or something. I'll find him."

Winslow set the dishtowel he had been using down on the counter, slipped into his plaid sport coat, and said he needed to get to the office. Before disappearing through the open doorway, Winslow winked at me, and then he was gone. I stared at the closed door for a minute and thought about the kindly country lawyer and his bright green eyes, then turned to join the hunt.

We searched the house from top to bottom, stopping

everywhere Calhoun was known to nap. Where could he be? Calling his name and teasing, "Here kitty, kitty" didn't bring him out of hiding.

Finally, I said, "I don't know what else to do."

Four scowled. "I'm sure he'll turn up."

Between the lingering effects of my hangover, the vigorous search, and my renewed addiction to tobacco, I felt like I needed something. "I'm going to make some coffee. Do you want anything from the kitchen, Four?"

He shook his head and stepped toward the stairway as the doorbell buzzed. Betty doted on Four before I could ask her if she would like a cup of coffee. I drifted toward the kitchen and Betty followed me a short time later. She sat at the table, and as I poured a pot of water into the Mr. Coffee machine, she said, "I noticed that Winslow's car was parked in the driveway early this morning."

My hand froze momentarily while retrieving coffee cups from the cupboard. "You are quite observant." I set the empty cups on the table and returned to the counter. I plucked a cigarette from the pack and poked it into the end of the holder, took a hearty puff, picked up an ashtray, and joined Betty at the kitchen table.

Betty watched me, clearly waiting for me to elaborate. There was no use in procrastinating. I would surely tell her anyway. "Last night I fell off the wagon. I got a call from California. Preston is dead, Betty." I paused for a minute. Betty looked at me intently but didn't say anything. I continued, "The next thing I remember is smoking cigarettes, drinking cocktails, and flirting with men at the Old Red Canoe. I should have stopped after one or two, but of course, I didn't. The next thing I knew, I woke with a thrashing headache. Then I discovered a man in the bathroom. Evidently, Winslow was called to rescue me and stayed the night."

Betty started to inquire. "Are you an…" She seemed at a loss for words. There were plenty of words to describe young people who entered into relationships, but there didn't seem to be a good way to talk about what happened when older people did. Betty finally concluded with the word *item*.

"Yes, I suppose we are an item. But so far our relationship remains chaste, in case you might be curious about that, honey." Many years ago we talked as schoolgirls and young women about boys and men. A lot of sand had passed through the proverbial hourglass since. I glanced at Betty, and the wrinkles on my friend's face were a keen reminder that I was far beyond my prime courting years. I said, "Oh, Betty. What am I doing, getting involved with a man at my age?"

Betty shrugged as if to say, "Why not," as the doorbell rang again.

It was a surprise to see Joanne at the front door. I couldn't remember her ever dropping by the house before. "I'm sorry to interrupt you at home, Misty."

"Don't be silly, honey. Come on in. Betty and I are having coffee in the kitchen. Would you like a cup?"

The young woman followed me into the kitchen. "I suppose half a cup would be okay." She looked distracted and out of sorts. I was unaccustomed to seeing the confident young woman look anything but self-assured. She wore a dress I hadn't seen before. The brightly-colored print featured pale yellow flowers, probably roses. I complimented her dress and she smiled. "It's a new pattern," she said proudly, but it looked the same as the other dresses she made. Her worries quickly returned to her face as I told Betty and Joanne about our missing cat.

Betty drained her coffee cup, tapped my hand, and said, "You working gals got important things to talk about. If you will allow me, Misty, I'll report Calhoun missing. I'll stop at the pound, place an ad in the Lake Placid News, and post a notice on all the bulletin boards in town."

Before she left, I said, "Betty, do you miss the decorating business? Are you glad you retired?"

Betty shifted her lips in a half-hearted frown, and said, "Sometimes I just want to buy a couch, flip through paint chips, or shuffle wallpaper and carpet samples. Most of the time, I'm glad to have my days to do what I want. Today, I feel like searching for a lost cat." Betty looked sadly into a corner of the kitchen and said, "I always loved Calhoun." When she used the past tense, I flinched. Betty blinked rapidly and added, "Calhoun the cat, that is. I always loved Calhoun the cat." I wondered why Betty repeated herself and emphasized missing the cat named Calhoun. It was as if she did not miss the man he was named after. With a sigh, she added, "Petting him reminds me of when AJ was alive."

I thanked Betty for her help and told her I still hoped that he'd show up within the house. We agreed it would be best to begin searching, nevertheless.

As Betty closed the door behind her, I yawned. My drinking had kept me up late and robbed me of my prime sleeping hours. My mind returned to thoughts of Calhoun. Initially, I loved the cat for the same reason Betty did, but before long I treasured the comfort and companionship that the good-natured feline offered.

Joanne and I sat back down at the table, and I said, "What's wrong, honey? You look worried. Maybe even scared."

"Oh. I didn't know it showed." The young woman with perfect posture crossed her legs, placed her elbows on the kitchen table, and her hands joined at the wrist, making her hands and arm into the shape of the letter Y. Then she perched her chin in the cup formed by her dainty hands. "I know that Doyle offered to take your shares of the company for nothing, so you could walk away free of the business." It wasn't like her to pout. Perhaps she couldn't help it. "I know you have every right, Misty but it would be such a shame. Nobody wants that to happen. Art is mad that Doyle made the offer on his own, without including him. The employee owners feel like Doyle is trying to pull the rug out from under them."

I stood up, walked to the cabinet, took out a glass, and filled it from the faucet. A moment later, a couple of aspirin spilled from a pill bottle and I hoped they would bring quick relief. "I'm sorry, Joanne. I've got such a headache this morning. Do you mind if I smoke?" After I lit another Winston, I said, "What do you and Rusty think?"

Joanne perked up, sat straight, and folded her hands in her lap. "We want to see you finish what you started, Misty. Our company was meant to go all the way to 100 percent, and it was meant to go the distance. If you give it to Doyle, it will go back to getting smaller every year. I don't know if you've noticed, but Rusty and Doyle argue a lot now and I'm afraid that Doyle is going to fire Rusty. He despises backtalking. If you finish the ESOP transformation, I'm sure we can make Adirondack Dowel into the business it was meant to become. I know we've got a long way to go and a short time to get there, but if we can complete Ithaca's order, will that show you that we deserve to be 100 percent?"

"It isn't that, honey. You always deserved it. I just wasn't able to lead you properly." I had much more to say, but Joanne cut me off.

"You're wrong, Misty. I'm sorry to interrupt, but don't *say* that. I believed in you. I still do."

"Here's the thing, Joanne. It isn't just the Ithaca order. It's also the bank. Even if we fill that order, the bank is determined to strangle the company. I should have told you sooner. I only found out recently myself." I told her the detailed story about my childhood rival, Lois Phelps, and then dropped the bomb about Lois' role as the Chairman of the bank's Board.

She tipped her head back, closed her eyes, and her mouth fell open for a second. Then she slowly returned to her usual posture, squinted at me, and said, "That explains a lot."

I thought about confronting her with a question. I couldn't shake the image of her snooping in Art's briefcase from my mind.

Joanne looked to the left and then to the right as if trying to decide whether to say something more to me. Perhaps she might have, only the doorbell rang once more. Of all days, why did everyone have to come calling on the one day in decades that I was hungover like a saloon girl in a television western?

Before I stood to answer, I asked Joanne to wait.

"I will, Misty. I brought checks for you to sign. I can't leave until you sign them."

When I opened the front door, the sad-looking man looked familiar. He had a long face, enormous earlobes, and droopy bags beneath his eyes. Altogether he looked like a basset hound in human form, and that association reminded me of who he was. It had been many years since I saw Kourtney Knox, though I wrote him a check every month.

The private investigator said, "I found them, Misty. It wasn't easy, but I located Bob Holstein's family. They have traveled to Lake Placid, and they want to meet you as soon as possible."

22

I hoped that Mr. Knox would bring them by tomorrow. I was eager to meet them but would prefer not to be hungover when they came calling.

At least the aspirin had blunted the ache in my head. I was far from feeling energetic, but caffeine kept me afloat. At almost 80, the zings were fierce, and too much caffeine made me jittery. I resolved never to have another hangover, as long as I lived. The thought hammered in my head, *I must quit the miserable habits of drinking and smoking, if it's the last thing I do. I should call my sponsor.*

Instead of signing the checks that Joanne had brought to the house, I checked on Four, who asked if he could visit with a nearby friend. I wanted to tell him *no* but it had been over a week since he had seen any of his classmates. He promised to return home if he became tired, and his friend was only a couple of blocks away from the house. Finally, I added, "If that pain in your leg returns, dial 911, and then call me at work."

When I arrived at Adirondack Dowel, I paused by the giant poster near the time clock. It had recently been updated. I frowned at the display. Three weeks had passed and five weeks remained before the largest order in the company's history had to be completed. It seemed even more impossible than it had when I first accepted Ithaca's order for three million dollars worth of our company's products. After subtracting one-third to be delivered by the contract manufacturer, of the remaining two million dollars, we had only managed to deliver $575,000 dollars or 29 percent. How could we possibly complete the order?

When I looked into the factory, I beamed with pride. Our employee owners always looked industrious to me, but with the extra help and high stakes, everyone worked even harder than ever before. Yet, it was not enough. If production continued at the pace of the previous week, we would still come up short. Over four hundred thousand dollars short. I turned and nodded at an employee passing by and didn't recognize them. The fact was, I didn't recognize many of the people I saw. Every slot in the time card holder was full, and several slots held multiple cards.

I stepped into the office, sat at my desk, and signed checks. Then I gathered the team to hold an unscheduled meeting. Art seemed agitated and I knew he disliked anything that disrupted his schedule. Doyle frowned. Many times in the past he had communicated what he thought about the negative value of meetings. I asked Joanne if she would find Rusty and bring him along as well. Doyle's eyebrows flashed angrily as if challenging my right to bring in one of his subordinates. I voiced, "He might have some ideas and I'd like to hear them."

When everyone was assembled, I praised the team for raising our production to $200,000 per week. "If we had produced at this rate from the start, we'd be closer to meeting Ithaca's challenge, but to catch up, we'll need more. Lot's more. What else can we do? Is there anything we've thought of that we haven't tried? Is there anything we haven't thought of? Is there anything we thought of but ruled out as impossible? Maybe we can find a way to make it happen, unlikely as it may seem."

Rusty grinned. "My uncles and cousins seem to be doing wonders. We could call in their uncles and cousins." He chuckled, tipped his head back, and said, "But it kind of reminds me of *The King, The Mice, and the Cheese.* I read that to the kids last night, and I'm reminded that sometimes, solving one problem creates another."

"It's worth the risk," I proclaimed. "We've got room for more tents in the field and more pallet stations outside the factory. Do they have woodworking equipment at home they can bring with them too?"

"Most do."

Joanne said that Stanley's brothers were hardworking. She added, "What if we asked him to bring his army friends? Many of them probably have their own equipment as well." Then Joanne turned to Doyle. She said, "You were also in the military. What if you asked your Veteran friends to work with us?"

Doyle nodded agreeably but didn't say anything. It was hard to disagree with Joanne, especially in public.

Then Joanne chirped, "I could ask some of the people who attended night school with me. I've kept in touch with many of them. They might be willing to help, but they probably don't know much about woodworking."

I said, "That's great Joanne. I'll ask Harold and Presto. Maybe they could help, and perhaps they work with people who could join us."

Doyle said, "What about the boy." He never liked to say my great-grandson's name. "He's a senior now, isn't he? Maybe he could send his friends down." Briefly, I tried to imagine Four and his Gothic friends mingling with the flannel and camo crowd of woodworkers.

I was glad to hear Doyle make a suggestion. I needed him on board to complete the order, but it was troublesome knowing that he'd stand a better chance of getting my stock for nothing if we failed. I realized that I hadn't given him my decision. Nor did I recall having formalized it myself, but after Joanne's plea, I returned to the company to do what I'd always done. Cheerleading.

Rusty said, "Let's hit Sears and snap up all the equipment we can." We researched the various stores we could visit and how far we'd have to drive to get there. Lake Placid wasn't near cities, plazas, malls, or department stores.

I asked the team, "What about the second and third shifts? Are they running at full speed? Are we producing around the clock?"

Doyle answered, "We never stop, but sometimes we slow down. People are getting tired, but we might be able to increase the overtime."

I wondered, "Would it make a difference if we made overtime double pay rather than time and a half?"

Art snarled. "If you do that, there won't be any profit on the business. What good is that?"

I nodded. "I know it's not good if we don't make a profit, but if we miss this deadline, we will lose our most important customer."

Art countered. "How about time and a half for the first 15 hours over, and double after that."

I turned to Doyle and then looked at Rusty, "Do you think that will make a difference?"

Rusty shrugged. Doyle said, "Let's give it a try. See how it goes."

I looked at Art, nodded, and said, "Thanks for the suggestion."

His nose twitched and it reminded me of Templeton the rat in the movie, *Charlotte's Web*. I tried to remember how old Four was when we saw that movie. Perhaps he was five or six years old at the time. I hadn't yet retired, and still lived in Washington, DC, but for some reason, I visited briefly while the movie was playing. For a moment, I wished that I had spent more time with him when he was little and forgot that I was in a business meeting.

Joanne sat forward, raised her eyebrows, and looked at everybody. She asked, "Can this really work?" She said something slightly different to each person. "It can, can't it?"

I nodded. The moment called for maximum optimism. I sprung to my feet. "Absolutely. It's just got to work." I felt light-headed and sat back down. I muttered, "Oh my," and told myself to leave the cheerleading to Joanne.

When everyone dispersed, Doyle remained behind. He

whispered, "You don't really believe it will work. You're putting it on, aren't you?"

I said, "It shall have to work, Doyle. We don't have a choice."

"What about my proposition?"

"I think you know the answer to that question, Doyle. Don't you?"

"I expect so. You've got moxie, I'll give you that, Lady Fingers."

Doyle stood to go, but I stopped him. "I know you're disappointed. It must have been difficult to expect one thing only to have something else happen. But I need you. Your company needs you. If this doesn't work out, your ESOP account will be worthless and you'll be unemployed, just like everybody else. Can I count on you? Can your fellow employee owners rely on your leadership?"

The man growled. "If they do what I say."

I said, "Are you referring to Rusty?"

Doyle snarled and nodded. "He used to be obedient and do as he was told, but ever since you started that ESOP he's grown increasingly uppity."

I rubbed my chin. "Uppity?"

Irritated, Doyle held his hands out beside him. "Like he's the only one that has the answers."

I smiled. "You know, Doyle. You've taught the man a lot through the years. Now he's proving what he learned. You won't agree with him all of the time, but that's the way it goes, don't you suppose?"

"I guess." Doyle frowned and tapped his wrist. "Gotta go. Clock's ticking. Work to do." Though he didn't say it, I heard, "Chop, chop!"

I turned and watched Art return to his desk. Joanne walked behind him, and as she did, I noticed that she turned her head and tried to focus on the papers at his desk. I tried to remember if I'd seen her do it previously and couldn't recall when it had ever happened before. I had always trusted Joanne completely. I thought that she was one in a million, the sort you could trust with anything. I believed that you could trust some people with your fortunes. You could trust some people with your secrets. You could trust some people with your dreams. You could trust some people with your heart and know they'd always be true. You could trust some people with your life. The people you could trust with anything were few and far between. I would have guaranteed Joanne was worthy of trust on every plane, but there she was. It looked like she was trying to spy on the company's confidential records, but what for?

My tongue passed across my teeth. My mouth still tasted awful and I supposed my breath was sour. As I searched my pocketbook for a mint, I thought, why would Joanne snoop? She has access to almost everything anyway. What was left? Maybe just payroll. I struggled to think of anything else that she didn't already get to see. Then I remembered telling Joanne about Lois, contrary to Winslow's instruction. I tried to remember her reaction, but my head began to ache again. I hated doubting the woman who made it clear to me that she saw me as her role model. If I were in her position, would I sneak a peak over Art's shoulder? I had to admit to myself that I *would* like to peek into his private property. Confound that mysterious briefcase. Why couldn't he leave the blasted thing at home?

***

When I left the office that night, I believed the employee owners could save the business. By the time I got home, I wasn't so sure. For better or worse, I had given Doyle my answer. Perhaps my family should have had a say in the matter. Adirondack Dowel was my problem, not theirs, but my decisions affected our personal finances.

Four got home shortly after I did. Presto had returned with

groceries and whipped up his specialty: spaghetti and meatballs with garlic bread and green beans. Harold returned home just as we were sitting down. The hearty meal improved my mood and settled my stomach. Even the dull headache that persisted despite the aspirin finally subsided. I felt better but weary and wished that I could climb in bed with Calhoun and call it an early evening. Instead, there was a knock on the door.

I had spent a decade looking forward to the moment when we would find Bob's family. They deserved to know what happened to him. I had forgotten that Mr. Knox had found Bob's loved ones, and now they were on the doorstep. I invited them in and offered them something to drink. I don't know what I expected. They were nothing like I had imagined. I figured they would be emotional. Perhaps they would weep. I thought they might even yell or scream, but they just sat on the sofa, stiff and wooden with eyes wide and unblinking. They reminded me of fish. They didn't look anything like the adorable scamp that wore a ski hat and worked at Adirondack Dowel a decade ago. They didn't ask questions or make noises that signified they heard or understood what I said. Sometimes they nodded, almost imperceptibly, so I went on. I told them everything I could recall about their lost son and brother, and then I started over and did it again. Finally, I said, "I don't know what else to tell you. I'm terribly sorry for your loss, but hopefully, you'll feel better knowing what happened to Bob."

Bob's mother meekly said, "His body was never found." It was hard to know whether she was making a statement or asking a question, though I had stated just that twice already. I nodded and they all stood, as if on cue, simultaneously.

All those years I prayed that we would find Bob's family, but as they stepped from the porch I thanked the heavens that they were gone. Still, the tragic loss of the young man pained me. A thousand times since he died, I wished that he were still alive so that I could mentor him and help him beat his addictions. Of all days to meet the Holsteins, it had to be the day following my relapse. And I still hadn't called my sponsor to let her know that I had succumbed to temptation.

I stepped to the dry bar and poured myself a large glass of brandy. I must quit all over again. Tomorrow I would give up booze. I didn't need my therapist's help to do that, after all. Did I? The day after, I would re-quit smoking. I carried my drink upstairs and sat at my dressing table and watched myself, drinking and smoking. I told myself, *This must never happen again.*

***

On Monday, three days later, I was served papers. I asked, "What is this?" It couldn't be good.

The process server said, "If you don't understand the documents, have your lawyer explain them to you." The advice seemed obvious. I asked Joanne to phone Winslow and see if he was available, and he told her that he could see me straight away.

When I arrived at Winslow's office, I handed him the beige mailer, unopened. I had no idea what the documents said, or who prepared them, but I felt an overwhelming sense of doom. I covered my mouth as he bent the metal clasp and unsealed the envelope. I turned away when Winslow removed the enclosed documents and stepped toward the window as he settled into the chair behind his desk.

I turned back for a moment and watched his face as he read and then sagged into the cushions of his sofa. A question came to my mind. Was it better to receive potentially bad news in a hurry or was it better to delay? Winslow's expressions were hard to describe, but I was sure I wasn't going to like it. Nobody had good news served in such a manner.

Winslow stood and made his way around his desk. "The Holsteins are suing you and the company for the wrongful death of Robert Jonquil Holstein. They claim you admitted as much, twice, and they have your statement recorded. Is this true?"

I told Winslow about their visit to the house and their strange behavior.

"Did you give them permission to make a recording?"

I strained to recall. "It was a long day and I was exhausted when the Holsteins stepped into my living room. Good heavens, Winslow, I might have said anything. It's not my fault that Bob is gone, is it?" I thought back to the bicentennial celebration and the sinking of our entry in the Moonlight Regatta. Did that qualify as business or pleasure? If Bob didn't work for Adirondack Dowel, he would never have been on that doomed craft. "Are they allowed to sue me?"

Winslow said, "It doesn't have to be your fault. Most anybody can sue, and sometimes the premises are weak. I'll have to think about this one, Misty." He sighed deeply and said, "Meanwhile, you'd better report this to the insurance company."

I knew enough about the law to ask about the statute of limitations. I asked, "Does the statute apply to wrongful death claims?"

Winslow winced as he answered. "I wish I knew, Misty. I don't handle these sorts of matters. I think so, but I'm unsure. The fact that the Holsteins only learned of their son's death might be a pertinent fact. And then there's the matter of a body. I think there has to be a body."

I said, "I don't care about your expertise, Winslow. I need you to take care of all my legal matters. Until this is over, I need to un-fire you, rehire you, and break up with you."

Winslow looked apprehensive and a little sad. "Are you sure, Misty?"

I covered my face and held in my tears. "Yes. Maybe when this is all over, I can re-fire you, and then we can fall in love again."

Winslow placed his hand between my shoulder blades and led me to the door. He said, "I haven't fallen *out of love* with you, but I understand, Misty. I know it is scary when somebody sues you. Try not to worry, alright darling?" I rested my head on his shoulder for several seconds and then I made my way down the steps and lit a smoke.

***

I returned to the offices of Adirondack Dowel after lunch in a dazed and frazzled state. I settled into the chair behind my desk and tried to think about what to do next.

In the next room, I heard a loud familiar voice. Joanne tried to stop him, but John Frederick Duncan said, "Don't bother to let her know I'm here, girlie. I'll show myself in."

I couldn't see through the walls but I could picture the man blustering down the hallway as if the walls were made of glass. He made himself comfortable in the guest chair and shuffled his posterior like a bird in a nest. I hadn't realized it previously, but his eyeballs seemed too big for his sockets. As he settled in, I imagined them popping out, and it was a gruesome visualization.

Gone was Mr. Duncan's usual pretense. "I'll get right to the point, Misty. The bank has been patient. We have waited years for the company to turn itself around." He looked around the office briefly, the way Betty looked at a room she had been hired to redecorate. Mr. Duncan continued, "I've explained to you at least half a dozen times what it would take to keep doing business with us. There's nothing more I can do to help you. The bank is calling your loans. You have ninety days to come up with the funds. If you don't pay the bank off by then, we shall foreclose."

The banker stood and shoved an envelope and a document on top of it across my desk. "Sign there."

"Why? What if I don't?"

He scoffed. "Read it, Misty. It's just a receipt. If you don't sign it, I'll have the papers served legally. You might as well just sign for it now."

I signed the paper and walked him to the door. We stopped beside the Xerox machine and I made a copy before letting him leave with the original.

I turned back toward my office, sat down, and stared at the

wall. The bank had called the loan. What would we do now? I thought, *Well, that's it then. In 90 days, we're done for.*

23

The first thing the next morning, I summoned the staff to another meeting. After a sleepless night of tossing and turning, my worried mind kept me awake most of the night. It was all I could do to get up in the morning and drag myself to work. It was time to tell the team the bad news.

Looking anybody in the eye was hard. Instead, I gazed at the floor in the center of the ring of chairs. Everyone was quiet, waiting for me to speak. My words sounded bleak even to me. "As you know, Mr. Duncan from the bank came to see me yesterday. The bank has called the loans. Now, we have 89 days to repay the bank or they will foreclose. Winslow has reviewed the documents. Our only hope is a miracle. I can't imagine where we'll find enough money to pay off the bank."

Rusty said, "What about the Ithaca order? When they pay us, won't we have enough money to pay the bank then?"

"We will have some, but we have a lot of debts to pay. We'll need half of it just to pay for the wood we purchased on credit. And who knows how quickly Ithaca will pay our invoice."

Joanne asked, "How much do we owe?"

"We owe about $200,000 for the mortgage on the land and building. Then there's $300,000 for the equipment loans. The worst part is our working capital line which funds our accounts receivable and inventory. We owe the bank $2,000,000 on the line. That totals $2.5 million."

"So, when Ithaca pays us $3 million, we'll have more than enough to pay the bank."

"No. First, we must pay the contract manufacturer a million, so we only stand to net $2,000,000. That leaves us half a million dollars short."

"What happens when the bank forecloses?"

"Winslow says that after foreclosure, the bank can operate the business, or sell off its assets. It will be up to them what happens when they take possession. Usually, banks prefer to liquidate everything and get as much money out as they can as quickly as possible. Winslow says we should expect that outcome."

The phone rang and our meeting ended. The caller was placed on hold and I retreated to my office to pick it up. It had been a while since I last spoke with the trustee and Mrs. Blankenfritter was hungry for an update. There was a lot to tell the woman. She didn't seem the slightest bit surprised to hear about our special order. How could she have already known about it?

Matter of factly, she asked, "What hope do you have of meeting the deadline?"

As I recounted our efforts to summon the forces and turn out the rod, I'm not sure I convinced myself let alone our skeptical trustee. Finally, I concluded, "We still have a long way to go and not much time to get it all done."

She grunted and then followed up with, "Is there anything else I should know?"

It was the sort of question a parent asked a child, and it was clear that she needed to know *everything*. First I told her about the Holstein family's lawsuit, and then I revealed Winslow's discovery which required telling the woman about Lois Phelps. Mrs. Blankenfritter was so quiet during our call that several times I had to ask if she was still there, which I hated to do.

"Of course I'm still here," she barked.

Then I told her about Mr. Duncan's visit and the bank's final demand.

"You already told me that." Mrs. Blankenfritter had had enough. Her voice boomed like thunder. "That's it. I'm coming to Lake Placid to put an end to all this nonsense." She slammed the phone and I pulled the receiver abruptly from my ear, looked at it for a moment, and then placed it on the rockers.

All I could think of was, *Now what?* Mrs. Blankenfritter was coming, but when? What did she mean? What would she do? What could she do? I knew what Mr. Duncan's vision of *the end* was, but what did Mrs. Blankenfritter mean when she said she planned to end the nonsense? The woman scared me and I think she had the same impact on everyone.

***

The phone rang again as the work day came to an end. A new gravestone had been installed in our cemetery plot. Replacing the vandalized monument right away should have been a higher priority, but I held out, hoping to install a towering obelisk. My dwindling savings forced me to accept a humble memorial. Instead of seating a larger headstone, the new marker was smaller than the one it replaced. There wasn't room on the stone tablet for extra sentiments or ornamentation, but at least everything was spelled correctly and the dates were right. It looked tidy and Father, Mother, and Johnny's names were deeply gouged into the surface.

After work, I visited the cemetery and spoke to the dead. "I'm sorry. I wish I could have done more for you. You deserve better than this." My knees sank to the spongy grass. With my open palms on the cold headstone, my head tipped forward, and a rare prayer on my lips, I shuddered as a wave of goosebumps fluttered across my skin. I got no farther than the salutation, "Dear God," before having the creepy feeling that somebody was watching me.

A raspy voice rattled behind me and made me scream. "I am going to destroy you."

It wasn't necessary to turn around to know who was there. I

pushed against the tombstone and stood. My body shook. In my imagination, the woman of my nightmares pulled a dagger from the folds of her cloak and thrust it into my chest. "What more can you do to me that you haven't done already?" I forced myself not to say her name.

She ignored my question. Her voice sounded closer. She must have stepped nearer. As I turned to face the woman who dreamed of my destruction, she said, "Why are you still here? You don't seem to get the message."

It didn't surprise me to see her shrouded in layers of loose black fabric. Draped over what looked like a nun's habit, was an overlay of intricate black lace. In the past, a sliver of her face and one of her eyes had been visible. Today I couldn't see her features. "All of this because of Preston Palmer? He's gone you know, and he never was worth all of this, to begin with."

"It's not about Preston anymore. Now it's about you. And it wasn't just my man. You stole my best friend and turned her against me too."

I didn't want to talk about Betty with Lois or hear about what imagined slight may have happened in grade school. "I know you are on the Board of Mirror Lake Bank."

Lois laughed with a deep rumble. "The bank may have given you 90 days, Misty. I'm not that generous. You have 24 hours. Get out now."

I gasped. Why didn't I think of it sooner? "That was you in the bathroom at Casa del Sol."

Hatred dripped from her words. "That's my favorite restaurant too."

"Those were the words on the brick that someone pitched through my window. Get out now." After repeating her ultimatum, I hesitated for a second and continued. "And scratched on the walls at Adirondack Dowel the night we were pillaged."

From the tone of Lois' voice, it sounded like she was gloating. "Who would do such things? If you are accusing me, I shall have to sue you for slander. It seems as if everybody wants to sue you, Misty." She venomously spat out my name. Then she whispered, "You'll never prove a thing. I don't commit crimes. I just wish them forth, but I'm tired of waiting. We're not getting any younger. I won't warn you again. Get. Out. Now."

A swift wind kicked up, a fog rolled in, and Lois backed into the mist. It was as if the whole thing was just my imagination but I pinched myself hard. It wasn't a dream. Lois had appeared in the cemetery and threatened me, again. Why didn't I tackle her when I had the chance? My head shook in disgust at the image in my mind of two old women in a physical battle to the death. It was like a horror scene from a gothic novel. I walked away from the cemetery toward the Mustang and thought of the books Four liked to read. I'd read far too many of his favorites.

I turned, looked back into the cemetery, and spoke to Father from the entrance. "Your soul will have to rest in peace. I don't know how, but I shall find a way to save the company. Not for your sake but for the sake of its current and future owners. I just wish I knew how."

***

The next twenty-four hours made me jumpy, but having survived Lois' latest curse, I began to relax.

Longing for Calhoun, and removing layers of makeup at the end of the day, made me face the facts. It was hard to accept that the cat was missing, yet the longer he was gone, the more hopeless the chances of finding him.

When the phone rang, I sprang from my chair. The calm moment I needed was interrupted and my nerves were frayed. Tranquility had merely been an illusion.

A relieved sigh parted my lips as Winslow's comforting voice greeted me. After exchanging pleasantries, he suggested asking Betty for a loan, certain that she'd be glad to help. Appealing to my oldest friend hadn't occurred to me, but why not? Since returning to the Adirondacks, Betty had become like a sister, if not a sister-in-law. Would asking for financial help be beyond the bounds of our friendship? Would she be willing to lend me the money?

Winslow thought the request would please her and chided me for calling the day over so early in the evening.

His hint wasn't lost on me. "Why don't I take a walk and ask her now?"

"That's a good idea, Misty."

After refreshing my makeup, and a couple of blocks stroll along the village sidewalks, my finger pressed the button and I heard Betty's doorbell chime. She didn't answer. There was no other sound from inside, so I knocked on her door. The lights were on and her car was in the driveway. Why didn't she come to the door?

Instead of returning home, Winslow's voice appeared in my head. "There's no time like the present."

With a glance at the flower box where Betty kept a spare key, my hand turned the doorknob and found that it wasn't locked. The hinges creaked as the antique door opened. I stepped inside and saw the back of Betty's head. She was sitting in her favorite chair and must have dozed off. The urge to tiptoe away was strong, but instead, my legs stepped forward. Hopefully, Betty would forgive me for the unplanned visit, letting myself in, and waking her from her after-dinner nap.

When I peered around the edge of her chair and saw the look on her face, I screamed and dropped my pocketbook. Despite my hysteria, Betty didn't move. The look of horror on her face made me shriek repeatedly. I backed away, but couldn't peel my eyes off of her. My clumsy legs tripped over an ottoman and I scrambled back to my feet. My hand covered my mouth and then I froze in place.

Betty was elegantly dressed in her favorite red gown. Her hair was freshly-dyed and she wore all of her most glamorous jewelry.

How strange, she never wore more than one or two well-chosen accessories at a time, and her favorite necklace, the one she wore every day, was missing. It wasn't like her to leave the door unlocked, but the hardest thing to comprehend was the horrified expression on her face. It looked like she had witnessed something so awful and shocking that it had scared her to death. But the way her arms and legs were positioned made it look like she had sat down to relax, tipped her head back, and peacefully expired. Her expression of terror indicated otherwise.

My eyelids fluttered but it wasn't possible to blink away my shock. I sucked in air so hard it forced a coughing spell.

How did this happen? I glanced at the telephone, then looked at the coffee table and saw a document titled Last Will and Testament next to a mostly empty teacup with Betty's lipstick on the brim. My hands reached for the vessel and I cradled the cold cup in my palms. How long had Betty been sitting there dead?

The reflection of my silhouette appeared on the surface of the liquid at the bottom of the old-fashioned cup and the room began to spin. The buzzing sound of an electrical current rattled me, but my grip on the delicate antique held firm. My eyes closed and I pictured the scene as if replaying a memory that seemed ancient and modern at the same time. Lois presided over a document signing, accompanied by four men. Behind Betty, one man poured liquid from a dark brown bottle. Another man held a gun pointed at Betty's chest. I watched as Betty nervously struggled with the pen in her hand, and then the other two men signed as witnesses. The man behind Betty delivered her beverage.

In my hallucination, Lois said, "Now there. That wasn't so hard, was it? Let's celebrate with a nice relaxing cup of tea. Drink up, Betty."

Obediently she sipped, her hand still shaking.

"That won't do. Why don't you drink it all? Then I'll leave you alone."

Betty gulped down three-quarters of the tea and set the cup on the table and said, "I don't feel so good."

"That's because of the poison, I suppose."

That's when Betty's expression froze in horror.

My hands shook as the teacup dropped onto its matching saucer. How barbaric. Poisoning an enemy seemed like something out of the middle ages, not modern times. Though my eyes had seen what happened, who would believe me? Was it shock or the toxicant that killed Betty? I hurried to the phone and dialed 911, then rang Winslow with the tragic news.

While waiting for the authorities to arrive, it occurred to me that my strange visions over the last ten years all connected objects to their past. The first time it had happened was with Johnny's cufflinks in Father's office. I thought back to the intricate picture frame in the banker's office and then, Four's discovery of the spiral medallion. I tried to recall other times it had happened. Would it be possible to concentrate on objects and conjure up their past intentionally?

After spending hours with the policemen, Winslow walked me home. I sputtered, "She seemed so healthy the last time I saw her. It seemed like she would outlive us all." It was hard to believe that Betty was gone. I don't remember how our conversation ended, but recall crawling under the blankets, curling up, and sobbing. It was tough to lose a cherished, childhood friend, even if we had drifted apart for a couple of decades before coming back together in our twilight years.

***

In the morning, the need to escape from town overwhelmed me. Perhaps that's just what Lois wanted. Whenever my eyes closed, the terror on Betty's face appeared in my mind. Would a few hours away make me feel better? Perhaps that was the only thing that could settle my nerves. My brain searched for a quick excuse.

Before long, I thought about how to show my appreciation to

the laborers who worked for Adirondack Dowel, and their friends and relatives who had joined up temporarily. They worked so hard, they deserved something special. Baking something special would be nice, but I wasn't in the mood to make lemon squares or brownies. Everyone appreciated fudge from the Candy Man in Jay when we celebrated the ESOP transaction. Why not make a short shopping excursion?

Four asked if he could come with me. He had his license but didn't get many chances behind the wheel. When he asked if he could drive the Mustang, I hesitated. I never liked riding shotgun and people complained about my behavior as a passenger. Preston hated riding with me so much, it was probably one of the reasons why he ran away to California with Eloise decades ago.

"Forget I asked," Four said.

I flung the keys at him and they hit his chest. He clutched them before they fell away. "Don't be silly. I want you to drive. But you know I'm a nervous passenger. I shall try to behave myself." Fortunately, Harold and Presto had taught Four to drive. I wouldn't have been able to stand doing that.

He said, "I don't get to drive the Mustang very often." Harold drove a pickup truck, Presto had an old sedan, and Four used whatever he could borrow at the moment. Mostly, Four walked to wherever he needed to go. He added, "Do you want me to put the top down, GiGi?"

"Why not?"

As a child, Four loved watching the top collapse behind the back seat, but as a teenager, he seemed far less impressed as he flipped the switch by his left leg.

I buckled my seatbelt as Four let off the clutch and hit the gas. My twelve-year-old steed belched and bucked forward into traffic. I gripped the armrest and gasped.

Four said, "Sorry, GiGi. I'm used to Dad's pokey jalopy."

I chuckled, glad there wasn't another car on our side street. "She's a wild one."

He glanced at me, raised an eyebrow, and said, "And powerful."

We waited for a while before we could pull onto Main Street, blocked by the summer traffic on Olympic Drive. We inched past the Speed Skating Oval, the Town Hall, and Art Devlin's Olympic Inn before we were able to pick up speed going out of town on Route 86.

Behind us, a pair of reckless drivers gunned past us on the straightaway, barely making it back in line and forcing the oncoming traffic to slow down. I thought I heard the drivers hoot and holler above blaring music. The brown Ford Fairmont reminded me of the car that sped away when I watched from the window after vandals pitched a brick through the window. I didn't recognize the red Chevy Impala. They screeched into the first parking area along the roadside, tires spinning, gravel flying, and the drivers added to the commotion by laying on the horns and yelling.

Four glanced nervously into the rearview mirror, and I was glad to leave the erratic drivers behind.

By the time we reached the turnoff to Connery Pond, the Fairmont and Impala were upon us again. They whizzed past us and slammed into the next pullover, this time on the left, just before the first crossing of the West Branch of the AuSable River. Four glanced out his window as we passed the motorists. The pitch of his voice elevated, and he said, "That jerk flipped us the bird."

As we passed River Road which would have taken us in the direction of Adirondack Dowel, I said. "Are you okay? Do you want to pull over?"

Four made a face, pitched his shoulders forward slightly, and continued along. He said, "I hope we've seen the last of *them*."

I blurted, "Me too."

By the time we reached Monument Falls, they were back. Four slowed down. The drivers left the pavement, darting between oncoming cars, roared along the short cutout where a historical mile marker commemorated the Adirondack Forest Preserve's centennial, and dashed back into line ahead of us, then braked, dangerously, forcing Four to slam the brake pedal. My head crashed into the dashboard and the wild motorists took off ahead of us. I complained, "It's a wonder nobody was killed, on the roadway or the pull-off. Tourists often amble about the monument. Slow down, honey."

Less than two minutes away, we saw the dunderheads again. "If I didn't know better, I'd say they were targeting us."

Frantically, Four said, "What should I do, GiGi? Stop? Turn around and go the other way?"

I had no idea what to tell him. Lamely, I said, "Whatever you want to do. We can shop another day." I didn't have a good feeling about the situation but was indecisive about whether my worries were ahead or behind us.

Four bravely decided. "I'll just go slow." He set his jaw and gripped the steering wheel tightly. I squirmed helplessly in the passenger seat. Four added, "If they want to zoom back and forth past us, they can. If it happens again, I'll turn around."

I was glad he chose and said, "Very well. Good idea."

The Fairmont ripped past us and the Impala nudged up behind us. The Fairmont braked and the driver behind us hit the gas. I cringed as the Mustang's bumpers crunched into the other cars. The Fairmont sped away as the Impala gunned past us. Four stopped in the middle of the road. I spied another vacant roadside pull-off just ahead and pointed. I said, "If the car still runs, pull over there, okay?"

Four hit the gas, forgetting to check for oncoming traffic. The Mustang flew across the road, just barely missing the front bumper of a logging truck. Within the safety of the parking area overlooking the river, Four collapsed onto the steering wheel with a relieved gasp. "Okay, okay. Okay. We made it."

I twisted about in my seat looking out the windows. "Do you think you can turn us around so we're facing in the other direction?

Then, when you feel up to it, let's go home."

The novice driver's nerves were shot. It wasn't a smooth maneuver. His delicate footwork on ice skates was nothing like his pedal mashing as he stomped on brakes, gas, and clutch, see-sawing us into position so we could return the way we came. Four was not fast enough.

One of the predatory drivers slammed into the back of the Mustang so forcefully, my car was pitched over the edge, head first into the swift currents of the icy river. Four screamed at the impact. The last thing I could remember was a sense of panic at the thought of drowning.

The next thing I knew, somebody was lightly tapping their fingers against my cheek. Sitting up and seeing my wrecked car partially submerged shocked me. The realization that I was sitting on a sandbar in the middle of the river came slowly. The fisherman beside me was a stranger. Did he pull me from the car? But what about Four? I looked back at the car, and nobody was there. I shrieked and the fisherman covered his ears. "The boy, is he alive?" My body crumpled and I sobbed into my hands. "Where is he?"

The stranger shook my shoulders gently and pointed up the riverbank. In a thick accent I couldn't recognize, he said, "I tink he vill be alright." Despite the stranger's assurance, I couldn't tell whether Four was dead or alive. He was strapped to a stretcher and a pair of medics trudged up a slippery slope to a waiting ambulance. My mouth hung open. How had I failed to hear the blaring sirens?

As the ambulance sped away, I lurched and pleaded with the fisherman. "Why didn't they take me too?" He told me they had another patient on board and would radio dispatch for another ambulance to get me.

My legs were wet. I shivered, crossed my arms, and huddled into my limbs. It didn't matter what happened to me anymore. I prayed like never before. "Please, God. Please take care of my baby." I glanced at the gold watch on my wrist, thought of the day they told me that Junior was dead, and wished for a stiff drink to appear in my hand.

Was Four alright? Did they know about his medical conditions? Certain he would not survive, I grieved his death beside the flowing river.

24

My injuries were limited to a couple of scratches and a mild concussion. After a quick check-up at the hospital, I was released.

The police noted everything we remembered about the boys who weaved through traffic. We didn't see whoever knocked us into the river, but there was hope the detectives would be able to track down the delinquents, based on our descriptions of the brown Fairmont and the red Impala.

The Mustang hit the river on Four's side of the car, and a giant boulder pressed into the car near his feet breaking his left leg and several bones in his right foot. Because of ongoing worries about blood clots, Four was re-admitted to the hospital. They wanted to make extra certain that his blood thinner dosage was properly balanced. Anything that might cause a blood clot concerned them, and they were afraid he had internal bleeding in addition to his broken bones. Four was furious when they said he might need to remain hospitalized for another week. The fact that his leg was broken again made him angrier still. He wanted to know who tried to kill us and why. So did I. Four's emotions bounced between anger and depression. Anger gave way to detachment and he frequently appeared vacant, as if he were elsewhere. When he did speak, he kept saying, "I'll never get to the Olympics, GiGi. It's not fair. How could this happen to me?"

I didn't have any answers for him and tried to get him to agree to see a psychologist. When he protested, I said, "It doesn't mean there's anything wrong with you, but it's helpful to have someone to talk to. Someone who you can share your most personal troubles with. Believe me, Four, it makes a big difference. There were a lot of hard times I wouldn't have survived if it weren't for my weekly appointments." I still hadn't spoken to my sponsor, though I had managed to quit drinking again on my own.

Four refused with a single word, despite my protest. "Don't decide so quickly. Give it some thought and we'll talk again." He didn't argue. Instead, he spent too much time on his back, with his hands resting on his chest, above the metallic pendant. Often he didn't seem to realize he had company and stared blankly at the ceiling.

My frequent trips to Bookstore Plus for dark epic fantasy novels provided Four's only distraction. Thankfully, the bestselling authors were prolific. What more could I do for him? I couldn't be away from work too long and tending to Betty's funeral was a troubling distraction.

Winslow demanded an autopsy and contested Betty's will. I didn't know that Winslow represented her until after she had died, but he was positive that the last will and testament she signed on her date of death did not represent her final wishes. He insisted the police interview the witnesses, but despite the addresses shown in the document, they could not be located.

***

Two weeks later, Mrs. Blankenfritter barreled through the front doors of Adirondack Dowel like a western gunslinger between batwing doors. She stood as if poised for a wrestling match in the middle of the waiting room and shouted, "What in the high Heavens is going on in this joint?" When I came around the corner from my office, Doyle, Art, and Joanne stood agape, not knowing what to do about the unexpected presence of our ESOP trustee. It

259

slipped my mind to tell them she was coming.

Her lip curled and she said, "In all my years of working with companies, I've never seen anything like this one." She sneered at Art and said, "I always said there's something fishy going on around here."

With a righteous sniffle, she planted her hands on her hips and turned to face Doyle. "The management here leaves a lot to be desired." She jutted her face forward at the general manager as if daring him to talk back to her.

Her expression softened as she turned toward Joanne. "Strangely, Adirondack Dowel is also my very favorite client. There's a wholesome goodness and heart beating beneath the surface, and you can feel the warmth of it when you walk through the doors."

Without looking at me, she pointed directly at me and said, "This poor woman deserves better. After all that she has done for you, this company, and its employees, she deserves far better than the lousy earnings this company makes. She shouldn't have to toil endlessly, long after her retirement. Did you all know that she works for free? Who does that? She doesn't even draw a salary from this company."

She slowly spun around until she was facing Joanne once more. "I've stood in that factory for hours and watched the employee owners at work. You have a better team than any other company I've ever set foot in. I don't know about those galoots outside, but that's another matter."

Mrs. Blankenfritter turned toward me. "Your customers love you, your employees adore you. People here work hard. You are in an important industry and the economy is good. This company should be making all kinds of money. Banks should be begging for your business, not demanding their loans be repaid. For the longest time, I couldn't figure out what was wrong with the place. Now I know. Get a chair and meet me in Misty's office."

Nobody moved. The trustee growled. It started with a low

grumble and ended with a roar and finally, she barked. "Now. Don't make me angry." If she wasn't already mad, I would hate to see what happens when she's furious.

Feebly, Art said, "I can't attend a meeting. I have important errands I have to run today."

Mrs. Blankenfritter made a face at him that I'd never seen before and curtly said, "If it's that important to you, you can go twice tomorrow. My meeting is *mandatory*." It was strange how she emphasized the first syllable of the word.

To Joanne, Mrs. Blankenfritter said, "A nice young man is standing near my car in the parking lot. Would you please send him in, and then get your husband as well? I think he should join us too."

Moments later, in my office, everyone cowered on their chairs with their backs against the wall. I had left my seat empty for the trustee since she was clearly in charge of this meeting. Mrs. Blankenfritter pointed at the empty chair and grunted. "You. Sit there." Rusty and Joanne filed into my crowded office and sat beside Doyle and Art who shivered like he was standing naked on the top of Whiteface Mountain during a blizzard in February.

Mrs. Blankenfritter turned impatiently and called out into the hall. "Confound it, where are you, man? There's never a cop around when you need one. Humph."

Officer Wideawake stepped into the room and stood in the corner where Father's bust once stood on a pedestal beneath a lacy tablecloth. Mrs. Blankenfritter said, "Attaboy, *Dumpling*."

Wilder Wideawake smiled. It was as if he knew what was coming. Had she known the policeman a long time or given him the doughy nickname only now?

I wondered where she would sit but it quickly became apparent that she intended to stand. She stood in the doorway blocking the exit like a prison guard. I was in awe of the powerful woman, though I had no idea what would happen next.

She spun her pinky finger in her ear, looked closely at a flake of earwax, and flicked it into the air.

Like most older people, I was usually cold, but it was beginning to get hot in my office. Had Mrs. Blankenfritter somehow managed to hit the thermostat?

Despite the heat, Art sat with his briefcase on his lap and shivered.

Mrs. Blankefritter said, "Let's begin."

I didn't dare to crack a smile but I was amused. Whatever was happening clearly began the moment she blasted through the front door.

She pinched her chin and said, "Where should I start?" Despite her words, I would have been shocked if she didn't have her agenda memorized.

"Let's start with this. When I first started coming here, I was so touched by everyone's generosity. Not just at Adirondack Dowel, but all of Lake Placid. Every year since I learned about the St. Kateri Orphanage, I've been making personal donations. Twice a year, at Easter and Christmas, I mailed a check. It warmed my heart to know that I was helping to provide for parentless Indian children. The last time I came to visit Adirondack Dowel, I allowed extra time before returning home. I took a long, circuitous route, and passed through the lovely town of Wanakena." The trustee looked directly at the business manager. Sweat beaded on his forehead. She continued. "Has anyone ever visited that town on Cranberry Lake? It's really quite beautiful. As much as you care about your charity, you *should* have visited the place."

Art stared at Mrs. Blankenfritter's shoes. He did not have the strength to meet her gaze.

Mrs. Blankenfritter continued with an uncharacteristic lilt. It was as if she were reading a fairy tale or telling children a story. "Guess what happened next?" She lifted her hand, formed a fist, and knocked on an invisible door. "I found the address where I had been mailing my donations and I rapped at the entrance. I met a woman named Lois and she did not invite me in."

Art closed his eyes and refused to open them.

"There is no orphanage and there never was. You've been hoodwinked. Gobsmacked. Swindled. Get the picture? You couldn't help yourselves. But me, I should have known better."

Art wobbled to his feet. "I have to get to the bank."

Through clenched teeth, Mrs. Blankenfritter said, "Sit down, Mr. Boykins." She emphasized his last name.

"I can't be held against my will."

"I agree. This is a free country. Do you work for Adirondack Dowel, or have you quit your job?"

Art didn't answer.

"I will assume, based on your silence, that you have not quit and therefore will continue to attend my mandatory meeting. If, at any time, your employment status changes, let me know." Mrs. Blankenfritter winked at me. It wasn't clandestine. I was certain everyone saw.

"Now, back to my story. When I got home, I hired a private investigator. He's really more of an auditor. I thought I might have a little work for him to do. You won't believe the things I've learned since the last time I was here."

The trustee had a way of leaving pauses and building suspense.

"You'd probably rather I skip the details and get to the good part. I found twelve vendors that don't exist. Misty signs checks for all the rest of the suppliers. Guess who signs the checks for twelve mysterious vendors that don't appear to exist anywhere on earth? But *I* know where those checks were sent. I also found a troublesome customer. It's one of your biggest. Instead of mailing checks to Adirondack Dowel in Lake Placid, somehow their payments arrive in Wanakena. The money does not end up in *your* bank account. You also have half a dozen employees you've never met. That's because they don't exist, except in Wanakena. Would you like to see pictures of the woman who picks up all of the mail at that address?"

Polaroids appeared in Mrs. Blankenfritter's hands like magic, and she slid them across the desk. It was unmistakably, Lois

Phelps. I passed the photos around the room.

"Guess where you can find the proof?"

Joanne pointed at Art's briefcase. "It's in there."

Art said, "I quit." He clutched his briefcase handle and stepped toward the door. "Excuse me," he pleaded.

Mrs. Blankenfritter said, "You may go but the briefcase stays here."

Art squeaked. "That's my personal property. I must insist that it remain with me."

"I disagree."

"I want to phone my lawyer."

The trustee said, "Wouldn't you rather call your mother?"

Art grimaced and his teeth chattered. "What's my mother got to do with anything?"

It was as if Mrs. Blankenfritter had punched him in the gut. She pulled an envelope from a skirt pocket, removed the contents, and unfolded an invoice and a copy of a check. "Last year when you got a new briefcase, the company paid for it, therefore the briefcase belongs to Adirondack Dowel. If you would like to open the attaché, we can go through its contents, and of course, you may take with you any personal belongings. Since you have chosen to resign, here's your letter of resignation."

She pulled another envelope from her pocket and he said, "I will not sign it."

"So be it, then," she said. "We have plenty of witnesses. Leave the briefcase on your chair." She stepped aside allowing him to pass. While he was still in range and able to hear her, she said, "Open the briefcase, Joanne. The combination on the left is 5-1-7 and on the right, it is 7-1-5."

Joanne said, "I know."

Mrs. Blankenfritter smiled. I had seen her do so before, but it did not happen often.

I could hear Art scurry away like mice in the walls of an old home. He cleared the front doorway before the second clasp flapped open. Mrs. Blankenfritter said, "Don't touch anything in the briefcase, dear. You'd better let the nice policeman have it. I believe it has become what you would call, *evidence*."

I shook my head as if in disbelief but hadn't the slightest doubt. "So all these years, Art has been embezzling money from the company."

"That's right. According to my calculations, last year alone, he got away with half a million dollars, and that doesn't count the fake charity contributions. What a racket?!"

"What was that bit about his mother?"

Mrs. Blankenfritter made a face at me that made me feel like I was the dumbest person on the planet. Perhaps it was so. "You still haven't figured it out, have you?"

My head shook.

"Art's mother is Lois Phelps. She was briefly married to Albert Boykins."

Several of us covered our mouths in surprise.

Mrs. Blankenfritter seemed to be enjoying herself immensely. "But wait, there's *more*. She also married a man named Alan Duncan. Lois is *also* your banker's mother." She turned to Officer Wilder Wideawake and said, "Are you ready for our next appointment? Let's drop by the bank, shall we, Dumplin'? Come along, Misty."

***

The trustee had planned her visit to the North Country very well. It was no accident that the Audit Committee of the Mirror Lake Bank's Board of Directors happened to be meeting at precisely the moment of our arrival. Our police escort convinced the receptionist to admit our entry. Lois was silent when we entered but John Frederick Duncan pronounced our presence, "Highly irregular."

Mrs. Blankenfritter stood inches from the furious banker and said, "Quite the contrary, Mr. President. It is most appropriate. You see, audit committees are most concerned about allegations of fraud, and I've got a beauty of a case to present."

I couldn't look directly at Lois but stole furtive glances. Her face was more heavily made than mine, yet still, I could see three deep scars on her cheek that I had never seen before. Perhaps they were recent and had become infected. She tried to tilt her head so that her hair would conceal that side of her face. It felt different being nearby and in brightly-lit commercial space. Her silence didn't fool me. I remembered every threat, spoken and implied.

As the trustee presented her case and backed it up with evidence, the other members of the Audit Committee became agitated and concerned. Lois's head lowered, bit by bit and her eyes drilled into me through the strands of her hair. She said nothing to anyone. I wouldn't have been surprised if she had the ability to melt a gaping hole in the wall of the bank with her smoldering stare. John Frederick inched his way toward the door, and Mrs. Blankenfritter pointed at him without turning around. Did she have eyes in the back of her head, a sixth sense, or extra sensory perception?

"Officer Wideawake, apprehend that suspect."

If she had instructed the policeman to shoot John Frederick Duncan, would he have emptied his revolver into the banker? It wasn't hard to imagine.

The vicechair of the bank demanded an immediate, emergency meeting of the full Board. Then he adjourned the Audit Committee's meeting and instructed the recording secretary to locate the Board Members' emergency contact information.

Officer Wideawake cuffed President Duncan and guided him to a comfortable chair in the corner. Then he radioed the precinct for reinforcements.

Lois finally found her voice and excused herself. "I must visit the ladies' room."

Mrs. Blankenfritter cheerfully said, "I as well. You know how us ladies are."

I wanted to warn the trustee about Lois. The more time went by, the more sure I was that she carried a sharp blade somewhere beneath the folds of her mysterious cloaks. But even with a dagger, I would bet on the trustee's physical advantage. Lois was, after all, as old as me.

Despite the irregularity, Mrs. Blankenfritter and I attended the entire special meeting of the bank's Board of Directors. After firing the bank president, the vicechair carefully traced his finger down the official bylaws of the bank, making certain to adhere to the strict rules required to expel Lois Phelps from the Board. The police escorted the accused mother and son from the building and, I hoped, put them behind bars.

Then Mrs. Blankenfritter asked if she might say a few words. "Given the personal vendetta of former Chair Phelps and former President Duncan, would the bank reconsider its action with respect to Adirondack Dowel? The bank and our company were both deceived, defrauded, and misled. If it weren't for embezzlement, the company would have made more than enough to meet the bank's customary lending requirements."

We watched as the Board voted the vicechair into the new position of chair. Then we were asked to step into the hallway while they decided what action to take regarding Adirondack Dowel's loans. When we returned, we learned that the bank was no longer calling our debt. I asked for a document for my lawyer, and then I gasped. "Good heavens, Winslow. I should have phoned him hours ago."

As we departed from the adjourned meeting, Mrs. Blankenfritter smiled and said, "You have a lot to tell the man."

"Would you help me?

"Only if you call me Alice from now on, partner."

I raised an eyebrow.

Alice shrugged. "We are partners, if you think about it, Misty.

You own half the company, and I represent the other half." She glanced at me briefly and said, "Has it hit you, Misty? Do you know what these revelations are going to do to the stock value?"

I shook my head. Guessing what the valuation firm would come up with never had been my forté.

Alice tipped her head forward like a schoolteacher and said, "If you add half a million dollars a year to your income projections, you're likely to find the value of the company comes in at two or three million dollars. But watch out, Misty. If I'm going to buy the other half of your company, it won't be easy. I'm a shrewd negotiator."

"If it weren't for you, Alice, this company wouldn't be worth a cent."

"I'm just a softie. You know that, don't you, dear?"

"Yes, in your own way. You are one in a million, Alice."

As we stepped onto the village sidewalk, Alice said, "It's time to name a successor, Misty."

"You are right, as usual, Alice."

"I know who the next president of Adirondack Dowel is going to be and you do too, don't you?"

"I've been turning it over in my head for years. It seems impossible, but I keep coming down to the same answer."

"Write it down. I'll do the same. Let's see if we agree."

We turned our backs to one another and recorded our votes.

25

We traded papers, and Mrs. Blankenfritter slowly unfolded her vote. Her fingers worked faster than mine and I heard a grunt of approval while reading the name she wrote: Joanne. I looked at the trustee and said, "No doubts? No hesitation?"

"No, Misty. She's *clearly* the one."

That night, Alice and I met Winslow for a late dinner at the Woodshed. He raised his eyebrow when he heard about selecting Joanne Buckpitt to lead the company. I praised her organizational skills and nurturing nature. Alice complimented Joanne's judgment, fearlessness, and inquisitiveness. Alice added, "When I told everyone there was something fishy going on, it was *that* girl who figured it out. One day she called me, told me what she knew, and what she suspected. After that, we spoke every couple of days. She worried about violating your trust, but I assured her that she was doing you a favor. As we built a mountain of evidence, I got to know the young woman very well. She's not just one of sixty-five employee owners. I think she's one in a million. We're lucky to have her."

Winslow nodded and the expression on his face communicated that Alice had convinced him.

After conveying the details of Alice's confrontations with the management and our visit to the bank, Winslow brought up the Holstein matter. He looked sympathetic and said, "I feel bad for them, but I don't think they have a case. I believe the statute of limitations protects the company in this matter. We could offer to settle, but I don't think there's much merit there."

I groaned and clutched my stomach. "Oh, Winslow. I don't want to fight with the Holsteins. Bob peddled our entry in the Moonlight Regatta entry. He may have been a volunteer, but it was *for* the company. Nothing can replace Bob, but I'd like to see the Holsteins get a good deal. It may not be the company's fault, but I should have insisted the float was safe. It *is* my fault. Bob was a little wild at times, but he would have outgrown it."

"But Misty, they're asking for $2,000,000."

My hands hit my cheeks with a slap. "Two million dollars! Good heavens, Winslow. I feel guilty about Bob and I'm sorry. So, so sorry. But that wouldn't leave anything for the employee owners or my family. What do you think the claim is worth?"

"I think 10,000 would be a generous offer."

I argued, "They should get more than that, Winslow. A lot more than that."

Alice interrupted. "Stay out of it, Misty. Let the lawyers negotiate the settlement. When they get to a final number, if you'd like to increase it we can talk about it then. Insurance should cover it anyway."

I slapped a hand to my face and glanced at Winslow. "I forgot to tell the insurance company. Winslow told me to notify them. I'll have Joanne type them a letter tomorrow."

***

As June came to an end, it was astonishing to see the crowds of people who showed up at Adirondack Dowel. I wandered, bewildered through a sea of woodworkers, inside and beyond the factory walls. I recognized a few of our employee owners among their families and friends. The mob chanted as they worked. "Save our company!" I frowned at the webs of extension cords strung across the lawn and gawked at the city of tents haphazardly pitched wherever lawn space could be found.

What earlier seemed impossible now seemed inevitable. I made my way to the poster by the time clock. Rusty stepped up beside me and said, "Get a load of that!" He pointed at yesterday's output and the cumulative total. "We're going over the top by the end of the day."

I turned toward Rusty and my head floated from side to side. I shook his good hand and said, "I can't believe it. Can you?"

He winked at me and said, "At first I wouldn't have, but a few days ago I began to. Radical, eh?"

My arm swept toward the industrious crew. "How many of them are related to you?"

"Gosh, Misty. My whole family tree showed up. I got relatives here I never met before." He laughed uproariously and said, "Call the truckers. It's time for a convoy. Look out Andy Branchport! Time to fill those warehouses."

Two days later, Adirondack Dowel looked like a TV western ghost town after the gold mine was played out. Somehow, we delivered the impossible order. The last truck departed for Ithaca, forty-eight hours shy of the deadline. Later, Doyle reported that Stuart Franklin phoned him with begrudging congratulations. We had protected our most important account from defecting to the competition.

***

I had hoped to consummate the final ESOP deal on the Fourth of July. Since our first transaction was inked on Independence Day, it seemed fitting, but it wasn't to be.

The trustee advised us to wait. "The pending lawsuit is bound to sink the appraisal."

Winslow told the trustee not to worry about the lawsuit, but

271

then a letter arrived from the insurance company. They had not received payment on our policy. After sending several notices, the policy had lapsed, and therefore, there was no coverage for the Holstein's wrongful death claim. Art blamed Joanne for being careless with the paperwork and Joanne claimed that she never saw any notices from the insurance company.

Ted Drake said, "Other than the valuation, everything is ready. All we have to do is fill in the blanks, dot the i's, and cross the t's."

Winslow still believed that the Holsteins claim would settle for a nominal amount, but the trustee insisted on waiting until the settlement amount was known.

At Adirondack Dowel, business had returned to normal within the factory walls. Outside, it would take weeks to clean up the garbage and abandoned possessions. I couldn't imagine the lovely lawn ever returning to the way it was, but it was worth it to see what our employee owners and those who care about them could do when their backs were against the wall.

Four was in a sour funk. He never had been a complainer, but his dark mood was evident. His head hung low, his gaze was perpetually dull, and he sat around with a Sony Walkman clamped to his head. He didn't feel like reading or helping me piece puzzles together. He never sought out conversations and said as little as possible whenever we tried to talk with him. He said he wasn't interested in the fireworks, complained about the tourists, and when I asked him to take me golfing, he said he didn't care for it anymore. "Alright," I suggested, "let's go to the movies. We could see *St. Elmo's Fire*, *Pale Rider*, or *Back to the Future*. Which would you prefer?"

Four responded in a monotone voice, "I don't care."

"May I choose?"

He shrugged.

"Let's go to the Palace and see *Back to the Future*." Somehow I nudged him from the house. I walked along as he swung his legs between the wooden crutches. The theater was several blocks from the house. Parking during the tourist seasons in Lake Placid was impossible, so driving wouldn't have helped.

I purchased a bucket of buttery popcorn and a couple of sodas. It seemed like Four was determined *not* to enjoy himself, but I hoped the movie would help him forget his troubles for a while. While we waited for the movies to begin, I said, "You don't seem yourself, lately."

"I guess I never will be."

"What do you mean?"

"I'm done. The coaches talked to my doctor and they said I didn't have a chance of making the Olympics, even if I hadn't broken my leg again."

"I'm sorry, honey. I know how much skating means to you. Couldn't you skate professionally without being in the Olympics? Maybe in ice shows or something?"

Four shrugged indifferently.

"What about college?"

"I'm not going."

"What will you do?"

"What difference does it make?"

I tried to convince him that if he could find something he enjoyed doing that it could make all the difference in the world. "I know skating was your dream, but you can find happiness in many places. You weren't built for just one thing. You can find another purpose, something else to love, wouldn't you say?"

"Skating was always my thing. I can't remember a time when I wanted to do anything else. Competing in the Olympics was my only dream. I don't know how to want anything else."

"Trust me, Four. You'll find you have other passions, you'll see. Be open to the possibilities."

"I'm not like that, GiGi. I'm…" The lights dimmed and Four frowned at me. He finished his sentence, "different," as the silver screen flickered to life and the speakers thumped. I was glad for the cover of darkness. When a loved one's dream dies, it's worse than mourning your own disappointments. Four watched the coming attractions with his head tipped forward and I tried to squelch my tears.

I was glad when the feature began. Immediately, I felt transported to a different world where strange things happened. I tried not to look at Four for a while, hoping that he would get caught up in the story as I did. Finally, when the DeLorean left a streak of flames in the wake of its first disappearance carrying Doc's pooch, after hitting **88** miles per hour, I stole a sideways glance and spied a glimmer of amusement. If that was it, the night was worth it.

By the next morning, gloom had re-consumed Four. I tried to pull him back by posing the question, "If time travel were real, when would you like to visit?"

"I'd go back to before I broke my leg and ribs. That's when it all began."

"Oh." I was about to poke holes in the theory that the blood clot was a result of his first injury, but I wasn't so sure myself. The phone rang and I flinched.

Officer Wideawake spoke quickly. "I've got bad news and good news." He didn't ask which I preferred to hear first. "The bad news is we have no suspects, leads, or clues as to who tried to run you off the road. We're beginning to think we may never find out who did that. I'm sorry, Misty. But the good news is, Calhoun has been found. I'll bring him right over."

"Where was he?"

"They found him when they searched Lois Phelps' house in Wanakena."

I gasped and dropped the phone on the rocker like it were a hot casserole.

***

It took a couple of days to get over the shock. Lois kidnapped our cat, but how? I remembered the scratches on her face that makeup could not conceal. Calhoun never bared his claws at anyone before. The good-tempered feline was as docile as a stuffed animal, but he seemed different after his homecoming. He spent most of his time lurking behind curtains and under beds. Whatever happened to the Turkish Angora, I hoped that in time, Calhoun would forget.

A week later, Winslow updated me on negotiations with the Holsteins. "They've come down from $2,000,000 to $1,000,000. We've gone up from $10,000 to $30,000."

"So they are down by half and we have tripled. What next, Winslow? When will this all be over?"

"I know it seems time consuming, Misty. If we move too fast, we leave money on the table."

I grumbled miserably and didn't ask for an update until a week later. Lois, Art, and John Frederick's arraignments distracted my lawsuit worries. I sat and watched as Judge Hornet commanded the room. The list of charges was much longer than I expected. Many of the crimes sounded the same, just with slightly different words. I suppose they wanted to increase the odds of substantial convictions. Murderous thoughts weren't on the list, but Lois had told me straight out she was guilty of them.

When Judge Hornet refused to set bail, Lois stood and screamed.

It was hard to make out everything she said. When she claimed that she married Albert Boykins to cover the fact that Art was Johnny's son, I gasped and covered my eyes. Could it be true? That would make me Art's aunt, but Johnny and Betty were a couple. Then I noticed that Lois wore Betty's favorite necklace, the one that Johnny had given her. I tried to recall whether my brother had ever been interested in Lois and my head started to hurt.

Lois shouted, "If anyone should have inherited the company, it was Johnny's boy." She pointed at Art. "Even AJ said so."

Judge Hornet banged the gavel repeatedly and shouted.

"Remove the defendant. Order in the court."

Lois struggled and put up quite a fight for her age. Before her removal was finished, Judge Hornet adjourned the session and promptly fled.

I couldn't get Lois' absurd claim out of my head. There didn't seem any resemblance between Art and anyone in my family, let alone Johnny, but what did that prove? Every person was unique. Even if it were true, that wouldn't justify the crimes that Lois, Art, and John Frederick had committed.

Maybe someday there would be a way to prove or disprove such outrageous paternity claims.

A couple of days later, I was pleased to learn that the Holsteins had offered $500,000. We were at $50,000. I asked, "Whose turn is it now?" Winslow said it was their turn.

The more time went on the more I worried we would have to wait another year to finish the ESOP. I told Winslow I'd gladly pay $250,000 to settle. He told me to be patient but I couldn't help pounding my fists on the table. It was unbecoming behavior and I apologized for my outburst. Winslow pleaded, "Give me another week, Misty. I suspect we'll be done by then."

A week later, they were at $300,000 and we were at $150,000. I said, "Just give it to them, Winslow."

"Are you sure? We could split the difference. Let me make one more counteroffer."

"No, I want them to have $300,000. No telling how much they'll get after they pay their attorney. Bob's life should count for something."

"Alright, Misty."

"Make sure it comes from my account, not the company's funds, Winslow. Only, make sure the settlement absolves the company and anyone that works there."

The settlement papers were quickly signed and a bank draft was delivered to the Holstein family. Whenever I pictured the fish-faced family, I imagined tiny, flapping fins on their cheeks and lost looks on their haunting, perpetually open round eyes. Picturing them like that always made me feel guilty and made me wish that I could have used the DeLorean to retrieve Bob from the past.

Yet I also remembered that Bob had run away from his family.

***

The stars finally aligned. The trustee determined that the company was worth $3,000,000. Winslow and Ted filled in the missing spaces in the legal documents and the parties gathered at Adirondack Dowel on the first day of August. The day I had longed for finally arrived.

I gave a grand speech and apologized for wasting so much time and effort building pillars dedicated to my Father. "I'm sure Adirondack Dowel's founder would be pleased to know what we have accomplished, but he never asked for paintings, sculptures, or monuments. I've been building castles out of peacock feathers, but the only legacy that matters is taking care of the company so that it can take care of you and those that will come afterward. If it were up to me, I'd declare Adirondack Dowel 'forever ESOP.' Wouldn't that be something? Just like the Adirondacks have been deemed 'forever wild,' what if we could remain forever ESOP?"

The first part of my speech drew raucous applause. When I announced my successor, Joanne's hands slapped her face. Alice stood and clapped enthusiastically. People stared at me, Joanne, and the trustee. They didn't know how to react.

I thought, *What's wrong with everybody*? It was so obvious to me and the trustee. Is it possible that nobody else thought of the possibility? Undaunted, Alice stood clapping as if everyone were applauding as well.

Finally, Doyle climbed to his feet, stepped to Alice's side, and cheered as loudly as she did. Four made a face, propped himself up with his crutches, and clapped as well. His expression looked as vacant as usual, but I appreciated his support.

When Rusty let out a howl and started clapping the fingers of his good hand against the palm of his other hand, the rest of the crowd ignited. I guess it was Rusty's approval they were looking for. I was proud of Doyle and Rusty, even though they were slow to respond.

When the crowd's cheers finally diminished, Stanley stepped forward and said, "Joanne taught me how to take care of people. I've never met anybody who was better at it than Joanne Sorely Buckpitt. Hooray! What good's a place if it doesn't take care of the people who love it? That's what I love about the ESOP. It takes care of all of us. But that's not all there is to it. We also have to take care of the ESOP and the company."

Everyone started clapping again. I scanned the audience, basking. Thank heavens for Stanley. The only dissent came from Buster who turned his back to the speakers. I shook my head and thought, if anybody can reform Buster, perhaps Rusty and Joanne can.

As the celebration waned, Stanley said, "My doctor wants me to retire, but I'm not nearly ready. Doc thinks I'm a miracle. Who knew I could live a second life as a rabbit?" The nightwatchman pulled a carrot stick from a flannel pocket and nibbled as he turned away.

I stood alone for a moment and congratulated myself. "How about that? It's done. I can't believe it's finally happened."

A comforting hand landed on my shoulder and Winslow eased up behind me. He kissed my cheek and looked into my eyes. "Congratulations, Misty. AJ would be proud of you. I sure am."

***

The next day, Winslow asked if I would join him for a day on the lake. Without knowing the details, or even which lake, I readily agreed. It was time to get away again. He said, "It will be relaxing, I promise."

We arrived mid-morning at the Lakeview Deli, across from Lake Flower in Saranac Lake. Did the proprietor know how loudly the music blared during the weekends? Two young men prepared for a busy day. They wore green aprons and matching ball caps with a prominent black mustache logo. Their name tags read, "Tim," and "Dave." While Tim loaded cigarettes into a large, overhead dispenser, Dave sliced cold cuts.

Winslow purchased ice, ordered a couple of sandwiches, and encouraged me to select drinks. I chose a couple of Oranginas, a ginger ale, and a small bag of chips. The door hadn't closed behind us when Tim and Dave chanted in unison, "We are the Deli Slugs coming to you live from Up the Lake." Perhaps they didn't know we could hear them. Maybe they didn't care. Then they busted into song, over singing, out of tune, and replacing the lyrics of a hit song by Paul Young with their own: "Every time you go away, you take a piece of cheese with you." I was pretty sure the real version of that song never mentioned cheese, but the young men did work in a delicatessen.

It was a beautiful day and a perfect date. When we got to the marina I was surprised when one of their staff boarded with us. Winslow introduced me to our craft's captain who was also a masseur. Then Winslow handed me a map depicting a chain of lakes, barely connected, and islands along the way. A strange X-shaped symbol appeared just off the shore and I asked him about it, pointing.

"It's a treasure map, Misty." Winslow's eyes sparkled and he said, "I hope it is still there. We must hurry."

We made ourselves comfortable near the front of the boat and Winslow wrapped his arm around me. Our boat zipped across Lake Flower and then up a series of lakes. After a while, Winslow said, "You better check the treasure map." The boatman slowed our craft and followed my directions as I tried to locate the correct cove. Finally, I spied it and pointed. The small island had a couple of luxury beach chairs, a small picnic table, and a massage bed, which looked ridiculously out of place.

Winslow set our cooler on the table, and said, "Now, let's see about that treasure. Can you find it?" He handed me the map. It showed twelve dashes before the X-shaped symbol. I stepped toward the middle of the island and spied a box wrapped in shiny gold paper with a sparkly bow. Winslow had followed me, and said, "That's for you, Misty." He carried it back to the picnic table for me and urged, "Open it."

Inside I found a bejeweled treasure chest. Inlaid gemstones glimmered as the midday sun shone on the gaudy box.

"Open it," Winslow said again. Music played when I lifted the lid. There was a small jewelry store box inside. I flipped its lid and lifted the box toward my eyes. There was nothing gaudy about the sparkling diamond ring inside. When I turned toward Winslow, his leg cracked as he dropped to a knee and asked me to marry him.

"Get up here, Winslow. Good heavens." I turned my head away from him and touched my cheek before glancing back at him. "Are you sure? Aren't we a little old for all this?" I couldn't get the words, *elderly newlyweds* out of my mind.

The attorney was a good negotiator and it didn't take him long to convince me that he *was* serious and that we *should* wed. We celebrated our engagement with massages and enjoyed a couple of hours on the lake before the boat skittled back across the water's surface.

It was the perfect date, with wonderful weather, and a dramatic engagement. Yet, something niggled in my head. I didn't doubt Winslow, however. It was Four that worried me.

***

Before Betty died, I bought tickets to see Tina Turner perform at the Olympic Arena. August 15th would have been Betty's 80th birthday. She adored the long-legged, wild-maned singer, and I also enjoyed listening to the icon's music. Four's cast was gone and he walked much better. I asked him if he would accompany me.

He said, "That's not really my kind of music, GiGi."

I tried everything I could think of to bust him out of the funk he was in but seldom succeeded. The last time he seemed to enjoy anything was a month earlier when we watched Live Aid together on television. He preferred the newer artists like Adam Ant and Ultravox, loved Queen, and even admitted enjoying watching Mick Jagger and Tina Turner perform. When I pleaded, "Let's do it for Betty," Four consented.

We arrived as the famous member of the Eagles, Glen Fry, took the stage as a solo performer. Near the end of Glen Fry's set, Four tapped his foot to "The Heat is On," and he rocked to the beat of "Heartache Tonight." Otherwise, Four seemed lost in his thoughts. Was he thinking about skating? I shouldn't have brought him to a venue built for the sport. He looked off blankly to where heavy sheets of ice normally covered concrete.

Tina Turner's show opened with a scantily clad, muscle-bound man banging an enormous gong followed by a film of Tina preparing for the show. I thought Betty would have loved this. I watched as Tina showed off her fingernails, teased her hair, painted her lips, left her dressing room, and exploded onto the stage in a tight white pantsuit, kicking the air. Her commanding presence matched her opening number, "Show Some Respect." As the minutes went by, Four perked up. The feisty performer and the wild crowd yanked him from his dull mood, and soon, Four was dancing and cheering along with the rest of the crowd.

When the first song ended, a raucous greeting and some air kisses were followed by Tina's trademark question, "Are you ready for me, Lake Placid? Well, I'm ready for *you*!" Then she lit into her second song which brought tears to my eyes. The words made me think of Four's ordeal. The song, "I Might Have Been Queen" made me think of overcoming odds and surviving impossible situations, which wasn't unlike the performer's personal traumas. I hoped that Four would draw inspiration from the performance. He needed to become a survivor too. Whether he was heeding the words or not, he rocked to the rhythm.

After the encore, I was sad that the show had come to an end, but the house lights did not brighten the stadium. The crowd roared and Tina returned to the stage for an unexpected second encore. She claimed that Bruce Springsteen had promised to write a song for her, but until he did, she said she would sing "Dancing in the Dark," instead.

Finally, when the show was over, Four said, "It was good to forget everything for a few hours, GiGi." His troubles seemed to return as he looked down at his feet. He mumbled, "I miss Betty," and we shuffled from the arena with the rest of the crowd.

I had attended many concerts through the years but never saw a better show than Tina Turner's.

***

Six weeks later, Four drove Presto's car to their cabin on a windy fall morning. He was dressed for the chill of autumn in a red and black flannel shirt, blue jeans, and blue sneakers. The modest house had been vacant and waited for Presto and Four to return. The 18-year-old dusted the tidy home as he drank whiskey from a bottle wrapped in a brown paper bag.

Four took a picture of his father and mother off of the wall and looked closely at them before squirting glass cleaner on its surface. His father had bright white teeth and thick blond hair, and his mother's hair was piled high on her head in a bouffant hairdo, just as I like to do. She wore a bright yellow dress with white trim and thick sunglasses covering her eyes, emulating her favorite entertainer, Doris Day. A medieval monk in a hazy fog looked on from the background. It was as if the developer had overlaid a second image on top of the first.

Four looked at the clock as if time mattered. Then he picked up an issue of The Old Farmer's Almanac from the year before and dusted beneath it. On another table, Four turned a radio on, and listened for a moment to *Dead Or Alive* sing "You Spin Me Around

(Like A Record)." He twiddled with the chain on a lamp and thought about how free he felt when spinning on the ice. Then he choked on a swig of rotgut.

When Four finished cleaning the cabin, he mowed the lawn, and then he sat beneath a maple tree, his arms resting on his knees and his head in his hands. A long thick rope coiled on his lap and overflowed onto the ground beside him. After a few minutes, he stretched his legs, leaned forward, made a loop, and fashioned a noose. When he was done, he stood and tied a knot around a stone at the opposite end of the rope. He pitched the rock up and over a thick branch of the maple tree, eighteen feet above the ground. The rope followed the rock which landed on the ground a short distance away. He untied the rope from the rock and attached it securely to a large boulder, ten feet distant. He kicked the ground and returned to the tree. He looked up into the tree and watched the noose sway in the breeze. The rope was the perfect length for what he had in mind.

Four took a long swig of whiskey, wiped his lips on his sleeve, and tossed the empty container into the woods. He didn't flinch at the sound of breaking glass as the bottle crashed into a tree.

He climbed until he was sitting on the branch that the noose hung from. Slowly he pulled the rope until he was holding the knot in his hands. He placed the noose over his head and pushed the knot tightly against his throat. He traced the continuous spiral on the medallion and then rose to his feet. His legs bent as he prepared to leap from the branch. He closed his eyes and imagined himself on skates, eternally spinning toward his Olympic destiny.

26

The stately maple's thick branch crashed to the ground. The healthy tree should have supported the teenager's meager weight. Four landed heavily on the ground. His breath was knocked from his lungs and he gasped for air like he had the will to live. Aside from scratches and bruises, Four was unharmed. What was happening?

The young man looked skyward. The large boulder hung over him. He shielded his head with his arm, then he rolled away so that the rock no longer hovered above him. He watched as it slowly descended, astonishment on his face. The hovering boulder floated directly in front of him, without touching the ground as smaller stones levitated from beneath the leaves on the forest floor. They gathered, swirling around beneath the maple like a slow-moving cyclone and Four was in the eye of the storm. His mouth hung open and his body shivered in fear. Was the whiskey responsible for his hallucination?

Finally, the weightless boulder eased to the ground. The flying stones dropped into a conical pile as he watched. Four squinted and turned his head slightly, innocently listening to a distant voice that he couldn't quite hear. He closed his eyes and saw the ghostly image of the bearded old monk from the background of his parent's wedding photograph. Four's shoulder shrank from the invisible touch of a stranger, and then his face filled with wonder and hopefulness. He sat still as a matching touch settled on his opposite shoulder. His eyes widened further and he crossed his arms over his chest to rest his hands on his shoulders, where he had felt the invisible touch.

Next, Four felt the invisible stranger's lips brush against one cheek and then the other. Four released his hold on his shoulders and his fingertips gently touched his cheeks. Though he was alone, Four spoke reverently. "I've been kissed by God. How can it be?" Then he cried into his hands, asking, "Oh, what have I done?" His hands tugged at the knot that pressed against his Adam's apple, loosening the rope's hold on his neck, and threw the cord aside.

An unseen presence's voice spoke to Four. He heard the words, "Share God's love with the world." Four nodded like he understood and watched intently as the presence trailed away, like a puff of smoke. Four's eyes followed the path that led from the cabin to the edge of the woods as if watching a departure. The apparition was no longer close by but had not dissipated. Four thought that he could see the ghostly fog near the cabin and then he watched in awe as the enormous rock took flight again, finally settling to one side of the cabin's front door. The pile of small stones followed and rested on the other side of the cabin door.

A swift autumn breeze swirled leaves at Four's feet and the presence near the cabin finally floated away. Four walked toward the familiar cabin he knew as home and stood beside the otherworldly rock garden. He thought for a moment and tried to decide whether it was God, a guardian angel, or an ancestor that had touched him. Perhaps he would never know. Had it all been a dream? Was it only his imagination? He rubbed his temples. Would they still be there when the intoxicant wore off? It would be impossible to enter the cabin without seeing the boulder and the cone of pebbles near the entrance.

It was as if the Heavens intended that he would always remember that moment, wonder about the miracles he had witnessed, and never forget what they meant to him.

***

DAVID FITZ-GERALD

One week later

Four's radical transformation surprised and delighted me. He still had no interest in attending college or getting a job, but the cloud that hung over him lifted. The morose teenager was gone. The young man that took his place was willing, helpful, and agreeable. When I asked him to assist me in America's attic, he readily agreed.

I called the storage area at the peak of the house America's attic because it was choked full of possessions, many of which had belonged to my grandmother. We never knew why she had been named America; it was an uncommon moniker. The woman had lived to the age of ninety-five and died just before the end of the Second World War. Someone had carefully boxed, wrapped, or covered her belongings, many of which I suspected came from earlier generations. It seemed a shame to let them go after keeping them in the family for so long, and yet, what good were they doing anybody stowed away for decades?

When Betty died and left her estate to St. Kateri's Orphanage, Winslow successfully challenged her will in favor of a document that he prepared for Betty months earlier. Betty's will surprised everyone. She left her bank account to the Adirondack Dowel and Spindle Company, and she bequeathed her home on Elm Street to me. Instead of moving from the house we loved, we took it off the market. I was about to make my dream of opening an antique shop come true. Betty's place was the perfect location.

As we climbed the worn wooden attic steps I made Four a business proposition. "Would you be my partner?" I was too old to be starting such an endeavor on my own, and he didn't have anything else to occupy his time.

His response surprised me. "I was hoping you'd ask me, GiGi. I've always been interested in history. I think it would be fun."

I was glad that I hadn't asked him sooner. It would have suited me to start right away after selling Adirondack Dowel to the ESOP but mentoring a new president of the company had consumed more time than expected. I didn't want to intrude but was curious about his new outlook on life.

At the top of the stairs, just to the right, a large object hid beneath a stiff blanket. It looked like an exercise bike shrouded in laundry. I said, "Let's begin with that." It was as if I were a child on Christmas morning and Four seemed as excited as me, hunting for attic treasures. The dust made Four sneeze as we unwrapped it. I gasped. "It's a spinning wheel. Oh, look, Four." It was in remarkably good shape. "Can you carry it down the stairs for me?"

He squatted, grasped the frame, and then jumped back, startled. He stared at his hands with a look of amazement on his face and then looked at me. I asked, "Static electricity?"

"I suppose."

When he tried a second time, it happened again but he didn't let go. It looked like an electrical current ran through him but his expression mirrored the look on his face whenever his blades drilled into the ice. Finally, he released the spinning wheel and stood up. "The most amazing thing happened, GiGi. I saw this spinning wheel. It was set up in a barn. A long-haired girl, about my age, sat on a stool and spun wool into thread. It happened so fast," he said breathlessly. "She enjoyed the spinning, but evil spirits haunted her." Four looked down the steps as if planning a hasty retreat then turned back to face me. "It was just like watching it on television, only I didn't just *see* it. I felt it too."

I reached forward and grasped his forearm. "Are you okay?"

He nodded. "I should be scared, but I kind of liked it. Maybe it's because of all those books I read."

My grip squeezed his arm a little more firmly. "We need to talk, honey. You are not alone. This happens to me sometimes. It's a little unnerving, and yet, exciting. I was much older when it began happening to me." My voice trailed as I finished. What would my life have been like if I had experienced the phenomenon at a younger age?

He asked, "Do you think we're related to this spinning girl? Wouldn't that be something?"

"It's in America's attic, so yes. There's a very good possibility she is one of our ancestors."

Four reached for a third try and I started to halt him, but that time he hefted the awkwardly shaped object and backed toward the stairs.

"Go slowly, Four. I'll be your eyes." I told him when to step and guided the bulky wheel as he descended, preventing it from scraping against the walls and the doorjamb at the bottom of the stairs. "Let's take it to the living room."

He raised an eyebrow and I knew he was thinking about hauling the wheel down another flight of steps.

When we reached Betty's living room, Four sat in a chair and watched as I filled the air with the scent of lemon Pledge furniture polish. Then I sat beside him and we admired the ancient artifact. Finally, Four said, "I'll bet it still works. Wouldn't it be rad to learn how to use it?"

"I hadn't thought about that. We could perform demonstrations in the antique shop."

"What should we call it?"

"The spinning wheel?"

"No, the store."

"I was thinking of calling it America's Attic. Isn't that cute?"

"Yeah. How about Magic Touch?" Four wiggled his digits as if trying to restore sensitivity to his fingertips.

My mouth tightened and I intoned, "Ooh. I like that."

We sat for a long, quiet spell. Maybe we were both imagining our future business partnership. Then, he began talking as if he were seeing ghosts. I sat, transfixed, and listened as he told me about his attempt to kill himself at the cabin and his remarkable revelations. When he was done, he said, "It was as if a wretched curse had lifted from my shoulders, GiGi."

***

It was hard to accept that Four had tried to hang himself. How could things have gotten so bad that he couldn't go on? I had tried to surround him with my unconditional love and affection, and had hoped to distract him from the hopelessness that enveloped him, but it wasn't enough. Having to picture it made me sick to my stomach, but the way he told the story, I couldn't help visualizing the scene. Days later, my skin still crawled as it replayed endlessly in my mind. I was grateful for the miracle he experienced but sickened to think how close we had come to losing Four at the edge of the woods.

We suspended mining for antiques in America's attic to appear before the Grand Jury in Elizabethtown. It seemed we had waited for ages since the arraignment. Perhaps the case against Lois, Art, and John Frederick was complicated. Maybe the defendants' high profiles made gathering evidence more difficult. We arrived early and waited for hours. The Grand Jury interviewed witnesses all day long, and I was exhausted by the time they called me in. I hadn't spent much time in a courtroom before and didn't know what a Grand Jury was for until Winslow explained their function. The blank faces of twenty jurors reminded me of Bob Holstein's family. Only one woman on the panel made sympathetic facial expressions as I testified. Walking away I doubted the outcome and feared the case against Lois, Art, and John Frederick would crumble. What would Lois do if she had another chance for revenge?

Lois testified after me, and I was surprised to see her in passing. Winslow said that defendants rarely testify before a Grand Jury. She mouthed, "I hate you," as she passed me. A chill spilled down my spine. Did evil people always see themselves as victims?

The next day, we got the news that all three defendants were indicted and promptly accepted plea bargain offers for reduced sentences. It was a tremendous relief, and yet, I feared what might happen if Lois were only sentenced to probation. Winslow didn't know whether they would incarcerate a woman of her age.

***

A couple of days later, I accompanied Four to his doctor's appointment. After the routine examination, Four told his physician that he wanted to get a tattoo. The man said, "I must advise against it, son."

Determined, Four said, "I've decided to do it. What precautions could I take?"

The doctor frowned and suggested a temporary modification to Four's blood thinner dosage.

Afterward, I said to Four, "Can I go with you?"

He looked confused. "When I get my tattoo?"

"Yes, I'd like to go too."

Four shrugged. "I suppose."

He bit his cheek. Would he rather that I didn't intrude? Tentatively, I asked, "Do you think they could fit me in as well?"

"You? You want a tattoo, GiGi?" He paused for a moment. What did his hesitation mean? Then he said, "What will you get?"

I smiled without answering and said, "Are you sure you don't mind if I come along?"

***

A week later, on our way to the tattoo parlor, we visited the cemetery. It was late in the year to leave flowers with the departed, but I couldn't help myself. After a couple of solemn minutes together, Four seemed ready to go. I said, "I just need a couple of minutes and then I'll be along."

"Take as long as you need, GiGi, I'll be in the car listening to the radio."

I watched as Four walked away. Once children reached a certain age, they always seemed to be walking away. I had to remind myself to be pleased as Four matured and became more independent, but such moments were bittersweet.

As if worshiping in church, I kneeled before Father's grave. With my hands on the stone, I leaned forward and kissed the cold granite, and then placed a single red rosebud on the top of the gravestone. My legs wobbled when I climbed back to my feet. My lips left an imprint on the marker's polished surface and my palms were pocked from having been planted on a rough section of stone. The soft fabric of my slacks soothed my hands and my thoughts drifted back to the many monuments I tried to build for Father. My heart glowed warm and a whisper from within told me he appreciated the lipstick and the flower. What folly it was to waste time and effort on paintings and sculptures? He just wanted me to take care of the things he loved.

Walking back to the car, I realized the symbolism. I couldn't have found something that better represented Joanne and the future of Adirondack Dowel than the crimson rose about to unfold. It represented the nurturing touch of a patient gardener. "That's it," I whispered into the breeze. "I'll get a tattoo of a rosebud."

Four drove from the cemetery to the edge of town. He parked in a small plaza in front of a sign that read, "Foot of the Mountains Tattoo Studio." The sign out front depicted a grotesque foot with misshaped toes and ragged nails. Four pulled the key from the ignition and the engine shook to a stop. He flared his eyes at me, excitedly. If he was afraid of the pain or the permanency of what was about to happen, it didn't show. I knew he had wanted a tattoo for many years, but it was not recommended for aspiring Olympians. A tear appeared in the corner of my eye as a blast of realization hit me like the back of a shovel. This was Four's consolation prize.

Four misread my emotions. "Are you scared, GiGi?"

"Not at all, honey. I can't wait."

Inside, the artist was glum. He said, "I should refuse," as we signed the forms releasing him from liability and promising to hold him harmless from any ill effects. Four handed him a note from the doctor and the man frowned. "I will not be held responsible if you do not like the outcome. I will give it a try if you insist, but you must understand and accept the risks." To Four, he said, "Your blood might not clot as it should, and that could ruin the artwork." To me, he said, "Our skin thins as it ages, and detailed tattoos are not recommended." With an exasperated sigh, the man said, "Who goes first?"

Four raised his hand and I felt excitement coarse through my body. It reminded me of when I brought him gifts from our nation's capital when I came to visit him as a child. Those moments when expressions of joy appeared on his face made my heart sing. I wished they happened more frequently and was glad that his demeanor had finally changed.

He removed his shirt and settled onto the tattoo artist's chair. He pointed to his chest, just above his heart, and I picked up a hot rod magazine as I eased into a chair to wait my turn. Now and then, I glanced at Four as the artist gouged my great-grandson's flesh. Four's expression was exuberant. It was as if he were a deified saint soaring through the clouds and I thought of the portrait Philomena painted.

A page of the well-worn magazine stopped me cold. I gawked at a bright blue, 1973 Ford Mustang. It was a dead ringer for my car. I forced myself not to think about the totaled automobile. It wasn't right to grieve over an inanimate object, but my heart lurched at the glossy image and I pined for my wrecked convertible, nevertheless. I remember telling Ted Drake a dozen years ago, *that* was my retirement vehicle. I missed the sports car and would never get used to driving Presto's ordinary sedan.

Guilt stabbed my heart and my skin flushed at the thought that Four's career-ending injuries were my fault. What if I hadn't picked a Mustang? Did I have to let Four drive that fateful day? Why didn't I just go by myself to the chocolatier? If I had surrendered the company to its management, perhaps Four's Olympic dream could have come true. The constant buzz of the ink slinger's gun lulled me into an afternoon nap as I tipped my head and dozed.

Our artist gently shook my shoulder and Four smiled proudly as I sat up with a start. Four's fingers quickly buttoned their way up his shirt, and I whined, "Let me see."

He shook his head and grinned, "Not now. In a couple of days, then you can see." He extended a hand and helped me rise from the plush chair's soft embrace.

I asked, "Did it hurt?"

His face puckered in memory of the pricking, scratching, and burning sensations, then he wrinkled his nose. "Not too bad, GiGi. Going to the dentist or the emergency room is worse, and none of it compares to spending all day on ice skates."

I raised my arms and hoped they believed me brave. "It's my turn now. My skin's not getting any thicker." I always tried to avoid the foolish phrase, 'I'm not getting any younger.'

"Have you decided what I'll be doing for you?"

As I described my request, he sketched it on a piece of paper. He said, "At your age, I must recommend thick lines rather than delicate work."

I never liked hearing the phrase, "At your age" but approved of the design.

When the artist was done pounding my skin, I had a long-stemmed rosebud surrounded by five small hearts. Each was a different color: green for my emerald-eyed attorney, Four's heart was purple, Presto's blue, Harold's yellow, and the white heart was for Calhoun. Beneath the flower and hearts, a flowing banner proclaimed the words: Forever, ESOP. That was for the future and the retirement vehicle that would carry generations of employee owners into *their* golden years.

The artist said that he was encouraged. The tattoos looked as they should. He told us they'd look better in a couple of days and explained how to take care of them. As we prepared to leave, he said, "I was worried about the two of you. I had you figured for fainters, but you were gnarly."

Four and the tattoo artist shared a high-five as we departed.

***

A week later, as Four was dressing to attend my hastily planned wedding, he showed me his tattoos. Five broken rings overlapped on his left breast. The circles mimicked the Olympic symbol, except for the fact that a chunk was missing from each one. Beside the incomplete, intertwined rings a small medallion hung from a lanyard like an Olympic medal, except instead of gold, silver, or bronze, the featured ornament was red and heart-shaped. Beneath the artwork were the words, "Pray and don't lose heart." I understood the meaning, but he explained, nevertheless. "Sometimes when you don't get what you thought you wanted, you wind up discovering something that means even more than what was denied."

I thought about what Four said. My failure to leave landmarks dedicated to Father represented my own unanswered prayer. Taking care of what Father loved, the company that he and his dedicated employees built, and then leaving it in better hands meant even more than any monument I could commission.

Winslow and I married in a small gathering at Casa del Sol, in Saranac Lake. I had come to realize that I had loved Winslow ever since Father's funeral. Couples were often asked about those special moments, such as, when: they first met, first kissed, and first knew they were destined to be together. I couldn't remember anyone who claimed they found their true love in a funeral home but looking back, I knew then. Ever since, Winslow has done nothing but prove himself the same kind, decent, loving man he appeared to be on that day in McCabe's Funeral Home.

After a short ceremony, we celebrated with a rich repast of chimichangas, rice, and beans on plates so hot they sizzled when set before us. After our wedding brunch, I used the ladies' room and couldn't help thinking of the time Lois shut off the lights and threatened me while I sat helpless in the narrow stall.

On my way back to our table, I glanced through an open door into the kitchen and saw an unexpected face. One of the cooks wore a ski hat and a white apron. I would have recognized the man anywhere, though nearly a decade had passed since he supposedly drowned. I smiled and waved at Bob Holstein. My shoulders lurched toward the kitchen, drawn to greet the man, but my brain talked my body out of it. As I returned to my family, my head shook in irrational amusement as goosebumps buzzed from limb to limb in waves. Somehow the man survived the Bicentennial Moonlight Regatta and persisted living in oblivion. He might never know that I paid his family hundreds of thousands of dollars on account of his wrongful death, but Bob was very much alive. In the years since, I've thought about the small fortune in compensation that I paid Bob's family for their loss. Three hundred thousand dollars is a lot of money, especially considering that Robert Jonquil Holstein wasn't dead. One night, after dining out, I snuck into the kitchen and shared a few words with Bob. He apologized for worrying me and I never told him about meeting his parents. I should have told Winslow about finding Bob, but decided not to. A woman shouldn't have to tell her husband everything.

Outside the stucco building, I kissed Harold, Presto, and Four and watched as they piled into the old bucket of bolts that frugal Presto refused to part with. I doted on Four with a long gaze into his eyes and whispered into his ears. He blushed and rebuked me halfheartedly when I told him I was proud of him.

When the boys were gone, Winslow and I drove further into town and parked across from the boat launch. Holding hands, we walked through Riverfront Park, along the shore of Lake Flower. I thought about Winslow's treasure map proposal and the glorious summer day we spent together.

As we sat on an inviting bench to gaze out over the water, I said to Winslow, "I have to tell you something I should have told you sooner."

"What's that, darling?"

"You're fired. I forgot to tell you that when you asked me to marry you, but just so you know, it's retroactive."

Winslow's eyes twinkled as he turned toward me. "You always were my favorite client." Our lips met briefly and then my husband reached an arm across my shoulders. Dry leaves fluttered by and the first snowflakes of the season wafted recklessly from the heavens.

The End

****

Thank you for reading *If It's the Last Thing I Do*.

Reviews are crucial for helping new readers discover me and decide whether to read my books. If you could take a moment to leave a review, I'd really appreciate it.

Recommending my work to other readers helps a lot too, so if you like this book, please consider spreading the word. Please let your family, friends, and followers know about my fiction.

About the Author

David Fitz-Gerald writes historical fiction, with the hope of transporting readers to another time and place. *If It's the Last Thing I Do* is his 7th novel.

Dave has worked for more than 30 years as an accountant, employee owner, and member of the management team at a "silver" ESOP (employee-owned) company. He has championed the cause in national, non-profit association leadership roles.

Dave's family roots run deep in the Adirondacks, going back generations. He attended college and worked at a deli in Saranac Lake during the 1980s. He portrayed an elf at Santa's Workshop on Whiteface Mountain in the 1970s and is an Adirondack 46-er, which means he has hiked all of New York's highest peaks.

Also by David Fitz-Gerald
Ghosts Along the Oregon Trail, coming in 2023

From **The Adirondack Spirit Series**
The Curse of Conchobar – A Prequel to the Adirondack Spirit Series
Wanders Far – An Unlikely Hero's Journey
She Sees Ghosts – The Story of a Woman Who Rescues Lost Souls
Waking Up Lost – A Mystical Fantasy Adventure
Caught in a Trance - A Tale of Hypnosis and Reincarnation

Not part of the Adirondack Spirit Series
In the Shadow of a Giant – Remembering Paleface Ski Center and Dude Ranch

Acknowledgements

Thank you to Lindsay Fitzgerald, my editor, collaborator, and cousin. My books would not be the same without you, nor would they be as much fun to create.

I'm grateful to the community of readers, reviewers, and authors for their encouragement and support. Special thanks to my Adirondack Spirit Guides group for your early feedback. If you'd like to join the club, you can find us on Facebook:

https://www.facebook.com/groups/adirondackspiritguides

My pastime has turned into an enormously pleasurable hobby. In the future, I hope to devote even more time to creating fiction. I couldn't do it without the support of readers like you and look forward to welcoming you back for *Ghosts Along the Oregon Trail*, coming in late 2023.

This is a work of fiction. Actual businesses, places, and historical characters have been fictionalized, including the Adirondack Dowel and Spindle Company and the village of Lake Placid, New York. As a reader and writer of historical fiction, I enjoy the coexistence of fact and fiction.

I am indebted to my earliest readers for their enthusiasm and enormously helpful suggestions which have made this book better. With gratitude, thank you so much to: Alberto Aguilar, Jim Bado, Ted Becker, Daphne Berry, Cecile Betit, Barbara Clough, Larry D. Compeau, Christie Kane, Gary Shorman, and Pat Wahler, author of *The Rose of Washington Square*.

This book was made possible by support from backers of a Kickstarter campaign, which funded this project into existence. It was fun to build reward packages featuring the themes in *If It's the Last Thing I Do*. I'm also delighted that the campaign funded a soundtrack album written and performed by my nephew, singer-songwriter, Kyle Hughes. You can find the music here: https://www.itsoag.com/last-thing-soundtrack

Thank you to the 41 backers who brought this project to life. It is an honor and a thrill to have your support. Special recognition and deep appreciation to the "BODACIOUS! Book Box" level supporters, Alberto Aguilar, Jim Bado, Daphne Berry, Barbara Fitz-Gerald, Bret Keisling, Katie Kimble, Aaron Moberger, Alex Moss, and David Sunderland; the "STELLAR! Olympic Bundle" level supporters, Barbara Clough, Ali Jamshidi, and Matt Kolb; and our "PATRON SPONSOR! Mentor" level supporter, Shawn Moody of Moody's Co-Worker Owned, headquartered in Gorham, Maine. The employee ownership movement is fortunate to have many champions, but I can't think of any more zealous, effective, and inspiring advocates than my friend, Shawn Moody. Thank you so much to Shawn, and all of the backers of *If It's the Last Thing I Do*.

It is my hope that this project will help spread the good word about employee ownership. It is truly a win-win model that creates a lasting legacy and helps every day working people build life-changing wealth through their work. If you'd like to learn more about employee ownership as an ownership succession model, please check out The Employee Ownership Foundation, The ESOP Association, and the National Center for Employee Ownership, for further information.

https://www.employeeownershipfoundation.org
https://www.esopassociation.org
https://www.nceo.org

Thank you for your interest in *If It's the Last Thing I Do* and spending time with the employee owners of the Adirondack Dowel and Spindle Company. The book is fiction, the company is make-believe, but my gratitude is as real as can be.

All the best,
Dave

HISTORIUM PRESS

www.historiumpress.com